Gathering Storm

For our lovely and much-loved daughter,
who makes the world a better place.

Acknowledgements

My grateful thanks to the following people:

my friend Naomi Tarrant, clothing historian, for giving me the benefit of her expertise and knowledge on the hairstyles and headgear of mid 18th century Scotland and for telling me about Dresden embroidery;

Leila Cruickshank of Kohl Publishing for very generously sharing with me some of her knowledge of printing and publishing;

jay [*sic*] Dixon, for her skilful and sensitive editing;

Hilary Johnson of the Hilary Johnson Authors' Advistory Service and her readers for their valuable critiques;

Tamise Totterdell, for her critique and telling comments.

the Open University, for creating and teaching their fascinating course A218, *Medicine and society in Europe, 1500–1930.*

Duncan Murchison, latter-day John Roy Stuart, costumed guide and historical weapons expert at Culloden and Fort George, for giving me the opportunity to fire a replica Doune Pistol.

to Senga Fairgrieve, for working her typesetting magic.

God bless the King! God bless the Faith's Defender!
God bless – no harm in blessing – the Pretender!
Who that Pretender is, and who that King –
God bless us all – is quite another thing!

Jacobite Toast

Prologue

He wanted a storm. Rumbling thunder. The flash and crack of lightning. Ragged, angry clouds. Lashing rain, falling, for preference, in Biblical torrents.

Instead, the haar was down as he sailed up the Forth, the cloudy air still as could be. Deceptively mild. Only when he jerked his head round in startled response to the shriek of a seagull did he feel the chill threat of winter in the air.

Rendering both shorelines invisible, the sea mist was making his return to Scotland – well, what, exactly? Despite his mood of growing trepidation, his mouth curved. He had always been able to laugh at himself. 'Twas one of his few saving graces. So he was perfectly happy to admit that this return of the prodigal was unimpressive. Dare he hope also for not as bad as he feared?

He gazed through the ghostly gloom pressing in on the small vessel which had been his home for the past six days, his portmanteau at his feet. He had wedged the well-travelled brown leather bag against the wooden rail of the ship to stop it from sliding across the creaking boards of the deck.

Under the long grey sweep of his military cloak his left hand rested on the hilt of his sword. He'd wrapped the fingers of his right around a taut rope to steady himself against the slow swell of the sea. A few feet away, eyes flickering up and down to the compass, the Captain with the neatly-trimmed auburn beard was at the helm, steering a careful course to harbour.

A sailor rang the ship's bell, alerting the crew of any other craft which might be gliding through this curtain of fog to their presence. The single seagull became a flock, wheeling and circling around the boat's masts, their harsh cries fighting the monotonous tolling of the bell. Pale and intent, the lookouts posted at bow and stern alternately called out depth soundings to the Captain and listened for the tell-tale slap of waves against treacherous rocks or the safety of harbour walls.

He lost focus, blinked to regain it, and saw that land was at last visible through the haar. Scotland was drawing closer. There was no going back now. He made out dockside buildings and a stone quay. An elegant black coach, fronted by a handsome pair of greys, stood on its gleaming cobbles, damp as those were from the mist.

As the ship's crew plunged into the well-rehearsed actions required to safely dock and tie up, a footman was helping an equally elegant gentleman in a long curly grey wig out of the coach. Bloody hell. The Lord President had come to greet him in person. He must be more important than he thought he was.

Duncan Forbes of Culloden scanned the small deck and spotted him. A smile spread across the cadaverous face. 'Laddie,' he called up, 'you're a sight for these sore old eyes and no mistake!'

The gangway was swung into place. Beckoned by the eager Lord President, he lifted his portmanteau and strode across it. He barely had both feet planted on Scottish soil before he found himself caught up in a great bear hug.

'Laddie,' Culloden said again, his voice gruff with emotion. 'You're home at last. Welcome home, my boy. Welcome home! I'll be able to sleep soundly in my bed tonight!'

Home at last. Welcome home. I'll be able to sleep soundly in my bed tonight.

He was glad the Lord President could not see his face.

She was in a strange mood today, restless, yet at the same time oddly dull, like a blunt pencil in need of sharpening. The weather wasn't helping, this haar which hadn't lifted all day. Making sweets for the shop with the girls, she was gossiping and laughing with them as she always did but her brain felt as cloudy as the fog pressing against the small square windows punched into the outside walls of the kitchen.

Their bottle-green glass panes were opaque from the inside too, steamed up by the heat of pans of tablet and the other sugary concoctions bubbling on the range. She walked across the flagstones to the kitchen door, turned the big brass handle and tugged it open. It shrieked its usual protest.

The younger of the two maidservants sent her a shy smile from under her neat white cap. 'Grand tae hae a wee breath o' air, Miss.'

'Aye,' she agreed, although she could have wished for a fresher breeze coming in off the Physic Garden. The air out there was too still today. She stood for a moment struggling to see the neat rows and drills which yielded so many of the herbs and plants she and her father used to treat their patients. Even the imposing bulk of Surgeons' Hall, no distance away on the other side of the garden, was lost in the mist. The little pagoda-roofed summer house set where the paths met in the middle of the gardens was no more than a shadowy shape.

'And whit do ye think ye're doing standing here, young lady?' came a demand from behind her. 'Trying to catch your death o' cold?'

She swung round and had to adjust her gaze downwards. Why did she always forget how short Betty was? It was years since she had outstripped the housekeeper in height.

'Just getting some fresh air. Nothing wrong with that, is there?'

'It's freezing oot there!'

'And it's boiling hot in here.'

'Which is why you're going to catch your death. Going frae ane to the ither without a cloak or a plaid. Come in, now.'

A concerned hand was already on the sleeve of her sprigged cream and blue gown, tugging her back into the kitchen. She shook it off. 'Leave me be, Betty. I'm needing to clear my head.'

'Are you already coming doon wi' something?' The older woman peered up into her face. 'Ye are looking a wee touch pale the day.'

'That's because I need some fresh air.'

'Aye ready wi' the smart answer, that's you, eh?'

'Leave me be,' the girl said again, trying the disarming smile. It usually worked. 'I promise I'll not bide here long. And there's nothing wrong. Dinna fash yourself about me.'

'Worry about you?' The hand left her arm, being required to complement its mate on the other side of Betty's hips. The posture was an invariable adjunct to scowling at her young mistress, or anyone else who roused her ire. 'Why in the name o' all that's holy would I do that?'

The disarming smile became a wry one. 'When do you ever stop worrying about me, Betty?'

The belligerent face and posture softened. 'Is it you that's worried about something, lass?'

Hard to come up with an answer to that when she didn't know it herself … and that was at least half a lie. For weeks now she'd been aware of a growing feeling of foreboding, as though some terrible storm were about to break —

'Aaargh!' cried the little maidservant. 'This tablet's boiling over!'

'Then slide it aff the heat!' Muttering direly about folk who dinna hae the sense they were born with, the housekeeper sped across the kitchen. Shaking her head to banish the uneasy thoughts, the girl laughed and followed her.

Edinburgh,

December, 1743.

1

Robert Catto swept out through the Bristo Port and wheeled left. Adjusting his steadying grip on the hilt of his sword, he proceeded to cover the newly-cobbled causeway behind Edinburgh University at a fast and loping stride. His eyes adapted now to the darkness, he was setting both the pace and the manner of approach for the detachment of the Town Guard sliding along at his heels.

Taking their cue from their Captain, they were closing in on Surgeons' Hall with admirable stealth and silence. Most of them were Highlanders. There was little need to spell out to anyone born north of the Tay the inherent advantage of leaving your quarry in blissful ignorance of your imminent arrival.

Catto led his troop along the line of the Flodden Wall, skirting the College, the Royal Infirmary and their respective policies. In a matter of moments they were past those grounds and had reached the spot where the causeway began to slope downwards towards the bastion which marked the south-eastern extremity of Edinburgh's defences.

Bringing his right hand up to the side of his head, he splayed his long fingers so everyone would be sure of seeing the signal to stop. As he came to a graceful halt, spinning round on the balls of his feet to face the men, the soft folds of his cloak billowed out around him. For a moment he might have been enveloped in the thick ribbons of smoke snaking up into the night sky from the hundreds of chimneys in the town on the other side of the wall. Even a waxing moon such as there was this frosty December evening was struggling to cast much illumination through all of that. Ideal conditions for tonight's endeavour.

A pack of wolves metamorphosing into men, the guards straightened up and awaited their orders. Obeying Catto's further silent commands, they began to scale the wall, with him bringing up the rear. There were a few suppressed grunts and some laboured breathing but they were all successfully completing the manoeuvre. He'd handpicked this group, selecting the youngest and fittest and putting them through a month's worth of relentless drilling and training. That was paying off tonight.

He too was negotiating the barrier without much difficulty, even if, or more accurately because, parts of the masonry were crumbling beneath his fingers, providing copious foot and hand holds. The parlous condition of Edinburgh's so-called defences was a bad joke. That their state of repair might be deliberate went far beyond one.

Still, 'twas only make-believe, was it not? The currents of history had left this country and this city far behind. The Lord President's fears notwithstanding, Catto had seen nothing over the past month to change his mind about that. With a bit of luck and a following wind, he'd be out of here sooner rather than later. 'Twas a glorious thought.

With a series of soft thuds, the men of the Town Guard jumped from the wall to land on the strip of rough grass on the other side of it. As Catto too hit the rock-hard ground a bolt of pain tore up his right thigh. Unable to suppress a ragged gasp and a muttered string of obscenities, he heard a whispered enquiry float across to him through the darkness of the night.

'You all right, Captain?'

Sergeant Livingstone. Apart from Catto himself, the only other real soldier in this ragtag troop he was doing his best to knock into shape.

'Fine,' he responded. The word was ground out through gritted teeth. Forced to give himself a moment, he rode the ricochets of pain as they careered around his knee and shot up into his thigh. When they had subsided from sheer fucking agony to no more than a gnawing bloody ache, he rose from the crouch into which the pain had locked him and drew one cautious breath. A second came more easily.

Doing his damnedest not to limp, he followed the men moving forward in the darkness to surround Surgeons' Hall, carrying out the orders he'd given them back at the guard-house. The foot of the Physic Garden on the other side of the hall was flanked by a pair of houses. The second Sergeant Catto had brought with him tonight was leading a separate troop of guards up the High School Wynd towards one of those dwellings.

A third troop under the command of Lieutenant Liddell should be ascending the steps which led up from the Cowgate into the High School Yards to surround the other house. It was shuttered and unoccupied but Liddell had been provided with its keys and instructed to make sure it was indeed empty. 'Twas as well to be thorough.

Rounding the gable end of Surgeons' Hall, Catto discerned through the gloom the shadowy figures of those two groups. Recognizable by his girth, Sergeant Crichton was waving his men into position around the occupied house. That was home to one Patrick Rankeillor, surgeon-apothecary, leading light of the Incorporation of Surgeons of Edinburgh, anatomist, professor at the town's College – and known Jacobite.

As the cordons formed around all three buildings, Catto allowed himself a small smile of satisfaction. He couldn't see the surgeon-apothecary managing to wriggle his way out of this. Especially not when accompanied by a gaggle of his students and a half-dissected corpse.

He turned his attention to Surgeons' Hall. The two-storey building looked to be in complete darkness, no lights showing at any of its windows. That meant nothing. Anyone engaged in cutting up a cadaver would have the shutters securely closed.

Approaching the front door, thinking about the procedure he was about to interrupt, he was forced to acknowledge both a frisson of distaste and a rush of excitement. 'Twas not only the frost hanging in the atmosphere which was making his fingers tingle. Flexing them, he curled his right hand under the guard and around the hilt of his sword before sliding it out of its scabbard.

However carefully you did that, there was always a whisper of sound. Like the sigh of a girl as you caressed her. Like the tiny breath of wind which brought you the perfume of grass and wild flowers as you steadied a nervous horse before battle. That sigh of pleasure never failed to excite. That tiny breath of wind always held the promise of action and the scent of adventure, the heady and intoxicating threat of danger.

The drilling of the men and the surveying of the city's walls apart, since he'd stepped ashore at a misty Leith four weeks ago today he'd spent far too much time sitting at a desk reading dossiers and poring over intercepted letters. One of those, written by an indiscreet student of Patrick Rankeillor's, had brought him here tonight. Before he'd come to Edinburgh there had been those long weeks of enforced idleness while he'd been recovering from the damage done by some misbegotten French bastard's musket ball.

He might rather have been anywhere else on earth this freezing December night than bloody Scotland. It still felt damn good to be out and about and doing again. It still felt damn' good to have his sword in his hand again. No doubt those feelings were entirely reprehensible in this day and age of reason, especially in someone who prided himself on being a modern man. Then again, if you came from a long line of Highland warriors, freebooters and cattle thieves, there were times when your forebears stood at your shoulder and would not be denied.

He should know. He had spent the greater part of his life trying to deny the whole bloody lot of them. Until, fool that he was, he had blurted out his big secret to possibly the worst person in the world in whom he could have confided. Pity he knew that now and hadn't before.

Pity the need to unburden himself had been so strong. Lesson learned. Price being paid right now: though hopefully not for much longer.

'Twas time to make a move. Everything was ready, the men poised for action. Their weaponry might look positively mediaeval to Catto's eyes – when he'd first seen them with their Lochaber axes he hadn't known whether to laugh or succumb to total despair – but he had to admit they presented a formidable picture. He was bloody glad they were all on his side. Or so he had to hope.

The axes themselves were fixed to the end of a long pole, on the other side of which was a hook. Scaling the city walls they had used those hooks as grappling irons. Now, eyes gleaming and unkempt beards bristling – their slovenly appearance was the next thing in his sights – the men held their ancient but vicious weapons across their chests, both hands gripping the long shafts.

Threading his way through the deadly forest of gleaming steel, Catto turned to face them. 'The anatomical theatre is on the first floor,' he murmured. 'You men,' he said, indicating the ones he meant, 'will follow me up there.' Another gesture of division and selection. 'Livingstone, you will take these guards and search the ground floor. Rintoul, you have your keys?'

'Always, Captain.' There was a smile in Davie Rintoul's voice. Thankfully the darkness of the night spared them the sight of his grin. Mouth like a badly-kept graveyard. 'Open any door or gate in Edinburgh, they will.'

'Then have Rintoul use his keys and search every room in here, Livingstone. Every cupboard, too. Once you've done that, proceed to the outhouses in the Physic Garden.' Catto swung round to address the remaining group of guards. 'You men will hold yourselves in readiness here and apprehend anyone who attempts to leave the building by this door.'

All three groups stepped forward readily enough, though the unease among the guards he had indicated should follow him up to the anatomical theatre was palpable. Strange how even men as rough and ready as this crew could fear the dead. Robert Catto had learned a long time ago there was only one way the dead could hurt you: if and when you allowed them to.

'Will you be wanting us to break the door down, Captain?' asked a lilting and hopeful voice. Obviously fear of the dead was warring with the pleasurable anticipation of the wanton destruction of property.

'Let's try opening it first.' Turning, he threaded the fingers of his free hand through the large brass ring which formed its handle. The metal was as cold as charity. 'Failing that—' But he didn't have to ask Rintoul to step forward and wield his skeleton keys. The handle turned as easily as the door surrendered to his touch, the heavy wood falling back into cavernous blackness. Careless of them to leave the place unlocked.

'Light the lanterns. As quietly as possible,' he warned in a low growl, hearing the clink of chains as small brass and glass lamps were unhooked from leather belts.

'You'll be wanting one too, Captain?'

'Aye.' The scrape of metal against metal as the lid of a tinder box was carefully opened. The scratch of steel against flint. A glow in the dark as the wick of the candle stub took the flame. The faint tinkle of glass against brass as the door of the lantern was closed, secured and proffered to him. He took it by the hook at the top of its chain and crossed the threshold into Surgeons' Hall.

He'd acquainted himself with the ground plan of the building a few days before and he knew his route. Up the broad staircase. Follow the banister round to the right. Or the left. Either direction would bring him to the double doors which opened into the anatomical theatre. Stealing up steps so hard and smooth they had to be marble, sword in one hand and lantern in the other, he chose to wheel to the left. The double doors lay a few inches ajar.

'N-o-w!' he yelled, his voice rising on each letter of the word as he lifted his foot and kicked the doors wide. 'Show yourselves!' he bellowed into the blackness. 'Show yourselves in the name of the King!'

The echoes of that imperious demand died away into silence. Then there was nothing. No shouts of alarm nor voices raised in panic. No frantic movement within the shadows of the room. No gasps or quick and hurried breathing. No sense of the exquisite tension of bodies held as still as humanly possible, aching to remain hidden and unnoticed. No sense of any living being at all lurking within the shadows of the anatomical theatre.

A discomforting thought danced into Catto's brain. That didn't necessarily mean the room was devoid of occupants. After all, a corpse could neither speak nor walk, could it? A prickle ran through the fine hairs bound by the black satin ribbon at the back of his neck. Mayhap he himself was not quite so sanguine about the power of the departed as he liked to believe.

He lifted his lantern high, resisted an unexpected impulse to cross himself in protection, took a deep breath and stepped into the featureless void.

2

The deep breath had been a mistake. The foul stink hanging like a tattered curtain in the atmosphere held the whiff of both the slaughterhouse and the privy. Pressing his lips together in a vain attempt to shut it out, Catto edged forward. He was in a lecture theatre. He didn't want to find himself stumbling and tumbling down stairs cut through descending rows of seats. The lanterns of the men clustering behind him were allowing him to make out the shape of those.

As the illumination increased, he saw a broad walkway around the curving back of the tiered seats and a succession of sconces set at regular intervals along a whitewashed wall. The lantern threw his shadow onto the stark surface, dramatically elongating his already tall frame. He had become a giant. Or a bogeyman designed to frighten children into scurrying into their beds and pulling the covers up over their quivering heads.

Walking first one way and then the other, his eyes swept along the rows of seats. He glanced down into the well of the lecture theatre, the focal point of the room. Set on a solid central plinth, a narrow white marble slab glowed dimly in the light spilling down onto it from the men's lanterns. Nothing lay on it. The whole damn room was empty, occupied by neither the dead nor the living—

Unless his quarry was concealed behind the curving wooden wall looming forward out of the deep shadows behind the marble slab. He knew what lay behind it, a small chamber which allowed for the discreet entry into the anatomical theatre of cadavers to be dissected. The entrance to it from the outside world was through a side door screened by trees on the ground floor of the building. He'd made sure to have men posted there, in the cordon he'd thrown around the place.

Disappointment at finding the anatomical theatre empty gave way to a bubbling excitement. He could feel it, fizzing through his veins at the thought of at least some action tonight, however unexciting his adversaries were likely to be. As he adjusted his stance, the cold steel in his hand shifted, glinting as it caught the light.

The men of the Town Guard thought they were here because of an illegal dissection. So he would continue to let them think that and in the process stretch the nerves of Patrick Rankeillor and whoever might be with him to breaking point. Those were his orders, after all.

'Come down hard on the man, Bob. God knows, he needs to be brought to his senses. I've tried reasoned argument. Until I'm blue in the face, forbye. If you have to turn his life and his household upside-down to drag the fool back from the brink of disaster, then so be it. I want you to put the fear of God into him, lad!'

Catto couldn't really see the need, but if that was what the Lord President wanted, then that was what the Lord President would get.

The foul aroma hanging in the air was overlaid with the fatty reek of candlewax. He stepped over to one of the wall sconces. All three of the white candles held within its black wrought-iron grasp were warm and soft to the touch.

'But recently extinguished,' he murmured to himself. 'I need these re-lit,' he announced in a louder voice. 'Now,' he added, placing his own lantern on a high wooden chair set against the back wall of the anatomical theatre and swinging round to the men gathered at its double doors, as little in the room as they could possibly be. As before, they moved immediately to do his bidding. Seconds later, he heard a muttered oath.

'God save us, Captain!' exclaimed the man, a lit spill burning down unheeded towards his fingers. 'This is an evil and wicked place, I'm thinking. A veritable cabinet of horrors.'

Following the direction of eyes brimming with shock and disgust, Catto stifled an oath of his own. He had to make himself walk along the curving wall to study the dark wooden shelves cunningly fitted into it.

A veritable cabinet of horrors. 'Twas an elegant description – especially when pronounced in that musical Highland accent – for the hideous battery which now confronted him. Suspended in liquid, presumably alcohol mixed with other preservatives, he was looking at all sorts of ... *productions*. He supposed that would be the correct word. A human foot, starkly white. A bubbling growth frothed out of it, some sort of canker. Apart from its washed-out colour it reminded him most unpleasantly of the curly kale Scots seemed to eat with such monotonous regularity.

Along from the foot, a deformed and crabbed hand floated in a tall glass jar. Claw-like in its disposition, the knuckles of the fingers were bent almost at right angles to each other. Impossible to tell whether this particular horror had once belonged to a man or a woman.

His eyes travelled along the shelf. Wanting to look. Not wanting to look. More sconces lighting up behind him. God Almighty. What he saw next could only be a human foetus, expelled from its mother's womb before its time. Revulsion. Quite visceral revulsion. That was what he was experiencing now.

There was no squeamishness in it. He was a soldier. As the boy he had been had fought his way to manhood across the battlefields of Europe, he had seen some terrible wounds, the sort that made you wish the poor bastard, be he friend or foe, had been killed outright. You knew he was never going to recover, the damage done to his body beyond repair. All he had left were hours, or if Providence or God or the fates or whoever decided these things was merciful, moments of agony.

If you could, if the heat of battle was not still raging, you stayed with him, tried to ease his passing the only way you could, give him some human contact in his final moments on this Earth, knowing that, but for the grace of God, he might have been doing the same for you. As you fought not to retch your own guts up at the sight of his spilling out over his belly, or his brains slithering in a slimy grey mess onto the fresh green grass.

You could never get rid of those pictures. They stayed in your head forever, flashed before your eyes at the most inopportune moments. As the sounds of men – and oh God, horses – dying in agony could scream in your ears for years afterwards, ambushing you when you least expected it.

No soldier Catto had ever met would choose to carry all that around in his head. Yet the men who gathered at Surgeons' Hall had made the choice to view the hideous specimens which surrounded him here. As they chose to dig people up out of their graves and dissect and pickle and study them. His mouth tightened. Time to reel the ghouls in.

'With me.' The three guards he'd indicated clattered down behind him as he descended the central flight of the three sets of stairs cut through the wooden benches of the anatomical theatre. His wounded thigh did not care for the repeated pressure of the downward journey.

'Stand back from the area around the plinth,' he ordered in a firm, clear voice. 'I am seeking evidence that an illegal dissection was indeed conducted here tonight.'

His words were for the benefit of Patrick Rankeillor and his students. Let them hope they were safe. Let them fear they were not. And he would not allow himself to dwell on the thought that they might still have the bloody and half-dissected cadaver with them.

As he approached the plinth, he observed with purely academic interest that the marble table had a raised lip round all four edges, turning it into a very shallow bath. Angled towards one end, it had a plughole stopped up with a cork, making it, he supposed, easier to clean, rinse and wipe dry afterwards.

Bending over the slab, he noticed some tiny soap bubbles clustered around the plughole. As he raised his head, moving the still air, a witches' brew of smells once more assaulted his senses. Intertwined with the smell of candlewax, the noxious aroma had to be a mixture of the cloying sweetness of decay and the freshness of hot, soapy water, the latter not quite masking the former.

Catto's capricious brain chose that moment to present him with a mental image of the object which must mere moments ago have been lying upon this cold white stone. The picture was so grotesquely vivid it was all he could do not to bring up the chicken fricassy he'd eaten for his supper.

'Most illuminating,' he pronounced.

Stepping back, he studied the wooden floor around the plinth. Some patches of wood looked darker than others. Crouching down, he laid his hand flat against one of those marks. It was damp to the touch. Lifting his hand to his nose, he sniffed his fingertips. They smelled clean and soapy. That the floorboards had not yet dried out from the water which had splashed on them was further proof, if he had needed any, that Patrick Rankeillor and his students had but recently made a hurried departure from the anatomical theatre. Most of them, at any rate.

He swung round to the three men awaiting his orders, placed one finger against his lips and pointed to the door of the small wooden chamber. Three unkempt heads nodded in return. Three pairs of hands took a firmer grip on those deadly Lochaber axes.

The door of the chamber had to open outwards. Catto marched over and flung it wide. Sword raised and ready for action, he strode inside – and found nothing but an empty room.

'These stairs over here, Captain?' The man who'd spoken was already heading there, his comrades clattering behind him.

'Leave me one of your lanterns,' Catto growled. His sword extended in front of him, he swung round, making sure he hadn't missed anything or anyone. Against the flat back wall of the chamber he spotted the ropes and mechanism of a pulley.

It was the work of seconds to raise the sturdy plank the length and width of a man's body. At one end a round wooden tray held a silver claret jug and three used wine glasses. On a board next to the tray sat the heel of a loaf, a bread knife, a mass of breadcrumbs, the remnants of a lump of cheese, a pat of butter and a spreading knife smeared with both those foodstuffs.

A small blue and white china bowl tucked between the tray and the breadboard contained nothing but clear water. Catto swore an obscene oath at the sight of it. To the right of the debris, as far away as the length of the board lift would allow, stood a loosely rolled coil of stiff paper. Next to it was a dark green leather cylinder with a narrow strap buckled to both ends. Laying his sword to one side, he leaned forward, checked the cylinder was empty and lifted the coiled paper.

He pulled it open, securing its topmost edge under the tray and holding the lower edge with his fingertips. He was looking at a map of Scotland, hand-drawn and meticulously done. Every town of any size was marked, as was every main route, military road and garrison, every major river, bridge, ford, ferry and coastal port.

For a moment he stood and stared at it, registering that England was no more than sketched in, shown only as far south as Carlisle in the west and Newcastle in the east. Out over the German Ocean, an elegant scroll had been drawn. It held a list, neat enough but done, he thought, by a different hand to the one which had made the map: *Garrison Strengths as at October 1743*. His eyes picked out a few names, linked by rows of full stops to other names and numbers on the left.

Dumbarton Castle .... *1 company, well below strength.*
Edinburgh Castle .... *General Guest, in Command of 80 Veterans & Invalids.*
Fort William .... *Walls badly in need of repair. Not easily defensible.*
Ruthven Barracks .... *1 Sargt. in Command of 24 Invalids.*

With the feeling of being in a dream, he released the map, slid it out from under the tray and straightened up. The stiff paper rolled itself back into the loose coil in which he had found it, bouncing and snapping as it came to rest. In the eerie stillness of the little room the sound cracked like a musket shot. A squadron of avenging angels, the sights and sounds and smells came swooping in.

Corsica. That surprise attack. Banditti swooping down from the shelter of dazzling, sun-baked rocks. No warning other than that first shot and the thin white plume of smoke rising from the musket which had fired it. A frantic scramble to pull one of his pistols from his belt with one hand and his sword from its scabbard with the other. A second crack and the whistle of stirred air inches from his head. Wheeling round to watch in horror as the young ensign next to him cried out and slumped in his saddle. The lad's life snuffed out in an instant.

Catto had roared out his fury at that. So had the men. Rage powered a vicious, bloody fightback. In a matter of moments every one of their attackers was dead. There was no mercy that day. The victors were left panting, dripping with sweat, splashed with the blood of the men they had killed, still warm from their veins: and Robert Catto had been left thinking yet again how thin the veneer of civilization and humanity was, how few steps man was away from barbarity. Himself included. All it took was one shot. The fires were always laid, and only ever needed one spark to set them off.

He was angry now. Only there was no enemy against whom he could raise his pistol or slash at with his sword, no superhuman physical effort to be made, no way he could use his strength to empty himself of his emotions. This battle called for different weapons.

He would have to find a different way to rid himself of the rage.

3

Pausing only to sheath his sword, roll up the map and slide it into its leather case, Catto flung out of the room. Sparing neither a glance nor a thought for the veritable cabinet of horrors, he took the stairs up through the wooden seats two at a time. There was no pain in his thigh now. Using the map case in a scooping motion, he indicated to the men that they should follow him up and out.

'Nobody on the ground floor or in the outbuildings in the Physic Garden, young Captain Catto,' announced Sergeant Livingstone, coming back inside with Davie Rintoul as their Captain ran nimbly down to the main doors of Surgeons' Hall.

'Nobody in the bagnio, either,' Rintoul offered.

'There's a bagnio?' Catto asked, surprised enough to be jolted out of his racing thoughts. That hadn't been marked on the plan he'd consulted. 'In the surgeons' meeting place?'

'Not that kind of a bagnio, Captain,' Livingstone said. 'This one really was just a bath-house.' He spoke with a primness which on another night and in another place would have had Catto wanting to howl with laughter. Well over sixty but a fine figure of a man still, Livingstone was married to a woman half his age and had proved his lusty vigour by fathering three children on her.

'That's no' the way my faither tells it,' Davie Rintoul said. 'Seemingly there was a time when some high jinks went on in there.

That's why they shut it doon. Fine ladies and fine gentlemen taking baths on the same day as each other.' Rintoul tapped the side of his nose. 'If ye ken whit I mean, sir.'

'Fascinating,' growled Catto. 'Just shows you the moral dangers posed by soap and water, eh?'

'Sir?' Rintoul asked, a puzzled frown replacing the knowing grin.

'Never mind. Go and put out the sconces in the anatomical theatre. Quick as you can.'

He spent the next few moments issuing orders, first dispatching a detail of the men he himself had led here tonight to the nearby Royal Infirmary. Two pairs were to stand guard at its front and rear doors, four others were to inspect the dead-room and the operating theatre. If they found nothing there, those four were then to mount a patrol of the exterior of the building, two circling it clockwise, two counter-clockwise.

He divided another group into small platoons and ordered them at once to reinforce the guard on Edinburgh's gates. Much fucking good though that might do. At this time of night those were locked and bolted anyway. The Bristo Port had been opened to let Catto and his troop out and immediately closed behind them. Given his own stupidity in creating a delay, might someone who wanted out of Edinburgh in a hurry already have left by a less orthodox route? Or was he only hoping that was the case?

Hoping. The word slammed into him. Winded by it, he bent forward, allowing the hand not holding the map case to slide down his leg to rest above his knee. He had been afraid of this. *Oh Christ Almighty, how he had been afraid of this...*

'That wound from Dettingen troubling you tonight, young Captain Catto?'

'Somewhat.' The pain was nothing now but better the Sergeant think that than anything else. 'One moment, Livingstone.'

Patrick Rankeillor and whoever might be with him.

No. He had no real reason to be thinking this. It went against sense. It went against self-preservation. Then again, when had that ever counted for anything? God in Heaven, hadn't everyone's safety and well-being been compromised? Except for that one precious, over-valued object, of course.

He drew in a breath of cold night air. He'd get nowhere if he allowed the anger to take him over. Logical and rational thought, that's what he needed now. Plus his instincts.

Honed over his years of soldiering, he had come to trust those. Experience too was playing its part, all those memories he wished he did not have but could never manage to erase, the ones which had come flooding back in that nasty little room tucked away behind the anatomical theatre.

'You bring certain very specific skills and advantages to this commission you so do not want, Bob.'

'I could wish them all to the Devil, sir.'

Unfortunately the Earl of Hell had no interest in what the Lord President had termed Catto's very specific skills and advantages. He was stuck with them, knew exactly what had been going on up there on the first floor, could almost hear those three glasses clinking in treasonable toast above that small china bowl. *Here's a health to the king over the water.*

He had not needed the Lord President to tell him there were dreamers and fools a-plenty in Scotland who carried out that hopelessly romantic ritual on a regular basis. Shaking his head, Duncan Forbes had described how some fought imaginary battles to restore the exiled Stuart king over their dinner tables, silver salt cellars and pepper pots standing in for the anticipated commanders of the opposing armies.

Catto had curled his lip at those stories, discovering nothing here in Edinburgh to persuade him anything more than such pathetic play-acting was going on. Until tonight.

Up in that nasty little room a man on the run had wolfed down a snatched meal. In the unpleasant setting of the anatomical theatre of Surgeons' Hall, a place of horror most people would go far out of their way to avoid. You would only sit down to eat there if you had no other choice. So here was a man who does not want to risk, or cannot afford to risk, being seen.

Two other men take a glass of wine with this man but leave the food to him, because he's a long way from his last meal and doesn't know where the next one's coming from. They give him bread and cheese, not anything cooked. However much a gnawing belly and a watering mouth crave steaming broth and tasty stew, hot food is something a man on the run can seldom have. Out in the open a fire signals your position. Indoors, in low-roofed houses and tall tenement lands, fragrant smells in odd places and at odd hours travel along corridors, drift upstairs and down, give the game away.

Second deduction, then. This is a man who has travelled to Edinburgh, not one who lives here. Although he is doing his utmost not to be noticed, he has to run the risk because he has an important message to pass on, and something to receive. The map. This bloody map around which Catto's fingers now coiled.

Beautifully drawn. Meticulously detailed. Listing the strengths of Government garrisons around the country. Protected in its own leather case, keeping it in perfect condition. Until it can be taken to a printer far from Edinburgh who will be paid handsomely to ask no questions and reproduce it one hundredfold so it can be distributed among the officers of an invading army?

The man who was now undoubtedly cursing himself for having left the map behind was also travelling in winter, the worst possible time to be moving around Scotland, which led to a third deduction. This is about something that is going to happen very soon. Not quite yet. Nobody in their right mind would launch a military campaign at this time of year, with winter about to close in—

A military campaign. Christ Almighty. Robert Catto snapped to attention as quickly as if the call to boot and saddle had been sounded. Bloody hell. Bloody fucking hell …

'Mr Catto, sir?'

'Other ways to get in and out of Edinburgh, wouldn't you say, Sergeant? Even when the gates are locked. As we have but recently demonstrated.' He hoped the reaction he had been unable to suppress had given nothing away. He couldn't be right about this. He couldn't be.

'You'd have to be gey fit to take them,' Livingstone said doubtfully. 'It'd be over hard a climb for most folk. Or too long a drop. Who are we after, young Captain Catto? Somehow I'm finding it hard to picture Professor Rankeillor dreeping a hundred feet down a wall.'

Catto shot him an appraising look. Livingstone was a smart man, in both senses of the word. His Captain had no complaints about his appearance. What was currently going on inside that handsome white-haired head was another matter. A swift answer, then. Or lack of one. 'His students would be more agile, though. Even if they were transporting a cadaver.'

'An awkward burden all the same. One they would be anxious to rid themselves of sooner rather than later, I'm thinking.' Livingstone spoke in the soft Highland accent years of soldiering in Europe followed by years of innkeeping in Edinburgh seemed not to have much altered. 'If you will permit me to speak my mind, young Captain Catto?'

Catto lifted a hand, granting the requested permission. He had the hospital and Rankeillor's house secured. It couldn't hurt to hear what Livingstone had to say.

'Would we not be better concentrating on the Royal Infirmary? That's somewhere they'll all ken, with a wheen of places to stow a body beyond the dead-room and the operating theatre.'

Catto didn't give a damn about where they might have hidden the cadaver. It was a live body he was interested in now, although the Sergeant wasn't wrong. The new hospital was vast, built on the grand scale, parts of it internally as yet unfinished, offering plenty of hiding places both for the quick and the dead. Three storeys high, it had an attic floor above those, plus cellars below.

Plenty of hiding places but plenty of escape routes too. The Infirmary's walls, including those of its two projecting wings, were studded with windows and doors. He couldn't be sure his guards front and back and his four-man patrol could cover all of those. The only way to secure such a building would be to surround it completely and search it from top to bottom.

He'd need every man jack in the Town Guard to do that and it would still be a stretch. He'd already considered the idea and rejected it. Too much of a risk to concentrate all his manpower in one place. Especially at night. Especially now he had lost the element of surprise. Especially as – and God damn this one to hell and back again – he had to be careful what he did when it came to the Royal Infirmary. Especially as the Jacobite messenger might equally have sought refuge in Rankeillor's house.

'Twould be a stupid place to run to but men scattering in a panic were not always thinking straight. So the surgeon-apothecary's house had to be at least a possibility. The thought brought a wave of nausea with it. Catto rid himself of that by focussing hard on the Sergeant, rehearsing what he knew about him.

Livingstone, Donald. Originally a native of the island of Lismore in Argyle. Looks not unlike a kindly Old Father Time or a wise and benevolent God. Still strong and wiry and fitter than many men half his age. Worked hard to persuade me to allow him to take part in the drilling and training. Spent twenty years in the Royal Scots and in his youth saw action during the War of the Spanish Succession, including at that bloodiest of battles: Malplaquet. Now runs a livery stable at the foot of the Canongate with that wife of his, who's a good thirty years younger than her husband but seems as devoted to him as he does to her.

None of which meant it couldn't have been Livingstone who'd delivered the warning to Rankeillor. Or dispatched someone less conspicuous than himself with it. Someone had alerted the professor and his mysterious visitor. The hurried departure from Surgeons Hall was evidence of that – and such a warning could only have come from the men.

Catto had told them their intended destination moments before they left the guard-house. Anyone else seeing the Town Guard on the move late this December evening could not have realized where they were headed until it was too late to do anything about it. He had not really been so naïve as to believe they were all on his side. Scotland was a place of conflicting loyalties. Aye, and shifting ones too.

Yet why any of the men would have been privy to tonight's meeting in Surgeons' Hall tonight, the one even more secret than the dissection, was a mystery. Plotting the return of the Stuarts was a gentlemen's game. Or those who, all evidence to the contrary, insisting on awarding themselves that designation. Catto's mouth tightened.

'Are you using me as a thinking-post, Captain?'

'Something like that.' Livingstone was looking back at him out of very blue eyes. As striking as everything else about his appearance, they were as clear and as innocent as a babe's. Shrewd too, though. Very, very shrewd. 'And what would you be thinking, Livingstone?'

'I'm thinking you're wondering if you can trust me, Mr Catto.'

'Can I?' The cold night air shimmered between them. Close by, the bough of a tree creaked. Livingstone cleared his throat. 'We're both soldiers, sir.'

'Comrades-in-arms?'

'Aye, young Captain Catto, sir.' The Sergeant's powerful head went up. 'Exactly that.'

Catto continued to meet the very blue eyes. 'Glad to hear it,' he murmured. Then, urgently, and truthfully: 'We don't have enough men to effectively seal and search the Royal Infirmary. The search of such a large building with so many potential entrances and exits could easily descend into a game of cat and mouse. Or utter farce. We cannot afford to run the risk of turning the Town Guard into a laughing stock.'

'Indeed no, Captain. Nor can we afford to take any men off the Professor's house. For those we seek might also have taken refuge there.'

That had been a quick climbdown. Deference to him as an officer, taking his point, or misdirection of his attention by first raising the hare of the Royal Infirmary and then dismissing it? Trust no one. Not even someone who's as good as told you he's on your side. Not even someone your gut tells you is with you. 'Twas a bleak thought.

'Those we seek might well have taken refuge in any number of hiding places,' he said, thinking of all those impossibly high tenement lands threaded through with a multiplicity of narrow closes snaking back from dark streets into darker courtyards. Even if he'd had a full regiment of regulars under his command, he hadn't a hope in hell of finding his quarry amongst that maze of rabbit warrens and rat holes.

So he had allowed a Jacobite messenger to slip through his fingers. How the Devil was he to explain that to the Lord President?

'Welcome home, my boy. I'll be able to sleep sound in my bed tonight.'

Not if he knew what was going on here, he wouldn't.

Catto glanced back up the marble stairs of Surgeons' Hall. Funny how light transformed a place. 'Twas simply a building now. No longer the yawning jaws of hell. Funny how your brain made room for irrelevant thoughts when you had vastly more important things to worry about. Like the decision heading towards you at a rate of knots, the one you absolutely did not want to have to make, the one which would force you out of the comfort of the shadows into lights as brilliant as the ones blazing on this staircase.

'Best extinguish these sconces here too before we go. We don't want to burn the place down. What's that?' he asked, swinging round to Livingstone, who had muttered something.

'I said it's a pity the good people who tried that back in '25 did not succeed, Captain,' the Sergeant said darkly.

'There was trouble over a dissection back then? Worse than last month's incident?'

'So I have been told. Although there is always trouble over dissections. As there should be. Such practices are not Christian. What is any poor creature cut to pieces by the anatomist's knife supposed to do come the Day of Judgement? We all have to be whole then.'

'Quite so,' Catto murmured, aware even in the midst of this developing disaster of his customary discomfort when confronted by genuine religious conviction. His own faith was of the pragmatic variety, brought out and dusted down only as required, chiefly when he struck the usual bargain with God before a battle or skirmish. So far, his wounded leg notwithstanding, the Almighty had kept his side of that bargain, even if Catto had not. Maybe that was why He was punishing him tonight.

Or maybe he only had his own stupidity to blame. He'd thought Duncan Forbes had brought him to Scotland on a fool's errand. Now it looked as though it was he who had been the fool. He hadn't wanted to believe the threat was real. He'd wanted to keep on thinking the Stuart Cause was dead and buried, six foot under, ashes and dust, the province of dreamers, fools and hatchers of hopeless plots. Bitterness rose like bile in his throat and he swallowed hard to banish it.

'Put the lights out and follow me over to the surgeon-apothecary's house. Leave these three men on guard at this door.'

'Outside o' it, Captain?' came a hopeful question from one of those men.

'Aye. Outside of it.'

Frosted pebbles crunched beneath his black buckled shoes as he marched out into the Physic Garden. He stopped and took a breath, drawing the night air deep into his lungs. After the stink of death and shit within Surgeons' Hall, he was grateful for its freshness, the open space also offering an escape from the acrid smoke of the surrounding chimneys.

He scanned the frozen garden in which he stood. It was criss-crossed by a grid of paths, the dull gleam of their white stone chips delineating dormant flower and vegetable beds. Where the paths met in the centre of the garden stood a little wooden summer house built in the shape of a Chinese pagoda.

'That been searched?' He used the captured mapcase to point towards it.

'Aye, Captain,' responded Rintoul, appearing at Catto's elbow. 'Not a living soul in there. Nor a dead one, either. We've had a keek in all the outhouses too, as ye ordered.' In his turn, Rintoul pointed towards those. Over to the right, against the city wall, stood a range of glass-houses and outbuildings. One or two panes in the former were catching what moonlight there was, reflecting it back to spill weakly over the path in front of them.

A messenger came running along that moonlit path. Stewart. A private. Catto reached for his first name and found two. William Angus. That was it. William Angus Stewart. Originally out of Appin in the West Highlands. Kinsman to Sergeant Livingstone. A caddie to trade, making him a foot soldier not only in the Town Guard but also in the army of Edinburgh's sedan chair carriers. Stewart belonged to a third force too, a rather more covert one.

'Sergeant Crichton's compliments, Captain,' came the lilting words. 'Lieutenant Liddell has ascertained that the second house is empty and asks if he and his men should remain there. The Sergeant also wishes to advise you that there's a chair coming along Infirmary Street. He cannot see who's in it but believes it to be heading for the surgeon-apothecary's house. It's passed all the closes in Infirmary Street.'

'I know who's in it,' Catto said. 'My compliments to Lieutenant Liddell. He is to bring himself and his men to Rankeillor's house with all dispatch. They are to enter it from the garden here, proceed up the back stairs to the attics and search every room closely, looking behind every door and inside every cupboard and working their way down to the ground floor. Tell me what I just told you.'

The messenger repeated the orders, and sped off. Watching him fade into the gloom, Catto wondered where else such a fleet-footed man might have run tonight. Trust no one. Not even a member of the Lord President's discreet Scotland-wide band of informers, observers and agents. Yet he was going to have to trust some people and William Angus Stewart was one of them. He couldn't do this on his own. Especially not now. Was that what you would call a calculated risk?

Heading along the garden's central path, he went round the little pagoda and made for the gates out into the High School Yards. Rintoul slid in front of him. Digging a set of keys out of his pocket, he flourished them like a magician performing some sleight-of-hand trick and had the lock open in a matter of seconds.

'Any door or gate in Edinburgh, Rintoul?' No matter what was going on, inside your head or out of it, there was always time for a word of encouragement. Nor was he going to make the mistake of believing they were all working against him. That way lay madness. He'd seen it happen to commanders who'd been too long in the field. 'You're a useful man to have around.'

'Glad tae be o' service tae ye, Captain.' Rintoul stepped back to allow Catto to go through the gate in front of him onto the plainstanes which ran in front of the Physic Garden and the two houses which flanked it. Suspended from a black wrought-iron archway at the foot of three wide and curving steps, a large glass lantern burned at Rankeillor's front door.

The three tall white candles within it lit up the oversized pestle and mortar hanging from a projecting bracket at the corner of the house, the universally recognized sign of the apothecary. Punctuated by a mullioned window on each of its two walls, Rankeillor's shop and dispensary occupied the front right-hand corner of his house.

The big lantern at the front door was illuminating something else, the sedan chair which had now reached the house. Its caddies looked a touch worried. Small wonder when they had emerged from the ill-lit tenement canyon of Infirmary Street into a phalanx of the Town Guard, all now holding bright lanterns aloft. Without saying anything, Catto indicated to the chairmen that they should lower their conveyance to the ground.

'What is going on?' asked its occupant. 'Why are there so many guards here?' She had a deep voice for a woman. Mellow. The caddies looked at Catto. He gave another wordless signal that they should open up the chair.

The roof was lifted up and back. The front was swung wide. Like a tightly-closed rosebud touched by the sun, a vast expanse of shimmering yellow silk blossomed out from the confines of the chair. The young woman in the middle of it had her dark head dipped as she prepared to emerge. What she was wearing must make that a tricky manoeuvre.

Walking forward, Catto transferred the map case to his left hand and extended his right. 'Mem?' he said, knowing she would think he was one of the caddies.

Her warm hand came to rest on top of his cold one.

4

'Twas the yellow gown which came out first, the articulated hoops of her petticoat continuing to expand as they escaped from the sedan chair. God knew how she had managed to cram all that in there in the first place. Her hand pressed down on his as she inched forward, readying herself to stand up.

Over her gown she wore a green velvet cloak. Its edges fell apart as she moved, providing Catto with an excellent view of her breasts. He was reminded of that summer in the south, when he had gorged himself on Italian girls and Italian peaches. Her skin had that same bloom. Her breasts had those same curves. Standing over her like this, gazing down the front of her dress, he could almost see the best bits, two little pools of shadow against that peachy skin. She looked up and he encountered for the first time the clear, if troubled, gaze of Miss Christian Rankeillor.

Had he raised his own eyes from her breasts in time? Did it matter? The hint of a sexual threat might prove a useful weapon here. The expression on the girl's face as she tilted her head up towards him was certainly one of alarm. Although, watching her closely, he was pretty sure it was his uniform which was provoking that reaction. The edges of his cloak too had fallen apart, allowing her to take in its rich dark red, crossed diagonally by his white leather sword belt.

'Is aught amiss?' she asked. 'Has there been some sort of a disturbance over at Surgeons' Hall?'

'Interesting you should pose that particular question, Miss Rankeillor.'

He saw the look, the one which meant *I wish I hadn't said that.* The alarm was still there too, clouding her eyes. They were as green as a summer meadow, her velvet cloak a perfect match for them. Curious that she had not asked how he knew her name. Used to being known, he supposed. Miss Rankeillor, the young Edinburgh lady. Miss Rankeillor, the surgeon-apothecary's daughter.

His mouth tightened. He could add two further designations to those. Miss Rankeillor, the graverobber's daughter. Miss Rankeillor, the Jacobite's daughter. If he had needed any more justification for what he was planning on doing next, he had it now.

The hand lying on top of his tensed. 'Has something happened to my father?'

This was too easy. He had her knocked off balance already. 'Step out of the chair and come into the house, Miss Rankeillor.'

The look of alarm intensified. 'I beg you, sir. If aught has happened to my father, pray tell me now!'

'Your concern for him touches me deeply. But I require you to step out of the chair.'

She stiffened, and her eyes widened. Clearly the little Jacobite Miss was not accustomed to being spoken to with such lack of deference. Well, she'd better get used to it. Much worse might be going to befall her. Bad things happened to people who had Jacobites for fathers. Especially those who were actively plotting armed rebellion. Once more Catto felt anger surge through him. It put steel into his voice. 'Step out of the chair, Miss Rankeillor. I won't tell you again.'

'I refuse to move until you tell me what is going on, who you are and what you are doing here.'

'Fine,' he said flatly. 'In which case I shall throw you over my shoulder and carry you into the house.'

She gasped and tried to withdraw her hand. He was too quick for her, turning his own so his fingers were gripping hers. Her eyes widened but her voice remained cool. 'Let go of my hand, sir.'

Used to telling the lower orders what to do, accustomed to being instantly obeyed. *Well, Miss Christian Rankeillor, your world's just changed.* He wondered if she had the faintest idea quite how much.

'I shall release your hand when you agree to walk of your own volition into the house. If you continue to refuse to cooperate with me, I shall do what I said I would and carry you in.'

'You wouldn't dare!'

'Oh, but I would. Believe me.'

How he would hoist her up onto his shoulder and keep her there when she was encased in the cane scaffolding of her petticoat and several yards of slippery silk he didn't know. If he had to do it he would find a way. He was always prepared to carry out his threats. Waiting for her to realize that, he treated himself to a leisurely survey of her lips. She had a nice mouth. Just the right size. She coloured up, drew in a quick breath, and stepped out of the sedan chair. 'I must pay the caddies.'

'By all means.' He released her hand and handed Rintoul the map case. 'Keep this for me. No-one is to open it. Including yourself.' He did not miss the glance Christian Rankeillor darted at the green leather cylinder, nor the tiny start she gave.

Once she had paid the chairmen and secured the drawstrings of her reticule, he made a sweeping and sardonic gesture of invitation, indicating that she should precede him into the house. The entrance steps were barely broad enough to accommodate her and her ridiculous skirts.

'I have not invited you into my house.'

'No,' he agreed, 'you have not. But I am coming in anyway. My men are already there.'

She looked through the open front door. It framed a press of red coats and that vicious forest of Lochaber axes. Rough male voices rumbled. Was there a flutter of panic, a tremble of those wide skirts as she took it all in? There had to be. Yet she said only, 'So I see,' and walked in front of him into her invaded home.

There were three females in the lobby, two young girls and one middle-aged woman. They were dressed for bed in all-encompassing dressing-gowns, their hair looped up in curling papers. Her demure brown wrapper topped by an incongruously colourful red and yellow shawl bearing a design of fanciful birds, the oldest of the three was directing a barrage of complaints against Sergeant Crichton. He was attempting to counter the verbal onslaught.

That was stupid. You didn't argue the toss with civilians who got in your way. You simply told them what you required them to do. If they showed the slightest disinclination to obey, you then told them what you would do to them if they didn't. The mere suggestion of physical aggression usually did the trick with females.

Following the turning heads of the Town Guard as Catto walked behind Christian Rankeillor into the lobby, the woman broke off. 'Miss Kirsty! Thank God ye're hame! The hoose is full o' these Hieland raggymuffins.' She jabbed her thumb towards the Sergeant. 'Matthew Crichton here – wha, being baith a Christian and an Edinburgh man born and bred, should ken better than to burst into honest, respectable folks' hooses in the dead o' night – is busy telling me he canna do anything without his Captain's authority. The lang lad wi' the chestnut hair.' She came bustling across the polished floorboards of the lobby to stand in front of Catto. 'That'll be you then, will it?'

He had to bend his head to look her in the eye. She was a good foot shorter than him. A belligerent sparrow. His face was impassive as he gazed down at her, his voice very cool. 'And who might you be?'

She lifted one hand and jabbed him in the chest with her index finger, an inch below the well-polished gorget he wore around his neck. A nod back to the days when soldiers wore armour, the half-moon brass disc was a symbol of his officer's rank. 'That's for me to ken and you to find out, young man.'

Not too taxing a puzzle. Judging by that *Miss Kirsty* and the bunch of keys dangling and jangling at her waist, she had to be the housekeeper.

'Betty,' Christian Rankeillor said, her voice rising, 'what is going on? Where is my father?'

'He's oot,' the little woman said. 'Ye ken fine he was going oot this evening, Miss Kirsty. Tae converse wi'— Weel, I canna just mind wha he was going tae converse wi'. Mr Hume perhaps, or maybe Provost Coutts. He kens that many gentlemen as knowledgeable and weel-read as himsel. Is that no' right, Miss Kirsty? Gie me your cloak now, lass.'

Wondering how much the two of them knew, deciding for the moment to head in one direction rather than the other, Catto curled his lip. 'I heard he was spending the evening with his students. And a cadaver.'

That chilling word didn't produce anything like the impact he'd been hoping for. Untying her green cloak, Christian Rankeillor allowed it to slip off her shoulders so the housekeeper could take it from her.

'Your father has been conducting an illegal dissection this evening, Miss Rankeillor. Am I not right?'

She raised gracefully arched eyebrows, dark as her hair. Pulled back at her temples to fall in soft ringlets around her face, that was more mahogany than chestnut. 'I can tell you nothing of that, sir. Although I might suggest you're more likely to find a cadaver in Surgeons' Hall than here. Give me the keys, Betty.'

Catto flipped the heavy folds of his grey cloak over one shoulder. 'We've already searched Surgeons' Hall. Now we're conducting a search of this house.'

The girl's chin flew up. Any higher and she'd topple backwards onto the floor. If a woman fell while she was wearing a hooped petticoat she was like a sheep stuck on its back. Miss Hoity-Toity Rankeillor would be completely helpless if that happened. At his mercy. He allowed himself to be diverted by the thought.

'You are not going to search this house!'

'We already are,' he told her smoothly.

'Not without these, you're not,' she said as the housekeeper gave her the keys.

'Which is why you're going to hand them over to me.'

That earned him a contemptuous flicker of the eyelids. 'I don't think so, sir.'

'Don't you?' He didn't need her keys. Not with Rintoul in his raiding party. Except that he did. This rapidly developing battle of wills had an audience, her household and his men. There could be only one winner of this contest.

Standing there in her evening finery, her yellow dress decorated with bows of white satin ribbon, she was a perfect picture of one of Edinburgh's Jacobite misses *en fête*. They were a type, one for which Catto had already come to nurse a healthy contempt. Professing support for the Stuart Cause was all the rage among the city's young ladies of fashion, the high spot of their social calendar the celebration of the Young Pretender's birthday.

The ongoing confusion between New Style and Old Style dating allowed Charles Edward Stuart two of those, 20th and 31st December. Judging by the letters Catto had intercepted over the past few weeks, the Jacobite misses took that as an excuse to thread their entire Yuletide festivities through with supper parties and soirées in celebration of their hero's birth.

Those letters sent by various breathless and indiscreet young ladies – in codes and ciphers laughably easy to break – had given him a clear picture of what was involved: sentimental songs, diabolically awful poetry and misty-eyed toasts to the king over the water and his son. Risible, faintly pathetic, and hardly likely to bring down the government or topple the Protestant Succession. What Christian Rankeillor's father and his mysterious visitor had been up to this evening might.

As neatly as though it had been rehearsed to occur at this

opportune moment, a voice floated down to the lobby from above his head. 'Nothing but servants' quarters in the attics, sir,' announced Lieutenant Liddell. 'All empty. Four room on this floor, three of those also empty. The fourth room would appear to be the young lady's bedchamber. Are we to search that too?'

Liddell, Archibald. Also one of the younger members of the Town Guard and by far the highest in terms of social status. Which is undoubtedly why he has scruples about invading the privacy of a young lady's bedchamber.

Barely glancing up to where the Lieutenant stood on the upstairs landing, his eyes fixed on Christian Rankeillor's face, Robert Catto spoke in a lazy drawl. 'Leave the young lady's bedchamber to me, Liddell. I'll undertake the search of that myself.'

5

He heard the shuffling of feet and the nervous adjustment of weapons. He glanced at Sergeant Crichton. The man was a veteran of the Town Guard, tough as old boots and rigorous when it came to enforcing the law, making no allowances Catto had yet distinguished for age, gender or social status. Yet even he was shifting uncomfortably.

The little maidservants looked stunned. The only person who didn't seem to be reacting was the one he was trying to provoke. The housekeeper squawked her protest. 'You will not ging into Miss Kirsty's bedchamber!' She put her hands on her hips. Not that she had any. She was as skinny as a rake. 'You will not!'

'That woman's beginning to give me a headache, Crichton,' Catto said languidly. 'Shut her up, would you?'

'Captain,' protested the Sergeant, 'how in the name of the Good Being am I to do that?'

'I don't much care. Find an apron or a cloth and gag her with it.'

That won him the reaction he'd been expecting. 'How dare you even suggest such a thing?' The silk skirts rustled as she swung round towards the housekeeper. 'Don't worry, Betty. He will not dare to do it. Not while I'm here to prevent it.'

Catto shrugged. 'One more word. Final warning.' He held out his hand. 'The keys.'

Her eyes flashed emerald fire. 'I do not give you permission to enter my bedchamber.'

'I don't need your permission, Miss Rankeillor. I am an officer of the law and I may go wherever I please.'

She glared at him. Then, nostrils flaring: 'The door to my bedchamber is not locked.'

'I expect the door to your father's shop is, though, and I wish to take a look at that before I go upstairs. I have neither the time nor the patience to stand here arguing with you, madam. The keys,' he said again.

She had slipped the metal ring which held them over her slim wrist. 'If I refuse?'

'Then I'll take them from you. With as much force as you oblige me to use.'

'*With as much force as I oblige you to use?*' Sparks flew off every disbelieving word.

'Exactly. Give me the keys. Now.'

She came straight back at him, pronouncing her words with the exaggerated precision which indicates blinding rage. 'Let me be sure that I understand you, sir. You are threatening to manhandle me if I refuse to hand over the keys?'

Manhandle her. Now there was another diverting thought. She was spoiling him. The peachy skin was rosy now, her face and throat flushed with anger. Her fury did not mask her fear. Her house was full of red-coated soldiers and she was scared. As well she might be.

He wasted no time in pressing his advantage, stepping forward so that he was too close to her, forcing her to tilt her head to look up at him. 'Be in no doubt that I shall do whatever I have to do, Miss Rankeillor.' He hardened his voice. 'The keys, madam. For the last time of asking. And tell me which one is for the shop.' When he allowed his eyes to drift to the housekeeper Christian Rankeillor drew the metal ring off her wrist, selected a key and thrust it at him.

She was holding the key she had picked out by its business end.

Clearly he was supposed to take it from her by its shank. So he made sure to confound her expectations. For the second time this evening, his fingers closed over her own. Her gasp of outrage gave him a jolt of pure satisfaction. As did the widening of her green eyes when he drew his sword.

Pretty certain there could be no one in her father's shop or they would be visible through the internal windows in the wall which separated it from the lobby, he nevertheless unlocked its double doors and went through into it.

Finding himself behind the counter, he walked around that obstacle and stepped onto a jewel-bright patterned rug in front of a red leather daybed set under the windows which overlooked the street. A folded screen stood against the wall at the foot of the couch. Catto turned and scrutinized his surroundings. There was plenty of light spilling in from the lobby, more than enough to see by. There was nobody here and the place was exactly as you would expect an apothecary's shop to be.

Behind the counter were banks of small deep wooden drawers with shelves above, the woodwork painted the shade he'd heard described as apple-green. The shelves held sets of brass scales and weights of varying sizes, wooden and porcelain pestles and mortars, crucibles and other dishes along with a multiplicity of green glass and blue and white pottery jars arranged in rows according to their varying shapes and sizes.

Blue and green should never be seen, not even on a fairy queen. The long-lost voice echoed around his head. It wasn't the first time in the last month he'd had the fancy he'd heard it. Not surprising when he was surrounded by so many soft Scottish voices. Harder to react logically when he both wanted it to keep talking and disappear like a puff of smoke and leave him alone.

Concentrating hard on the shelves behind the counter, Catto found himself looking at six tall glass jars full of sweets. One of them held small straw-coloured squares. Tablet. He'd forgotten all about tablet in his years away from Scotland. This time the memories clutched at his heart. Only one way the dead can hurt you. They were laying into him now.

Emotion coursed through him, powerful enough to freeze him to the spot. He blinked, looked up, and saw that Christian Rankeillor was gazing at him through the internal windows, a curious look on her face. He gave himself a silent order. *Move, Catto. Shift your sorry arse. Now would be good.*

He focussed hard, saw green and gold brocade curtains covering the back wall of the room. Drawing them back revealed another set of double doors. He struck lucky with the key. Or maybe there was some logic at work here. It was the next one on the ring.

He found himself in a library. No surprises here either. Floor-to-ceiling shelves, two big carved wooden chairs with seats and backs upholstered in the same green and gold stuff as the curtains on the other side of the door and a large square table serving as a desk in the middle of the room. Piled high with books and papers, it was as untidy a one as he'd ever seen. Quite impressive in its own horrific way, although he'd never understood how people could work like that.

He took a quick breath. Good. He was once more back on an even keel. Or as even as that keel could be after what he had discovered tonight.

The third set of double doors proved to be unlocked and led, as they had to, out into the lobby and the twin glares of Mistress Belligerent Sparrow and the Hoity-Toity Jacobite Miss. Mistress and maid united. So sure of themselves. So sure of their place in their safe little world. Especially the young mistress. Condescending little cunt.

She'd be a lot less sure of herself if he let the men loose on the house. He'd have them tramp all over it, their heavy brogues working more dirt and ice into the floors and the rugs than they already had, use their Lochaber axes to rip open stuffed chairs and feather pillows, ransack those neat little drawers in Patrick Rankeillor's shop, empty all the lotions and potions onto the floor, throw the jars of tablet and sweets onto the bright rug and stamp the glass and sugary confections into it, turn it all into sludge, make a right fucking mess. She'd be on her knees in front of him then, begging him to stop—

Catto caught himself on, shaken by the venom he was feeling towards this girl. She was nothing to him, merely a means to an end. To achieve that end he would go as far as he dared, hammer home more harshly still the message being delivered by this invasion of her home.

Moving with slow and graceful deliberation, he raised his sword in front of his face in mocking salute to his girl adversary. Beyond the rising glint of the blade he could see every head in the lobby follow its progress as he lowered it again. This must be how actors on the stage felt, each member of the audience focussed on their every move.

He stretched out his arm before turning the sword flat and using its tip to describe a semi-circle in the charged air. A rather roguish *maître d'armes* had taught him this trick. Whenever he used it he always heard the voice of his old fencing master in his head. 'Not many people are prepared to argue with a man who has a sword in his hand, young *Robert*.' The man had always pronounced his name in the French way. Naturally enough. 'Especially one who holds his weapon with control, wields it with grace and looks as if he knows how to use it.'

He knew how to use it, all right. Observing the reactions, he heard the two young maids whimper, saw them clutch each other's arms. Even the housekeeper couldn't stop herself from shrinking back. Only Christian Rankeillor stood her ground. He could tell by those expressive eyes that he was frightening her. Yet she did not budge, even managed the air of haughty disdain. 'Isn't this a little theatrical, sir? Tell me, do you really expect to find a cadaver in my bedchamber?'

'I have no idea what I might find in your bedchamber, Miss Rankeillor. I've always found it good policy in such situations for a man to be armed.' He looked her up and down, taking his time about it, judging from her blush that she had understood the all-too-obvious double entendre. No innocent miss, then.

Liddell and his platoon had arranged themselves on the stairs.

'We've lit the sconces on the upstairs landing, sir.' Taking the steps two at a time, Catto gave the Lieutenant a nod of acknowledgement.

The housekeeper couldn't resist one last protest, shouting it up after him. 'Call yourself a gentleman? Yet you're going tae breenge into a young lady's bedroom! Wi' your sword drawn and a'! You should think black burning shame on yourself, young man!'

Wondering if the little woman was objecting to the violence inherent in his drawn sword or its phallic symbolism, Catto swung round as he reached the upstairs landing and pointed the offending weapon at her. 'She's had the warning, Crichton. Take her through to the kitchens and gag her. Take the girls as well. One word out of either of them and they get the same treatment.'

'Does that go for me too?'

'You,' he told Christian Rankeillor, meeting her eyes as she glared up at him, 'will stay where you are until I am ready to speak to you. Watch her, Liddell. You personally, I mean. She is not to move from the lobby. Your men stay here in case I need them.'

'Sir.' Already descending the stairs he might be but the Lieutenant's distaste for the task he'd been set was obvious. Well, it had been his choice to join the Town Guard. He had to take the rough with the smooth, even if he did move in the same circles as the young woman he'd just been ordered to guard—

Bloody hell. Could it have been Liddell who had warned Rankeillor? Catto had not immediately thought of him because somehow you didn't think about Liddell. Yet didn't the people whom other people seldom notice make the best spies? He added that to his mental list of matters to be thought about later.

'Found nothing up here or in the attic?' he murmured to two men of Liddell's platoon standing on the landing.

'No' so much as a mouse, Captain.'

Catto divided a searching glance between the two of them. 'Checked everywhere?'

'Behind every door and inside every cupboard, sir.'

'Show me.'

A few moments later he returned to the landing. 'The other house?'

'Empty, Captain. No sign o' ony disturbance, forbye.'

Satisfied, he curled his free hand around the balustrade of the landing and looked down at Christian Rankeillor. Standing there in her yellow silk, looking back up at him, she was shimmering with barely-controlled fury. Fighting for control. Good. That was exactly how he wanted her.

Call himself a gentleman? He couldn't remember when he'd last done that.

He shut the lid of the deep wooden chest in Christian Rankeillor's closet and leaned against it, lowering the point of his sword to the floor. In the silence surrounding him he could hear his own breathing, coming a little too fast and a little too shallow.

No need for that now. Other than the small cat, more white than black, curled up on the sumptuous four-poster out in the bedchamber, he had found nothing and nobody up here, neither dead nor alive. So he was not going to end the evening by apprehending a Jacobite spy and covering himself in glory. Or eternal damnation.

His gaze drifted over petticoats and bodices, frills and furbelows. The little Jacobite Miss kept them all very neatly. If he wasn't mistaken, seeing them as he was only by the light flickering in from the fire in her bedroom, she also stored them in logical order of their colour and hue. Curious. Then again, if you had nothing to do all day but sit around taking tea with your friends he supposed you were always looking for ways of passing the time. The necessary paraphernalia for making that most fashionable of drinks sat to one side of the blue-tiled fireplace out in her bedroom.

For two pins he'd leave Miss nose-in-the-air Rankeillor something to remember him by, here in her most private place, her inner sanctum.

He could raise his sword and slash her pretty things to ribbons, throw her neat disposition of them into disorder, strew them all over the floor. Wasn't that what tonight's mission had originally been about, to turn the Rankeillor household upside down and make a great noise while doing it? Even if the Lord President had issued a caveat, tempering his robust orders to come down hard on the man.

'Not too hard, mind. For the reasons we've already discussed and another, forbye. The common folk might have no time for anatomists but Rankeillor's an apothecary too, treats them and their children for free. He and his daughter are gey popular. The last thing we want is to rouse the Edinburgh mob. Did ye ever hear the story of Captain Porteous, Bob?'

He hadn't recognized the name and the Lord President had not elaborated further. Catto had seen the violent disorder the Edinburgh mob was capable of unleashing, although he didn't doubt he and the men could quell them. A few gunshots over the heads of the crowd or to the feet of the main troublemakers usually did the trick.

He blew out a breath, stood up and walked out into Christian Rankeillor's bedchamber, past her four-poster bed. The little cat curled up in the middle of the quilt raised its head and blinked at him. Small though it was, it looked like a warrior. The scratches across its nose and the split in one ear were something of a giveaway.

'Go back to sleep, baudrons,' he murmured, remembering the affectionate name by which all Scottish cats were addressed. 'You and I have no quarrel with each other.' He watched as it lowered its head and closed its eyes again. Clearly he hadn't struck terror into its tiny heart. A bubble of grim humour bobbed to the surface. He'd have to do a lot better than that with the cat's mistress.

For a moment he stood gazing at the other creatures which adorned Christian Rankeillor's bed, carved into its wooden posts. Luxurious blue velvet curtains were fastened neatly to those by ivory tasselled cords, allowing glimpses of a long-eared hare, a bushy-tailed squirrel, a surprised deer. Burning behind a brass mesh guard, the flickering flames of the fire cast its light over them all, the warmth bringing out the delicious smell of beeswax.

A small high table stood next to the head of the bed. It held a candelabra and three books, stacked in a neat pile. She must indulge in the dangerous habit of reading in bed. How many fires had that started? All it took was a breeze to stir the bed curtains and bring them too close to the candle flame.

He picked up the books, scanning their titles. *A Discourse on our Ideas of Truth and Beauty* by one Francis Hutcheson. The name was vaguely familiar. *A Treatise on the Multifarious Benefits to be Derived From the Cultivation in North Britain of the Vegetable Known as the Potato.* On the frontispiece of that one someone had neatly scored two lines through North Britain and written Scotland above it. How very predictable.

Underneath both those worthy tomes he found *Fantomina; or, Love in a Maze* by some female scribbler called Eliza Haywood. That curled his lip. Clearly a romance and therefore rubbish. Not that he'd ever read any. Probably the little Jacobite Miss only actually read such novels and kept the other books to hand in the hope of impressing her friends when they took tea with her in her bedroom.

He set the books down separately on the table, one overlapping the other. She should know he had touched her things. About to leave the *Discourse* face down and open on top of the other two, he found he couldn't do it. He had no quarrel with the book either. He settled for leaving it next to the other two, and askew.

He walked over to the casement, parted the curtains which matched those on the bed and looked out. The garden was dotted with pinpricks of light from the men's lanterns. Beyond the garden, once more in darkness save for those other pinpricks of light from the men he had left on guard there, was Surgeons' Hall. Not visible from here but not far beyond Surgeons' Hall lay the Royal Infirmary.

His quarry might be skulking there right now. His quarry might be in any one of all those other hiding places, even have left the city altogether. Highland blood or not, Catto wasn't fey enough to know that. 'Twould be one thing to recall the men from the gates, mount that full-scale search of the hospital and discover a Jacobite plotter. 'Twould be quite another to turn the place upside down and find nobody.

As Duncan Forbes had warned him, the Royal Infirmary was the pet project of too many important people. Catto might need at least one of them as an ally this week. He certainly could not risk antagonizing George Drummond, former and very likely future lord provost of Edinburgh and, so the Lord President had told him, the man above all whose dream the Royal Infirmary had been.

Leaning forward, he pressed his forehead against the cool lead and glass of the window. How had he so offended the fates that the storm had tossed him onto this beach? What the Devil was he doing here in Edinburgh, hunting Jacobites? How had he so further offended those fates that he seemed to have found some?

Anywhere but here. Dear God, let him be anywhere else but here. If he started walking now he could probably reach Leith within the hour. He would go along the quayside and offer the first Captain he met whatever they agreed was a fair price to take him wherever the ship was headed.

If only. Or if only all he had to do was face down an angry mob. Keep your nerve, give the men the confidence to hold the line and that was easy. Or at least straightforward. His standing orders from the Lord President compelled him to follow a more subtle and infinitely more complex path.

Raising his head from the windowpane, Catto swore viciously and went downstairs to put the fear of God into Miss Christian Rankeillor.

6

'Miss Rankeillor, you will accompany me to your father's library.'

She looked up at him as he descended the stairs and spat out her refusal. 'I don't think so, sir.'

Stepping onto the now damp and dirty floorboards of the lobby, he walked across to where she stood next to Archie Liddell. Only when he was as close to her as those extravagant skirts allowed did he speak. 'I could have you brought, madam. If you prefer.' He had to mentally count only to three before she answered him.

'Very well,' she said. 'I shall come. But under protest.'

'Your protest is duly noted.'

'And ignored,' she countered, giving her head a defiant little toss. His eyes went from her artfully-dressed hair to his Lieutenant.

'Are you going to issue a protest, too, Liddell?'

The Lieutenant swallowed. 'I was wondering if Miss Rankeillor should have a chaperone, sir. Perhaps I might go and fetch the housekeeper?'

Catto looked at him. 'Let me make something clear, Liddell. We are here to investigate wrong-doing. We are here in the execution of our duties as the keepers of Edinburgh's peace.' He loaded his voice with sarcasm. 'We are not here to take tea. This is not a social visit. Is that understood, Lieutenant?'

The young man's eyes met those of Christian Rankeillor. 'Yes, sir,' he said miserably.

'Rintoul?' Catto said, holding out his hand for the map case. Once again he saw the girl react to it. He wondered how much she knew. Not much, probably. Rankeillor would surely shield his darling little daughter from the realities of life. Although something about this leather cylinder certainly bothered her.

He led the way into the library, not allowing the lady of the house to precede him as manners would have dictated. Compounding the offence, he closed the doors into the shop, tossed the map case onto her father's table and threw himself down into one of the big armchairs in front of the library fireplace.

She remained where she was, glowering across the room at him. If looks could kill he'd be lying bleeding to death on the Oriental rug beneath his feet. Standing framed in the double doorway, she looked like a painting come to life. *Portrait of a Lady.* Portrait of a very angry lady. There was real passion here.

What was that to him? These days he preferred his women compliant, preferably bought and paid for. It made life so very much simpler. He gazed back at her over the spectacularly untidy desk, making sure to do so with an air of amused contempt. That wasn't difficult. Not while she was wearing those clothes. How could you take any female seriously who chose to imprison herself in one of those cages?

Keeping her waiting before he spoke, he considered what he knew about her. From the dossier he'd had from the Lord President he'd learned that her mother had died only days after giving birth to her. She had been the first and only child and Rankeillor had never remarried. He and his daughter were said to be very close. How very nice for them.

From her own letters which he had intercepted over the past couple of weeks, Catto knew she had at least two close female friends, one in Glasgow and one in the north. Both girls were coming to Edinburgh next week and were looking forward to going to the Daft Friday Ball at the Assembly Rooms with her. Oh God, the Daft Friday Ball. There was another horror lying in wait for him.

The letters between Christian Rankeillor and her friends were affectionate and gossipy and all three girls had included little drawings in them. He supposed most young ladies dabbled. There had been paints and an easel set on a square table in front of the window in Christian Rankeillor's bedroom. Another of the pastimes with which useless chits like her filled their endless free hours.

She claimed in her letters to her friends to spend a great deal of time helping her father, preparing physic for the shop and serving behind the counter. The first letter of hers he'd read had been about making sweets for it, with a comic drawing of a pan boiling over and the differing reactions to that of herself, the housekeeper, Mary and Tibby. They'd be the maidservants, he presumed, and the sweets would include the tablet he'd seen, which was entirely irrelevant to anything.

What might be highly relevant was that one of Christian Rankeillor's two friends had some very interesting relatives. He'd got that not from the Lord President's dossiers but from Culloden's apparently limitless knowledge of who was who in Scottish society. It seemed everyone in Scotland was related to everyone else, although Catto had already known that.

'I'm curious, sir,' Christian Rankeillor bit out. 'This evening you have chosen to unleash the full force of the Town Guard upon us. Yet when three of my father's students were set upon by the mob a month since, the Town Guard was conspicuous by its absence. Pray explain to me why you chose on that occasion to turn a blind eye to unprovoked assault.'

The Lucky Kennedy affair. That was what she was referring to. Catto had witnessed its aftermath, a demonstration of the power of the Edinburgh mob. The late and unfortunate Mistress Kennedy, landlady of an oyster cellar in Leith Wynd, had taken exception to some wealthy young oafs pawing her daughter, a girl of only thirteen. The ensuing argument had blazed up out of control, ending only when one of the young gentlemen lay dead on the floor, Lucky Kennedy standing over him with a bloody kitchen knife clutched in her trembling hand.

Notorious though he already was for his drinking and whoring, the victim had been the son of one of Leith's wealthiest wine merchants, well-connected through the port, Edinburgh and beyond. So the outcome of the landlady's trial had never been in any doubt.

In what many had seen as evidence of heartless spite, the judge had sentenced her not only to hang but for her body to be given over to the anatomists. It was the only legal way corpses for dissection could be got and then only if the relatives did not or were not allowed to claim the body.

Incensed on behalf of Lucky Kennedy and her motherless daughter, the mob had roared into Surgeons' Hall intent on retrieving the body and giving it Christian burial. In the ensuing mêlée, three blameless medical students had been badly beaten.

It had all happened only three days after Catto had disembarked at Leith, still finding his feet along with his land-legs. He'd heard about the riot at Surgeons' Hall too late to prevent it, hadn't made the connections with the Lord President's intelligence network he was rapidly building now. Not that he was going to justify himself to the little Jacobite Miss currently standing in the open doorway looking down her nose at him.

'I take it you are aware, sir, that being in possession of a cadaver breaks no actual statute?'

'It does if you dig it up out of its grave,' he told her with a bland smile.

'Actually,' she said, sounding like a petticoated professor lecturing a group of raw students fresh up from the country, 'that's not the case. As long as you leave the mort-clothes behind. Only then are you committing theft.'

'Actually,' he responded, tossing back both the word and the superior attitude, 'that's a common misconception. Those who violate a grave are committing the offence of desecrating a sepulchre. Care to tell me where you've been this evening, Miss Rankeillor?' He already knew the answer from his monitoring of her mail but she didn't need to know that.

'Where I have spent the evening is no concern of the Town Guard.'

At odds with the extreme femininity of her clothes, she stood as a man might, planted in the doorway, ready to take him on. He was pretty sure she didn't realize her aggressively-folded arms were pushing up the shapely breasts already so enticingly on display in the low-cut evening gown. He didn't doubt she could play the coquette when she wanted to. He was in absolutely no doubt that she would not be choosing to do so with him. He was looking at Miss Outraged.

She sucked in a breath, offering another tantalizing lift of creamy breasts. 'I insist on my housekeeper being freed of the restraint you have ordered to be placed on her. I insist on being able to dismiss the maid-servants so they may go to their beds. They must by now be completely overwrought.' She stressed the word, her eyes widening as she said it. They were still as intensely green as the cloak she was no longer wearing. 'And,' – another captured breath – 'I insist upon you dismissing your men and withdrawing from this house. I insist upon it, sir.'

Nice try, he had to admit. Not that it was going to get her anywhere. 'You're in no position to insist upon anything, Miss Rankeillor. Come into the room, close the doors and sit down. If you please,' he added perfunctorily.

'And if I don't please?' Red, yellow and green, the toe of an embroidered slipper peeped out from beneath the big skirts. It was tapping. Any minute now she'd start threatening him with her influential friends and relations. Her sort always did.

Where I have spent the evening is no concern of the Town Guard. She had pronounced those words with such studied contempt. Yet his blood was as good as any man's. Any woman's too.

Who the hell did she think she was anyway? Nothing more than the daughter of a sawbones and hawker of lotions and potions to the gentry. Catto sat back in the chair and crossed his legs, making himself at home in her home. Another way to rile her. He saw by the expression on her face that he had. She was no good at hiding her feelings.

'Sit down, Miss Rankeillor. Over there,' he added, pointing to the chair opposite his own.

She threw him a pitying look. 'I can do no more than perch on that chair when I'm wearing this gown.'

'Then you shouldn't wear such stupid clothes. You do realize that you are obliged by law to answer my questions?'

'No. I don't. By what right do you put them to me, pray? By what right do you force your way into my house and browbeat my servants? Gag and restrain them? How dare you, sir!'

'As I have already informed you, madam, I am an officer of the law. I do everything that I do in the name of the King.'

'Your king.' The words were accompanied by another toss of the head, shaking the big ringlet which lay against her neck. Its darkness emphasized the peaches and cream tones of her skin. 'Not mine.'

Oh, he really must have riled her to make her fire back a reply as indiscreet as that one! If he gave her a little more rope, would she hang herself? 'Loyal Britons can have but one king, madam.'

'I agree with you, sir.' The haughty chin went up again. 'And his name is James.'

'Have a care, miss,' he growled. 'You are talking treason. For which I could arrest you. Have you ever seen the inside of the Tolbooth?' He watched with satisfaction as everything she had ever heard about the horrors of the grim building set in the middle of Edinburgh's High Street was mirrored in her face.

'That cat of yours got your tongue, Miss Rankeillor?'

'How did you know—' She stopped herself. Now he was studying her realization of how he knew she had a cat. Watching her rosy face, he was as sure as he could be that she was visualizing him in her luxurious bedchamber. Good. He wanted her to feel embarrassed and uneasy. She was a haughty bitch – Christ, to have had the gall to say the name *James* to him and expect to get away with it – and she stood in need of being taken down a peg or two.

Fear darted through her eyes. 'Have you hurt my cat?'

He did not answer her. Instead, once more taking his time about it, he looked her up and down. He'd seen plenty of women naked. He could easily imagine what she looked like stripped of all those layers of clothes, nothing between her and him but that peachy skin.

She did not drop her eyes but her face, throat and breasts were growing more flushed by the second. *More like a strawberry than a peach now, eh, little Miss Jacobite?* He locked eyes with her and imagined himself back in her bedroom, taking her there with him. He knew it had worked when her skin grew redder still. Too easy. She really was far too easy. 'Come into the room, Miss Rankeillor. Now.'

'I asked you about my cat.'

'And I did not answer you.'

Would there be pleas and tears now? No. She changed tack. So much for the cat.

'You are new to Edinburgh sir, am I not right?

Another toss of the head. Another icy look. She probably wielded that weapon with some frequency, a technique guaranteed to freeze the balls off any over-familiar admirers. He could see her rehearsing its effect in the big cheval glass in her bedchamber. In his imagination, he chose now to dress her, though only in the nightgown which had been draped over the soft white pillows of her fairytale bed. That garment had been made of the finest Picardy cambric, the sort of material which clings to soft curves and reveals as much as it conceals…

Feeling the stirrings, he adjusted his position in the big wing chair. 'Twould be as well if his own miserable cadaver did not spring into response to her undoubted charms.

'I'm asking the questions this evening, Miss Rankeillor. Apart from which, I fail to see the relevance of yours.'

'Its relevance is this, sir. You seem to be unaware that for some years now those of us in Edinburgh of differing political opinions have found ourselves able to rub along together quite amicably. I cannot recall when I last heard of someone being arrested merely for the expressing of political views.'

She had grown in confidence over the course of that little speech, ending it with a smug little smile curving her lips. Catto was surprised by the emotion which seized him then. If something really was afoot, she knew nothing about it. He could almost feel sorry for the haughty little bitch.

7

He mustn't find the other sketches. That was what mattered now.

She couldn't be sure the green document cylinder held any of them but she had a horrible feeling it might. He had meant that talk of treason and the Tolbooth to frighten her – and, oh God in Heaven, it had – but she knew he must be here because of tonight's dissection. Och, but she had thought it was too soon to have one after what had happened last month!

She could see the other drawings perfectly well, albeit out of the corner of her eye. Only the edge of the red leather portfolio containing them was visible, peeping out from under the guddle of papers on her father's perpetually untidy desk. They were no distance from this unnerving man's well-shaped but much too inquisitive nose.

Thinking of the neat and betraying date in the bottom right hand corner of each of the preliminary studies she had done of the undissected corpse this morning, Christian felt panic grip her chest. That she and not Patrick Rankeillor was the executor of the sketches which were such a help to him and his students was a secret well-kept by both father and daughter. The only other people who knew were Jamie – as her father's apprentice it would have been impossible to keep it from him – and Betty, and they were both sworn to secrecy.

The formidable ladies who governed the manners of Edinburgh society would be appalled if they ever found out that a girl within their own social circles drew the naked cadavers of both men and women.

Or they would pretend to be. A story like that would keep them and their daughters gossiping over their teacups for months.

On the edges of those social circles as she was, Christian could have put up with that. It was the damage such a revelation might do to the Infirmary that worried her. The wonderful new hospital of which her father was one of the managers was dependent on the patronage of Edinburgh society: not that they used it themselves, of course. When they were ill they were treated at home, fussed over by physicians who attended them there.

The Infirmary was for the poor, allowing medical men and the students they taught a collection of patients on whom they might practice and perfect their skills. The people who donated the money which paid the Infirmary's bills and fed its patients wielded considerable power and influence throughout Edinburgh, and they knew it.

Take the Liddells, prominent members of the East Lothian gentry and fabulously wealthy into the bargain, much of that wealth coming from the coal mines on their estates out at Tranent. Archie, hovering uncomfortably in the lobby behind Christian, was one of their poor relations, which was undoubtedly why she had always felt a sense of comradeship with him.

She had spent the evening at the Liddells' Edinburgh town house in the Potterrow. She couldn't say she had enjoyed herself. There was only so much diabolically awful poetry a woman of taste and discernment could take. She wasn't sure why she had been invited anyway. Charlotte Liddell had always made it abundantly clear she considered Christian one of her many social inferiors.

Nor was she sure why her father had been so set on her spending the evening with Charlotte Liddell and her friends. He had to be polite to the Liddells for the sake of the hospital but she knew he had no time for most of that family on a personal level. Patrick Rankeillor gave no automatic respect to lords, lairds and ladies but only where it was due. He had brought his daughter up to feel the same.

Not content with encouraging the assault on her guests' ears, Miss full-of-herself Liddell had also assaulted their eyes. With a ridiculously dramatic swearing to secrecy and much pretended modesty, she had unveiled a portrait she had painted of Charles Edward Stuart. Ye gods. Diabolically awful didn't begin to cover that. Did the exiled Stuart prince not have enough to contend with without being made to look like a turnip with a face?

Every other girl there had admired the painting, praising it to the skies. Listening to their sycophantic prattle, Christian had found herself struggling not to yield to a wild impulse.

You must all come round and see my drawings sometime. I'm particularly pleased with how I've captured the male organs of generation in my last series of sketches.

She was feeling no such impulse at the moment. Aware of how closely she was being watched, she was too worried she might betray the location of the sketch book by an anxious dart of her eyes in its direction. She had to distract his attention from the table. Better yet, she had to get him out of the house, send him home empty-handed, with no evidence at all of anything untoward having happened over at Surgeons' Hall tonight.

How she was to accomplish this remarkable feat she had no idea. She stood alone here. He had armed men backing up his powerful presence. Her stomach lurched. *God Almighty, the Town Guard is occupying the house. God Almighty.* She could not and would not allow herself to imagine the damage this body of men might do to her home if their Captain chose to fully unleash them. Her only defence was to continue to play the haughty young lady.

Little though she cared for these stupid rules, she knew she should not go into any room alone with a man who was not a relative, safely much older than her or a close family friend. Especially not this man. He had already been in her bedroom. That alone could leave her reputation in tatters. Dear God, how much worse was the story going to become after it had been told and retold by every member of the Town Guard here tonight?

Desperate situations called for desperate remedies. Christian strode into the library, kicking her yellow skirts out in front of her. They crackled like fallen autumn leaves as she headed for the tapestry bell-pull which hung to one side of the fire. 'This has gone far enough. Much too far. You will leave now, sir. I require your name before you do. Forthwith,' she added crisply, giving each syllable of the word its full weight. 'I also require the name of your superior officer. Rest assured that I shall be making a complaint to him as regards this intrusion first thing in the morning.'

'I am the superior officer of the Town Guard, madam.'

Her hand reaching towards the bell-pull, Christian stopped and turned to look at him. The eyes so steadily returning her gaze shone like well-polished gunmetal. He had enjoyed saying that and they both knew it.

Gazing into those wintry depths, she found herself wondering how his life had led him to where he was tonight. He was younger than she had originally thought, perhaps only a year or two older than herself. 'Twas strange how much authority a uniform could confer, especially when, as in this case, it was worn with considerable style.

Neither the officers nor the men of the Town Guard were known for their sartorial elegance. The town rats. That was the nickname for this despised brigade, usually as rough in their appearance as they were brutal in the execution of their duties in the keeping of Edinburgh's peace.

This new Captain – for surely he must be new or she would have noticed him around the town – was an exception to that rule. Under his grey military cloak she could see that his dark red uniform coat was made from the finest of cloths. His white waistcoat and knee-breeches were spotless, as was the stiff white stock which closed his shirt at the neck.

Running round that deep collar, tied in a bow exactly in the middle of it, was the thin black silk ribbon known as a solitaire. The brass gorget which indicated his rank was suspended by another length of black ribbon exactly the same width as the solitaire. Perfectly finishing off his dauntingly elegant appearance, he wore his hair in a bagwig of quite ferocious neatness.

That wasn't a wig at all, of course. Pulled back from his face, the chestnut strands of what was clearly his own hair were secured at the nape of his neck by a stiffened black satin ribbon, part of a larger bow-shaped bag into which the rest of his hair was tucked. Judging by the soft fullness, he had rather a lot of it.

What would he look like with all that gleaming hair tumbling about his face and curling on his shoulders? Softer, perhaps. More human. Even though his features were rather angular. A perfectly straight nose, broadening towards the base. High forehead and cheekbones. A wide mouth and a strong chin. He had good teeth too, white and evenly shaped.

Overall, there was something of a Nordic cast to his face, elements in it which put Christian in mind of the Norwegian and Swedish students who occasionally passed through her father's classes at the university. Yet he was clearly not from either of those countries. He sounded like an Englishman and yet at the same time he didn't. She was sure she could hear the occasional Scottish cadence in his voice: which would make him the worst kind of Scotsman, the sort who wore the red coat of England.

'You will know me again, Miss Rankeillor.'

Curse her artist's habit of studying faces and figures. She would hate this man to think her interest in him had any other basis. 'This conversation is over, sir.' Hot with embarrassment, she turned and reached once again for the tapestry bell-pull.

'I'm afraid you cannot dismiss me like one of your servants, madam.' He spoke with infuriating calmness. 'I am commissioned by the highest authority to undertake these enquiries. I fear I must also remind you that your servants are not free to answer your summons.'

Damn, damn, damn. Nor were they. She had therefore just made a prize fool of herself. The only way to recover was to continue to act the condescending young miss. *Be as haughty as you can be, Kirsty Rankeillor.* 'Then I shall show you out myself, sir.'

Turning again, she found herself fighting her skirts. That drew from him a look of sardonic and very male amusement which served only to deepen her embarrassment. Moving too fast towards the library door, her hoops swung wide, catching around the bulbous wooden leg of the small upholstered footstool which crouched beside one of the green and gold armchairs.

She wanted to scream with frustration. She wanted to burst into tears. She wanted him not to be watching her with that knowing little smile playing about his mouth. Wrapping the fingers of one hand around her slippery skirts, she tugged. Her hand was slippery too, slick with sweat.

'You're at the wrong angle to do that, Miss Rankeillor,' came the cool voice. 'I'm assuming you are trying to free yourself?'

She ignored him and tugged harder. If she wasn't careful she would rip the material of her overdress. Right at this moment that seemed a small price to pay. She tugged again. Nothing happened. Stuck fast, she muttered angry words. 'Och, damn and blast the bloody thing!'

'Language, Miss Rankeillor. Language!'

She threw him a black look, saw him make a steeple of his hands, tap his fingertips against his mouth and survey her over them. Pure malice. That was what shone in those grey eyes now.

'Want some help?'

'I think it must be obvious even to someone of the meanest intelligence that I need some help.'

He let out a laugh which seemed to surprise him as much as it did her, allowing as he rose from the chair, 'It's a pretty distinction, madam.' One long stride and he was at her feet, crouching down to disentangle the slippery silk of the gown and the cane and cambric of the petticoat beneath it.

'There now,' he said as he succeeded in freeing her from the grip of the footstool. 'I'll only come after you and bring you back but do feel free to flounce out of the room if that's what you really want to do.'

She slanted a wary glance down at him. 'Very droll.'

'I'm glad you appreciate my wit,' he said, looking up at her as she was looking down at him. Laughter had relaxed his features, softening those forbidding good looks. 'I was beginning to get the distinct impression that you don't like me very much.'

'I was beginning to get the distinct impression you were going out of your way to provoke exactly such a response from me. I would know your name, sir.'

'Catto, madam. My name is Catto.'

'You are also in possession of a Christian name, I take it?'

'Not one as Christian as yours.'

'More wit,' she commented drily. 'May I have the answer to my question?'

'Robert,' he supplied. 'Robert Catto. Captain of the Town Guard.' Springing to his feet, he placed one hand over his heart and made her a little bow. 'At your service.'

'But that is what you are patently not, Mr Robert Catto.' She frowned at him. 'You are at someone else's service, are you not? Nor are you are in this house tonight because you wish me or my father well.'

'I do not wish you any ill, Miss Rankeillor. Quite the contrary.' Something flared deep within his eyes. She did not recognize the emotion, knew only 'twas not the malice she had seen there before. Yet the memory of that remained strong enough to sharpen her temper and her tongue.

'You do not wish me any ill?' she repeated. 'You occupy my house, terrorize my servants, violate the privacy of my bedchamber—' her voice shook on those words – 'and yet you say you do not wish me any ill?'

'You do not understand my meaning.' In contrast to her own, his voice was very flat. The animation had faded from his face, rendering it once again an impenetrable mask.

'No. I do not.' She was angry again, both with him and with herself. She had no business seeing this man as a human being, capable of amusement and emotion. She did not want to speculate on what his life history had been or why he and she were standing alone together in a room in Edinburgh late on a December evening or what had brought him to the position he was in today. Or what he might look like with his hair loose.

Captain Robert Catto, most definitely not at her service, had brought the Town Guard into the house and had them tramp all over it. He had ordered Betty to be gagged, terrified Mary and Tibby. He had gone out of his way to invade the privacy of her own bedchamber. It would be she who would pay for that studied insult, which was obviously why he had done it – and he had the effrontery to tell her he did not wish her any ill?

For all those reasons what she wanted to do was cordially detest him. For all those reasons what she wanted to do was draw some blood.

'Tell me, Mr Catto, do you have many friends? Or are your evenings too taken up with harassing and terrifying innocent women and girls? Your mother must be so proud of you.'

For a split second he simply looked at her. Then his hand shot out to grab her wrist. Standing too close to her as it was, the movement brought him closer still, his legs pressing not only against her yellow silk skirts but the cane hoops of the petticoat beneath them, pushing those against her shins. He must know he was doing that. He must know he was hurting her more than a little.

'Let me go, sir. Let me go right now! And I demand that you and your men withdraw from this house without further delay.'

'Damn your eyes, madam,' he snapped back. 'I'll decide when this interview is over. Not you!'

'You may be the superior officer of the Town Guard, sir, but my father is one of Edinburgh's most prominent citizens. He is intimately acquainted with the Lord Provost and many of the city's bailies. The people who pay your wages? Why, the Lord President himself is one of his most intimate friends.'

'Predictable,' Catto said flatly. 'I knew you would say that. How shockingly conventional of you, Miss Rankeillor. I'd have expected more from a girl whose father spends his evenings cutting up mouldy old corpses.'

'It wasn't mouldy,' she said indignantly, 'it was perfectly fresh—Oh!'

He gave her a chilly little smile, flexed his fingers and took a firmer grip of her wrist. 'Care to repeat what you said there, Miss Rankeillor?'

'I said nothing! It'll be your word against mine if you try to claim otherwise!' She hoped he could not feel the pounding pulse beneath his fingers and was horribly sure that he could. He was a man who noticed everything, every last little detail. What was she going to do if he would not let her go?

'I demand that you leave this house, sir. I demand that you do so right now!' She raised the hand which was not a prisoner of his. 'The kitchen door lies yonder.'

'The kitchen door?' he flung back. 'The kitchen door? You really are a condescending little cunt, aren't you?'

She went very still. He couldn't have said what she thought he had. He couldn't have.

For a moment they stood frozen together, eyes locked. Then she saw him look over her head towards the lobby. A commotion had erupted out there.

Relief. A huge, crashing wave of it. Her father was home.

8

Her respected parent was singing a bawdy song, the one about the sailor who wanted to show the fair maiden his bonnie wee bird. Anxiety swamped relief. Her father never sang bawdy songs. Patrick Rankeillor wasn't that kind of man. She heard him stop – mid-vulgarity – and a rough but authoritative voice telling him that no, he could not go and find his daughter. She was with young Captain Catto in the library—

'And wha' the De'il micht young Captain Catto be, if you please?'

Christian winced. Her father had a lovely voice, deep and warm. It had rasped like a blunt saw cutting through wet wood when he had roared out that question. Already ajar, the double doors which separated the library from the lobby were thrust wide.

'Kirsty Rankeillor!' he bellowed as he breenged in. 'What's this I hear about you being closeted alone in the library wi' a young man for a good quarter o' an hour and more? Have ye no sense o' the proprieties, lassie?'

His full-bottomed wig, a riot of fair curls reaching down his back and in two separate flaps to the middle of his chest, was askew, his complexion a trifle ruddy. Neither of these flaws diminished in any way the dramatic impact of his entrance. He wheeled round to glower at the Town Guard Captain. 'Sir, I'll be needing an explanation for your behaviour!'

That her father had downed, or spilled, at least one glass of wine was evidenced by the purple stain on the front of his cravat. Christian knew he couldn't have had the time to imbibe much more than one glass, nor the inclination either. He was acting the part. Och, but this was a gey risky strategy!

Following him into the room, Jamie was acting too, striving to convey by a series of half-smiles and apologetic glances his apparent embarrassment at returning a father to a daughter in this liquid state. Bringing up the rear was Archie Liddell and the man she had already vaguely recognized as being a Sergeant in the Town Guard, the one whose Captain had told him to gag Betty.

'Mr C-Catto, s-sir,' Archie Liddell stammered. 'Captain. I'm s-sorry. We could not hold the Professor back!'

'No matter.' Robert Catto waved both Archie and the Sergeant away. 'Leave us. And close the library doors.'

Jamie was already making the introductions, identifying himself as Patrick Rankeillor's apprentice and giving the Redcoat Captain what he always referred to as his full Sunday name, James Buchan of Balnamoon. He launched into a rambling tale punctuated at frequent intervals by noisy interruptions from his master. Despite Patrick Rankeillor's apparent inebriation, between them they managed to communicate that they had sat down with some other gentlemen at a table in *The Blue Blanket* in the Canongate at six of the clock that evening and risen from it a mere quarter of an hour before.

Arms folded across his scarlet chest, eyes flickering from one speaker to the other, the Town Guard Captain listened to the whole rigmarole in stony silence. Watching him, Christian was in an agony of indecision. If only she had not blurted out that comment about the cadaver. She could deny it all she liked now but it meant he knew very well the story being offered up to him was a pack of lies. Yet, if she interrupted Jamie, what could she possibly say? When he at last stopped speaking three pairs of eyes swivelled round to take the measure of the reaction.

'So you'd both swear to this?' The tone of voice was almost pleasant. 'Before a magistrate, if required?'

'Before Duncan Forbes of Culloden himself, laddie!'

'Well, that's impressive.' The response came with an inclination of the head which an unobservant person might have taken to mean that Robert Catto really was impressed. 'I have already heard you are most intimately acquainted with the esteemed Lord President, sir.'

'Aye,' Patrick said. 'Maist intimately indeed!' He released a stoater of a belch. That too was completely out of character. Despite the broadness of his speech, he was a man of refined manners.

Christian sent out a silent plea. *You're trying too hard. Please don't either of you say anything more. He's not stupid and he knows you're making this up. Can neither of you see that? Did neither of you hear the mockery in what he said about the Lord President?*

Evidently not. To her dismay, her father spoke again. 'My great friend Sandy would swear to it too.'

'Professor Alexander Monro,' Jamie chipped in, an idiotically helpful look on his face. 'Holder of the Chair of Anatomy at the University. He too was at *The Blue Blanket* this evening.'

'You astonish me. Along with a number of other eminent medical gentlemen, no doubt. With all of whom Professor Rankeillor is also, of course, intimately acquainted, and with whose names and directions he or you can supply me.'

'If you require them,' Jamie said after a tiny pause.

'Aye,' Patrick Rankeillor said a little too hurriedly, 'we've all had a grand evening trading tales of the surgeon's knife.' He clapped Jamie on the shoulder. 'Including your own, Jamie, lad. Now ye're walking the wards, ye're gathering a grand fund o' stories. The hours fair flew by. It seems no time at all since we sat doon.' He shot Robert Catto a glance far too shrewd for a man in his cups. 'When was that again, Jamie?'

'Six of the clock,' his interrogator supplied. 'A piece of information which has now been offered to me four times over. I don't, of course, believe a word of this fairy tale. Tell me,' he said expansively, 'do you all think this is some sort of a game?'

She had not moved, but somehow Christian felt herself miss a step, lose her footing, feel the solid floor beneath her shift and sway. Robert Catto addressed his next words to Patrick Rankeillor alone.

'I'd be obliged if you would now give me the truth, sir. I'm sure you can manage to do so without slurring your words.'

'I cannot believe you found any evidence of a dissection having taken place tonight,' Jamie said quickly.

'Then you're mistaken, Mr Buchan of Balnamoon. My eyes are keen.' The mobile mouth set itself into a grimace of distaste. 'As are my other senses.' He looked Jamie up and down. 'Yours must have become blunted. Although what interests me about Professor Rankeillor's activities this evening has to do with a quite separate matter.'

He glanced once more at Christian before turning that implacable grey gaze back onto her father. 'I don't suppose,' he said, his voice as smooth as silk, 'that you trust your daughter with any of the real secrets. Am I right, sir?'

9

A tableau vivant. That's what they must look like now. One of those entertainments Charlotte Liddell and her horrible brother Cosmo liked to put on of scenes from history, legend and myth. *The Kings and Queens of Scotland. The Heroes of Ancient Greece.* They and the other young men and women who made up their inner circle draped themselves in what they fondly imagined to be the appropriate costumes and struck poses, remaining as still as statues for minutes on end. The young and not so young people who ached to be in that inner circle then showered them with rapturous applause.

What would the title of this tableau be? Christian's racing brain came up with three. *The Cat Let Out of The Bag. The Stunned Silence. A Daughter's Accusing Glance: Father, What are these Real Secrets of which this Mysterious Stranger Speaks*? Those tumbling thoughts hurtled her towards the answer to that question. Oh, dear God in Heaven. It couldn't be. Could it?

It didn't surprise her one jot when it was Robert Catto who broke the silence. The part of her mind still available for rational thought was realizing too late that his pursuit of an illegal dissection had been nothing more than a ruse, an excuse to bring the Town Guard down upon them. This house's Jacobite sympathies had never been a secret. This occupation of it was about more even than those. She was growing more sure of that by the second.

Unfolding his arms, the Redcoat Captain walked forward to stand only a foot away from her father. Too close. He'd used the same technique on her too, she realized, an unspoken but clear physical threat. She wanted to loathe this man. She could not dismiss him. He had presence, and a crackling energy all the more potent for being kept rigorously under control. Although he had lost control for a few seconds when he had grabbed her wrist and flung that obscenity at her, that foul word she could hardly bear even to silently pronounce inside her own head. He was totally in command of himself now.

'A question,' he said crisply. 'Addressed to you, Professor Rankeillor. Pray tell me the name of the third party you and Mr Buchan met with earlier this evening over at Surgeons' Hall.'

The tension in the room was already unbearable. That question wound it up to breaking point. Her head spinning with the implications of it, Christian gazed mutely at her father, willing him to know what to say, what to do.

It was Jamie who spoke. 'What makes you think my master and I met anyone over at Surgeons' Hall this evening?'

'I don't think it.' Robert Catto answered Jamie without taking his eyes off her father's face. 'I know it. The answer to my question, Professor. If you please.'

'Allow me to answer for my master-'

'No.' Robert Catto still had not looked at Jamie, simply put out one hand to stop his words. 'I find myself vastly curious to hear an answer from Mr Rankeillor's own lips.' His voice hardened. 'The name of your guest, Professor. If you please. Also his business with you and your business with him.'

Raised though it was like a shield against him, Jamie ignored that commanding hand. One word tumbled over the other in his haste to speak. 'The Professor is not at liberty to answer your question, sir. Everyone he sees in his capacity as surgeon or apothecary he does so under the cloak of confidentiality and anonymity.'

Robert Catto at last turned towards him. The two young men

exchanged an odd look, the meaning of which Christian could not decipher.

'Especially,' Jamie said, pretending to throw her an embarrassed glance, 'when the ailment is what might be called a sensitive one and the patient is a weel-kent face around Edinburgh. Also,' he added, 'a person of some influence.'

'I don't care if the professor was treating God himself.' Robert Catto's voice dripped with contempt. 'Or the Archangel Gabriel. Are you also going to tell me the ethics of your calling do not permit you to answer me, Professor? Or do those ethics vary according to how wealthy or influential the patient is?'

The colour drained from Patrick's face. 'You insult me, laddie.' His tone of voice was both too quiet and too angry for a man trying to pass himself off as an amiable drunk.

'Do I?' came the brisk response. 'Tell me, Professor, do these names mean anything to you?'

The four or five names he rattled out meant nothing to Christian. Nor could she decide whether Jamie or her father demonstrated any recognition of them. Neither of them was behaving very naturally this evening. They were both too … alert. That was the word which sprang to mind.

Robert Catto did not wait for an answer, following up one question with another. 'Is it one of these gentlemen with whom you have been associating, Professor Rankeillor? Mr Buchan of Balnamoon? You have perhaps been acting *in concert* with them?'

Another pause. Christian had no idea why those two subtly emphasized words were significant, only that they clearly were. Waiting for what seemed an eternity before her father answered, she darted a glance at Robert Catto's shuttered face. Strange how different he had looked before, when he had helped her untangle her skirts, when she had asked him for his first name and he had commented on hers.

Why the two of them had declared that momentary truce she did not know. 'Twas hard to believe he might have felt sorry for her. She knew only that there were deep waters here. Deep and troubled and dangerous. Troubled? Why should she care if he were that?

'I have been associating with a patient, laddie. An occupational hazard in my trade.'

Robert Catto stirred the air with his finger, as though he were puzzling out some interesting conundrum. 'You saw this patient before or after these convivial hours at *The Blue Blanket* of which you have been telling us?'

'Before, laddie, before. I prefer no' to treat my patients when I'm a wee bit the waur o' the wear.'

'Indeed? How very commendable, sir. As is your determination to keep the name of your patient to yourself.'

'That is a requirement of my trade.'

'So you have said, sir.' Then, the words couched once again in that falsely pleasant voice: 'I take it you realize that my trade gives me the authority to arrest you and Mr Buchan of Balnamoon? Carry you to the Tolbooth and keep you confined there until you give me the answers I seek?' His smile was chilling. 'I do have some very effective means of – well, shall we say *persuasion*? – at my disposal.

Once more he let the silence stretch. Once more it was he who broke it. 'Professor Rankeillor. I shall spare us all the embarrassing spectacle of you having to decide whether or not to continue to play the drunkard. You travel to Glasgow and the West tomorrow, am I not right?'

'How do you know that?' The question was surprised out of Christian, the warning glance Jamie threw her coming too late to stop it.

'How I know that is neither here nor there, Miss Rankeillor.' His attention focussed on her father, the reply was tossed over his shoulder. 'Am I not right, sir?'

Patrick Rankeillor drew in a breath and nodded his bewigged head.

'A straight answer to a straight question,' Robert Catto said sarcastically. 'There's a novelty in this day and age. Whilst you are on your travels, I would advise you most strongly to confine yourself to the company of medical men and the discussion of medical matters. Any discussion of or involvement in politics could be … hazardous. Do I make myself clear, Professor?'

Whilst you are on your travels. So he wasn't going to arrest them? Relief threatened to overwhelm Christian, except she knew it was too soon to surrender to that emotion. Dreadful danger hovered all around. It hung like invisible swords above their heads, bright deadly steel waiting to fall.

'What,' asked Patrick Rankeillor, gathering his considerable dignity around him, 'if I were to tell you I have nae idea what ye're talking about, laddie?'

'Then I'd call you a liar,' came the uncompromising reply. 'Tell me something, sir. Do you really have no idea of the risks you're running? What the consequences of the path you are choosing to tread might be not only for yourself but also for your daughter? You stand to lose everything, sir. As does she. Are you really prepared to risk that? Do you know what can happen to girls and women in times of war, sir?'

Anger flashed across Patrick's face. Dangerously quiet words came from Jamie. 'You go too far, sir.'

'No,' came the sombre response. 'I do not. But others may. Be warned, sir,' he said to Patrick Rankeillor. 'Be aware that your activities are known. And know this, sir. If you continue on your present course you can expect to be met by the full force of the law. The full force,' he repeated. 'I take it you are aware of the penalty for treason.'

Patrick paled but remained composed. 'Aye, laddie. I'm aware o' it.'

'Then be warned, sir,' Robert Catto said again. 'Actions have consequences. I should particularly advise you to drink no more claret over the map of Scotland with mysterious gentlemen who come in out of the night and snatch a makeshift meal before moving further along a path which can lead only to ruin.'

Patrick said nothing in response to that. Jamie only blinked.

The map. That was what was in the document cylinder. Not one of her anatomical drawings but the map of Scotland her father had asked her to create some six months since. They both loved maps. She had always drawn them. Maps were objects of beauty. Maps provided information too, showing towns and cities and roads and ports and harbours and military garrisons—

All the information an army needed.

Be warned, sir.

Come to your senses before it is too late.

I take it you are aware of the penalty for treason.

Do you know what can happen to girls and women in times of war, sir?

Once more the solid floor beneath Christian's feet began to shift and sway. She might have been on the deck of a storm-tossed ship, pitching and rolling on the waves of a swelling sea, and with no chart to guide her to a safe harbour.

10

She stepped forward to grip the back of her father's chair, anchoring herself. Horribly dizzy, she closed her eyes, fighting to keep the sensation at bay. The three men were focussed on one another. They would not notice what she did. She heard the library doors being pulled open.

'Sergeant,' came that cool voice again, 'withdraw the men from the house. Liddell, round up those who are out in the physic garden. Send word to the guards on Surgeon's Hall and the Royal Infirmary that they are to remain there overnight and remain vigilant. They will be relieved by a fresh detail at six o'clock tomorrow morning. Send word also round the city gates to tell the extra men there that they too are to remain at their posts overnight and remain vigilant. They may stand down one hour after first light tomorrow morning. Everyone else is to assemble at the top of the High School Wynd now to await my further orders.'

Christian had the impression that he whirled back round then, the achingly still air in the room stirred by the swing of his cloak as he delivered his parting shot. 'I shall send a message to the West Port that you are to be allowed to leave Edinburgh tomorrow morning, Professor Rankeillor.'

Her father's voice still held that dangerously quiet edge. 'I dinna think I need your permission to go in or out o' Edinburgh, young man.'

'You do now,' came the steely response. 'As does your daughter, all members of your household and Mr Buchan of Balnamoon. All members of your household,' he repeated, 'and anyone who comes to Edinburgh to visit it. That's written permission. Oh, and by the way, from now on each and every dissection in Edinburgh will also require my express and written permission before it can proceed.'

'Such matters are outwith the remit of the Town Guard,' she heard Jamie say hotly.

'Not any more they're not, Mr Buchan.' The satisfaction in the voice whose origins were so hard to pinpoint was unmistakeable. 'Your master and his daughter aren't the only people who have friends in high places. I'll see myself out,' he added. 'I know my way to the front door.'

Christian's eyes flew open. Those words had been directed at her, she knew they had. She caught only a flash of grey cloak and green map case as he swept out of the library, leaving the three of them once more standing in a silent tableau vivant. She listened to the sound of his retreating footsteps and then, louder and less defined, those of his men. The front door was pulled shut behind them.

Patrick Rankeillor raised his eyebrows. 'Somebody wi' some manners.'

'Archie Liddell, probably,' Jamie murmured. 'But let us be a wee bit careful here.' Placing one finger against his lips, he walked out into the lobby, returning within seconds to the library. 'Coast's clear. But I'd jalouse he's going to leave someone watching the house. So I should not stay too long.' He groaned. 'Damn him for taking the map.'

'I'll draw another one,' Christian said, stepping out from behind the library chair and gliding across the floor to join the two men.

'Not yet awhile,' Jamie said quickly. 'For the moment we must keep the gentleman who just left as much in the dark as possible. So no purchasing of large sheets of parchment, Kirsty. No drawing attention to your skills of draughtsmanship.'

'You think he will be watching us that closely?'

Jamie shrugged. 'They watch us. We watch them.'

'Catto,' she supplied. 'His name is Robert Catto.'

'Useful to know.'

'Jamie lad,' Patrick asked anxiously, 'how much do you think he does knows?'

'Too much. I also think we can guess from whom he gained his knowledge.'

'Culloden,' Patrick agreed. 'That must be who he meant by friends in high places. So it was my maist intimate friend Duncan Forbes of Culloden wha sent the Town Guard here tonight?' His expression grew thoughtful. 'There's something about that young man ...'

'Definitely a cut above the usual run of Town Guard Captains,' Jamie agreed. 'For a moment there I was even beginning to wonder whose side he was on.'

'Not ours.' Patrick gave his head a decisive shake, making his wig slide into an even more ridiculous position. 'If he's working for the Lord President, definitely not ours.'

Jamie ran a hand through his dark waves, pulling them free of the neck ribbon which always struggled to confine them, especially by this time of day. 'Then why in the name of God,' he demanded, 'did he not arrest us?'

He and his master looked at each other. Patrick's answer was expelled on a sigh of incomprehension. 'I don't know, lad. That one's puzzling me too.'

'Here's another conundrum to go with it. Why did he not try harder to get the identity of our visitor out of us?'

'We would not have told him,' Patrick said stoutly.

'He could have tried some of those means of persuasion he was talking about. Without carrying us off to the Tolbooth, either. He does not strike me as a man who would scruple to use his fists. Or whatever else came to hand.'

Patrick darted a glance at his daughter.

'I'm going to check on Betty and Mary and Tibby,' she announced.

The cat too, she thought a little wildly, and Lucy the cat. 'So you'll not be heading to the Infirmary yet, Jamie. When I come back it'll be me who's looking for some straight answers to some straight questions.' She looked from one man to the other, lifted her hands and adjusted Patrick's wig. 'From both of you.'

Jamie laid a hand on her arm. 'You shall have those straight answers now, Kirsty.'

From somewhere deep in his throat Patrick made an inarticulate sound of protest.

'We have no choice, Professor,' Jamie said. 'Not any more.' He hadn't looked at his master, sought no permission before he spoke again. 'Kirsty,' he said urgently, 'there is something we must ask you to do.'

Catto stood and watched as the men stepped into the shadows and disappeared into the night. Continuing the pretence as to what the raid had been about, he had told the assembled guards that while they might not have caught the anatomists in the act they had made it clear the Town Guard was ready, willing and able to be vigilant about such matters and to police them with vigour.

That would play well in the howffs, oyster cellars and humbler homes of Edinburgh. In candlelit dining rooms citizens of the higher echelons of society would be uneasily aware that it might have been Patrick Rankeillor's politics which had brought the Town Guard down upon his head. As well they might. As well they bloody might.

Back there in the surgeon-apothecary's library, Catto had recognized the one emotion above all others hanging in the air. Even knowing the deadly danger in which they stood, neither Rankeillor nor Jamie Buchan had been quite able to suppress their excitement: the wild, passionate, unreasoning excitement of men with a cause. He spat out an exclamation of disgust. Dreamers and fools. Idiots who knew nothing of the realities of war. Even greater idiots who did but were blessed with short memories, allowing them to refuse to acknowledge the horror of the genie they proposed to release from the bottle.

He was convinced now that his instincts were right. The thought afforded him no satisfaction. The thought made him want to throw his head back and bay at the moon like a wolf out in one of the great forests of Saxony.

Do you know what can happen to girls and women in times of war, sir?

He did. Oh, dear God, he did. As he plunged into the blackness of Robertson's Close, he was back there. At the farmhouse.

He'd been part of a scouting party from Guise's. All of them, officers and men, had grown uneasy as they drew near to the farm buildings. Afterwards he had realized it was the lack of noise which had unsettled them. No lowing cattle or clucking chickens, no barking dogs, no children playing, no women laughing and talking or slapping laundry against a flat stone in the nearby river.

They were all dead, the family and their animals. It was a dog they spotted first. Its throat had been cut, the blood which had flowed from the hideous wound congealed and buzzing with flies. Then they saw the old man lying next to the beast, his hand on its back. The dog's master, they agreed, making a last vain attempt to save its life.

Whoever had killed his animal had meted out the same treatment to him. Only they hadn't slit his throat but cut his balls and prick off and allowed him to bleed to death. As an added refinement, they had stuffed his privates into his mouth.

Leaving the youngest of his troopers vomiting over a fence, Catto responded to Fred Scott, who was beckoning him to enter the farmhouse. Sometimes he dreamt of that moment, the one before he stooped to go through the low doorway and found himself in the seventh circle of hell. He always saw himself then as the boy he had been before he had lost any vestiges of innocence or belief in human goodness.

A mother and her three daughters. All dead, their bodies beginning to decay and smell inside the stuffy house. That hideous, sickly sweet smell. A boy of about twelve tied to a chair. They'd killed him the same way they'd killed his grandfather.

Although probably not till they made him watch while they ploughed his mother and his sisters. That's what Fred Scott said. All the women had been raped, including the youngest, a girl Catto had judged to be no more than eight or nine. Their simple linen skirts and bodices, bright embroidery red and sticky with blood, had been ripped to shreds.

With broken bottles.

I can see that.

Catto was standing in front of the bodies of the two older girls when those observations were exchanged. Broken glass had been used to cut flesh as well as cloth, naked breasts lacerated. When he saw the jagged neck of a bottle sticking out between the legs of one of the girls he wanted to be sick too, but spewed out words instead.

Bastards. Sick, fucking bastards.

Those were the mildest of the words he used.

Very effective message to send, though.

He stared in disbelief at Fred Scott.

Policing action, I expect. Extremely effective warning to any other would-be rebels.

An old man, a boy, a woman and her daughters?

A shrug. *People should consider what happens if they take sides.*

Punishing a man by slaughtering his whole family? Violating his wife and his daughters?

Can't make an omelette without breaking eggs, Catto. Come on, nothing for us to do here.

Yes there is. We bury them.

What for? We won't be back this way again. Never going to need the house.

For common decency, that's what for.

He helped dig the grave himself, one big pit in which to lay the whole family to rest. He put the dog in there too, laying it alongside the old man, in the crook of his arm. Fred Scott laughed at that. None of the men did. That night, in a tavern as faraway as they could get from the farmhouse, they and Catto set about drinking themselves senseless: and at some point during that evening he spilled his guts while a much more sober Fred Scott listened.

That was why he was here now, in this benighted town in this benighted country he had hoped with all his heart never to set foot in again. Simply being here was bad enough, the voices which reminded him of other voices, the memories which ambushed him at every turn. After tonight it could only get worse. Who knew what might be lying in wait for him now, lurking around the next corner, waiting to step out of the shadows with a nasty little smile on its face?

He wanted to hit something. He wanted to hit someone. The Jacobite messenger would do nicely. None better. He was one of the bastards who was preying on the dreamers and fools, one of those who lurked in the shadows. Dark places. Lonely places. The great black void which could open up in front of you when you least expected it. Like a soldier's memories. Like the pain and loneliness of a lost child, sobbing in the depths of the night.

Suddenly – no reservations now, no, not a one – Robert Catto wanted to find the Jacobite messenger, known or unknown, throw him up against a wall, punch him in the face till the bastard was drinking his own blood and choking on his own teeth, slam his fist hard into his stomach a few times, watch him slide down to the ground, broken and bloodied and beaten.

Once he was satisfied he'd made mincemeat of him he would haul him off to the Tolbooth – aye, and Rankeillor and Balnamoon too, clap all three of them in the heaviest, rustiest –fetters he could find, leave them in the dank horror of that place for days on end, alone in the darkness with the rats and the dirt and the human filth. The girl could beg him all she liked to let them go but he wouldn't budge—

He stopped dead, aware for the second time this evening that his breath was coming too fast, floating up like white smoke out of his mouth and spiralling heavenwards into the freezing midnight air. The hairs on the back of his neck began to prickle. Someone was watching him.

11

'Daft Friday,' Christian said.

'Has to be,' Jamie agreed. 'Our only chance of getting him out of Edinburgh and on his way north.'

'Will he be fit to travel by Friday?' For, as he had just told her, the mysterious stranger had fallen in the pell-mell dash from Surgeons' Hall and badly twisted his ankle.

'He'll have to be,' Jamie said grimly. 'There are gentlemen in the north with whom he must speak as a matter of urgency if matters are to unfold as we wish them to. One he must speak to in Edinburgh before he leaves.'

Christian swallowed hard. 'There is to be an attempt in the spring?'

'Maybe even earlier. Surprise always make for good tactics when it comes to military manoeuvres.'

'Military manoeuvres?' she repeated, feeling her blood run cold. 'You mean fighting, Jamie.'

'Aye. I mean fighting.' He gave her a look which mixed fear with excitement. 'We must have the stomach for it, Kirsty.'

'But you will not fight. Jamie, please tell me you do not intend to strap on a sword!'

'I cannot ask other men to do what I will not.'

'But you're a surgeon, Jamie, and a healer!'

'It is as such that I hope to serve the Cause but what will be will be.

We may all have to do things we would never have contemplated before this is all over. Kirsty, I must go. If I tarry any longer 'twill look like we're conspiring. Talking treason and sedition.'

'We are, aren't we?' she said crisply. 'By their lights. I might have done so all the sooner given the opportunity.'

'I wanted to tell you long since. Your father wouldn't hear of it. He will tell you the rest. Or I will tomorrow. You understand what you have to do?'

'Take sustenance and medical aid to our visitor. Not be seen while I'm doing it.' She raised her eyebrows. 'Therein will lie the difficulty.'

'People are used to seeing you around the hospital. Yet also not noticing you.'

'Thanks. 'Tis nice to know I am invisible.'

'You know what I mean, Kirsty. Women are much less noticed than men as they go about their daily business. Few folk are inclined to visit that part of the hospital, either. Not since—' He broke off.

Not since that poor boy hanged himself there last year. Those were the words Jamie had left unsaid. People were beginning to tell stories about that quiet corridor at the back of the infirmary. Lined with locked cells designed for the safe custody of lunatics, its first and so far only occupant had been a troubled young man. Last summer he had chosen to end his life there.

'Try to look confident, Kirsty. Act as though you have every right to be there. If anyone does notice and asks what you're doing, have a story ready.'

'I might say that boy's mother thinks he left something there, a notebook with some lines of verse or little sketches. Of no monetary value but precious to her. I might even make such an object and carry it with me.'

'Good idea. As long as nobody sees you doing that. Kirsty, I really must go!'

She laid a hand on the sleeve of his threadbare coat. 'One last question. How are we to get our visitor out of Edinburgh when the hospital's under guard, we're probably all being watched and we now need permission to leave the city, written permission at that?'

He smiled at her from under the untidy hair. 'Dammit, Miss Rankeillor, you always have had the tendency to ask awkward questions.'

'You haven't worked that out yet?'

'No, but I will. Goodnight, Kirsty.'

She gazed after him as he strode out of the library. Tired though he clearly was, there was purpose and determination in every step. She had never seen him look so alive.

Never so alive.

I take it you are aware of the penalty for treason.

Fear crouched beside her, coiled and ready to strike. Nausea rose in her throat.

She drew in a deep breath, forced the nausea down. She did not have time to be scared now. She was needed elsewhere. Flattening her cumbersome skirts in readiness, she hurried out of the library toward the narrow passageway that led to the kitchen.

Catto curled his fingers round the hilt of his sword and spoke into the shadows. 'I know you're there. Come forward and show yourself.'

'You look sad, mannie.'

His fingers relaxed. 'You can tell that in the dark?'

'Ah can tell a lot o' things in the dark. That's where ah maistly practise ma trade.'

'Ah. So that's why a young lady like yourself is out and about at this time of night.'

'Aye.' There was a smile in her voice. 'And aiblins ah hae the cure for whitever ails ye. I'll mebbe can cheer ye up, mannie.'

He shouldn't do this. But he was already hardening. 'Are you clean?'

'As a crimson-tippit gowan,' the trollop said cheerfully, walking forward to join him where he stood in the moonlight. As she allowed her all-enveloping plaid to slip from her shoulders, he saw she was a bit thin for his taste. Pretty face, though. Funny how that still mattered when all you wanted was a female body. There was less chimney smoke now fires had been closed in for the night. He could see her well enough to realize that she was very young. If she was even eighteen years old, he was a Dutchman.

He hesitated. No young girls. No girls who seemed in the least measure unwilling. When it came to satisfying his baser instincts those were two of the few rules he had for himself. But she would take him away from the farmhouse. She would take him away from what he had discovered tonight. She would take him away from his own black heart.

She laid a small white hand on his arm. 'Whaur shall we ging, dearie? Your lodgings?'

She was experienced. He could tell that from her attitude and the knowing expression on her pretty face. No innocent, then. Although she might have been a couple of years back when a father or an uncle had pressed her into plying this trade ... but it wasn't his principles that were in control of him right now.

'Not my lodgings.' His breath quickened. 'I want it here. Now. Against the wall.'

She laughed. 'Ye're ower tall for that, mannie. We'll no' manage tae fit thegither.'

'Find something to stand on. I'll pay you a bit extra.'

'How much?'

He dug into the pocket of his red coat, brought out his purse, pushed its leather drawstring open, found a florin and tossed it to her. She caught and held the coin in one practised movement before peering at it to make sure of its value. She stowed the money in the wash-leather pouch she wore at her waist and waved an arm towards the shadows from which she had emerged. 'There's a doorway ower here wi' some lang steps in front o' it. Ye'll hae tae tread carefully, mind.

Ye'll no' be wanting to get any nastiness on your fine shoon. Walk where I dae and ye'll be fine.'

He did as he was bid, noticing as he followed her that despite the chill of the winter's night the girl herself was barefoot. He thought about the word she had used. *Nastiness.* It was one euphemism the good citizens of Edinburgh used to describe the filth they flung into the street every night at ten o'clock: vegetable debris, ashes and the contents of chamber pots alike. *The flowers o' Edinburgh.* That was the other name for it.

Following the girl, Catto picked his way round a pile of shit, taking a stride rather than a step to avoid the stagnant half-frozen puddle of rank urine oozing out of the stinking mess. Next to the filth, a rat gnawed on a cabbage leaf. Eyes gleaming like glass beads, the creature didn't move as Catto and the girl passed it. Stretched out behind it, its curling tail was as long as its body.

The trollop climbed up onto a stone step and turned. 'Will this dae ye? I'm thinking it'll work fine if ye staun' on the causeway in front o' me.'

He reached for her waist under her plaid. Far too skinny for his liking. Far too cold. His splayed fingers were encountering too many bones and not nearly enough warm female flesh. 'Move alang a wee bittie,' he told her. 'Careful, mind. There's some mair shite here.' Funny how, after all these years away, he had discovered he still had a guid Scots tongue in his heid.

The girl giggled when he lifted her bodily over the shit and allowed him to guide her to the clean end of the step. It was a nice sound, simple and unaffected. 'Ye like tae tak' a lassie wha's got her back against something solid?'

'I like that fine,' Catto agreed. 'And I like it fine when a lassie opens her legs wide. As wide as they'll go.' He hooked one hand under her thigh. 'We'll lift this leg a wee bit too.'

She giggled again and twisted awkwardly to accommodate his

stated requirements. She must be bloody uncomfortable. She wasn't complaining.

'I'm needing tae growp your breists as weel,' he said, once more couching the demand in the *patois* of the street. He pushed his sword and the map cylinder he had slung across his body out of the way and lifted his hands to part the fronts of her plaid, taking her compliance for granted. Her own hands came up to stop him.

'Another sixpence?' she wheedled. 'It's a gey cauld night for this kind o' cairy-on.'

He fumbled in his pocket, pushed his purse open again and found another shilling. Once the girl had it in her purse, she pulled back her plaid. 'Will I undo ma bodice or will you?'

'I'll do it. Ye'll no' mind if I'm a wee bittie rough.' Was he asking her, or telling her? He didn't know.

As he untied the already loosened laces, she tilted her head back against the wall. 'For three shillings ye can dae anything ye want tae me,' she murmured.

Her breasts gleamed in the moonlight. Small, soft and white. One pair was as good as any other. His hand found a nipple, stiffened already as hard as a musket ball in the freezing December air. He pinched it between his thumb and fingers, squeezing it and the breast beneath it hard. The girl whimpered, swiftly transforming the sound of pain into a moan of pleasure. Aye, she was experienced, all right. She shivered.

'Cold?'

When she nodded, Catto gripped the soft folds of his grey cloak with his free hand and wrapped it round them both. 'Better?'

'Aye,' she sighed, her breath a white string of smoke in the night air. 'That's a lot better, mannie.'

After that it was all hardness, himself as stiff and unyielding as the barrel of a Doune pistol, his thrusts so forceful they were lifting her slight frame. Consciously using his far superior height and weight, he pushed her back against the stone surround of the doorway. He needed to feel resistance and the girl herself was too slight to offer much.

This was he wanted right now, this was what he needed. Fucking a girl he'd never met before in the midst of all of this filth and nastiness. Fucking her *hard.*

The moans sounded more genuine now. Was he making her come? Or, like all her kind, had she learned early on it was a good idea to make a man think that? Her breath, at least, was warm. The words were sighed into his ear. 'It's no often I have a big handsome chiel the size o' you up me.'

In the darkness, Catto's mouth curved into a cynical smile. Pay three times the going rate and you could not only use them as you pleased, you'd bought yourself some flattery too. However inelegantly phrased it might be.

On his way back up the High Street, he called in at what had become his usual howff, asking the landlady to sell him a bottle of claret and a bottle of brandy.

'Ye're no' wanting company wi' your refreshment the night, young Captain Catto?'

'No,' he said, throwing the payment down on the counter, 'I'm not.' He turned on his heel and went back out into the chilly night, wondering why so many people here had to preface his name with that bloody adjective. He was damn sure none of them knew an old Captain Catto.

The guard-house squatted in the middle of the High Street, halfway between the Netherbow Port and St Giles' Cathedral. It was a long, low and unprepossessing building, resembling a tumbledown, if oversized, cottar house way out in the country somewhere. A wooden horse, designed for the punishment and humiliation of guards guilty of insubordination or other misdemeanours, stood at one end of the building. Tied there for a few hours, they would be subject to catcalling and the occasional projectile. There was little love lost between Edinburgh's citizens and the Town Guard. A dingy timber lean-to at the other was used by the city's chimney sweeps to stow their brushes and ladders overnight and on the Sabbath.

Catto gave the day's password to the sentry on duty at the stable-like door and exchanged a few words with the corporal in charge of the night-watch. Only one drunk and disorderly citizen locked up in the guard-house's cell tonight and he was already sleeping it off.

'Ye shouldna be disturbed, Mr Catto, sir. Except by the snoring, mebbe. Naebody in the Deid-Room, forbye. That's a relief, Captain, eh? Ah dinna ken aboot you, but ah'm no' just awfy fond o' spending the night wi' the departed. We've had ower many o' them in here recently, eh?'

Stepping through the small internal courtyard, Catto pushed open the door of the flagstoned kitchen around which the life of the guard-house revolved. Slumped over the big table which occupied the centre of the room, he found Geordie Maxwell the cook-boy. His ocean of golden waves resting on skinny white arms, coarse linen shirt-sleeves rolled up to the elbows as they always were, the child was fast asleep. Catto shook his shoulder to wake him up.

'Did I not say you weren't to wait up for me? Get away to your bed.'

The boy looked all too wide awake, coming from sleep to full alertness in a matter of seconds as Catto had learned he invariably did. 'Shall I no' make ye some supper, Captain?' he asked eagerly. 'Did it go well tonight? Can you tell me now where ye were?'

Placing the claret and brandy bottles on the table, Catto divested himself of his cloak and sword. 'I'll tell you tomorrow. And I'm not hungry. Is the fire banked up for the night?'

'Aye, and the one in your bedchamber too, Mr Catto,' the boy said, his clear young eyes sliding to the bottles. 'Ye'd be the better o' some food to soak a' that up, sir.'

Catto fetched a corkscrew from the massive smoke-blackened

dresser which took up most of the back wall of the kitchen, opened the bottle of claret, put it to his lips and took a swig. Geordie shot him a reproachful look, slid off his chair and hurried round the table. When he reached the dresser he stretched up to lift a battered but well-polished pewter tankard off one of the brass hooks screwed into its bottom shelf.

'Thank you,' Catto said icily. He was in the blackest of moods now, and he knew who he had to blame for it. Men with a cause. God damn men with a cause to hell. That was where they belonged.

Condescending smart-mouthed little Jacobite bitches. *Do you have many friends, Mr Catto? Your mother must be so proud of you. The kitchen door lies yonder.* God damn her to hell too. Why he had felt at all sorry for her he did not know. Why the hell he had allowed her to make him laugh he did not know. That was truly incomprehensible. Well, he'd got his revenge for that, although any small pain he'd inflicted upon Christian Rankeillor was currently being paid back with interest, his damn thigh once more throbbing with pain. That was all he bloody needed.

He sloshed half the bottle of wine into the tankard. A few drops escaped and spilled onto the table. Geordie went off again, returning with a cloth to mop them up. Catto put a hand to the back of his neck and pulled open the ribbon which secured his hair. Yanking the black satin folds clear of it, he shook his head to free his gleaming chestnut waves.

'Shite, Geordie,' he growled, throwing the bagwig onto the table, 'you're like an old woman sometimes. Just bloody leave it, all right? And get away to your bed. I'll not tell you again.' He put the tankard to his lips and downed another gulp of claret.

'It'll only take a wee minutie.' The boy leaned forward, wiped up the splashed wine and stood looking anxiously up at Catto. 'I'll easy mak ye some supper, Captain. It's nae bother. I've some soup in the pot, or I could redd up the fire again and toast ye some bread and cheese.'

'I hate cheese,' Catto snapped, turning the full force of his stare onto him. Confound it. Why did the boy himself have to possess such expressive eyes? Blue as a summer sky. As Christian Rankeillor's were green as a summer meadow. They had clouded with fear when she had realized what was going on. Why should he care about that?

'Bed,' he said softly. 'Now.'

'But it's really nae bother—'

Catto's free hand went up and back. He stopped himself just in time, although not before Geordie had flinched violently away from him. Man and boy stared at each other. Then Catto dropped his hand. 'Away to your bed,' he growled. 'Now.'

The lad stood where he was for a few seconds more before obeying him, slinking away to the box bed in the corner of the kitchen. His master watched him climb up into it, put out the lights – the lantern which hung from the rafters over the table and the one which stood on a stand next to the dresser – picked up his bagwig, sword, claret and brandy and went through to his bedchamber.

The room was warm from the banked-up fire. Stripping down to his breeches, waistcoat and shirt, he took a spill from the smoke-blackened mantelpiece and bent down to slide the tip of it into the mound of coals and dross. Once it ignited, he straightened up and stepped across to the table under the window which served him as a desk, lighting the branched candlestick which stood there. There was always paperwork.

He and the Lord President had agreed that his log should be a simple recording of the facts, and only the most basic of those. Edinburgh's current Lord Provost was going to want to read his log for tonight too. His absence from Edinburgh on a visit to his wife's family in Berwickshire had been an important factor in allowing tonight's raid to go ahead.

Culloden had given Catto the names of certain gentlemen who were not under any circumstances to be trusted. Lord Provost Coutts was one of them. The man denied any Jacobite sympathies but the suspicion remained. Nor had it escaped Catto's attention that Rankeillor's housekeeper had tried to bandy Coutts' name in defence of her master.

He wrote up a skeletal account of tonight's mission, blotted the page, closed the ledger and slid it to one side. He pulled a loose sheet of paper towards him from the neatly ordered paper tray at the back of the desk and dipped his quill once more into the pewter inkwell.

He had written to Culloden's principal agent in Glasgow at the beginning of the week, asking her to keep an eye on Patrick Rankeillor while that gentleman was through in the West. He wrote a brief second letter, asking her to "kindly redouble your efforts in the matter previously discussed." Careful wording was always a good idea when you were forced to entrust a letter to the public mails. Codes and ciphers could be a double-edged sword, demonstrating to your enemies that you had something to hide.

His private and fuller dispatch to the Lord President was to be carried north by a trusted pair of hands a week on Monday, two days after the Daft Friday ball. Culloden had sailed from Leith yesterday, heading up the east coast to keep Christmas at his estate near Inverness. A widower with one son on whom he doted, he was also the paterfamilias to his wider family, which included several nieces and nephews. Some domestic emergency within that extended family had called him home to Inverness earlier than he had intended to go.

He had known tonight's raid was going ahead, had assured Catto he had every confidence in him carrying it out successfully, felt certain he would have a lot more to tell him after word of the raid got around the town, and after the Daft Friday ball. Catto had news for the Lord President now. He could entrust it to the public mails only if he worded his message so that his meaning was clear to Duncan Forbes but gave nothing away to anyone who might intercept the letter.

As he sat there in the candlelight, quill poised as he considered what that wording should be, it came to him that he was about to pen his own death warrant. Or, at the very least, the warrant for his incarceration without limit of time. Once the Lord President knew his own fears were justified, the earlier promise he had given that Catto need stay in Scotland for only three months would fly out of the window. Culloden would undoutedly keep him here for as long as he thought he needed him.

There was an even worse possibility. His stay in Scotland might be all too short.

The quill fell from his fingers, spattering ink over the paper beneath his hand. Catto did not react to the calamity, only sat staring into space. Then he reached for the claret and brandy bottles and set about drinking himself into a stupor.

The prostitute was back in the Grassmarket, her usual stamping ground. As instructed, she made her way down into the oyster cellar, sliding her way between sweaty bodies and slapping away wandering hands. Not unless and until they'd paid for the privilege, that was her philosophy.

He was sitting in the inglenook of the big stone fireplace. He even had a tassie of geneva waiting for her. A gentleman, she thought with a little thrill. Like the one she'd just had. She was coming up in the world. Maybe she could rise above the misfortunes which had beset her throughout this awful year.

First there had been the man who had nominated himself her protector, the one who had claimed to love her, running out on her, taking all the money she had earned forbye. As if that hadn't been enough, she'd then discovered she had the pox. She was clear of that now, thank God. She could work and build up some money again.

Once there was enough in the kitty she would leave the overcrowded and smelly lodging house where she stayed and find herself a nice wee room where a select band of gentlemen would come to her. They would make an arrangement to visit her on a certain day and at a certain time and they would be handsome and kind and treat her decently.

Some of them might even bring her little presents. A wee posy of flowers, maybe. Or a length of silk to fashion into a bonnie gown. She longed for nice clothes. The Town Guard Captain had been well-dressed, his uniform cut from the finest cloth. The material had felt lovely and soft against the bare skin of her arms and breasts.

'You've done the needful?'

'That was our arrangement, was it no'? That I was tae keep him occupied for a wee while?'

'Aye. That was our arrangement.' The man who'd been waiting for her slid over to allow her to join him on the bench. 'How was he?'

'Hard,' she murmured, taking a deep breath and relishing the warmth of the fire after her walk through the frosty chill of the December night.

He chuckled and reached a hand to her chin, grasping it between his thumb and forefingers. 'You enjoyed it then, my wee strumpet?'

'Of course I did.' She'd learned her trade the hard way. Even if you'd hated every second of it, you never said so. It was funny how even the men and women who ran you wanted to think you were in this trade through inclination rather than desperation, that you weren't selling yourself because there were damn few other ways for a lassie alone in the world to earn her daily bread.

'How much did he pay you?'

She thought quickly. Say too much and he might renege on the original bargain to double the money, say too little and she'd lose the profit that would go towards funding the dream of a wee room of her own. 'Two shillings,' she said, unable to keep a tinge of pride out of her voice as she thought what the real sum had been. The tall and handsome young Captain of the Guard had wanted her so badly he'd been prepared to pay well over the odds. He'd been kind too, wrapping his cloak about her when she'd shivered. She'd felt real warm after that.

Before they'd parted he'd even asked if she was all right, waiting for her reply and wishing her goodnight before he swept off. *I'll bid you goodnight then, lass.* She'd liked that, him taking his leave of her in a proper manner. Lots of them went without a word. Or used her hard and flung foul words at her as they left.

The slim fingers gripping her chin tightened painfully. 'Lying wee hure.' He raised the pitch of his voice, mimicking her. '*For three shillings ye can dae anything ye want tae me.*'

Her eyes widened. 'Ye were watching?'

'Maybe I wanted to see what he was made of.'

'Or maybe ye just like to watch,' she suggested. 'Instead o' daein it.'

The fingers gripped even tighter. 'Careful. You want some more money, don't you?'

She nodded. He released her chin and threw a shilling on the table. 'It's all you're worth.'

'Look,' she said, 'gie me the three shillings and you can have me too. Anyway ye like. A' the different ways ye like.'

He laughed. It was a pleasant sound, merry and warm, horribly at odds with the words which followed it. 'I like 'em a lot less used than you are, sweetheart.'

She'd thought he was different. Now she saw he was no better than all the rest. They thought they could say whatever they wanted to you. That was almost as bad as them thinking they could do whatever they pleased to you, disgusting things, sometimes.

She turned from him to stare into the flames dancing and flickering in the fireplace. She was getting those memories she hated, the ones she tried so hard to suppress. The feelings they aroused swamped and overwhelmed her. Shame. Helplessness. A rage that washed over her, leaving her breathless, trembling and empty.

She'd only been a wee lassie when it had started. How could they have let those men do what they had done to a young girl, their own flesh and blood, forbye? She'd never been able to understand that. It had hurt, hurt so sore, and all everyone had done was laugh. *Breaking her in good and proper. She's a right dirty wee hure now.* The jeering words, leers and laughter had never left her head.

Yet she would not allow the memories to defeat her. She'd managed to escape, hadn't she? She'd run away, traded herself for a lift from a carter who had brought her to Edinburgh. She'd made her own way here in this bustling place and she'd been promised that money, double of whatever the Town Guard Captain had paid her. She'd earned it, fair and square.

The girl took a sip of her gin, felt the spirit warm her throat and chest. 'Maybe I should ging tae the guard-hoose and tell yon young gentleman that you asked me tae waylay him,' she said softly, placing her cup on the rough wooden table. 'D'ye no' think he might be interested in knowing that? D'ye no' think he might be interested in some other things I ken aboot?'

'And what would those be?'

She told him, wondering if she was seeing admiration in his face at what she had made it her business to know. He was certainly studying her very thoughtfully. She had the daftest idea he wasn't seeing only what lay on the surface but what was inside her too. His smile was reassuring. 'All right, then. I'll pay you your money. But let's complete our transaction elsewhere. There's ower many folk bothered by their noses in this place.'

She smiled, relieved that it had been so easy. 'Can I hae another geneva wherever we're going?'

He slid his arm about her thin shoulders. She liked it when men did that. It made her feel warm and safe and protected. 'Of course you can, my wee strumpet. Of course you can.'

12

Her room felt tainted. Invaded and sullied. As she walked round the bed to her closet, Christian spotted the books on her bedside table. The disarray in which he had left them had to be deliberate. There was something tidy about the untidiness of how it had been done. He had wanted her to know he had picked up and handled her books. Touched them. As he had touched her. With malice aforethought.

She hadn't noticed the books when she'd been up here earlier, too concerned with changing hastily out of her cumbersome evening gown into her night clothes so she could go back downstairs to the girls. Despite what she'd been put through this evening, Betty had come up with her and helped her change. The two of them had hurried back downstairs to calm Mary and Tibby and put them to bed, relieving Patrick Rankeillor, who was coaxing both white-faced girls to sip some warm milk laced with honey and nutmeg.

Now, with the Rankeillor household at last settling down for the night, Christian stood quietly, trying to absorb what had happened here this evening. Reeling though she was from what Jamie had told her and asked her to do, she could not rid herself of the sense of Robert Catto's presence. Powerful. Hostile. Male. Contemptuous of her and everything about her. Bringing the reek and clamour of the battlefield into her home, her very bedchamber and closet, her most precious and private place.

She could see him here, that grey military cloak swirling about him as he turned and looked at her things. Inspected them. Sneered at them. Sneered at her. He had meant his invasion of her bedchamber to be a violation, not only of the room but of her. He did not know her but he despised her.

She sank back against the edge of her high bed. Now there was no longer the need to put a brave face on it for the sake of Mary and Tibby, the energy was draining out of her. Her head fell forward, and she wrapped one arm around the post at the bottom of the bed. Her fingers trace the carvings on it, following the bushy tail of a squirrel.

She loved this bed that had been specially made for her. She loved this bedchamber. Other than Betty and the girls and now and again her father, only her closest friends ever came here. Here she could withdraw from the busy world to read and think and dream and draw. Here she could be most truly herself. Only now her private world had been violated and intruded upon. That had been done with malice aforethought too.

The sound of footsteps on the stairs brought her head up. Sliding onto her feet, she made a dash for the head of the bed. She had the books on her bedside table back in their usual neat pile only seconds before Betty came bustling through the door.

'What are you up to?' the housekeeper demanded.

'Nothing. Betty,' she protested, walking down the side of the bed towards the housekeeper, 'why don't you get away to your bed? I can easily brush my own hair.' The evening wig was on its stand in the closet now.

'No ye canna. I've brushed your hair every night o' your life. I'm no' going to stop now. And you've a gey guilty look on your face for someone who's no been up tae onything.'

Betty wasn't going to get this one out of her. She might disapprove of Christian reading in bed but she'd have been outraged if she'd known Robert Catto had touched the books. She knew the older woman felt that sense of violation too, had done from the moment he had announced his intention of personally searching her bedchamber.

Betty Gilchrist guarded Christian Rankeillor's reputation as though it were a precious jewel.

'I'd rather you just went to your bed.' She walked to her dressing table where Betty was leaning forward to pick up the hairbrush. 'You need your rest after what you've been through tonight. Are Mary and Tibby asleep now?'

'Aye. And it would tak mair than callants like yon tae frichten me. Sit doon.'

It would tak mair than callants like yon tae frichten me. Swallowing the lump in her throat, Christian obeyed her. Lucy the cat leapt onto her lap. The little creature had come padding down the stairs as she had hurried from the library, clearly none the worse for her encounter with the Town Guard Captain. He'd only been trying to frighten her by letting her think he'd harmed the cat.

'What did ye say?'

Christian raised her eyebrows at their combined reflections in the mirror. 'Charming fellow. The Town Guard Captain, I mean.'

'Aye,' Betty said grimly. 'Charming.'

'Ow! Dinna take it out on my hair, Betty. Or my poor heid.'

'It's all tuggy. It aye is after it's been dressed. I need tae smoothe these ringlets oot if you're no' going tae lie on them all night and gie yersel a headache.'

Christian threw her a smile. 'It was tuggy when I was a wee lassie, Betty. Before I ever had my hair dressed. Do you mind how I used to greet when you brushed my hair? And you'd tell me you had to smooth it so it would be bonnie and I would be bonnie and give me a wee sweetie to dry my tears.'

Betty's fierce expression softened. 'Aye,' she said. 'I remember.'

Their eyes met in the mirror. 'I think we're in trouble, Betty.'

Betty's busy fingers stilled. 'Aye,' she said, laying the hand not holding the hairbrush on Christian's shoulder. 'I think we are.'

The girl was cold, so very cold. She wore only her shift and a plaid she had stolen from that terrible woman. Dried now and rubbing against her bare skin, her legs and the back of her shift were stained with blood. The pain between her legs was as sharp as broken glass.

But she had got away. That was what she had to hold on to. She was out of their clutches. She had stumbled blindly through this unfamiliar landscape of soaring tenements and dark closes, wanting only to put as much distance as possible between herself and that house to which she had been taken, carried thither bound and covered in the back of a cart. Emerging without warning into an open space, she yelped as she stubbed her toes against a block of stone.

Her eyes accustomed now to the gloom, she saw that she was standing in front of a half-built wall. It seemed to bound the gardens of a large building. A huge building. Bigger than any she had ever seen. Bar one – but she would not think about that place now.

Her heart leapt into her mouth when she heard male voices. Hardly daring to look, she saw four men standing together some distance away with their backs towards her. She could make out uniforms and the glint of weapons. Soft laughter. The smell of pipe tobacco.

Silent as a mouse, she backed away, following the wall along until she found a corner. Slipping round the hard stone she came to another corner with bushes and trees in front of it. She'd be well hidden behind them. Drawing her legs up, she tucked the plaid over her feet, securing the material with her toes.

Once she saw dawn beginning to break, she would go and find her brother. She would arrange her plaid so nobody would guess she only had her blood-stained shift on beneath it. She'd have to ask for directions. A kind-looking, respectable housewife. That was who she would approach, some nice lady out early to buy fish or meat from one of the markets.

She bent her head and brought her arms up over it, making sure to keep them covered by the folds of cloth. What if that kind-looking, respectable housewife was able to tell what had happened to her? What if she looked into her eyes and immediately saw her shame?

It wasn't her fault. What had happened to her wasn't her fault. Only it was. The girl curled in on herself, a tight little ball of misery. She'd been a fool, a daft, stupid gowk—

Footsteps. Coming towards her. Her head shot up and she barely managed to suppress a whimper of fear. When she made out two of the guards she'd seen earlier coming round the corner of the building she wet herself, and had to stuff her hand into her mouth to stop the cry of pain at the sting of the warm urine on her wounded flesh.

'Waste o' bloody time, this,' muttered one of the guards as they passed a few feet away from her.

'Aye,' came the low-voiced answer. 'Quiet as Greyfriars kirkyard here. He'll no ken if we knock off noo, will he?'

'I'm no' so sure about that. Eyes in the back o' his heid, that one.'

'How about we find a wee corner inside yon front porch and do a final circuit o' the place about half-past five? The others'll no' clype on us.'

'Good idea. Bloody freezing tonight, is it no'?'

They passed and she strained her ears until she could hear their voices no longer. She let out a sigh of relief: until she once more heard the sound of approaching footsteps.

Please God, let this not be the guards coming back to get me. Please God, let this not be those terrible people coming back to get me. Please God, anything but that!

She wanted to close her eyes. Fear kept them open. She saw one man, labouring under a burden. It looked like a big bolt of cloth. With a grunt of exertion, he lowered it to the ground. The girl's eyes widened further still. That wasn't a bolt of cloth.

As he rolled it in under the bushes, mere yards from where she sat, a stiff white hand flopped out. The girl froze, and became as still as a stone statue.

'Miss Kirsty! Miss Kirsty!'

Christian snapped upright, provoking a growl from Lucy, curled up next to her on the big bed. 'What's the matter? What's happened?'

The two girls launched themselves onto her bed, one on either side of her, drawing their knees up, making themselves as small as they could be. 'The Town Guard are back in the hoose!' Mary cried. 'Listen!'

Downstairs something crashed. Tibby whimpered and drew even closer to Christian. 'They're in the shop!'

Christian put an arm about each trembling girl. More crashing from downstairs. They were smashing pottery and breaking glass, spoiling and destroying. Catching the fear, the frantic cat pressed itself against her breast. She had no hand to spare for Lucy, no chance to try to soothe the little creature. Where were Betty and her father? Oh God, where were they?

Consumed by panic, the cat scratched her, drew blood, sent red spots spattering down the front of her nightdress. She bent her head and stared stupidly at them.

Male footsteps were mounting the stairs. One man. Christian looked up and towards the door. Tibby and Mary screamed when Robert Catto flung the bedroom door wide. His sword was drawn, his concentration on Christian and Christian alone. He locked eyes with her and walked slowly towards the bed—

'No!' she cried, and once more snapped upright. This time she was awake.

Breathing as though she'd been running a desperate race, her breasts and her shoulders were heaving. 'Mary?' she asked over the thumping of her heart. 'Tibby?'

Only the cat answered, giving her a trill of greeting. Her trembling hand found the warm fur, and the purring started up. 'A nightmare, baudrons? Was that all it was?'

It took her a few moments to be sure. Only when her breathing had slowed right down did she lie back against her pillows. She left her hand resting lightly on the warm and purring cat.

13

It was early, still dark outside, but the fire in Christian's bedchamber had already been stirred back into life, she in the wing chair to one side of its red glow and her father in the other. While she was still in her nightclothes and quilted wrapper, he was more or less dressed for the day.

He'd already tugged on his riding boots. Now all he had to do was put on his wig and tricorne hat and exchange his long blue damask dressing gown for his frock coat and heavy winter cloak. Those lay on the foot of Christian's bed, along with his portmanteau. His larger valise was to be collected tomorrow to be carried through to Glasgow on the mail coach.

Betty was already up and about and had gone back downstairs a moment before after bringing bowls of porridge up to Christian and her father. Lucy the cat had followed her down on the promise of a nice bowl of milk waiting in the kitchen.

'Has she left the lassies tae sleep, though?' Patrick asked between one fragrant spoonful and the next.

'Aye,' Christian said, busying herself with making tea for both of them and glad of the task. She'd taken only two mouthfuls of her own porridge and knew she wouldn't be fit to eat the rest. 'You ken what she's like. Aye harder on herself than anybody else.' The lustrous brown curls Betty had brushed the night before slid down over the deep flounces of her dressing gown as she bent forward to pick up the little brass kettle from its stand.

'Will you take your tea now, Father?'

'Thank you, my dear,' he said, setting his wooden porridge bowl and horn spoon down on the small table Betty had placed next to his elbow. 'I shall indeed take the vile drug and contemptible beverage—Oh!'

Christian's mouth twisted. It was Duncan Forbes of Culloden who gave that disparaging description to tea. Considering the heroic amounts of claret and brandy he routinely quaffed, she and her father had always found it funny. Nothing about the Lord President seemed remotely amusing this morning.

'Ach, lass,' Patrick said, 'let's have a toast in tea.' The two dainty china cups met. 'May times mend.'

'And down with the bloody Brunswickers,' Christian supplied, managing to return the smile lighting up her father's face. This toast had long been a private joke between them, the only occasion when as a young girl she had ever been encouraged to swear.

'I trust that young man last night offered you no insult. Other than searching your bedchamber, that is.' Patrick's voice had grown very dry. He had gone white-faced with anger when Betty had poured out that part of the story to him last night. 'He didna deal with you personally in any way inappropriately?'

How was she to answer that?

He called me the worst name a man can call a woman. He touched me, grabbed my wrist. So hard that I have a bruise there this morning. He pressed the hoops of my petticoat against my legs and knew he was doing it. He stood too close to me. He looked at my mouth.

She had looked at his. And if it was inappropriate for a man's eyes to drop to your breasts when he was talking to you then a large proportion of all the men she had ever met were guilty of the offence. 'Not unless you count him telling me that I was wearing stupid clothes.'

'I might be with him there, lass. Fancy him having Betty gagged.' Patrick pretended to shudder. 'He's a braver man than I am. Although I canna say the thought's never crossed my mind over the years.'

'Now you're doing it too.'

'Doing what?'

'Trying to make light of things.'

'Best way,' he said blithely, and continued to drink his tea. Studying him, it occurred to Christian that she was one of the few people who ever saw him in his *déshabille*, without the protective panoply of wig and academic robes. He could look quite formidable in those.

She was always trying to persuade him to exchange his full-bottomed wig for a more modern short one, tied back in a queue. He was always telling her, with a twinkle in his eye, that his big old-fashioned wig gave him the presence which allowed him to terrify his students. His own fair hair was cut short, turning the imposing Professor Rankeillor into a boyishly handsome man. He was not so very old, after all, but four-and-forty, in his prime – and as easily broken as any other man.

I take it you are aware of the penalty for treason.

Made clumsy by fear, she set her cup on the little table at her elbow so that it rocked before it came to rest, a splash of tea leaping onto her thumb. She let out a yelp of pain. Her father was up out of his chair within seconds, crouching in front of hers to take her trembling hand in his, lifting her thumb to his lips.

'There,' he said, 'that'll make it better. Best physic there is. Do we no' baith ken that?' He rose to his feet long enough to kick a footstool into place, sat down on it and took both her hands in his. 'So like your mother,' he murmured. 'Bonnie and bright and never content until ye ken the hale truth.'

Her brimming eyes searched his well-loved face. 'You have brought me up to love the truth, Father.'

'Aye. That I have.'

'Yet you have kept this secret from me. You and Jamie both. Did you not trust me?'

'I would trust you with my life, lass. We sought only to protect you.' His voice grew heavy with regret. 'And now we have to ask you to put yourself in danger. How I wish there was another way. How I wish I did not have to go to Glasgow. But I must.'

Was there a question in his voice? That she could not allow.

'Indeed you must. You always go to Glasgow in December. 'Twould only look more suspicious if you changed your mind now. And,' she added earnestly, squeezing the hands which held hers, 'I would play my part, Father. Neither you nor Jamie can help our visitor. Were either of you to be seen heading for that part of the hospital, people would immediately notice and ask why.'

'I ken that fine. I still dinna like it. Kirsty,' he went on, 'there are a few things I must tell you afore I set off for Glasgow and I want you to listen to me carefully. If the worst should come to the worst, ye must ken that I have made some preparations. This hoose, as ye well ken, belongs to the Incorporation of Surgeons of Edinburgh but the shop is mine and soon it will be yours. I've spoken to our man o' business, and he is drawing up the documents to put everything in your name. As there will be enough siller in the bank, also in your name, to allow you and Betty to set yourselves up in a smaller hoose and give the girls a wee something to tide them over till they find a new position if ye canna afford to keep them on. Gin ye want to establish the shop elsewhere, I see no reason why that shouldna be possible. After all, when it comes to the preparing and prescribing o' physic, ye've aye been as much my apprentice as Jamie.'

Christian stared at him. 'But where does that leave Jamie? After all this time as your apprentice he would be entitled to have—'

'Expectations?'

She nodded. 'I think you have had expectations too, Father. Regarding Jamie and me. That one day we might make a match of it.'

'I'd have liked that fine, lass.' Plain as day, the regret was there in his face for her to see. 'But there's no spark between the two o' ye. Is there?'

'Och, Father …' She slid her hands out of his, turned her head away to gaze into the fire. 'We are very fond of each other, Jamie and me.'

'But you do not love each other. Not as a husband and wife should.' Patrick's voice grew very soft. 'Not as your mother and I loved each other.'

She turned her head away from the fire. 'I think I am very lucky to have a father like you.'

'Because I shall never tell my daughter who she must wed and brook no argument as to the choice of bridegroom?'

'That, and so much more.' She knew there were many parents who did not consider love a prerequisite for marriage, who would laugh at the very notion. Such people viewed wedlock as a business contract, a desirable partner for their son or daughter one who would increase a family's wealth or social status. Patrick Rankeillor was not one of those parents.

'I'm sorry, Father,' she said awkwardly.

'Dinna be that. I have already discussed this with Jamie, and he agrees we must protect you and your interests. My concern is that whatever might befall me or him you shall be safe and sound. That if things dinna go the way we hope, and if there are reprisals afterwards – as there were back in '15 – then you will be protected. Say something, Kirsty.'

'I'm all right, Father. It's only that I do not think I ever fully realized – and it sounds so stupid to say so – I do not think I ever fully realized that … that blood might be spilt over this.'

The words were out now. She could not call them back. Typically, Patrick did not try to brush them aside. 'Blood might well be spilt over this. I shall tell you no lies on that score, Kirsty. Although maybe, just maybe, if we can get enough people on our side, if we can sway them to our way of thinking—'

'You really think that might be possible?' she asked eagerly.

'No blood was shed back in '88. That is one reason why the Whigs call it the Glorious Revolution, is it not?' He gave her a wry smile. 'What the French call a *coup d'état*. Ye ken the term?'

'Yes. Where power changes hands without any fighting, often by stealth. People wake up the next morning and find they have a new king. Who will remain on his throne if enough people want him to.'

'And if the initiators of the *coup d'état* move quickly to occupy and secure the positions of power and arrest those who occupy them.'

She looked at him. 'Arrest?'

'They might hope German Geordie and his family will do the decent thing and flee. Take himself and his family back to Hanover.'

'They will not risk that. Given what happened in reverse back in '88. They will have to kill him, will they not? His family too. So he will be fighting not only for his throne but for his life. As all those corrupt politicians and venal placemen who have profited from his reign will be fighting like wild dogs to hold on to what they have.'

'An astute analysis,' her father said. 'If not a very comfortable one.'

'London will be the target, then?' she asked after a moment.

'Aye. With we in Scotland poised to respond. If we can get the Highland chiefs to declare, and as many gentlemen of the Lowlands as possible, who knows what we might achieve without fighting and bloodshed? That is why it is so important that our visitor heads north as soon as possible. He is a persuasive man and he comes to us directly from Rome.'

'From the court-in-exile?' Her eyes widened. 'Our visitor is not...?' She stopped herself before she could say the words. *The Prince.* Even to refer to Charles Edward Stuart as such was an act of treason. So why had she openly owned his father James last night? Stupid, stupid, stupid. All she had done was hand Robert Catto more ammunition.

'Gin that had been the case, I think we might have had to tell you his name afore ye came face to face wi' him in the Infirmary. Wouldna want ye having a fit o' the vapours.' Patrick laughed, acknowledging that his daughter was not the type of young woman likely to succumb to such a ridiculous complaint.

'I'm not sure I would recognize him if I saw him,' she responded, thinking of Charlotte Liddell's terrible portrait.

'Few of us probably would. Especially if he were dressed in simple clothes, as he likely will be when he comes. Incognito, they cry it, after the Italian fashion.'

'When he comes,' Christian repeated. 'It's really going to happen, then?'

'It seems like it, lass. Excited?'

'Excited and scared all at the same time.'

'Aye. I ken whit ye mean. But no, our visitor is not the Young Gentleman himself but someone very close to him. Very close indeed.'

'He must be a Highlander,' she said shrewdly. 'I do not think the clan chiefs would listen to someone who is not.'

'Ye canna ken his name, Kirsty.'

'I do not ask for it.'

'But ye're curious, as well ye micht be. His real name is a dangerous one tae ken. A dangerous one tae bear, forbye. He already has a price on his head. If he is discovered, and you alang wi' him, ye must plead ignorance of who he is and what his business is here in Edinburgh. Hopefully such an eventuality will no' arise. If it does, ye'll tell yon Captain o' the Town Guard or anyone else wha asks that I commanded you to tend to the gentleman and ye didna dare disobey me.'

She jerked upright. 'I will do no such thing! That would be to betray *you*!'

'Christian,' Patrick said sternly. 'How often have I asked you to give me unquestioning obedience such as some fathers demand from their children? As, for example, in the matter we were discussing a few moments ago regarding Jamie and you? Christian?' he asked again when she hesitated.

'Never,' she allowed, knowing what was coming next. 'Hardly ever.'

'Only when?' prompted her father.

'Only when I was wee and did not know any better than to go too close to the fire or play too close to the top of the stairs. Only when it was to do with my own safety.'

'Exactly. Christian, I am already implicated. You would be telling any interrogator nothing they didna ken very well already.'

Once again she did not reply. Patrick fixed her with a stern look. 'You will do this, Christian. For me. I will have your promise on it.'

She looked at him. Then, crossing her fingers in the folds of her dressing gown so the lie wouldn't count: 'Very well, Father. You have my promise on it. If I am discovered and questioned I shall tell them you commanded me to do it. Now will you please finish your breakfast?'

She watched as he rose to his feet before sitting down again in the armchair opposite her and lifted his porridge. 'You are not going to Glasgow only to give your usual lectures and demonstrations, are you? You are going to talk to people to try to sway them to our way of thinking. That is why you are going now, later than you normally do. That is why you are missing the Daft Friday ball for the first time in years. You have been waiting for this messenger.'

He finished his porridge before he answered her, dispatching it in two generous spoonfuls. 'That and more, Kirsty. I am seeking also to secure pledges of money and goods from the manufactories in Glasgow.'

'Goods?'

'Shoes. An army might well march on its stomach but good stout shoes come in handy too. Bedding. Tents. The makings of field kitchens. Pots and pans and the dishes from which to eat the rations.'

'Weapons too? Pistols and muskets and swords?'

'An army canna march without those. Unfortunately. Even if it hopes never to have to use them.'

She drew in a breath. Armed rebellion. Whether those weapons were used or not, that was what they were talking about. Rising in armed rebellion. 'You will be careful who you speak to about all of this?'

'I shall be very careful. As you also must be. Betty alone can know about our visitor.'

'We could not hope to keep it from her. Not least because she always knows to the last ounce of cheese and the last bottle of ale what we have in the pantry and the cellar.'

'Aye,' her father said with a soft laugh. 'Although I have told her only that he is a friend in trouble. For her own safety she must know no more than that.'

She's not daft. She'll guess the rest. Probably already has. Her father knew that as well as she did.

'I wish to God we could keep this from her,' he said, his face troubled. 'They would not necessarily believe how little she knows, and they would be harder on her than on you, Kirsty. Much harder.'

'I know,' she said, thinking of the rough treatment meted out to Betty the night before. 'They would not go easy on you either, Father.'

'We'll cross that bridge when we come to it. If we come to it.'

'You'll be crossing a fair few bridges today. When you are riding to Glasgow rather than waiting for the mail coach tomorrow because you are testing yourself. To see whether you can still withstand the rigours of long rides.'

'Aye. Feart I might have grown soft wi' all this fancy living. Too well looked after by you and Betty and the lassies, that's my trouble.' He slapped his hands on his knees and inched forward in the chair, readying himself to stand up.

His daughter ignored both that and his further attempt to lighten the mood. 'So,' she said flatly, 'you are planning to go out on campaign. When the fighting starts. Please tell me you too do not intend to belt on a sword, Father. As Jamie says he must.'

'If I do it'll only be for the show o' the thing. I'd likely be mair o' a danger to myself than anybody else. The only blades I plan and hope not to wield in this endeavour are those of my surgical instruments. And mind that it's if the fighting starts, Kirsty.'

'There's a gey few *ifs* in all of this.'

'As in life,' Patrick replied, but once again his daughter was not to be side-tracked.

'You encouraged me to accept Charlotte Liddell's invitation last night because the Liddells are a powerful family and you think a time may be coming when I shall stand in need of their protection. Am I not right?'

'We must all keep our options open, Kirsty.'

'As the Liddells will do.'

'Oh, aye,' Patrick agreed. 'They will undoubtedly choose the winning side.' He arched a cynical eyebrow. 'Whichever that turns out to be.'

'You are not keeping your options open,' she observed. 'You are nailing your colours to the mast.'

He gave her an outrageous wink as he rose to his feet. 'Aye, but naebody's looking in that direction yet!'

'The Town Guard Captain is,' she said as she stood up with him.

'He knows nothing for sure.' Patrick walked over to the foot of the bed. Shrugging his shoulders out of his dressing gown, he laid it down and picked up his frock coat. 'We have to make sure he learns nothing more from us. While finding out as much as we can about him.'

Jamie had said the same thing last night. 'Twas fast becoming an article of faith. Christian thought of the penetrating gaze of Robert Catto's grey eyes and the sharp intelligence which clearly lay behind them and had to convert a shiver of fear into movement. Joining her father at the foot of the bed, she helped him into his coat, handed him his wig and let him place it on his head before she adjusted it. 'Cloak,' she said, and adjusted the flaps of the wig again once he had swung that about his shoulders.

'Will I do? Fit to be seen?'

'You'll do. You will put up at that inn at Kilsyth tonight, the one with the friendly landlord? You should have a clean shirt in here for tomorrow.' As she rummaged in his bag, her fingers found cold metal. 'Oh,' she said. 'You're taking your pistols.' Pushing the folds of his spare shirt aside, she looked down at the guns, a gift from a grateful patient.

They were not full-sized. They were still potentially lethal: whichever end of them you were on. Lifting her hands out of the bag, she turned and looked at Patrick.

'For protection only, Kirsty,' he said. 'For protection only. Come here, lass. Ye'll be fine while I'm away?' he asked as she stepped into his arms. 'Make sure you and Betty lock everything up tight as soon as it gets dark? Close and snib all the windows?'

She hoped he wasn't expecting an answer to that. Locked doors and windows wouldn't keep the Town Guard out. If they were refused entry they would simply break the door down or smash the windows in. Her stomach lurched. If they weren't too busy searching the Royal Infirmary. The Royal Infirmary where they were concealing a man with a price on his head. God Almighty. That had to be a hanging offence.

'Heaven knows,' Patrick murmured into her hair, 'I dinna want to go and leave the four o' you without a man in the hoose after what happened last night. But 'twould not do to have Jamie staying here overnight while I am away.'

No, that would not do at all. There was going to be enough gossip as it was. She had always known gossip could be malicious. Now she realized it could be dangerous too, drawing that attention they did not want to the Rankeillor household.

'I could wish Miss Meg and Miss Anna were staying here while they're in town for the ball.'

'Or maybe not,' Christian said wryly. 'Given what Meg's politics are. Wouldn't want her offering to come across to the Infirmary with me on the mornings she's in Edinburgh. Going to have to watch what I say to her, am I not?'

Patrick's voice was soft with understanding. 'And you lassies have aye told each other everything?'

She nodded against his chest, remembering. Whispered conversations and fits of the giggles at dead of night when all three of them had been girls sharing a bedchamber, their parents happily assuming them to be sound asleep. Light-hearted chats about fashion and young men as they had grown up. More serious talks about love, life, the world they lived in, and what the future might hold for each of them. Vows, whatever that might be, wherever life might take them, that they would stay friends forever. Forever and a day, as Anna Gordon always put it …

Oh, dear God. Were she and Anna now to regard Meg as the enemy? Never that, please God. How could the world have changed so much in one day?

Only yesterday she had been happily anticipating Meg and Anna's visit. They were staying in the Potterrow, at the town house of the Duffs, but the three girls were getting ready for the Daft Friday ball here. Her father and Betty had agreed they might open the bagnio, light the fires to heat the bath water, luxuriate in there before Betty, Mary and Tibby helped them dress in all their finery— Christian stiffened.

'What?' her father asked as she pulled out of his embrace.

'Am I to keep this from Anna too?'

'She may already know.'

'Her father is also a member of this Association, this Concert of Gentlemen? Is he one of those in the North with whom our visitor must speak?'

'Kirsty,' her father protested, 'I've already told you too much.'

Her question had not been an idle one. Other words trembled on her tongue. They were scaring her out of her wits but they had to be spoken. She had to put this to her father.

'Good God, lass,' he said with sudden passion, 'the last thing I want is for you to put yourself in danger! I could never forgive myself if anything were to happen to you or your friends—' He stopped himself, his breathing coming fast and shallow.

It was Christian who spoke first. 'I shall be very careful, Father. I give you my solemn promise on that. As I shall be very careful with Meg and Anna.' She lifted her chin. 'We must find a new path through all of this, must we not?'

'Aye,' Patrick agreed, calmer now. 'As we must find our courage. Because what we are doing is worth the candle.'

'Because when the King comes into his own again, Scotland will too. Our ancient kingdom will regain the independence our nobles and gentry so shamefully surrendered and once more take her rightful place among the nations of Europe.' Her voice shook with emotion. 'We shall no longer be this pathetic apology for a country, this mere North Britain.' Now there was contempt in her voice. 'As though we are unruly children who must not only be harshly governed but continually put in our place and reminded daily how insignificant we are to those who now govern us. They have stolen even our name from us.'

From her childhood they had discussed this, on summer days on plant-collecting forays in the fresh air and hills outside the city far from listening ears, by the fire on winter nights, speaking in low voices. Her father had shown and taught her so much, about the healing properties of plants, about nature and human nature, about the beauty of the world. He had taught her about Scotland too, inspired her with tales of its heroes and heroines. Betty too had played her part, singing her the old songs and ballads of love and war, dreaming poets and tragic queens, fairy folk and seal-people.

'What are you thinking?'

'I should not hold you back any longer.'

'A few moments will make no difference.'

'I am remembering what William Wallace's uncle said to him, what Wallace is said to have repeated to his men before the Battle of Falkirk.' She quoted softly. '*I have brought you to the ring. Dance according to your skill.* We have been brought to the ring, have we not? Where we must rise to meet the moment. Now you really must go, Father. The sooner you leave, the sooner we'll have you back.'

'You told me earlier you were very lucky to have a father like me. I think I am a very lucky man to have a daughter like you.' His eyes full of love, Patrick dropped a kiss on her forehead. 'Dinna come downstairs wi' me, lass. It's ower cold there yet.'

She stood for a few moments by her bedroom door, listening to his footsteps going down the stairs, the low murmur of voices floating up from the lobby as he took his farewell of Betty, the door closing behind him. That was it, then. He was gone. She was on her own.

No. She had Betty at home and Jamie within reach, Jamie to whom she would take the idea which had leapt into her mind moments before as to how they might get their visitor out of Edinburgh. Her father did not need to know anything until it was all over. He had enough to deal with during his visit to Glasgow without having to worry any more about her, or her friends.

There was a miaow from behind her. Lucy had returned from the kitchen. Christian stooped and picked her up, wrapping her arms about the cat to hold her close. 'The world has changed, baudrons,' she murmured. 'The world has changed.'

She looked up. Betty was standing in the doorway of her bedroom, Betty who had left Mary and Tibby to sleep late after their ordeal last night but risen early herself to cook porridge for Christian and her father. *It would tak mair than callants like yon tae frichten me!* As she stood looking at Christian, the housekeeper's face was filled with a mixture of emotions. Love. Tenderness. Fear. Yet she spoke calmly as she came into the room.

'Time ye were getting dressed, lass. I've prepared your basket. There's a cloth over whit's in the bottom o' it and then the first layer o' physic. Ye'll ken better than me whit comes after the usual preparations. That's how we'll do it for the next few days.'

Christian nodded, set Lucy down on the bed, stepped forward and put her arms around the older woman. 'Whatever would we do without you, Betty?'

'I canna imagine. It's a question I often ask masel.' Betty spoke briskly but stood for a moment before patting her young mistress on the back and disengaging herself. 'Come on now, lass. The sooner ye get across tae the Infirmary, the sooner we'll have ye safely hame.' Christian felt a lump come to her throat. That was what she had just said to her father.

'Why,' demanded Betty, 'have ye no' put your shift and your petticoats out here to get a wee warm by the fire afore ye put them on?'

Their eyes met in silent agreement, the message exchanged nothing to do with the customary affectionate scolding.

Be careful. Be very careful.

I will. I promise.

Betty turned, heading for the closet to fetch Christian's clothes. She made another silent promise to that bustling back. *I'll be careful, and I'll do whatever I have to do to protect my own.*

They were all scared. The thing to do now was not to give in to the fear. That was the only way they were going to be able to achieve what had been dreamt of for so long. Freedom. The first step in achieving that was to send their visitor on his way north. As that was the only way to keep her father and Jamie safe. If only for a while.

Christian straightened up and drew in a deep breath. She too would not cross her bridges until she came to them. What she needed was strength and courage for today, for the next hour of it. She could be brave for an hour.

I have brought you to the ring. Dance according to your skill.

She would do her utmost.

14

The wee man with the big hammer was hard at work. He was doing his level best to demolish Robert Catto's skull. Shard by splintered shard. Blow by pounding blow. His victim groaned, and cautiously opened his eyes. The room was dark, although a few streaks of grey were beginning to show through the ill-fitting shutters. Yawning hugely, Catto registered that his mouth was as dry as one of the famed deserts of Araby. He needed a gallon or two of water down his gullet—

Like a river bursting its banks, the memory of the night before came rushing in. He was back in Surgeons' Hall, staring down at the map. He was back in Patrick Rankeillor's library, sensing the excitement the surgeon-apothecary and Jamie Buchan of Balnamoon had been unable to suppress. He was putting two and two together and trying to deny that they made four. Knowing that they did. He hadn't been having a nightmare, then. This was real.

His headache spiked, propelling him upright to swing his legs over the side of the bed, one hand coming up to dash away tears of pain. 'Bloody hell,' he muttered. '*Bloody* hell …' Kicking him while he was down, the private playhouse within his brain moved in for the kill, presenting him with a vivid recreation of the other events of the previous night.

What in God's name had possessed him, coupling in the street like a drunken trooper? With an unknown and barefoot lass at that, in the midst of a nastiness of filth and muck? He thought about the rat nibbling on the cabbage leaf. He thought about how he had taken the girl standing, pushing her bony little body hard against the stone of the doorway. There had been nastiness in more ways than one last night. He could add the clout he had so very nearly given Geordie to the tally.

Your mother must be so proud of you. He didn't need that voice in his head to be able to admit he had used the girl pretty hard and this morning he was sorry for it. Maybe he would try to find her again, give her another few shillings in compensation. 'Twould serve him right if he had earned himself a pair of Canongate breeks. That was what they called the most hideous of ailments in these parts. He'd be lucky if it hadn't already invaded his parts.

Between his legs, his cock was half standing up to greet him in its usual good morning fashion. He addressed a muttered question to it through the gloom of his bedchamber. 'Have you no shame?'

A standing prick has no conscience. That was the old saying. The girl had stepped into his path last night and he had taken what she was offering. She had been nothing more than an empty vessel into which he could pour his anger and frustration. Disgusted with himself, he fell back against his pillows. Sometimes he despised the whole of his sex.

How we all use women. How we all use our strength to bully and dominate.

Your mother must be so proud of you.

'Bugger off,' he muttered. 'You deserved everything you got last night. Which was as nothing compared to what some of your sex suffer.'

Those thoughts took him whirling back to the farmhouse in Saxony, to the murdered and violated mother and daughters, to the boy and grandfather who had been unable to protect their womenfolk. He didn't want to go there again, didn't want to start imagining that what had happened in Saxony might happen in Scotland, didn't want to think about evil genies emerging from broken bottles. Oh, dear God, no, he certainly didn't want to think about broken bottles ...

He didn't want to think that he cared, either. Only he knew he did.

Daft Friday: when the world went mad. Boys put on their sister's dresses, girls pulled on their brothers' breeches. Drunken revellers danced through the graveyard, cocking a snook at death itself. Ne'er-do-wells and the lowest of people spoke back to their betters and, on this one day and night of the year, expected to get away with it. On Daft Friday everything turned tapsil-teery. The normal conventions did not apply.

Edinburgh taverns and closes would be full of drinking, sweating, shouting humanity. Stumbling out of one howff heading for another, laughing crowds would be singing, joking and intent on mischief. Up at the Assembly Rooms at the top of the West Bow, some of those merry folk would gather as they always did to gawp at the guests arriving for the Daft Friday ball, held every year to raise funds for the Royal Infirmary. Raucous commentaries on the looks and finery worn by those guests would be tossed backwards and forward. Sedan chairs would be everywhere, struggling to navigate their way through the crowds.

As the evening wore on, drink-fuelled mischief could turn ugly. Some bright spark might pick up a stone and hurl it at a window, laughing crazily as the glass shattered. Someone else would deem it rare fun to set something alight, a cart maybe, or a bale of hay. One reveller might look the wrong way at another and, before you knew what was happening, a circle would form, egging on the two men now throwing vicious punches at each other. More sober heads would be taking advantage of the chaos. There were always robberies on Daft Friday.

And who would be dealing with all of this? The Town Guard. Their Captain was going to need every man at his disposal to do so, including those who were watching the Royal Infirmary, especially if trouble erupted close to the hospital. So they were going to have to make sure it did. Jamie had probably already thought of that.

While that engineered disturbance was being dealt with, she would escort their visitor from the Infirmary to Surgeons' Hall. Once he was safely in the bagnio, they could disguise him in women's clothes and Anna Gordon could escort him to the nearby Cowgate Port, with a pass to leave Edinburgh signed by someone much more powerful than the Captain of the Town Guard.

As a member of the mighty Duff family, Anna had more than enough influence to be able to secure such a pass. She could ask Provost Coutts to write and sign one for herself and one other. No individual guard or official was going to question that, nor have much interest in a young woman and her maidservant, especially if they dressed the latter to look like an older woman, a faithful family retainer. Anna could then slip back into the city at the Netherbow Port and return to the bagnio.

Jamie would know how to get their fugitive down to Leith, as he would know who might hide him there. The name of one redoubtable old Jacobite lady sprang immediately to mind. From there he could sail north with Anna when she embarked for Banff on the Monday following the Daft Friday ball, again posing as her maidservant.

There were a few wee flaws in the plan. Christian could see them all too clearly. Provost Coutts was away this week, not due to return to Edinburgh until Friday, in time for the ball. Robert Catto might have organized extra guards down at Leith. What if a gust of wind blew back the frills of an old-fashioned mutch to reveal a male rather than a female face? A pass signed by the Lord Provost would be no help then.

There would be problems before they left the bagnio. Betty and the girls would want to wave them off, and what were they to do about Meg? They couldn't expect her to come in on the plan. Then there was Anna herself. Christian didn't doubt for one second that she would help, which meant the biggest problem with her plan was that it would put Anna in danger. This must be how her father felt about what she was doing right now.

A woman is much less noticed than a man as she goes about her daily business. As she approached the main door of the Royal Infirmary, Christian could only hope that was true. There were two guards standing there. Her mouth went dry, and she had the oddest fancy her basket had magically transformed from wicker to glass, displaying its betraying contents for all the world to see. She had to stop herself from shifting her plaid to conceal it.

'Your business in the hospital this morning, Miss? Why, it's Miss Rankeillor, isn't it? It'll be your faither's turn to supply physic tae the Infirmary?'

'Aye,' she agreed, relieved beyond measure to see a friendly face. She had successfully treated this man's young grandson and granddaughter for croup last winter.

'Away you go in then, lass,' he said, and held one of the big doors open for her. 'Still gey cold, eh? Although they say it's tae be a fine day once the sun comes up.'

Heeding the advice Jamie had given her last night to look confident, she forced herself to set out boldly. The guards on the door weren't to know she would normally go through the entrance lobby and straightaway turn left for the dispensary. Besides which, although she was indeed bringing in physic this morning, and thank God for the timing of that, she was often in the hospital on other errands. She might legitimately be going somewhere else inside the building.

The deserted corridor at the back of the building was not quite so deserted now, although it felt eerily still as she walked through into it. The door which separated it from the rest of the hospital swung shut behind her with nothing more than an unnerving whisper of wood upon stone. Darkness enveloped her.

She set her basket on the floor and felt within it for the small lantern she had put there. Her fingers were trembling, fumbling with the brass and glass, fumbling again as she sought the tinder box she had also brought with her. She opened it, found its components with her fingers and struck flint against metal. It took her three attempts to catch the spark and put it to the wick of the candle stub. A small flame blossomed and she closed the lantern and let out a relieved breath.

The lantern remained a very little light in the darkness pressing in around her, the deep shadows it cast almost as unnerving as the previous total blackness. No matter. A very little light was all she could have. She dug for a second time into her basket and came up with the ring of keys Jamie had given her last night, those which secured the many doors in this corridor and which normally hung behind the main door through which she'd just come. They jangled as she brought them out, the noise horribly loud. Ruing her lack of foresight, she squeezed her fingers around the keys to silence them.

Straightening up on unsteady legs, she took her basket in one hand and the lantern in the other. She had gone only a few cautious steps along the corridor before she let out a shriek. Something was scuttling along beside her, hidden in the shadows. She stood for a moment, heart pounding. All was silent. She wondered if the creature was sitting in the impenetrable shadows, watching her. With the lantern allowing her to see only a few feet in front of herself, anyone or anything could be hiding there.

Including a troubled spirit?

Fear washed through her. Blood pounded in her ears – until she reminded herself that she was an intelligent woman, a rational human being and a daughter of the Age of Reason. She did not believe in ghosts. She said those words out loud.

'I do not believe in ghosts.' The shadows around her did not grow any less opaque, but she put one foot in front of the other and walked on.

The fifth cell on the right. That was where she was headed. She counted the doors as she passed them in the gloom. They would all be locked. Jamie had told her how he'd blindly grabbed the keys from their hook when he and her father had hustled their visitor in here. Those keys had to go back now. 'Twas unlikely, but they could not risk someone taking it into their heads to make an inspection of this corridor.

The door to the fifth cell on the right lay ajar. Should she knock? No. That was another noise someone inside or outside the building might be able to hear. She placed her hand against the solid wood and gave it a push. Before she could announce herself, a voice spoke from the shadows.

'Who goes there? Speak, before I shoot you where you stand.'

The soft-voiced threat froze her to the spot, her eyes seeing nothing but the dull gleam of the pistol barrel aimed straight at her heart.

15

'I thank you, lass,' said the man whose face remained in shadow. He had lowered the pistol the instant he had seen her, apologized profusely – 'a man in my position cannot be too careful' – and laid the weapon on the bed, next to its mate. Pistols always came as a brace. Miss the first time and you had a second shot in reserve. Or so she had been told.

These pistols were much larger than the pair her father had taken to Glasgow with him. While both were made entirely of steel, lock, stock and barrel, Mr Fox's were also elaborately decorated. It had always seemed strange to her that people embellished weapons: especially with the carved hearts she could make out as her eyes adjusted to the gloom.

'I am indeed most grateful to you for your skilled and gentle hands and this kind medical attention. Not to mention these victuals,' he added, a smile entering his voice. His accent mixed a Highland lilt with the hint of a long residence in France.

'You passed a hungry night, sir?' Christian's heart was still beating too fast but carrying out familiar tasks was calming her down. After she had dressed the stranger's ankle, she had found pillows and blankets in the press in the corridor and a chamber pot in the necessary house at the other end of it. This she now deposited wordlessly close to the bunk on which her new patient lay.

She was her father's daughter, brought up to be matter-of-fact about the body's functions. Betty loved to tell the story of how she had once found the five-year-old Christian peering into her own chamber pot to see if she could diagnose why she wasn't feeling too well. The adult Christian was glad all the same of the dim light on this occasion.

That it would have to be her who emptied the chamber pot was a bridge she would cross when she came to it. She'd done it often enough for female patients and children but never for a grown man. What her new male patient had done last night was a thought best left alone, especially when she doubted he could walk very far. 'Twas as well that this cell was an airy one.

'I passed a safe one,' he said graciously. 'I am indeed most grateful also to Professor–' He broke off. 'Now then, 'twould be as well for no names to be used between us, am I not right?'

Christian finished laying out the loaf, piece of cold boiled beef, slab of cheese and small pottery flask of ale Betty had placed in the bottom of her basket onto the rough-hewn small table fastened by a fetter and chain to the wall next to the head of the bed. 'I have been told to call you Mr Fox, sir.' That had been Jamie's suggestion when Christian had said she had to call him something. She dug once more into her basket and brought out a handful of candle ends and the tinder box, before glancing at the pistols on the bed. 'Shall I put those on the table too?'

Her patient's hand went possessively to his decorated weapons. 'Prefer to keep these close. They've helped me out of a few tight corners. Mr Fox?' Another smile flashed in the gloom, followed by an easy laugh. 'Ah. I think I can see where my new *nom de guerre* might have come from.'

Christian thought she might too, having caught, as he occasionally made a cautious shift of position, the gleam of red hair. 'Please do not let me stop you from eating your breakfast, sir,' she said as she cleared away the paraphernalia attendant on cleaning and redressing her patient's swollen ankle.

Privately alarmed by how puffy it was, she'd said nothing to him, only exchanged the soft and rather battered leather portmanteau on which his foot rested for two of the pillows she'd found in the wall press. Whether he would be fit to leave this hiding place by Friday was debatable. He certainly wouldn't be leaving disguised as a woman. Even sitting down as he was, she could see he was far too tall. A fairly major blow to her plan. She gestured towards the food.

'Please eat, sir,' she said again. 'There is no need to wait for me to go. Although I fear this must also serve as your meridian and your supper so you would be best to split it into thirds. I am sorry I cannot return later in the day. It is unusual for me to be in the hospital in the evening.'

'So we cannot have you suddenly changing that pattern.'

'Or drawing attention to this corridor. When I have no legitimate reason to be here. Sir?' she added, for although he had said nothing, she sensed that he wanted to.

'Despite what you have said, I am wondering if I might persuade you to stay a little longer. A few moments? Perhaps you could quickly tell me what happened after I was bundled in here.'

She hesitated. There had been a pleading note in his voice, although there was a powerful and attractive charm here too. She was a wee touch wary of it. Yet she knew he must have passed an anxious night and was now facing another lonely day and night. 'What would you like to know?'

'There was a raid? On Surgeons' Hall?'

'Yes. Mounted by the Town Guard. Ostensibly they were in pursuit of an illegal dissection but that was only an excuse.'

'You know that for certain?'

'The Captain of the Town Guard made that very plain. Eventually.'

'Kept his cards close to his chest to begin with?'

'Aye. Made me feel a bit of a fool,' she confessed, and wondered why she had confided that to a complete stranger.

'Older and wilier than you, I expect.'

'Not much older than me.' Her basket repacked, the ring of keys lying on top of it, she stood holding it in her two hands. 'A year or two perhaps.'

'Someone you know?'

'Someone I met for the first time last night.' Her mouth tightened. 'And if I never see Captain Robert Catto again, it'll be too soon. Now I really must go, sir.' She transferred her basket to her right hand. 'I shall endeavour to bring you some newssheets and reading material when I return tomorrow morning. If you keep the lantern I brought you in the little niche where I have placed it I think you may safely read without fear of being discovered.' Which meant she was going to have to negotiate the corridor without a light. Although it was growing brighter now as the late winter dawn began to break.

'Sir?' He was staring at her, albeit in a way that made her think his thoughts were elsewhere. Miles away.

'Sir?' she queried again.

He blinked, and smiled at her. 'Some newssheets and reading material would be most acceptable, lass. I thank you very kindly in advance.'

'Is there aught else I can bring you, sir?'

'Paper and pen, a few sheets of the former? If that is not too difficult?'

'Not too difficult at all. Only …'

'Only what?' he queried.

'I am thinking it might be a wee bit risky for Ja—' Like Mr Fox, she caught herself on before she could say the name. 'For the person who most likely would be the one to deliver your correspondence. I fear he is being closely watched.'

A look of regret crossed Mr Fox's face. 'I am bringing you all a wheen of trouble, am I not, lass?'

'You must not think that, sir. Indeed, we are all more than glad to help you on your way. Och, but I did not mean that the way it sounded!'

'I should not blame you if you did, lass. I have become very used over my life to being regarded as something of a poisoned chalice. Which has always been a source of great regret to me.'

'I'm sorry, sir.'

'Don't be,' he said immediately. 'I would not have such a brave and bonnie lass as yourself cast down on my account. Now go, and try to forget for a few hours about your troublesome visitor.' His eyes dropped to her basket. 'Will you leave those keys with me?'

'They should be where they normally are kept,' she explained. 'At the end of the corridor. Where I do not think you should go. You must put as little weight as possible on your injured ankle. Rest and elevation is what it needs, sir.'

His eyes rose once again to her face. 'I do not want to find myself being elevated in a more permanent fashion, lass. My mission is too important to fail on the simple matter of an unlocked door. When you return tomorrow please knock or call softly so I know who is waiting outside the door.' His smile was wry. 'I would not have you once again at the point of a pistol.'

The action Catto now had to take contradicted everything he understood the word to mean, went against every one of his soldier's instincts, carried a huge personal risk too. An observer unaware of the tightrope last night's discoveries obliged him to walk might well see what he was going to do today as a dereliction of duty. A hostile observer could make a meal of it, call his loyalty into question. Good bloody job Fred Scott wasn't in Edinburgh.

He stood up and walked across to the armoire where he kept his clothes and yanked the door open. His eyes lit on the dressing gown he'd had made by a seamstress in Antwerp two years before but which had always seemed too good to wear. Fashioned out of Chinese silk, the pattern was of red and turquoise dragons rising up out of a yellow background. He pulled it from the shelf, shook out the heavy folds and swung the dragons on over his nightshirt. Geordie first. Here at least was something he could fix with a few well-chosen words. If he was lucky.

Presiding over his pots and pans, Geordie's eyes ran up and down the dressing-gown. He'd been very taken with the robe when he had helped Catto unpack his things on his arrival at the guard-house back at the beginning of November. This morning the boy made no comment on it, only brought a pewter jug and tankard to the table. Catto was careful to use the latter before he drank, although it did not take him long to empty it.

'More?' The boy's voice was dull. 'Or will ye wash now?'

'In a minute. I've something to say to you first. Would you look at me, Geordie?'

He did not like what he saw when that question was silently answered. The blue eyes were full of something worse even than fear. Resignation. Young though he was, had the lad already learned it was foolish to hope for anything other than harsh words and rough treatment from his elders?

'A promise. I won't beat you and I won't hit you.' Catto tried a smile. 'All right? I was in a foul temper last night but I shouldn't have taken it out on you. Things didn't exactly go as planned.' He raised his eyebrows, hoping for a reaction. 'Given my luck, 'tis entirely possible such a situation may arise again. So I can't guarantee I won't ever be in a foul temper again. Can't guarantee I won't shout or swear at you sometimes but the promise holds.'

The boy said nothing, only kept looking up at him out of those clear eyes. Catto found himself wondering what they might have seen. He had a shrewd suspicion Geordie was a runaway of some sort. Up until last night at least, the boy had come to relax in Catto's company, although there remained always a watchfulness, more than a hint of wariness.

His and Geordie's paths were probably destined to cross only briefly. Yet it came to him that he could make a difference to this child's life, if only by treating him with some respect and consideration during the time they would spend together, kindness too. 'Twas a much underrated virtue.

'All right?' he said again. 'Shall we shake on it?'

Geordie looked at Catto's outstretched hand, then looked up at him. Catto realized that he was holding his breath. This mattered. Forgiveness from this boy mattered.

Geordie gave it, smiling shyly and extending his own hand. Catto smiled back as he gripped the small fingers, gave them a firm squeeze and released them. He didn't deserve it, but the day had started with a gift. Despite everything, he felt his spirits lift in response.

'I'll wash now,' he said, leading the way out into the chilly courtyard. Although it caught the sun in the afternoon, at this time on a winter's morning it was as cold as the grave. Dark and shadowy too, though with enough yellow light spilling through the kitchen window to see by.

Used now to his routine, Geordie was there as soon as he emerged from the privy. The boy had a folded towel over one shoulder and was struggling with a large pitcher full of water which he placed halfway up a flight of stone steps. They had given access to an ancient part of the guard-house which had collapsed fifty years previously, killing one man who'd been inside it at the time. As Geordie had told Catto, clearly relishing the telling of the tale, the body had never been recovered from the debris.

Whether that was true or not was anybody's guess. Edinburgh did like its tall tales and gruesome stories. A vigorous holly bush crowned the crumbling steps now, clinging onto a patch of scrubby earth at their top and tumbling over the side. It was the only thing that grew out here.

'I've some hot water by the fire. Shall I bring it out and warm up what's in the basin?'

Catto shook his still unkempt head. He needed the shock of the cold water this morning. Deserved it too, after what he had done on his way back to the guard-house last night.

'Shall I take the dressing gown back inside, Captain?'

'Aye, Geordie.' His back to the boy, he allowed him to remove the silk robe and heard him run inside with it. With a muttered, 'One, two, three,' Catto stripped off his nightshirt, rolled it up into a ball and threw it to one side. Plunging his face into the basin, he came up gasping, dunked the soap in the water and began to lather himself all over.

'Now, sir?' asked the boy, returned to the courtyard.

'The sooner the better, Geordie.' Catto's teeth were chattering and his wayward member had been put firmly in its place. He didn't want it to turn blue and fall off. He needed it for an appointment he had on Tuesday night with one Miss Lizzie Gibson. She was an energetic girl. The world might be falling to pieces around him but the pleasures of the flesh remained. Thank God for a warm and willing woman.

Geordie took the basin and clambered to the top of the steps. Catto moved to stand below him, avoiding the prickly green and yellow leaves of the holly bush, and the lad tipped the water over his head. His master yelped but stood his ground until the deluge was spent, using his hands to speed the rinsing process and thinking longingly how nice it would be to have a good long soak in a hot bath. Pity the bagnio at Surgeons' Hall was all locked up. Wrapping himself in the towel, he ran for the kitchen.

His clean linen was warming on a chair close to the fire, his brown breeches and waistcoat laid over another one. A bowl of hot water and his shaving kit stood on the big dresser, a small mirror propped up behind them. Geordie looked after him well. He reached out a hand to ruffle the boy's gleaming blond waves, pleased when the lad did not flinch away. Catto too had been a boy in a man's world and he knew it could be a lonely place to be.

'What are you cooking for our supper tonight?' he asked as he dried himself and stepped into his clean linen.

'Beef and pancakes. If that's a' right wi' you, Captain. These top clothes fine for today, sir?'

'Grand,' Catto said. 'Beef and pancakes it is.' He soaped his chin and lifted his razor. 'Will you be needing more money for supplies tomorrow?'

The boy shook his head. 'I've plenty o' siller left over from what you gave me last week.' That was another thing. Despite the temptations to which he was exposed, Geordie Maxwell was as honest as the day was long. Each week he insisted on giving Catto a detailed account of his expenditure. Priding himself on the bargains he struck at the markets, any money he saved went back into the housekeeping.

'Are you off to the kirk now?' Catto seldom set foot inside a church himself but he never mocked anyone who did.

'Once you're ready, Captain.'

Finishing his toilette, Catto rinsed his shaving brush and razor and dried the blade before shrugging into a clean shirt. He tied his cravat loosely about his neck and drew a comb through his damp hair, gathering the exuberant nut-brown waves back with a simple black satin ribbon. When he had finished dressing he wolfed down a bowl of porridge, remaining standing while he ate it. His grandfather had always done that, his mother had brought him up to do the same and since he'd been back in Scotland he'd found it impossible not to revert to the old custom.

As his mother had told it, it was the warlike Border Reivers who had started it. Even first thing in the morning you had to be ready to meet the enemy, who were quite likely also to be your neighbours from over the next hill. Too close for comfort. You never knew when they might turn up.

He didn't know when his enemies were going to turn up either. Or from which direction they might come. What he did know was that they wouldn't announce their approach with the blood-curdling shouts, mad pounding of hooves or clash of swords like the old feuding Borderers. His enemies were going to be doing their damnedest to remain in the shadows. If only he could leave them there. No longer an option.

'Apples, Captain,' Geordie said, emerging from the pantry in the corner.

'Apples?'

'Ye aye take apples on a Sunday. For the cuddy. Tam is it, that they cry him?'

'Aye. I'll need to take you down to see him and the other horses sometime. Would you like that?'

'I'd like that fine, sir. Stables are right cosy places.'

Catto lifted his tan leather horseman's coat from its peg beside the front door, ready to set off for Donnie Livingstone's livery stable. Livingstone kept the Sabbath, but, albeit with the air of bestowing a huge favour, had agreed to stretch a point for the sake of his Captain. With a murmur of thanks, Catto took the apples from Geordie and slid them into the pockets of his coat.

After his master had left, Geordie cleared away the wooden bowl and the horn spoon he had used, rinsed them out and left them to dry and air beside his own. Then he pulled on a bonnet and muffler and set out for St Giles. He'd be late if he didn't hurry. He got no more than the second close down the High Street from the guard-house before he heard his name being called.

It rooted him to the spot. For so many long months he hadn't heard that well-loved voice. He wasn't sure he was really hearing it now. Maybe he was dreaming, the pain of separation and longing for what had been lost strong enough to stoke the fires of his imagination. Turning, he peered into the dimness of the close. When he saw who was standing there, his sharp-featured little face lit up with joy.

16

Halfway to Duddingston and Catto was beginning to think he might just live. A brisk walk round Edinburgh's gates had helped. The wee man with the big hammer was administering only the very occasional blow.

On his tour of the gates he had reinforced his restrictions on the Rankeillor household and his further orders for the day. Any unknown travellers who sought to leave or enter the city were to be closely questioned. If they could not give their place of abode, who they had been or were intending to visit in Edinburgh, a good reason for being out and about on the Sabbath or simply seemed in the least wise suspicious, they were to be detained until he returned. No exceptions.

How long he was going to get away with that was debatable. He'd have to hope at least until Friday, when Provost Coutts returned to town. He'd called at former Provost Drummond's house this morning, only to learn that he too had been unexpectedly called away. His servants were not sure if he was going to be back in time for the Daft Friday ball.

'Up here, Tam,' he told his mount, geeing the horse up a grassy slope, thawing out to a rich green under the bright winter sun. 'Let's give ourselves a little perspective. And,' he added in a soft murmur, 'also allow whoever is watching us this morning to get as good a view as possible. We'll have to hope to God they were in too great a state of confusion to be watching me on my way back to the guard-house last night, eh?'

Harder to follow a man out here in the open, of course, somewhat inept to use a spy-glass on a day as sunny as this one. Catto caught the winking flash of brightness for the fourth time out of the corner of his eye, way over to the left. 'Not very smart, Tam. Although it suits our book today.'

Catto's brother officers in Guise's would have hooted with derision to see him on the back of this sturdy garron rather than a sleek and powerful cavalry horse. Especially one of those brother officers. Catto's mouth tightened. If it hadn't been for Fred Scott, he might not have been sitting here looking over Edinburgh. Although he supposed Duncan Forbes had to shoulder the lion's share of the blame.

Did a young man obliged by fate to make his own way in the world turn down a direct appeal from the Lord President of the Court of Session of Scotland? No, of course he didn't. Oh, the letter to Catto's commanding officer had been couched as a request, full of flowery phrases.

I wonder if I might prevail upon your kindness. May I beg you most humbly to make me a loan, as it were, of Lieutenant Catto? I stand in urgent need of a soldier, engineer and military officer of high intelligence and high calibre, so he more than fits the bill. I should be prodigious grateful if you might help me persuade him to undertake this commission.

All finished off with the usual extravagant courtesies: *I beg to remain, sir, your most humble and obedient servant,* and the rest. Funny how the grandest of people went in for all that supposed humility.

The personal letter to him had been a lot less formal. *My very dear Bob, I hope you are recovering from the wound I was so distressed to hear you had sustained on the field at Dettingen. I understand you acquitted yourself with admirable courage before and after that lamentable event – I refer to your injury rather than our glorious victory! – not to mention 0exhibiting exemplary coolness under fire. Mentioned in dispatches, I hear. Your mother would have been proud of you.*

Somehow Catto doubted that. His grandfather, maybe. Or, considering on which side his grandson fought, maybe not.

Your mother would have been proud of you. Those words had acquired an uncomfortable resonance, but he would not allow them to lead him back to Christian Rankeillor. He had more to worry about today than her.

Culloden was a clever man, and a canny one. He had sweetened the pill. Whilst seconded to Edinburgh's Town Guard, Lieutenant Robert Catto would have the status of Captain. When he returned to the regular army he would do so with a real Captain's commission in his pocket.

Yet even the promise of that longed-for promotion – by God, had he not earned it a hundred times over? – had not persuaded Catto, his reluctance to return to Scotland so strong. God Almighty, he had vowed never to return. He'd been on the point of trying to convince his colonel that Guise's needed him a lot more than Edinburgh's Town Guard and apparently crumbling city walls when Fred Scott had stuck his oar in.

Standing behind their commander as he sat at the map table in his campaign tent, Fred Scott had looked over that gentleman's head at Catto. Such a sly look it had been, too. Sleekit. That was the Scottish word. It seemed appropriate. The message had been only too clear. *Want me to tell him what you told me that drunken night? That'll ruin your military career at a stroke, Catto. They'll never trust you again.*

So he'd had no choice but to come to Scotland, where he so viscerally, desperately, passionately did not want to be. There were too many memories here. Painful reminders of all he had lost. He had felt that acutely in Rankeillor's house last night, aware even as he was doing his damnedest to set it by the ears of its comfort and warmth. The mutual concern had been tangible, a circle of care and affection binding everyone together, from the little maidservants to the mistress of the house – but he was refusing to think about her today, was he not? As he was refusing to raise his eyes towards the north, to all that lay beyond the Forth. That at least he could spare himself.

Leaning forward, he slid one hand under the rough hair of the horse's mane, clapped the beast's warm neck and murmured some soothing words. Tam twitched his ears and tossed his head in response, setting his bridle and reins ringing like fairy bells.

'All right,' Catto said. 'I know what you want.' Digging into the deep pocket of his riding coat, he came up first with his pen-knife and then an apple, leaning down one side of the pony's neck to offer the beast each sliced piece in turn from the flat of his hand. The soft mouth was warm on his palm, a contrast to the crisp air surrounding man and horse.

He straightened up again. Edinburgh lay beneath him like one of those maps which offered you a bird's eye view, much like the one pinned to the wall above his desk. He had an excellent map of Scotland to pin up next to it now. Or perhaps he too should preserve it in pristine condition. In case his own side might need working copies.

Unease tugged at him. Scotland alone, with only the very north of England sketched in. Whether as a response to what might be going to happen in London or not, whatever was being planned here was being planned to happen here. Yet the map itself was not enough proof of that and 'twas proof the Lord President needed.

Catto's eyes followed the line of the High Street. Heart and spine of the city, that straggled down the long tail of the crag whose summit was crowned by Edinburgh Castle. The great fortress had stood sentinel on its rugged rock for centuries, offering fierce and proud resistance to the Auld Enemy. Those days were over. Nowadays the castle was home to a company of redcoats.

He'd been going through the motions when he'd attempted to have a discussion with the commander as to the state of the defences up there, not too worried when he didn't get very far. General Guest was as old as Methuselah and away with the fairies into the bargain.

Catto had a different view on the importance of Edinburgh Castle now. Given sufficient supplies, the garrison could probably close the gates and hold out for several weeks or even months. Understrength and mainly composed of veterans and invalids, it had no hope of preventing a Jacobite army from occupying Edinburgh. If the veterans fired off their cannons the balls would hit as many citizens as they would Jacobites. That was assuming any of the old crocks had a steady enough hand to be able to light the fuses. Or that Methuselah wasn't too gaga to issue the relevant orders.

No, Edinburgh's best physical defence was its city walls. Hah! In which case all was already lost. Especially if that section near Rankeillor's house was allowed to further deteriorate or actively weakened by some brute force and a heavy hammer or two.

His eyes dropped from the castle to the wall, following it round. When he came to the Royal Infirmary he blew out a breath, a ribbon of smoke in the cold air. He had left orders that the guard on the hospital was to be stood down at one o'clock. Too late now to wonder if he had done the right thing.

He was already having the building and the Rankeillor house covertly watched by William Angus Stewart and two more of the Lord President's agents. They all lived in tenements around the hospital. Stewart had a wife and mother who took a keen interest in what their neighbours were up to and a battalion of young children, all of whom acted as his eyes and ears.

There was of course the small matter of whether Catto could trust Stewart and his comrades to report what they did see, not tell anyone else what they were up to either. He'd have to hope to hell that he could. As he would have to hope he had tightened security enough on the gates so anyone now in Edinburgh was going to find it bloody difficult to get out of the place. If the man he sought hadn't already left.

Livingstone was right. You'd have to be pretty damn fit to contemplate a departure via the walls. In most places the height you'd have to drop was considerable, dangerous in itself and with a high chance of being seen or heard while you were attempting it. It wasn't impossible, though. Catto could not know for sure that the Jacobite messenger was still here. Frustrating.

His eyes continued to roam over Edinburgh. For centuries fear of invasion by an English army had made her citizens huddle inside the city wall for protection, building upwards rather than outwards. There was a tenement in Old Parliament Close which stood a remarkable fourteen storeys tall, many others dotted throughout the town which stretched to six, eight or ten floors. Nowhere in the world, an English visitor had once observed, did so many people live in such little space as in Edinburgh.

A town which needed to sprawl had been forced to squeeze itself ever more tightly together, everyone obliged to live cheek by jowl with their neighbours. In one tenement you might find a shopkeeper on the ground floor, a laird and his lady on the first, a merchant on the third, a dressmaker on the fourth and a prostitute in the attic.

There were plans now for Edinburgh to expand, spilling much farther outside the city walls than it already did, to the north as well as the south. He had attended a lecture given by former Provost Drummond in the Assembly Rooms the week before where the proposals had been put forward. The noxious swamp which was all that remained of the Nor' Loch would have to be drained before any expansion could take place. That unpleasant entity, artificially created hundreds of years ago to give the castle even more protection than its dramatic rock, festered at the bottom of the deep gully which separated the High Street from the fields and orchards which stretched northwards to the Forth.

High up as he was, Catto could see those fields and orchards over the pall of smoke rising from Edinburgh's multiplicity of chimneys. That smoke had earned the Scottish capital her most famous sobriquet: Auld Reekie. Beyond the foul yellow cloud, with Fife and the hills of the north as the backdrop – where he was still determinedly not directing his gaze – lay the fishing villages of Grantown and Newhaven and to the east of them the port of Leith – as he had discovered, a right nest of Jacobites – and then Musselburgh.

Stoneyhill in Musselburgh: the comfortable house which served as Culloden's Edinburgh lodgings. That was where he had taken Robert Catto when he had swept him up from the quay at Leith, four short weeks ago …

17

One Month Before

'Drink up, Bob. Otherwise I'll think ye dinna like my claret.' The Lord President raised one bony finger under the froth of lace at his wrist. The signal brought the impassive footman forward to top up both wine glasses.

'It's very fine, sir,' Catto assured his host. Although he would prefer not to slide under the table quite yet. Something was telling him he needed to keep a clear head. So far the conversation had covered Dettingen, the leg wound Catto had taken there and how it was healing, the latter in some detail. The Lord President fancied himself as something of an amateur physician. He'd moved on to quiz Catto on the progress of the war in Europe and his opinion of the various commanders and their respective strategies.

'Now, Bob,' Culloden said, coming at last to the point. 'Your opinion on the Disaffected.'

'The Disaffected?'

'You know who I mean, Bob. Jacobites. Supporters of the House of Stuart.'

'Yesterday's men.' Catto gave a dismissive flick of his long fingers. 'Irrelevant.'

'You heard nothing while you were on the Continent to change your mind about that?'

'Only the usual rumours.'

'To the effect that?'

'There was talk of the French assembling a fleet.' He spoke slowly, reluctant to give the words even the credence of speaking them aloud.

'Those rumours have reached me too.'

Catto glanced up at the footman, standing next to a long sideboard with his back to the wainscoting.

'We may speak freely in front of Fergus.'

Out of nowhere, a flash of memory came to Catto, his grandfather telling his mother that Culloden's servants were all devoted to him. The silent Fergus was a somewhat unnerving presence all the same.

'Have there not been such stories before, sir? Without anything coming of them?'

'Aye. But this time I am sorely afraid they may prove to be true.'

'Surely 'twas all laid to rest some thirty years' since.' Catto blew out an exasperated breath. 'Did the fiasco of the '19 not see it off once and for all? There's a new generation come up since then.'

'Too many of whom have been infected with the same malady,' Culloden said, his voice sombre. 'Inoculated with it, you might say. As surgeons deliberately infect people with the smallpox.' He sat with one elbow on the white damask cloth, his glass in his hand. The crystal twinkled red and yellow in the light of the three-branched silver candelabra he had earlier lifted down the table so it did not obscure his and his young guest's view of each other. 'As you should know better than anyone, Bob.'

'Inoculation is designed to equip one to resist the malady, sir.'

'And in your case, the inoculation took?' Duncan Forbes did not wait for an answer. Knowing Robert Catto's history as so few people did, he did not need one. 'The government is deeply unpopular, Bob.'

'The London government, you mean?'

'That's the only one we've got, lad.'

'Do you regret that, sir?' Catto did not like the direction in which the conversation was heading but he could not ignore the wistful note in the older man's voice. It spoke to something in himself. He didn't like that very much either. He stretched his legs out under the table, trying to rid himself of the tension which had gripped his limbs. Unease had crept into the room, lurking in the shadows where the candlelight did not penetrate.

'Ach,' said the Lord President, 'only insofar as 'twas the end o' an old song.' He sighed. 'And those who accuse too many of Scotland's nobles and gentry of selling the country for English gold are not wrong. But Scotland's future lies with the Union. Our country's fate is bound up now with that of England's. That is where our future fortune and prosperity lie.'

'But not everyone sees it that way?'

'No. There are those who believe the way forward is for Scotland to regain her independence and once more take her place among the kingdoms of Europe. I do not agree with them but I understand the sentiment. As you may do yourself, lad.'

'I have no opinion on the matter, sir.' Catto's chair creaked as he rolled his shoulders and shifted position. Now he was back on solid ground. 'I'm a soldier. I obey my orders and I do my duty. I take no interest in politics.'

Culloden looked at him. 'Aye,' he said drily. 'I see. Politics may well take an interest in you, however. It's often the way. What you must know is that the London government does not always act wisely. Scots now think themselves over-taxed, under-represented and without anywhere to direct their complaints about any and all of that. I'm afraid I also have to tell you that the Town Guard is not exactly popular. Did you ever hear the story of Captain Porteous, lad?'

Catto shook his head. 'I have been away from Scotland for so long, sir.' By and large he'd been away from Scots too, with their interminable telling and re-telling of their own stories. That was no loss. 'What happened to Captain Porteous?'

'I'll tell you another time.' Culloden gestured once more to the manservant.

'You are saying there is much discontent in Scotland over the Union with England?'

'Aye. That's what I'm saying. Also that a restoration of the House of Stuart offers a focus for that discontent.'

'You believe support would come from more than the Highlands and the North?'

'I do. There are disparate groups throughout Scotland whose members might well make common cause in the hope of bringing about such an eventuality.'

'To restore a Stuart monarch who would also be a Catholic monarch?' Catto's voice was sharp. 'Surely that would be an insurmountable stumbling block for most of these disparate groups?'

'Not if that monarch or his son – who will undoubtedly be the figurehead this time – were wise enough to guarantee freedom of worship to all his subjects. I understand the Young Pretender to be more than ready to make the compromise. Paris is worth a mass. He also has advisors wise enough to tell him he must guarantee other rights and freedoms if he is to win supporters in these islands.' Culloden's smile held both malice and mischief. 'Although for public consumption we shall paint him as the worst kind of autocrat and more Catholic than the Jesuits.'

'You said *in these islands*, sir. You think there is significant support for the Stuarts other than in Scotland?'

Culloden took another swig of claret. 'More than is comfortable for the friends of the government to contemplate. Not only where you might expect it – in Northumberland, Oxford and Wales – either. Whisper it softly, but there may even be covert Jacobites in London itself.'

'Which surely makes it likely that any attack would be directed against London,' Catto said, more confident now. 'We all know Charles Stuart cannot mount an attempt without French help. The French would certainly be happy to see a Stuart king on the British throne but they would want to achieve that as quickly and with as little cost to themselves in men and time as possible. Were they to sail up the Thames under cover of darkness, they could land troops within a short march of London. Although I have to say the French would much prefer a Catholic to a Protestant Stuart.'

'Indeed they would,' agreed his host. 'Which is only one of the difficulties with which the Young Gentleman will have to contend. May he suffer many more.' A second malicious little smile flashed. 'I too believe London will be the first choice. But we in Scotland cannot afford to be complacent. Old loyalties die hard here. The French could land troops in the Highlands or somewhere on the East Coast, Montrose or Aberdeen or Peterhead or a myriad of smaller harbours. Support for the Stuarts remains as strong as ever it was in Angus and Buchan. They're a stubborn lot in the north-east. Gey thrawn, as they themselves would say. From either location, a Jacobite army supported by French troops could easily sweep south and take Edinburgh.'

The Lord President raised his pepper-and-salt eyebrows. 'With appalling ease, given the almost complete lack of local militias or army garrisons to stand in their way. Not to mention the state of Edinburgh's defences, the parlous condition of which might well be compounded by the assistance of the Disaffected of Edinburgh.'

'You fear they might act the part of the horse of Troy?'

'That is what we need to know. What would they do if push comes to shove? How far are they prepared to go? It's one thing to drink toasts to the King over the water. It's quite another to pick up pistol and sword and rise in armed rebellion.'

Catto nodded. 'Those who make a great song and dance about their views are often less dangerous than those who contrive to remain in the shadows.'

This time the smile was wintry. 'You are wise beyond your years, Bob.'

'The fruits of experience, sir. I have observed the phenomenon several times in several places. Yet surely 'twould be suicide for anyone in any part of the British Isles to rise in armed rebellion. I cannot believe there are many who would be willing to take the risk.'

'There are those who feel they have little to lose, especially here in Scotland. Who lost much of what they held dear back in '15 and who are now willing to risk everything on one last throw of the dice.'

'Then they are fools,' Catto said harshly.

Culloden fixed him with his unwavering gaze. 'Maybe so. But they are fools who may take others who are not fools to perdition with them, fools who may well lead all Scotland to disaster. In the vain hope of regaining Scotland's nationhood.'

Catto raised his brows in a gesture of profound cynicism. 'I am afraid I see a fault in your logic, sir. Charles Stuart does not want Scotland alone. He has been raised since birth to believe himself heir to all his father's phantom titles.'

'I agree with you, Bob. Scotland alone will not be enough for that young man. But Scottish loyalty to his family could give him a powerful base from which to launch an attack on England, and Scotland is currently undefended. Wide open. As you know, the army is at full stretch in Europe, and wants our Highland companies too, those which were very effectively policing the Great Glen until they were marched south.'

The Lord President looked suddenly weary. 'Men who were of the Highlands, knew the country, spoke the Gaelic, kept their ears to the ground. The men who would be the most effective intelligencers were a Jacobite threat to materialize. We all know what happens when the cat's away.'

'If such a threat were to materialize, surely the Highland companies would be sent back north. Or regular troops would be recalled from the Continent and dispatched thither.'

'That's what worries me,' Culloden said grimly. 'I fear the threat would be dealt with once and for all. For centuries England has seen

Scotland as a thorn in its flesh. Forcing the army to turn its attention from Europe to Scotland would rouse the ire of its commanders and the government. They might see it as both a necessity and an opportunity to rip that thorn out and trample it into the ground forever. That is what I am most afraid of, Bob. That the wounds of centuries of warfare, which have begun to heal, could be ripped open again and bleed for generations to come!'

Duncan Forbes' voice shook with emotion. Catto went very still. What was he supposed to say now? *If this benighted bloody country does want to hurl itself to hell in a handcart, am I really supposed to give a fucking damn?* He counted himself lucky when Culloden regained his composure before he had to say anything.

'We'll move over to the fire. Fergus, put the brandy and the glasses at my elbow, will you? Then you may leave us to our own devices.'

Belying his lack of land-legs and the amount of alcohol he had been encouraged into consuming, Catto sprang to his feet and walked round the table to stand by the Lord President's chair. 'May I assist you, sir?'

Culloden looked up at him. 'You think I'm an ancient old man, don't you? Seeing ghosts and bogles where they don't exist?'

'I think you're the most astute man I've ever met, sir. And you're hardly ancient.'

Forbes rose painfully to his feet. 'Is that why you look so troubled, lad? Because despite your belief that the Jacobites are a spent force a small fear remains that I may be right? On my other side, if you please. The left elbow aches marginally less than the right. Give me the support of your strong young hand there. And I'm fifty-eight. Today is my birthday.'

'Then I wish you many happy returns.'

The older man seemed amused. 'Thank you kindly, laddie. Unfortunately, my joints do feel ancient. Help me over to the fire and sit yourself down opposite me.'

Once they were both settled, the door closed behind the manservant and the brandy poured, Culloden spoke again. 'You are much the same age as the Young Gentleman, Bob. You know how swiftly the blood runs in young veins. As you have observed, he has been raised from birth to believe it is his destiny to restore his family to the throne. I hear he is a very handsome young man. Like yourself. Ach, dinna colour up at that, lad! I'd jalouse you ken better than anybody that the lassies find your figure and your fisog easy on the eye.'

'You were saying, sir,' Catto managed. 'About Charles Stuart?'

'I was saying that by all reports he is a handsome chiel, possessed also of a considerable amount of charm. Both these things you know very well, of course. In fact,' Culloden went on, looking Catto straight in the eye, 'you must be one of the few people who knows what he looks like outside the romantic portraits with which his father and the Stuart court-in-exile try to tempt the more foolish princesses of Europe and their equally foolish parents that one of them should marry him.'

For a moment the only sound in the room was the crackling of the coal in the grate. It came, so Culloden had told Catto earlier, from Tranent, where one of the many coal mines which littered the hinterland of East Lothian was situated, stretching back from the coastal towns of Musselburgh and Prestonpans and Port Seton.

Catto looked across to the windows, thought of all the people out there beyond the darkness, living their lives in their little houses, sitting around their fires and their cookpots, making their plans. Man proposes, and God disposes. As do men of destiny, or those who have been encouraged by everyone around them to think that's what they are. He brought his gaze back to the Lord President, waiting patiently on the other side of the fireplace for him to speak.

'Is that why you summoned me to Scotland, sir? Because I know what Charles Stuart looks like?'

'Let's hope 'twill not reach that stage. Not if we can nip it in the bud. Nor need you fear an unexpected meeting.' Culloden moved his free hand in a gesture of adjustment. 'Or perhaps unanticipated would be a better word. A close eye is kept on the Young Gentleman's movements.

He remains still with his father and brother at the Palazzo Muti in Rome. If he leaves it for more than a few hours we shall know within a matter of days of his absence from there.'

The Palazzo Muti. The name sent memories chasing one another through Robert Catto's head. Sunshine. Laughter. Boasts about prowess at fencing and shooting. Boasts about girls. A proud father measuring his son's height against those of his friends, making the laughing boys stand back-to-back to see who was the tallest. A proud father. As fierce as it was unwelcome, bitterness rose in Robert Catto's throat. He'd put all this behind him years ago. Or so he had thought.

'What about my name, sir?' he asked, his voice carefully neutral.

'The name you go by now, Bob?'

Catto's chin went up. Some reactions were too hard to control. 'The only name I have been willing to bear for many years now. Ever since I had the choice.'

'A fine, distinctive name it is too. Especially for anyone curious enough to do a little digging.' Culloden raised his glass. 'To your mother, Bob, a brave and a bonnie lass. God rest her soul.'

He didn't want his mother brought into this. He could not refuse to drink to her memory. Lifting his own glass, he took a sip of brandy.

Especially for anyone curious enough to do a little digging.

He'd been wrong to think that the Lord President had come to the point a few moments ago. They'd only arrived at it now.

18

'The fire is in want of coal,' he said, rising to his feet to carry out the task. Lifting the brass poker from its stand by the side of the hearth, he raked the bright glow before swapping the poker for its companion tongs. Hunkering down, he transferred a few lumps from the scuttle to the fire. A small flame immediately licked its way up over one of the new coals, claiming it. Out of the corner of his eye he could see the Lord President watching him.

'Would I be right in thinking you are not going to ask me to adopt a different *nom de guerre*, sir?'

'Bravo, Bob,' Culloden said softly. 'I knew you'd get there before me.'

'You think it might be an advantage for them to find out my connections. They might think I'm playing a deep game. Which could muddy the waters and also encourage indiscreet admissions of loyalty. Or should that be disloyalty?'

His voice was rock steady. He supposed he owed that to years of learning how to hide his anger, a whole bloody lifetime of masking his deepest feelings so nobody would guess they even existed. The Lord President had brought him here for this?

'Aye, well,' said that gentleman with a wry twist of the lips. 'Loyalty or disloyalty? There's the thing. There's the danger. Men and women acting out of loyalty are a wheen more dangerous than those acting out of pure self-interest.'

'Dangerous to those they sacrifice to that loyalty too. Who have neither say nor choice in the matter.'

There was nothing more he could do to the fire. As he sprang to his feet, he saw that Culloden's glass was once again empty. The older man refilled it, leaned forward and offered the bottle to Catto. 'Have some more brandy, man,' he urged.

When Catto made no move to lift his glass or resume his seat, Duncan Forbes spoke gently. 'If I could have left you in peace I would have, Bob. I find, however, that I have to use every weapon in my armoury. You are who you are, lad. There's no getting away from that. You bring certain very specific skills and advantages to this commission you so do not want.'

'I could wish all those skills and advantages to the Devil, sir.' Catto laid one hand on the high mantelpiece and stood gazing down into the fire.

'I ken that fine, Bob.' There was compassion for him in the Lord President's voice but something else too. Determination. Or maybe ruthlessness would be a better word.

Here was another man of destiny, one who believed Scotland stood at a crossroads in her history, one who thought that gave him the right to lean down like one of the gods from Mount Olympus and intervene in other people's lives: Robert Catto's life.

And for what? A chimera, a will o' the wisp, a lost cause, that damned, cursed Stuart Cause, domain of dreamers and fools, dead but it won't lie down. Was he to be sacrificed to the bloody ghost of it? Not without a fight. Or at least a protest.

'I have spent years taking great pains to conceal who I am. As you choose to put it, sir. I no longer think of it that way.' He was beginning to see pictures in the fire. A line of redcoated soldiers. A rearing horse. A row of tents with campfires burning in front of them. Scenes from his world. He longed to be back there.

'I know I cannot rid myself of my connections but I never speak of them to anybody.' Well, only that once when he'd been blind drunk – and distressed beyond measure – but he would never admit to that either. 'I cannot think they would ever work to my advantage within the ranks of the British army. Nor can I think my career there is going to work to my advantage where I think you are asking me to go.'

'No? I seem to recall that someone very close to you followed a very similar path.'

Robert Catto drew in a breath, raised his head and looked at Culloden. 'He went in the opposite direction to me, sir.'

'Aye,' Culloden said. 'More's the pity. But what's done is done and we must start from where that has left us. Use it to our advantage. Play that deep game.'

'I'm a simple soldier, sir. I don't think I'm cut out to play a deep game. You are asking me to play two very different roles here. Contradictory roles.'

'Aye,' Culloden agreed, 'and you must be just as convincing in one as the other. Come down hard on those who need to be scared away from personal ruin and national disaster yet retain enough ambivalence to plant seeds of doubt in the bolder spirits as to where your own loyalties lie. You must walk a tightrope, lad. Although I have absolutely no doubt that you can do that.'

Catto shook his head. 'I'm not so sure, sir. It may be that I shall fail you here.'

'You underestimate yourself, Bob. There's a damn fine head on those young shoulders of yours. Besides which, it's you I need. No one else will do.'

A good head on his shoulders … and a heart that was sinking into his boots. The Lord President kept on talking. Implacable. Was that the word?

'We shall tread very cautiously, Bob. I was careful to request your colonel to send you to me purely for the training of the Town Guard and the surveying of the city walls prior to their repair. Neither he nor your brother officers will learn anything of this other business from me. That is the story for the Lord Provost and the Town Council too, aye even for George Drummond, though he's a good man and on our side. Go to him if you have to, though. He'll back you up if you need him to. Ostensibly you report to his successor, Mr Coutts. In reality you report to me. Another tightrope you will have to walk.'

Catto did not immediately reply. He was dwelling on the sheer bloody irony of it all. Against his will, against every instinct, he had been coerced into coming here. All in the hope of concealing something the Lord President was now asking him to be prepared to reveal.

It was all very well to speak of caution but once a secret was told, who was to say whose ears it would eventually reach? *Three men can keep a secret if twa o' them are deid.* Catto gripped the mantelpiece hard. God in Heaven, was he never to be rid of this unwanted inheritance?

'You have another safeguard, lad. The people we seek to wrongfoot operate within a labyrinth, a place of smoke and mirrors. If we are to defeat them we too must enter the labyrinth, raise the smoke and tilt the mirrors. That affords benefits as well as presenting difficulties. Like us, they will want to keep any meetings or communications as clandestine as possible.'

Tightropes and labyrinths. This was going to make him dizzy.

'For our part, we shall be discretion itself, commit to paper only what must be told, and then only alluded to, or in code. Fergus Chisholm shall be our messenger as and when required. You can trust him implicitly. Be wary of anyone else. Even those who present themselves to you in the guise of friends.' The salt and pepper eyebrows rose over the intelligent eyes. 'Aiblins especially those who purport to be your friends. Ye ken what Niccolo Machiavelli said about that.'

'Keep your friends close,' Catto supplied, 'and your enemies even closer.' His face grown too warm, he took his hand from the mantelpiece and a step or two away from the fire.

'Aye. Sometimes it's gey hard to tell which is which,' Duncan Forbes said with cheerful cynicism. 'Give me the next three months, lad. That's all I ask. Chapter and verse, that's what I need you to get for me. Those buggers in London won't shift their arses unless I can show them solid proof.'

'And if that proof isn't there to be found?'

'Then I shall be happy to let you go back to the life you have chosen for yourself.' The soft voice grew softer still. 'Not the one you inherited by an accident of birth. Maybe you are right and I am wrong, Bob. Maybe there is nothing to be found out. In which case you shall go back to Guise's with your Captain's commission and nobody will be any the wiser as to why you really were in Scotland.'

Oh, aye, that would be bloody right. Catto might hold his host in high esteem but he had as little faith in a politician's promise as the next man. Those three months was being dangled like a sweetmeat and would dissolve as quickly if it suited Culloden's purpose.

'Have some more brandy, man,' the older man said again. His lips twitched. 'And sit down, if you please. I'm getting a crick in my neck from looking up at you and God knows I dinna need any more aches and pains.'

'Do you think I might need it, sir?' Catto asked drily. 'The brandy, I mean?' For there was more to come. Worse to come. He knew that. Deep down hadn't he known why the Lord President had summoned him home? Home? Where had that treacherous little word come from?

'Might need it? Very good, Bob. Very good indeed.' Culloden refilled both glasses, sloshing the spirit in, and set the decanter down. 'Aye, I think you might very well need it.' Waving Catto to his chair, he sat back in his own, moving less cautiously than before. The brandy must be easing the aches and pains. No doubt the copious amounts of claret were also helping.

'Allow me to give you some of the background. There is a group which calls itself the Association. Or sometimes the Concert of

Gentlemen. Individually they are known as Associators. Their aim is the restoration of the House of Stuart.'

'To Scotland or England?'

'Both. The whole of the British Isles. Although we are not sure how close the links are between the Scottish and English Associators. We suspect, however, that the Scottish Association may now be widening its activities. Seeking new allies.'

'It includes the man you wish me to go after?'

'That is something I should dearly like to know. He is one of those who makes no secret of his political views and never has done. Which, as you have observed, might make us disinclined to suspect he poses any real threat. Except that he is a man of science and logic, one whose support for the Jacobites has more to do with what he believes Scotland might achieve under a Stuart king than any ancient loyalty to that family. There are others who may be willing to be convinced of that, lawyers and bankers who feel Edinburgh now has the status of a backwater and who see advancement for themselves in the restoration of a Stuart king, especially if Edinburgh once more were the seat of a royal court.'

Forbes raised a hand. 'I know what you're going to say, Bob. Not what the Young Gentleman wants. Yet we must not underestimate the longing for it in Scotland. This man of whom I speak is too an honest and well-respected man, whose opinions and actions may influence other honest and well-respected men, most dangerously here in the Lowlands.' Culloden blew out a breath. 'If the Lowlands fall to the Stuarts, we're all buggered. So he needs to be both warned and watched. If he has any dealings with the following, we need to know. There are some names here which you may recognize.'

So here it came at last. Catto sat and listened to the list. Was this how it felt to hear yourself sentenced to hang?

'John Murray of Broughton,' Culloden began, 'a gentleman from Peebles in the Borders. John Gordon of Glenbucket.' He grimaced. 'A man who ought to be old enough to know better. No fool like an old fool. William Robertson of Balhaldy. In reality William MacGregor of Balhaldy, Robertson being his preferred *nom de guerre.* We believe Murray of Broughton to be the main liaison between the Associators and the Old and Young Pretenders, chief carrier of messages betwixt Scotland and Rome. Someone else who is known to have done the same in recent years is an impoverished Highland gentleman by the name of John Roy Stuart. He spells his surname in the French style.'

Catto took a sip of his brandy and met the Lord President's gaze over the rim of the glass. 'Yes,' he said evenly, 'there are names there that are known to me.'

'They are hard men to track. They could turn up in Scotland. Despite the fact that one of them has a price on his head. Although he is a foolhardy man. So he cannot be trusted to stay safely away. We understand him currently to be very much in the confidence of the Young Gentleman.'

Ruthless. Aye, that was the word for the Lord President all right. Catto lowered his brandy glass from his lips. His hand was shaking. He commanded it to become still.

'We need to know if any of these conspirators fetch up on our shores. As we need to know who they are visiting while they are in Scotland, on whom they are exercising their influence, their powers of persuasion and,' Duncan Forbes added carefully, 'their silver tongues.' The compassion evident in his face was only making this worse. 'We need, of course, also to stop them before they can spread the poison too far.'

'So,' Catto said, running one fingertip around the rim of his glass, steadying himself and it, 'you need someone who knows what they look like too. Although I have to point out that more than one of these men you have mentioned,' – he would not say gentlemen – 'also knows what I look like. One at least will recognize my name.'

'Which could work to our advantage.'

Not to his advantage, though. He was fighting the urge to hurl his glass into the fireplace, watch it smash into a thousand razor-edged shards, release his rage and frustration. His restraint was wasted. The Lord President knew him too well.

'You are thinking that I am asking you to place yourself somewhere between the Devil and the deep blue sea, Bob, are you not?'

There was only one possible answer to that question. Robert Catto raised his eyes from his glass, looked Culloden full in the face. 'I'm a soldier, sir. As I have already told you, I obey my orders and I do my duty. To the best of my ability. Without fear or favour.'

'Never think that I doubt it.' The Lord President's voice was warm. 'I know your worth, lad, and I know your mettle. But if I am right, that mettle and that noble credo may well be sorely tested. Are you ready for that, Bob?'

He wasn't being offered a choice about this. There was none. *The Devil or the deep blue sea. That noble credo sorely tested?* Sweet Jesus.

'I have answered your question, sir. Now let us move on, if you please.'

Not something a young man should say to an older one. Not something anyone should say to a man of the status of Duncan Forbes. He issued no rebuke, only observed: 'You're angry, Bob.' Then, when Catto did not reply: 'Poor consolation this may be, but you could find yourself in the position of being able to prove your mettle beyond any doubt. In which case you will revert to one role and one role only, loyal Captain of the Town Guard and soldier of the crown. Putting not only your mettle but also your loyalty beyond any doubt whatsoever.'

Oh, that was a low blow … but one that hit home. Catto kept his gaze on the long-case clock which stood in one corner of the dining room. Even above the crackling of the fire, he could hear its tick-tock.

'A Devil's bargain, to be sure,' the soft voice went on. 'One which I regret beyond measure having to offer you. Believe me, Bob, I do so only because I have been forced to it.'

Christ, Culloden was reaching for the brandy again. Blink though he did at how quickly Duncan Forbes had emptied his glass, Catto quaffed some more from his own still well-filled one and held it out to his host. He had no choice about this either. For the next three months he had no choice about anything. So he might as well drink to this Devil's bargain.

Only three short months. They would pass quickly enough. Then he would shake the dust of Scotland from his feet forever.

19

Three short months. What a poor bloody fool he had been. He threw his head back to gaze up at the sky, blue as a summer's day, the sun warm on his face. That was another of the things he'd forgotten about Scotland, how winter days could often be so bright and sunny. His treacherous heart betrayed him then, lowering his head and his eyes to look across the river and over the Firth, silvery in the winter sunshine, up to the hills of Fife, knowing that beyond them lay the Tay and Dundee and then the north, Aberdeen, Banff and Inverness.

All those names held memories, flooding into his head before he could raise any defences against them. He gave way to the remembered faces, places and voices, having no choice but to surrender to the pain and the sadness. These feelings were old friends and old foes – and in that instant he realized why the name *Balnamoon* was familiar to him.

A corner of the windswept uplands of Banffshire. A little stone bridge over a burn. A burnt-out laird's house, no more than a mile or two from his own grandfather's house. A sunny winter's day like this one, and clumps of nodding white snowdrops on a sward of frosty green grass.

How odd. Could he and Jamie Buchan of Balnamoon have known each other as children? There had been so sign of recognition from Balnamoon last night, as he himself had been aware of none for him. That might come, though. In which case Balnamoon would definitely uncover his connections. Those rolling wheels would roll faster still and more steps would be taken along the labyrinth of which the Lord President had spoken, drawing Catto ever more deeply in.

The wheels were already in motion. He had set them rolling last night, when he hadn't arrested Rankeillor and Balnamoon. The latter had unwittingly given him the excuse not to press them for the name of Rankeillor's alleged patient, feeble though that excuse had been.

Given how brutally he had invaded Rankeillor's house, the rough treatment he'd had meted out to the housekeeper and the series of insults he'd inflicted on Rankeillor's daughter, did they really think he would have scrupled to go further? As if he'd have had any respect for medical confidentiality if he had really wanted to get that name out of them…and he was trying very hard to ignore the small voice telling him he hadn't pressed them for it because there was one name above all others that he did not want to hear.

He'd confused them, that was what mattered. Seeming to take the guard off the Royal Infirmary would reinforce the message he was at least ambivalent about what he was doing. As would riding out to the country inn where he'd come every Sunday since he'd been here, following his usual pattern. If he was to be equally convincing in his contradictory roles, he had to go a lot further. He had to convince them he would be prepared to help them.

Shifting his position in the saddle, he earned himself a whinny of rebuke from Tam as the movement caused him to pull on the reins and the bit within the horse's soft mouth. Another apple should sort that grievance out. He leaned forward and slid one hand under the wiry black mane to clap the soft neck underneath, offering a reassuring murmur. 'When we get down to the inn and you can have a good chomp, Tam. We'll be there soon.'

Trust no one. He would have to hope they were not experienced enough plotters to have yet learned that lesson ... and his eyes had returned yet again to the Royal Infirmary. Bloody hell. Daft Friday. If the Jacobite messenger was in the hospital, that would be when they would try to move him.

Daft Friday, when Catto had been warned by Crichton and Livingstone to expect trouble across Edinburgh, pranks, idiocies and drunken brawls threaded through the celebrations of the start of Yule. The plotters might add a few distractions to the mix, further diverting attention from what they were up to.

So he would keep the gates well-guarded and maintain the covert surveillance of the hospital while subtly presenting himself as someone who might be willing to turn a blind eye. He would go out there and play the role, spend time in the taverns, make himself visible and available. He would be open but enigmatic, a raised eyebrow here, a brief observation here, a failure to comment there, and he would listen more than he spoke.

He'd have to tread a fine line, walk that tightrope. He couldn't afford for any of this to come back to haunt him. He'd also have to allow Balnamoon and any of his fellow plotters who might approach him to get to know him a little. Or maybe not. As obsessed as they were with their prince and their plots, why should Edinburgh's Disaffected be interested in him other than because of his contradictory actions last night and this morning?

Did it matter to them who his relatives might be? His own supposed or suspected political sympathies need have nothing to do with those. If they thought he was in a position of some authority as Captain of the Town Guard yet had Jacobite sympathies, that might be enough.

He was well used to guarding his tongue when it came to who he was and where he came from. Hellfire, he'd spent half his life in the army and, apart from that one occasion, had managed to keep his family connections to himself. Why should he not be able to do so here and still obtain those indiscreet expressions of loyalty to the Stuart Cause, an admission the Jacobite plotter was still in Edinburgh or even a plea for his help in getting the man out?

As sudden as it was unexpected, a spark of hope flared in Catto's breast. This could work. This could absolutely bloody work, and get him a lot more than the chapter and verse the Lord President needed. This could get him the Jacobite messenger and allow him to flush more of Edinburgh's Disaffected out of the woodwork. Who else might the messenger have talked to last night, tried to win over to the Stuart Cause?

If the Lowlands fall to the Stuarts, we're all buggered.

The Liddells. The name shot into Catto's head. They owned great swathes of the land he was looking out at now, terrain rich in the coal which gave them their wealth. He had a coded letter from one of them tucked into the inside pocket of his riding coat, a copy he'd made from the original he'd purloined for an hour or two last week before returning it to the post office.

It had drawn his attention because of the red wax seal bearing the Liddell family crest and, when he had opened it, because it was written in code or, more accurately, a cipher. He had yet to tackle that, although he knew who had written the letter, one of the most prominent members of the powerful and influential Liddell family. Not the sharpest knife in the drawer to have closed his epistle with his family seal, or to have signed his own name, uncoded, at the bottom of the message. Or perhaps this scion of the house of Liddell was too cocky to care.

The Lord President certainly wanted the Liddells watched, albeit subtly. '*Kid gloves, Bob. They have a gey high opinion of themselves and they're quick to take offence. The sort who might choose sides on a whim, thinking their wealth protects them from any sort of consequence, and who might also be hoping for glory and honours. From whichever side as long as it's the winning one. Nor would I have them take agin you personally, lad. Their influence is far-reaching. Stretches as far as the army.*'

It bloody would, wouldn't it? Catto felt the same irritation he had experienced when Duncan Forbes had told him that. How many times had he come up against this, the useless young sprig of the aristocracy promoted over his head, the social dismissal of himself because he could not or would not bandy about the names of influential relatives?

He slid his hand into his pocket and brought out the copy of the letter. Might it have been passing on word about a meeting? Unfolding the paper, he stared at the symbols he hadn't yet had time to decipher. As he hadn't yet had time to think about who had sent the warning to Rankeillor and Balnamoon last night. Could it have been Liddell?

Catto lifted his head from the letter. Lieutenant Liddell. Closely related to the powerful and wealthy Liddells. Cousin to the man who had written this letter. Did that have implications? He might be closer to an answer once he knew what the letter said. He would have to squeeze out the time to decipher it sometime this week.

Given the opportunity, and who knew what other information might come to him over these next few days, he would strike hard and he would strike fast. He had freedom of action until Friday. Once the Lord Provost returned to Edinburgh he could not be sure the man would not countermand his orders, order a reduction of the security on the town's gates, relax the restrictions on the Rankeillor household.

Catto could not allow that to happen until after the Daft Friday ball. So he would have to call on Provost Coutts on Friday as soon as he got back and make sure none of that happened. He might suggest it could call Coutts' loyalty into question. Aye, that could work.

He could do this. He could do all of this. Last night he had looked into the abyss and seen himself looking back out. A natural reaction to events, none of which were of his making. 'Twas not his actions and choices which had created this set of circumstances. He would hope not to have to confront his past in too familiar a form but he would do his duty whatever fate threw at him. He would do his duty without fear or favour.

In return he might have the chance of nipping this in the bud, saving Scotland from itself and getting out of the bloody place before he was very much older. He laughed out loud. Nothing like being ambitious. Taking a firmer grip on Tam's reins, he squeezed the horse's flanks with his thighs, geed him up and rode down the hill.

'There's some mair bread tae ye, sir,' said the barmaid, transferring two doughy slices from the tray she carried to the rectangular wooden platter in front of Catto's soup plate. He was in the *Sheep Heid* tavern in the village of Duddingston, about to start on his second helping of the famous broth from which, so he'd been told, the inn had taken its name.

'Ye'll be for some mair ale too?' she queried, lifting a large earthenware pitcher off her tray. Catto put his hand over his tankard. 'Something wrang wi' the ale, sir? Ye'll no' be telling me it's wersh, I hope?'

'It's as sweet as a nut,' he assured her, giving her a smile. She was a bonnie girl. Once more, he found himself slipping back into Scots both in thought and speech. 'But there was something wrang wi' ma heid when I woke up this morning.'

'Ah!' The girl laid the pitcher down and took her tray in both hands. 'So that's the way of it. Perhaps we should start serving foreign muck instead.' She affected a hoity-toity voice. 'Apparently yon *tea* does not occasion inebriation.'

Catto laughed. He was in a good mood now. Hopeful. For the first time in weeks. 'Och, ye'd be awfy polite gin ye did that, lass. All the fine young ladies would flock to the *Sheep Heid*.'

Her eyes sparkled. 'I'd wager ye ken a thing or two aboot fine young ladies, sir.'

'You think so, sweetheart?'

'I'd put money on it,' she said, throwing him a cheeky smile over her shoulder. Enjoying the sway of her hips as she moved off, he wondered idly if she was available. In Edinburgh, tavern girls who were prepared to service as well as serve you wore a belt of oyster shells about their waists. It was harder to know what might be on offer on top of food and drink in a country inn like this one. You could get your face slapped for propositioning the wrong girl. If she turned out to be the landlord's daughter you could find yourself out on the street, sprawled there on your hands and knees if her father really took exception to you. He'd seen it happen.

A few satisfying moments later he used the last morsel of bread to soak up the last drop of soup. That should keep him going until Geordie's beef and pancakes. He took a little more ale to wash it down, sat back on the bench seat and stretched his legs out under the table. He laid one hand on his leather coat, folded beside him on the wooden bench. Perhaps he would have a little snooze before he started back to Edinburgh, allow himself some calm before the storm.

As soon as his eyelids fluttered shut Christian Rankeillor was there, glaring at him. 'Not you again,' he muttered. 'Get out of my head, Miss Jacobite.'

'First sign of madness, sir,' came an amused male drawl. 'Isn't that what they say about talking to oneself?'

Catto drew his legs back and opened his eyes. His interlocutor, a dark-haired and strikingly handsome young man about the same age as himself, stood in the middle of a group of other young men. It was clear from their poses they had been walking past his booth on their way to somewhere else in the rambling building occupied by the *Sheep Heid*.

'It's Captain Robert Catto, am I not right?' A friendly smile. A hand offered across the table. 'Cosmo Liddell, sir,' the dark-haired young man announced. 'At your service.'

Cosmo Liddell. The Honourable Cosmo Liddell. The author of the original of the letter lying under Catto's hand. Well, well, well. That was fortuitous.

Or a bloody quick response.

20

'All right?' Jamie murmured as Christian walked into the dispensary, glancing up from the ledger in which he was writing.

She answered him in similarly low tones. 'Not exactly. His ankle is very swollen. I do not think he will be able to walk easily for quite some time. Jamie—'

'Kirsty,' he growled. 'There must be as little talk of this as possible.'

'You asked me,' she protested.

'And now you have told me. So if you please, no more on this subject.'

He lowered his dark head to the ledger, leaving her blinking at him, wounded by the sharp tone. They had to speak about this. How else were they get Mr Fox out of here and on his way? She had a question for Jamie too, one which could not wait. Today might be the Sabbath but she didn't think that would bother the Town Guard Captain. How could they know he wouldn't take it into his head to fetch up at the Infirmary today with his men and mount a search of the building?

She put that to him in a low and urgent voice, and then: 'Jamie, should I not therefore go and call on Mr Drummond and alert him and the other hospital managers to the possibility of a search of the hospital so we might prevent that from going ahead?'

'How would you explain to them our anxiety that such a search should not go ahead?'

'On medical grounds. Because we do not want the patients disturbed.'

'Mr Drummond is away, Kirsty. Besides which, he is no friend to our Cause. The other managers will already have heard about the raid on Surgeons' Hall and your house. Given that everyone knows what your father's politics are, do you not think they will put two and two together if you now draw their attention to the Royal Infirmary? Suspect something is afoot here, that we do have something to hide?'

'But Jamie, what will we do if the Town Guard turn up at the front door—'

His hand sliced through the air, cutting her off. 'Enough, Kirsty. Enough!'

She turned away, began busying herself with emptying her basket and putting the medicines within it where they belonged in the dispensary.

Weak at the knees. Now she knew where that expression came from, understood why her father often stated that the mind ruled the body. The relief that she was no longer carrying food and sustenance to a man with a price on his head was physical. That was one day they had got away with it. What about tomorrow and all the days till Friday when the risk would have to be run again? Fighting the panic, Christian heard herself blurt out another dangerous question. 'What happened to the subject?'

The subject. That was always the word they used when they spoke of dissections. Never the *body*. Never the *cadaver*. She knew how to be discreet about those things which required discretion.

'Professor Monro's demonstrator has it stowed away in the Old College,' Jamie said shortly. 'The dissection will take place tonight.'

That brought her head up from the stowing away of the physic. 'Without the Town Guard Captain's permission?'

'Do you want to be the one to tell Professor Monro that express and written permission from the Captain of the Town Guard is now required before a dissection can proceed?' Jamie snapped.

Her own temper flared. 'What if Professor Monro is discovered in the middle of the dissection? If that Captain was having you watched last night he's probably still having you watched today.'

'You think I don't know that?' Jamie didn't look up, his quill continuing to move across the page of the patients' ledger.

'So what are we going to do, Jamie?'

The quill stopped. 'I don't know, Kirsty.' He looked up at last, and their eyes met. What she saw in his made her walk across to the table to stand next to him.

She was dressed simply today, wearing a bluey-green tartan plaid over a dark blue gown. Its only ornamention came from the quilted patterns on its underskirt and split overskirt. Stitched flowers and leaves held together the layers of fabric that were keeping her warm. Beneath that she wore no hoops but two simple petticoats, one of linen and one of red wool. In the winter Betty wouldn't let her out of the house without that one.

'Jamie …' she began, thinking how tired he looked. He often did. Now she knew the burden included so much more than his work here at the hospital and as her father's apprentice. Jamie Buchan of Balnamoon's devotion to the Stuart Cause was exactly that. While he agreed with the Rankeillors on the benefits they were convinced would flow from a restoration, the wellspring of his support for the Jacobite Cause was that old loyalty to the House of Stuart. Instinctive. Unswerving. Woven into a miasma of history, religion, blind faith and myth.

She knew too that he was prepared to sacrifice everything for it, as his father and grandfather had before him, even his hopes for advancement in the profession to which he was also so devoted, even the hopes he must have had that one day he might take over at least part of her father's business as an apothecary.

It came to her what the odd look he and Robert Catto had exchanged last night had meant. It had been a recognition that James Buchan of Balnamoon was much more than he seemed, a worthy adversary, in his own way as much a soldier as he was. If Robert Catto realized that, he knew a lot more than they thought he did. Dear God, the risks they were running here…

Jamie laid down the quill and rose from the table, walking across to stand looking out of the window which overlooked the Infirmary's grounds. He half-turned, peering up the side of the building, although all he could be seeing was the coal store. An adjunct to the main hospital building, it projected out from it.

'What are you looking at out there which is so prodigiously fascinating?'

He pointed. 'Beneath that rowan tree.'

She joined him at the window and focussed on the spot he had indicated, in front of the shorter wall of the coal store, where it formed a corner with the wall of the main hospital building. 'Checks,' she said. 'Tartan. A plaid?'

Jamie grabbed her arm. 'It's more than a plaid. Kirsty, come on!'

Catto shook the hand he was being offered. 'I think we've already met, sir,' he said, curious as to what response the reminder was going to get him. 'At the lecture ten days' since on the plans for the expansion of Edinburgh.' *At which, as soon as you found out that I was merely the Captain of the Town Guard, you were really rather dismissive of me. Quite de haut en bas, you dandified prick.*

The Honourable Cosmo Liddell smiled at Catto, a gesture of such apparent openness and friendliness he found himself in real danger of being disarmed by it. 'Didn't know the cut of your jib then, sir. Didn't know you were on the field at Dettingen. My cousin Archie has subsequently filled me in. Honoured to meet a veteran of Dettingen, sir. Truly honoured.'

He spoke like an Englishman. No, he spoke like a Scotsman trying to sound like an Englishman and almost succeeding. It occurred to Catto that he himself probably sounded like an Englishman, although in his case that had just happened somewhere along the way. He didn't think anything about how Cosmo Liddell presented himself to the world was accidental.

He was surprised by how firm Liddell's grip was. Not that the man struck him as being a molly. He was a fop though, albeit one with a mercifully restrained sense of style. His silk waistcoat was something to behold all the same, an extravagantly embroidered fantasy of stylized flowers rendered in sky blue and gold thread against a black background. His dark blue coat and black breeches were of the finest quality and cut but understated in style.

Aping military fashion, he wore his cravat in a Steinkirk knot. No soldier would have worn his hair the way the Honourable Cosmo Liddell did, though. Tied back at the nape of his neck by a ribbon which perfectly matched the blue of his frock coat – and, Catto registered, the colour of his rather striking eyes – it was artfully arranged at the front into a mass of black curls. He looked like a handsome gypsy, or perhaps a bored young artistocrat's idea of one.

Since the hair at his nape was perfectly straight, it could only be assumed the curls owed their existence to artifice. Catto had never understood how any man could be bothered with that sort of primping and preening – best left to the female of the species, in his considered opinion. Liddell dropped his hand at last.

'I admire your courage, sir. Should have realized the first time we met that you were the genuine article. A real military man.' He turned to his friends. Or maybe acolytes would be a better word. Popping of its own accord into Catto's head, the description seemed all too appropriate, especially when every last one rushed to agree with their aristocratic friend.

'Evident from his very bearing that he's a military man,' one of them said.

Evident from his very bearing even when he was sitting slouched at a tavern table? Flattery would get them absolutely nowhere.

The young man who had commented on his supposed military

bearing was Hector Grant of Soutra. 'Honoured to make your acquaintance, sir,' he gushed. 'Deeply honoured.'

Next to introduce himself was Arthur Menzies of Edmonstone. He was the recipient of the coded letter. 'At your service, sir,' he said, sketching Catto a rather too extravagant bow. That he modelled himself on Cosmo Liddell, both in style and the arch manner, was obvious.

They were all *of* somewhere. As he himself had once been, a long time ago and a lifetime away. Currently he was *Robert Catto of the High Street of Edinburgh*. Didn't have quite the same ring to it. After everyone had been introduced, Cosmo Liddell raised one hand in a casual gesture of command. 'The invitation, Hector. Kindly extend the invitation to Captain Catto.'

'Sir,' Grant began. 'I have the honour to be the secretary of the Tuesday Club. Whose most faithful members you see around you here.'

'Even though it's a Sunday,' said one of the acolytes, a comment which provoked an outbreak of guffaws.

'We of the Tuesday Club,' Hector Grant continued, 'should esteem it a great honour if you would come and give us your account of Dettingen. Would you do that, sir? Dare we hope that you would honour us? We convene in the Black Bull Tavern at the top of Leith Wynd on–'

'—a Tuesday?'

'Very droll, sir. Oh, very droll.' Everyone laughed. As before, Catto noticed they only did so after they had first glanced at Cosmo Liddell and seen whether he was laughing.

'Might you possibly favour us with an acceptance?' Hector Grant looked not unlike one of the bright-eyed squirrels carved into the posts of Christian Rankeillor's bed. All he lacked was the bushy tail. 'We can promise you an attentive audience. Your supper too, of course.'

He'd rather have stuck burning needles into his eyes. He'd rather have eaten a bowl of mud. He'd rather have walked naked up the High Street with feathers and bells dangling on pretty pink ribbons from his manly attributes.

'I'd be delighted,' he said. 'Absolutely delighted.'

'That's settled, then,' Cosmo Liddell said, breaking in on Hector Grant's effusive thanks. 'Fancy a game of skittles?'

Catto blinked. That had been very brisk and no-nonsense. He answered in like vein, sliding along the bench seat until he was clear of the table and could stand up. 'I don't mind if I do. There's an alley here?'

'Through at the back.' Liddell pointed at Catto's coat. 'I'd bring that with you. Pack of thieves and vagabonds in this place.'

Catto swung back to the table, scooped up his coat and followed the group through.

'She's dead, Jamie?'

Kneeling beside the body, he nodded as he rose to his feet. 'For some hours, I'd say. The stiffening is well advanced. Although the cold might have accelerated that, of course.'

'She's only young,' Christian observed sadly, studying the white face above the colourful plaid. 'Younger than us.'

'Aye,' he agreed, and for a moment neither of them spoke, simply stood on either side of the dead girl, looking down at her. Somewhere nearby a blackbird begin to sing. Yesterday this lost soul at their feet might have heard that sweet song. Now she would hear nothing more.

'How do you think she died? I can't see anything obvious. Can you?'

'Not without further examination. The question is, what are we going to do with her?'

Christian looked across the body at him, confused as to what he meant. 'I suppose we will have her carried to the dead-room and report what we have found.'

'Report to whom, Kirsty?'

'Ah,' she said. ''Tis the Town Guard who must be informed, is it not?'

'The very same. In the person of Captain Robert Catto. Rather unfortunate, under the circumstances.'

'We cannot not report the death.'

'Of course not. But it means we are once again drawing attention to ourselves. Not to mention bringing Robert Catto into the Infirmary.'

Christian shivered. That was certainly not a prospect to be relished. Then, with a little gasp: 'Jamie, what if we could make a virtue out of necessity?'

'I understand,' Cosmo Liddell said, standing beside Catto as the other members of the group whooped and cheered as each of them rolled the ball down the skittle alley, 'that the Town Guard is now worth the watching.'

'Indeed, sir?' Pretending to concentrate on the game, Catto folded his arms across his brown waistcoat – his very plain brown waistcoat. This must be what hens felt like when they stood next to cockerels. Liddell clapped him on the shoulder.

'Why so modest, man? The story of last night's raid is all around the town.'

'News does travel fast.'

'Especially after the churches empty on a Sunday morning. Sometimes I think I should attend more often if only to hear the gossip. My cousin Archie is also most impressed by you, Captain Catto. Says you've really taken hold of the Town Guard.'

'It's needed a shake-up for years,' chipped in Hector Grant. 'Trouble is, everyone's been scared to do it. After what happened to Captain Porteous.'

'What did happen to Captain Porteous?' Catto asked. 'No one seems to want to tell me.'

'We won't dwell on that,' murmured Cosmo Liddell. 'Catto,' he mused. 'Can't say I've heard the name before. Might I ask where your family originates from, sir?'

He might, but there was no bloody way he was going to get an answer. If Liddell really wanted to know, he could find out for himself. If he didn't already know. Catto felt a prickle of unease. 'Here and there.

We're rather dispersed. Looks like it's my turn.' After he'd taken it he found himself standing next to Arthur Menzies of Edmonstone. Somehow he didn't think that was accidental.

'You're not from Edinburgh, Mr Catto?'

'No,' he agreed. 'My stay here is temporary.'

Well, it hadn't been difficult to turn aside that none-too-subtle follow-up question but he still wasn't sure he was cut out for this cloak and dagger stuff. He would never wish himself back on a battlefield but at least there you knew who was friend and who was foe. Not like here. Were this lot cultivating him because they had stars in their eyes about soldiers, or had they a more serious intent?

He glanced past Arthur Menzies at Cosmo Liddell. That foppish air was definitely an affectation but whether it was covering hidden depths or hidden shallows was debatable.

'Do you anticipate your stay in Edinburgh being a long one, sir?'

'That's rather in the lap of the gods.' Represented here on Earth, he thought with a flash of amusement, by Duncan Forbes of Culloden, Lord President of the Court of Session of Scotland.

'Indeed? You must make sure you waste no time getting to know the place.'

'I'm contriving to do so.'

'You must lose no opportunity to do so. Isn't that right, Cosmo?'

'What's that?' asked Liddell, tossing his head to throw back a stray curl which had fallen forward over his brow. He clearly thought the gesture an attractive one.

'I'm saying that Mr Catto should lose no opportunity to get to know Edinburgh.'

'Indeed not,' Liddell said. 'An excellent piece of advice.' He clapped Catto on the shoulder. 'Lose no opportunity. A good maxim for life, I've always thought.' His eyes slid to the barmaid, moving among the skittles players taking orders. He was studying her breasts, not her face. Definitely not a molly.

'Where,' Liddell asked, dragging his eyes off the girl, 'do your tastes run when it comes to the fair sex, Captain?'

'Oh,' Catto said, 'I'm a simple man. As long as all the usual components are in all the usual places, I'm happy.'

Liddell laughed. 'Very well put, sir.' He glanced at Arthur Menzies of Edmonstone and Hector Grant of Soutra before looking back at Catto. 'Tell me, sir, would you describe yourself as a broad-minded man?'

'Kirsty, this is not a good idea.' They were back in the dispensary, Jamie once more standing at the window, although there was nothing to see out there now. Two porters had removed the body to the dead-room a few moments before.

'Even if it persuades the Town Guard Captain we have nothing to hide?' She had not told Jamie – he had not given her the opportunity – of how Mr Fox had been waiting for her this morning, a pistol trained upon her breast. If he had seen Robert Catto standing there he would have shot him dead. She was sure of that.

'Twas not only that there was a ruthlessness underlying the charm or the way he had spoken of his mission, as something sacred. He would have had no other choice, could not have afforded to be merciful, to shoot only to wound and disable. This must be what war meant, that men who had no personal quarrel with each other had to make a split-second decision: him or me.

Whatever she thought of Robert Catto, he didn't deserve that. Oh and dear God, to have such a thing happen in the Infirmary, a place dedicated to the healing of wounds and the saving of lives. There had to be something they could do to stop such a thing happening. There had to be a different way of going about this.

'Even if it persuades him to change his mind about that …' She paused, searching for the right word. '… that *edict* he issued last night?'

'Captain Catto does not strike me as a man who changes his mind very easily.'

'No,' she agreed. 'He seems very strong-minded.'

'Although also troubled,' Jamie said, turning at last away from the window.

'I think that too. Although I do not see how we can use that to our advantage.'

'I am thinking more that it may be revealing. Perhaps he is troubled because he has divided loyalties. Perhaps he feels torn between them.'

She shook her head. 'I wish I could think that, Jamie, but I can't. That man despises us and everything about us. How in any case would you ever find out?'

'By asking him.'

'Jamie, you must not do that! 'Twould be far too risky!'

'I meant subtly, Kirsty. I am not planning to ask him outright.'

'Then how are you planning to approach him?'

'I think we were talking about the ban on dissections. Let us return to it. Even though 'tis not a subject I relish.'

'Because you know how Professor Monro is going to react when he hears.'

'He will be incandescent with rage.'

'As will all the other anatomists. Professor Monro will undoubtedly shoot the messenger.'

'Oh, aye,' Jamie said with weary resignation. 'There's no two doubts about that. Or that it'll be me in the firing line.'

'You could do without that.'

'You might say that,' came the dry response.

'So surely it makes sense to take this opportunity both of trying to change Captain Catto's mind and persuading him we do not fear him coming to the hospital?' She added a reluctant: 'Meeting him again in less hostile circumstances might also give you the chance of getting his measure. So you might judge whether or not you could sound him out.'

He gave her a faint smile. 'You're persistent, Kirsty, I'll give you that.'

'Does that mean you'll agree to this? And listen to my idea about how Anna Gordon might help us get Mr Fox out of Edinburgh?'

21

Catto dismounted from Tam, gave him a final clap on his warm neck, threw the reins to Donald Livingstone's eldest son and walked up to the Netherbow Port. Davie Rintoul was on guard.

'Urgent message for ye, Captain,' he announced, giving Catto a passably decent salute. He didn't yet have them running on full military discipline but he was getting there. 'Sergeant Crichton's compliments and he'd be obliged gin ye could mak your way tae to the Infirmary forthwith. It's another deid boady, sir,' Rintoul added, displaying all the relish usual to a bearer of grisly tidings.

'Not too unusual to find one of those at the Infirmary, surely,' Catto responded. 'Anyone I should know about been in or out today? Apart from Professor Patrick Rankeillor by the West Port, I mean. I know he left for Glasgow from there this morning.'

'Aye, sir. Here's the list you asked to be taken from a' the gates o' today's activity. We're keeping quiet about daeing that as well, as ye requested. Naebody we didna ken. It's been the usual quiet Sabbath. And it's a wee touch mair unusual for a corpse to turn up at the Infirmary if someone finds it half-hidden in the bushes at the side o' the building.'

'Ah,' Catto said, raising his head from the sheet of paper Rintoul had handed him. 'I take your point. Bloody hell,' he added, 'does that make six sudden and violent deaths since I arrived in Edinburgh? Is it always this bad?'

Rintoul grinned, treating Catto to the sight of his mouthful of quite disgusting teeth. 'Are ye keeping a tally, Captain?'

'Well, I had all but one of them resting for a night or two under the same roof as me when they were in the dead-room at the guard-house. Tends to fix them in the mind. What is it this time?' He lifted his hands and began counting off on his fingers. 'So far we've had the two drinking companions who managed to slay each other while they were both too rat-arsed to know what they were doing, one respectable merchant who succeeded in drinking himself to death after – so I'm told – years of trying. Lucky Kennedy and the student, of course and-' He transferred the reckoning to his other hand, then paused, struggling to remember who the sixth *deid boady* had been.

'Yon wifie who stepped out of her house for a wee minutie,' Rintoul supplied. The disgusting teeth were once more on display. 'The only trouble being that she lived twelve storeys above the Parliament Close.'

'How could I have forgotten that one? We had to scrape her off the causeway. What do we have this time?'

Rintoul shook his unkempt head. 'I canna tell ye any more, Captain. Other than it was Lieutenant Liddell who was first tae deal wi' the body. He subsequently called Sergeant Crichton oot and the Sergeant says he needs tae speak tae ye urgently.'

'Does he suspect foul play?'

'He wouldna say.' Rintoul sounded disappointed. 'Only asked if you would go to the Infirmary as soon as you got back tae the toun. Yon wee Geordie tellt him ye were away for the day but he didna ken where. We knew ye'd left by the Netherbow Port but that didna mean ye were going tae come back by it, so the Sergeant pit word round a' the gates. The first one o' us to see ye was tae send a message tae the Sergeant's hoose and he'll be there wi' Lieutenant Liddell tae meet ye.'

Since it was still light, Catto went the back way, out of the city gate, along St Mary's Wynd, round the foot of the Cowgate and up the High School Wynd. He'd made it his business to explore all these short cuts, including this one which had been employed to such good effect last night. As he turned the corner into Infirmary Street he glanced down towards Patrick Rankeillor's house. He didn't spare a thought for the surgeon-apothecary's daughter. Not much of a one, at any rate.

Red in the face – he'd clearly made haste to get here – Sergeant Crichton was waiting for him in the quadrangle of the Infimary, standing a few feet in front of the hospital's austere Grecian portico. He was haranguing a miserable looking Lieutenant Liddell.

'What's going on here?'

Crichton roared at Liddell. 'Why don't you answer the Captain's question, young sir?'

Liddell swallowed hard but didn't speak.

'Lieutenant,' Catto barked. 'What the Devil's the matter with you?'

'Mr C-Catto, sir. C-Captain.' Liddell gulped, and got the words out without a further stutter. 'I've-given-permission-for-the-body-to-be-dissected, sir. By-Mr-Buchan-of-Balnamoon.'

'You've what?'

'Miss Rankeillor was very persuasive, Captain. She said it would be much better for Jamie to start the dissection while he might still work by daylight.'

'Miss Rankeillor? What the fuck does she have to do with this? Since when does the Town Guard do what some chit of a girl says? *Miss Rankeillor?*' he howled. 'What in the name of God Al-fucking-mighty was the point of last night's raid if you're now taking orders from the target of it? Do you take orders from Miss Rankeillor, Liddell?'

'No, s-sir,' Liddell stammered. 'Of course not, s-sir. I take orders from you. But Kirsty was very persuasive, and I was feeling really bad about what had happened last night. I'm s-sorry, s-sir.'

That Jamie had been bad enough, but it was the Kirsty that did it. Catto lost the battle to hold on to his temper. 'Sorry? Sorry? What's the use of being fucking sorry? Do you realize you might have undone everything we achieved last night? I could discipline you for this, Liddell.'

The young man paled. 'Don't put me on the horse, Captain. My mother would die of shame!'

'Actions have consequences, Liddell,' Catto snapped. 'Go home and think about that. I'll speak to you later in the week. Crichton, follow me. Where are we going?' he asked as they stepped into the entrance hall, stopping so abruptly the Sergeant barely managed to avoid crashing into him.

'Top floor, sir. To the operating theatre. Seemingly they're doing the dissection up there. Tae try tae keep it quiet, like.'

'That's the triumph of hope over experience if ever I heard it,' Catto growled, taking the wide central staircase two steps at a time. It did nothing for his temper when he found the doors to the operating theatre on the top floor closed but unlocked. If they were trying to keep this quiet why the fuck didn't they lock the fucking doors, for Christ's fucking sake?

The operating theatre was almost identical to the anatomical theatre in Surgeons' Hall. Jamie Buchan of Balnamoon stood in the well of it. On the marble slab in front of him, covered in an unbleached calico sheet, lay an unmistakeable shape. Could there be a hope in hell the dark stains on it were old and not new and he had arrived in time to stop this? Balnamoon looked up, startled by the interruption.

He had a female with him, a woman in a plain blue dress, a capacious white apron and matching linen cap. It couldn't be, could it? God Almighty, it was. What kind of an unnatural female was she that she chose to participate in such a hideous undertaking as this?

'I forbid this,' he said as he clattered down the steps between the tiers of seats, too heavily for the wound in his thigh to ignore it, even if he managed to. 'This body is not to be touched.'

Jamie Buchan had a scalpel in his right hand. Was he poised to cut or had he already done so? Catto was aware of feeling a trifle queasy. That was daft. He was a soldier. He'd encountered death many times, often violent, terrified and contorted death, the stench of it lingering in his nostrils for days and weeks, seeping into his very pores.

All was calm here. Yet in a different way there was something profoundly disquieting about this. A sense of intrusion. The dead person had no voice, no say in what was about to happen to his or her mortal remains.

'Did you hear me, Mr Buchan of Balnamoon? This procedure will stop now. Do I make myself clear?'

'What if Mr Buchan can help you ascertain the cause of death, Captain Catto?'

'I wasn't addressing you, Miss Rankeillor.'

'No,' she said after a tiny pause, 'but I was addressing you. In the hope perhaps of assisting you, sir.'

'Assisting me?' He swung round to look at her. 'How do you propose to accomplish that remarkable feat, madam?' *And why would you want to when I've given you every reason to hate my guts?* The answer wasn't hard to find. She wanted something from him, no doubt a reversal of his decision on dissections. The need to appear ambivalent or not, he wasn't prepared to let her win this one.

'As I said, Mr Catto,' she said quietly, 'possibly by helping you discover the cause of the subject's death.'

'There are no obvious signs of injury?' Catto turned away from her, directing the question at Balnamoon.

'No. The subject is young and appears healthy. A little undernourished, 'tis true, but otherwise healthy.'

'Healthy,' Catto repeated, unable to resist a sarcastic: 'Apart from being dead, that is. How did you think the *subject's* people are going to react when they find out that the body has been dissected?'

'I don't think we're going to find she had any family, Captain,' Balnamoon said. 'Your Sergeant Crichton recognized our cadaver. As did I.'

Catto wheeled round to Crichton, one eyebrow raised. The

Sergeant nodded. 'There'll no' be ony folk wanting to claim this one, Captain. I'm pretty sure o' that. Ah dinna hae a name for ye, I'm afraid, but ah kent the poor cratur by sight.'

'As I recall treating her. Although I'm afraid I cannot give you a name either.' Balnamoon glanced at Christian Rankeillor. 'We treat rather a lot of people in the Salivating Rooms. I could go through the ledgers but 'twould take some time and I might not be able to match the name to the face. She may not have given us her real name, anyway.'

'Salivating Rooms,' Catto repeated briskly. 'Suffered from the pox, then.' If Christian Rankeillor was prepared to assist at a dissection, she must surely be prepared to hear some plain speaking.

'Aye,' Balnamoon said. 'Undoubtedly contracted in the course of earning a living. Her purse contains six shillings, implying she had six—' Balnamoon coughed again. 'Six encounters on the day or evening of her death. Which I estimate as being sometime last night or in the early hours of this morning.'

Filing away the not-too-surprising information that Jamie Buchan knew how much a street prostitute cost and thinking how he himself had vastly overpaid the girl with whom he'd had an encounter last night, Catto posed another question. 'Isn't that mere supposition? A deduction as to how she might have earned her living?'

'I have already performed an examination of her vulva. It would appear to contain a fair amount of—' Once again Balnamoon glanced at Christian Rankeillor. 'It would appear that several gentlemen made love to her yesterday evening. But aiblins we should let you take a look for yourself,' he continued, sweeping back the sheet covering the body.

At which point Robert Catto saw that what was surely unnecessary delicacy in front of his master's daughter had made Jamie Buchan choose entirely the wrong words. No one had made love to this girl last night. Several had coupled with her, taking their pleasure and release with selfish and loveless unconcern for the person providing it. He had been one of them.

22

'Mr Catto? Are you all right?' Concerned – as she would be for anyone who had gone quite so pale quite so quickly as he had – Christian found herself laying a solicitous hand on the sleeve of his leather riding coat. She could well understand that walking in on a scene such as this might prove a shock even for the most hardened of men. His Sergeant was already backing away. 'Mr Catto, s-sir,' he stuttered. 'C-Captain … I've g-got to … I c-canna …'

Robert Catto waved him away. 'Wait for me outside, Crichton.'

'Aye, sir,' the Sergeant managed, and wasted no time in obeying the order.

Christian gestured towards a tall window in the corner of the operating theatre. 'Sir, if you would like to step over here, I shall open the casement and let you have some fresh air.'

Robert Catto looked at her, looked down at his arm, and pointedly took a step back. 'I am not in need of fresh air. I have seen worse sights than this in my time.'

Christian allowed her hand to slide off his arm. He lifted his head in a gesture directed towards the body, although she could not help but notice that he did not turn his eyes towards it. 'What I am in need of is an explanation as to why this procedure has gone ahead without my permission. Mr Buchan?'

'Don't blame Jamie! 'Twas I who persuaded him to do it!'

'Do you always let her answer for you, Mr Buchan?'

Despite that exasperated question, Christian couldn't stop herself from jumping in again. Carrying out a full examination and partial dissection of the body had seemed such a good idea a few short hours ago. Now it seemed like a very bad idea. Mr Fox might be some distance away, in an entirely different part of the hospital, but pursuer and quarry were still under the same roof. Her heart was pounding so hard she felt sure Robert Catto must be able to hear it.

She schooled her features into a calm mask. They were committed now, the dissection all but over. It had been a disappointment when an orderly had returned from the guard-house with the message that Captain Robert Catto was away for the day and nobody knew where. Then at one o'clock Archie Liddell had turned up to stand down the guard on the hospital. He had also offered a stumbling apology for the previous night's raid. Christian had taken immediate advantage, easily persuading him into giving his permission for the dissection to go ahead.

She walked across to a small writing desk and lifted the paper on which she'd been taking down the notes of his findings Jamie had been dictating to her. She willed Robert Catto to look at her and the sheet of paper she was holding up for his scrutiny. 'We had thought perhaps to help you in your investigations, Captain Catto.'

He didn't look at her, although he did respond, even if it was only with a terse: 'What investigations?'

'Surely, as the senior officer of the Town Guard, you will be investigating the circumstances of this poor young woman's death.'

'I do not think those circumstances need detain us long,' he said dismissively, glancing again at the body, leading Christian to the wry conclusion that looking at a cadaver was preferable to looking at her. Under the leather riding coat, she saw his shoulders rise in a shrug. 'Do you really think 'tis so unusual for a girl of this stamp to make such an end as this?'

'A girl of this stamp?' she repeated, her voice rising. Jamie was sending her one of his warning glances. She had privately resolved she would not let herself be riled by anything Robert Catto might say or do. Knocked off-balance by the events of the past twenty-four hours, she found she could not stop herself from responding.

'If you cannot find it within yourself to have compassion for a fellow human being whose life has been cut so cruelly short, may I ask if you are so sanguine as to the possibility of us having a murderer in our midst? Even if his victim is a girl *of this stamp*?' she finished, tossing his own words back to him.

'You're making quite an assumption there, Miss Rankeillor,' he said, and directed another question across the corpse at Jamie. 'Have you found any evidence to indicate she might have been done away with?'

Christian waved the sheet of notes. 'His observations are all in here. I can make a fair copy and have it delivered to you at the guard-house—'

She had his full attention now, all right. Wheeling round, he bunched his hands into fists at his waist and yelled his next words into her face. 'For pity's sake, woman, will you keep your mouth shut and let Mr Buchan of Balnamoon speak?'

Woman. It was nothing compared to what he had called her last night. It was insultingly dismissive all the same. That didn't mean she was going to cower in front of him. She gave him back glare for glare, looking deep into the stormy grey eyes. What she saw there brought her up short. Mr Robert Catto wasn't nearly so unmoved as he was pretending to be. Jamie coughed.

'My examination—' He coughed again. '—and partial dissection of the body has perhaps thrown up more questions than answers.'

'Why do you say that? Because the body is not marked in any way?'

In his waistcoat with his shirt sleeves rolled up to the elbows, Jamie folded his arms across his chest and inclined his auburn head first one way and then the other in the balancing gesture so characteristic of him. 'To say the body is not marked in any way is not strictly true. Her back is a little bruised. I would turn the body over and show you but perhaps I should stitch her up first. It could get a wee touch messy otherwise.' He appended a cheerful: 'Blood and guts tipping out all over the place, you know.'

Christian narrowed her eyes at him. As utterly at home with the dead as he was, she had never been able to decide if he went out of his way deliberately to disgust the unwary or if the gallows humour was a necessary release for himself and his own finer feelings.

Having regained some colour, Robert Catto had now paled again, although his voice remained cool and apparently unconcerned. 'I shall wait until you do so, Mr Buchan. Tell me now, if you please, what conclusions you draw from the bruising on her back?'

'I would hazard a guess that it might be consistent with her profession. If you get my meaning, sir. Standing up while working.' This time the look he sent Christian was an embarrassed one. As frank as he was about death, he could be surprisingly coy about other subjects. 'Probably involving the somewhat unforgiving combination of a stone wall and … um … a forceful partner.'

'I get your meaning, Mr Buchan,' Robert Catto said drily. 'There is no need to elaborate further. I presume the lack of any other bruising precludes the possibility of an accident.'

'I would not wish to commit myself on that. Although 'tis true that the site of the body's discovery has yielded nothing to indicate an accident.'

'This site is close by the Infirmary?'

'On the north side of the building, halfway along one of the projecting wings. In front of the coal store, which projects out further again, forming a small corner a few yards up from the dispensary.'

'Describe this corner to me.'

'There is a single rowan tree and a row of some half-dozen whin bushes. She was lying there. Between the tree and the bushes.'

'Not hidden by them?'

'Only partially.'

'She could not have fallen from a window in the building? Or jumped from the roof? With the bushes breaking her fall?'

Listening to this rapid-fire exchange of questions and answers, Christian wondered if he was thinking about the poor woman who had jumped to her death from high above the Parliament Close. She knew the Town Guard had dealt with that and wondered now if Robert Catto had been directly involved. Was that one of the worse sights of which he had spoken? Or did he mean on the battlefields of Europe?

He had to be a soldier, a real one, not simply the Captain of a local militia. Everything about him – his bearing, his manner, his precision – indicated that as his profession. So they had brought him to Edinburgh because they already knew something was afoot and they needed a professional soldier to help deal with it?

She wondered how much this unsettling man really did know. Those eyes seemed to see everything while giving little away about what was going on behind them. What if he could see inside her head, know where she had been this morning, see the long, unused corridor and the fugitive concealed there?

'If she had fallen,' Jamie was saying, 'or jumped, I do not think she could have avoided sustaining some cuts and scratches from the thorns and twigs of the bushes.'

'On her face or hands or feet, you mean?'

'Aye. More than likely through her clothes as well. Miss Rankeillor has already examined those and found no rips or tears. If you will step forward and inspect the body at closer quarters you will observe for yourself the lack of cuts and scratches on the subject.'

Was there a second's hesitation before he responded to Jamie's request to move closer to the body? Christian was sure of it, even more so when after inspecting the hands and feet, Jamie had to say, 'the face, too' before Robert Catto turned his attention to it. He did gaze on it for a few unflinching seconds. Straightening up, he took a step back, then another one.

'How was the body discovered? And by whom?'

'Miss Rankeillor and I spotted something out of the window when we were conversing this morning. A flash of colour which turned out to be the girl's plaid.'

'Where were the two of you doing this conversing?'

'In the dispensary. At the front of the north wing.'

'Was anyone else there with the two of you?'

Jamie shook his head. Ridiculously, Christian felt herself blush. There was nothing wrong with Jamie and her having been alone together in the dispensary. 'Twas a common enough occurrence. Although she never went out of her way to mention it to Betty.

'The girl could not have crawled in under these bushes by herself? Perhaps died of the cold during the night?'

That explanation had occurred to Christian too. Poor girl if that were true. Poor girl whatever the circumstances of her demise.

'It's a possibility,' Jamie allowed. 'There was a hard frost last night.'

'But she had those six shillings in her purse,' Christian put in, judging she might now be able to speak without having her head bitten off. 'Even if she had no permanent lodgings, she had more than enough to secure a bed for the night somewhere. Why would she choose to be outside in the dark and the cold?'

'She might have been round the side of the Infirmary in the course of her business, Kirsty.' Jamie shot her another embarrassed glance.

'And stayed out there after the man had left? Why would she do that on such a cold night?'

Christian answered Robert Catto's question with one of her own. 'Because he had rendered her incapable of leaving?'

He looked at her and raised one hand to rub the back of his neck, under his tied-back hair, which was neat but not so neat as the night before. 'That's another possibility, I suppose. By administering some form of poison perhaps.'

Jamie demurred. 'Poison tends to be a weapon of the rich, not the poor.'

'Why do you assume her assailant – if such a person exists – was poor? That might not necessarily be the case.'

'It seems a fair enough conclusion to draw. Why would a man of any status have anything to do with a street girl? Bit squalid, don't you think?'

Robert Catto didn't answer Jamie's question. He put another of his own. 'Asphyxiation then? Using her plaid perhaps?'

'Think that through, Captain Catto. How would you react if someone were trying to asphyxiate you?'

'I'd fight them off, of course. I imagine a woman would kick and scratch– Ah,' he said, tapping one long finger against his mouth, 'I see what you mean. Such a struggle would show up on her hands and feet?'

Jamie nodded. 'Defensive wounds. As we have all already observed, she has no such marks. Such a struggle might also, of course, show up in her facial expression, but she looks so calm. Quite child-like and innocent,' he added softly, gazing down at the girl. 'As though she had slept peacefully away.'

He put one hand out and smoothed the girl's hair back from her brow. He might occasionally make ill-considered jests about the bodies with which he dealt but he was not nearly so hard-hearted as he would have you believe. He lifted his hand from the girl's hair and looked up again. 'Which might well be the case. Especially when you consider how much gin she had imbibed.' He made a beckoning gesture. 'Once more if you can stand it. Over the stomach this time. The smell has dissipated somewhat but you can still get a fair whiff of it.'

'Gin,' Robert Catto agreed a few seconds later, looking decidedly queasy. 'Would the consumption of a considerable amount of alcohol not have protected her from the cold?'

'A popular misconception. In reality, alcohol drains heat from the body.'

'So,' came the response, clearly being thought out as he went along, 'she might have got drunk, lost her way home, fallen asleep in the lee of the hospital and at some time during the night have died of the cold?'

'I think we have to consider that as a possibility.'

Christian was gazing at the girl's face. Jamie was right. She did look peaceful and innocent, which was ironic when you considered what her profession had been. How awful that a young girl should have led such a squalid life and come to such a sad and lonely end.

Her fingers ached to draw that still face. She could hardly do so while the Town Guard Captain was here. Glancing at him as he watched Jamie sew up the long incision between the girl's small breasts, she noticed that he was standing in an apparently casual pose. His right leg a little extended, he had raised the toe of his buckled black shoe as though he were about to start tapping it.

Something made Christian look at his hands. Under the ruffle of his shirt cuff, he was gripping his left wrist so tightly with his right hand that the fingers beneath it had turned white. She was right, then. Captain Robert Catto was not nearly so unmoved as he was pretending to be.

'There's really no need for you to see me off the premises, madam.' As they walked together down the wide staircase he shot her a look as sharp as broken glass. 'I believe I can manage to find my own way out.'

'I'm sure you can, sir, but we always like to escort our guests to the door.'

'We?'

'Those of us who are involved with the Infirmary think of ourselves as a family.'

'Indeed? How very fascinating.' They had reached the entrance hall. It was austere in decoration but grand in scale. His eyes went in turn to two inscriptions carved on stone tablets fixed to the walls. Christian knew them off by heart.

I was a stranger and ye took Me in.

I was sick and ye visited Me.

'Good afternoon, Miss Rankeillor,' the Town Guard Captain said, his eyes on the Biblical texts. 'I shall arrange for the body to be fetched tomorrow morning for burial.'

'Mr Catto,' she said. 'Captain. May I ask you to step into the dispensary for a moment? It's along this corridor here.'

He followed her pointing finger before swinging back round to look at her. 'Why would I do that?'

'I had thought to offer you some refreshment. A glass of wine and a biscuit, perhaps. We keep a supply of both commodities on hand. Sometimes they can be as effective as physic.'

He was staring at her as though she were a halfwit. 'A glass of wine and a biscuit,' he repeated. 'Why the Devil would you offer me a glass of wine and a biscuit, Miss Rankeillor?'

She flushed. He was making her offer of refreshment sound ridiculous. 'Because I fear Mr Buchan and I have subjected you to a rather unpleasant experience.'

'As I told you, Miss Rankeillor, I have seen worse. Much, much worse.' He looked her up and down in a way which told her that by whatever scale he was measuring her, she was being tried and found wanting. 'Horrors of which a privileged and protected young lady such as yourself could not possibly conceive. Good afternoon, Miss Rankeillor,' he said again.

A privileged and protected young lady. The words stung. As he had intended them to. Even if he did not and could not know what she was coping with at the moment – right under his very nose – he had seen her assist at a dissection. Did a privileged and protected young lady do that? Had he really no idea that by inviting him to step into the dispensary she was risking even more gossip than was probably already circulating about her?

She watched him as he walked out under the Infirmary's portico. Waiting for him in the darkening quadrangle, his Sergeant straightened up and looked expectantly towards him. In another few seconds he would be gone. She walked out after him. 'Please wait a moment. There is something I must ask you.'

'Really?' He sounded bored. 'Then pray ask it with all possible dispatch. I am a very busy man and I must be on my way.'

She gazed up at him as the two of them stood under the portico lamp, lit and flickering as day gave way to evening. Those cool grey eyes, guarded now, were giving her no encouragement. 'Will you please reconsider your decision to impose yet more restrictions on dissections?'

'Why would I do that?'

'Because it is so very important for the students to be able to study the human body.'

'Is a dissection ever anything more than a gory spectacle?'

'Oh, yes,' she said earnestly. 'So very much more. Have you never attended a public dissection, sir? One is held each year in Edinburgh. 'Tis hoped to have the next one in January. I am sure you would find it most educational and illuminating.'

'Educational?' The grey gaze slid past her. He seemed to be studying something he couldn't possibly see, something which lay in the shadows beyond his Sergeant. Snow was beginning to swirl around the quadrangle, tiny white dots too light to fall straight to the ground. 'I once attended such a demonstration in Paris. The *beau monde* was in attendance. Treating the whole thing as they might have done a comic play. Laughing and flirting while something which had once been a human being like them was hacked to pieces before their eyes.'

Christian winced. 'I have heard of such barbarities. I am thankful I have never been present at one. I think you must agree that Mr Buchan's approach is quite different. He may jest about it but he has respect for the deceased. As does my father. As do all of Edinburgh's anatomists.' She crossed the fingers of one hand behind her back as she said that. The anatomists were respectful, their students not always so.

'It still seems like the final indignity for that girl lying up there in the operating theatre. To be violated in death as she must so often have been violated in life.' He sent Christian a swift glance, as though afraid he might have given something away. As indeed he had. Convinced he had betrayed his true feelings, she spoke again.

'But by examining her body we have found out things about her. Was it not of use to you to find out how she may have died?'

'It doesn't make her any less dead. She was a whore, Miss Rankeillor. Nobody cares anyway. Nobody cared when she was alive and nobody cares now that she is dead.'

For the second time that afternoon, Christian found herself laying a hand on his arm. 'I care. And I think you do too.'

For a moment she was sure she could feel a softening in the strong arm under her fingers: until he snarled at her. 'How many whores do you think there are in Edinburgh, Miss Rankeillor? How many do you think lead squalid lives and meet with early and unfortunate ends? Do you care about all of them, too?'

She held his steely gaze. 'Do you yourself not find it unbearably sad that a girl of such tender years should lead such a squalid life and meet such an untimely and lonely death? Or that her family may never find out what became of her? That is something you might accomplish, sir. If you were to make some enquiries—'

He cut her off. 'I have enough to do as it is. In any case, such enquiries could lead nowhere without a likeness of the girl. What?' For Christian's fingers had tightened on the smooth leather of his sleeve.

'Nothing,' she said, and hastily removed her hand.

'Is there aught else, madam?' he demanded.

'It would seem not. Apart from the body being collected tomorrow morning.' She could not resist one final plea to his better self, always assuming he had one. 'To take it to Greyfriars where she will be buried in common ground before dawn tomorrow. With no marker or memorial to tell the world she ever lived at all. We do not even know her name.'

'Will any of us be remembered in a hundred years' time?' Harsh already, his voice grew harsher still. 'Will you remember her in one year's time? Or even one month's time? Will you talk about her as you take tea with your friends or pull a string along the floor for your cat to chase? Will you give her even a passing thought as you continue with your safe and comfortable life?'

'My safe and comfortable life?' she flashed back. '*My safe and comfortable life?* You know nothing at all about my life, sir. You know nothing at all about me. Och,' she said, losing the precarious hold she had on her temper, 'I give up on you! You're impossible!'

He glared down at her from her under the flickering light of the portico's lamp. '*I'm* impossible?' he yelled. 'That's the pot calling the kettle black if ever I heard it!'

'Don't shout at me! Don't you dare shout at me!' she yelled back and, to her utter horror, felt her eyes fill up with tears.

23

She had whirled round, turning her back on him. Now she wrapped her arms about herself and bowed her head, presenting him with a view of the nape of her neck under the white linen cap into which all her hair was tucked. Only one tendril of those mahogany locks had escaped its starched clutches.

Tears. The deadliest and most unfair of weapons. The hardest for a man to withstand.

He didn't doubt she was genuinely distressed, as much by what she had learned last night as by the death of the girl. Add one to the other and it was only to be expected that she would be upset. Good. That was what he wanted, wasn't it? He had invaded her life yesterday precisely for that reason, to make her and her father and Jamie Buchan of Balnamoon and every other misguided fool of a Jacobite face up to reality. 'Twas not his fault if that reality had turned her world upside down.

Yet, as he studied the back of her head and her trembling shoulders, Robert Catto found himself seized by an impulse which threatened to overwhelm him. He wanted to step forward, smooth that stray curl to one side and press his lips to the creamy skin beneath it. He wanted to put his hands on her shoulders and stroke the side of her neck with his thumbs. He wanted to give her an encouraging little shake.

Because he wanted to do that so very, very much, he put ice into his voice, punishing them both for his weakness. God in Heaven, he had known her for less than a day. Her feelings were not his responsibility. He could not care how she felt!

'Must be hard for you to find a man who's impervious to your feminine charms, Miss Rankeillor.'

That brought her spinning back round to face him, dried her tears too. 'There you go again! Making assumptions about me! How dare you, Mr Robert Catto? Just who do you think you are to sit in judgement upon me?'

'Oh, so we've dropped the Captain, have we? Now you no longer want something from me? Good afternoon for the third and last time, Miss Rankeillor. I'd like to say I hope we won't meet again. I fear, however, that it's more or less inevitable. And my decision about dissections stands.'

She hurried back up the main staircase of the hospital before her courage could desert her. Jamie would probably shoot the messenger too, which was no more than she deserved. As she pushed open one half of the double doors of the operating theatre, Christian was miserably aware that she had made matters worse, not better.

Looking down into the well of the room, her fingers curved round the edge of the door, she saw that the only occupant was the dead girl, her slight form covered by a white sheet. So still. So gone from this world. Yet sometimes it was unsettling when you couldn't see the faces of the dead. Had you imagining all sorts of things. That they would suddenly sit up, throw off the sheet, swing their legs over the side of their temporary bier and come walking towards you …

Like Robert Catto walking towards her in her dream, his sword drawn, a soldier of an advancing army. If the plotting swirling around them now spilled over into warfare, there would be hundreds of soldiers walking forward with swords drawn and muskets raised. Blood would indeed be shed. If there were a battle for Edinburgh, the bodies of the fallen might well be carried here to the Royal Infirmary.

For a moment her vivid imagination presented her with an operating theatre filled with those bodies. Still as the girl down there and as gone from this world. Covered in sheets which would become their shrouds. Young and vital men one day and corpses the next. Sacrifices to the cause of Scotland's freedom. Would that be any consolation to their mothers, wives and daughters?

She took a step back, onto the landing. Her palm had grown moist. It slid off the door. She grabbed for its brass handle but missed. The door banged shut, the noise reverberating up and down the broad staircase. A porter on the floor below looked up in alarm. 'Miss Kirsty? Is everything all right?'

'I let the door go by mistake,' she called down, stepping closer to the banister and giving him a smile and wave of reassurance. He returned both and went on his way. She was doing a grand job of not drawing attention to herself.

She found Jamie in the female surgical ward, taking the pulse of a middle-aged woman who'd been admitted to have the stone removed the week before. He looked up and saw her and she mouthed, 'When you're finished.'

He threw her a long-suffering look before his attention returned to his patient. Of course it would be when he had finished. The patient always came first. This woman had been a nervous one and still was, even after a successful operation. As she hung back and watched, Christian saw her begin to relax under Jamie's gentle examination. He was good at that, judging the right approach to take with different patients. Some needed to cover their own fears with bluff jests and enjoyed it when the doctor responded in the same way. Others, like this woman, needed a soft voice and a soft touch.

'Come out onto the landing,' he murmured a few moments later. When they got there, she told him in a low voice what had transpired between her and Robert Catto. Maybe not exactly everything, but enough for Jamie's expression to stiffen. 'So you have antagonized him further?'

'I didn't mean to,' she said painfully. 'It just sort of happened.'

There was no softness in his brown eyes now. 'Just sort of happened? This isn't a game, Kirsty. We cannot allow things to *just sort of happen.*'

She flushed. 'I'm sorry, Jamie.'

'Kindly prove that by not meddling any further, Kirsty. Kindly do not approach Captain Catto again either. Over the matter of dissections or anything else. The two of you clearly strike sparks off each other. I shall deal with the matter of how we are to move our friend on to his next destination. So leave this alone now. Do what you have been asked to do and no more. Don't say anything to Anna Gordon either. If I find that I need her help I shall speak to her myself.' Turning on his heel, he strode back through to the ward.

'Captain? Are you all right, sir?'

'I'm fine,' Catto said, coming only then to a realization of where he was. Geordie was at his elbow, looking up at him out of anxious eyes.

'You're gey pale, sir.'

'I'm fine,' Catto said again, sinking down into a chair. He glanced across at the door. His leather coat was hanging on the back of it. He had no recollection of taking it off. As he had no recollection of his walk back from the hospital.

'Was it nasty, sir?'

'Was what nasty?'

'The body, Captain. Is that no' where you've been – attending to the body found at the Infirmary?'

'That's no business of yours. Go and attend to what is.'

The boy looked at him. Then he turned and went over to the cooking range. Catto spoke to his stiff back. 'What's for supper?'

'I tellt ye that this morning, sir. Beef and pancakes. There's some soup to start.'

'I don't want any soup.' He was back in the operating theatre, listening as Balnamoon enumerated the contents of the girl's stomach, indicating the half-digested oysters with a wooden pointer he must keep for that purpose, more or less stirring the stinking mess around … Oh God, no, he didn't want any soup.

'It's real good soup, Captain. I made it the way you like it. So you can stand your spoon up in it.'

'For Christ's sake, Geordie,' Catto roared. 'Take a telling! I don't want any fucking soup!'

She did not believe in ghosts. She had no real fear of the dead. As long as she could see their faces. 'Twas true that even then her imagination sometimes ran away with her, had her fancy she saw a tiny movement in the cadaver she was drawing. Her breath would come faster and she would have to force herself to keep looking until she was absolutely sure the body was still. She had no doubt this girl was dead. She had flipped back the sheet and been gazing at her face for some time now. Yet she kept thinking she was going to open her eyes, look up at her, and speak.

The eyes in the white and lifeless face had been closed when they found her. Only the hair still looked alive, a thick and glossy brown. She had been a bonnie girl – one condemned to a life of squalor beyond imagining. Christian had read of courtezans past and present who traded their bodies and their favours for comfort and riches. The bargains this girl had struck had been nothing like that. You could tell that from her threadbare clothes and her bare and dirty feet. Whatever she had earned by allowing men to make free of her body had not been very much.

Seized by the sadness of it, Christian fell to wondering how she had looked in life. Had she smiled and laughed and told funny stories? Had she had friends or family or a sweetheart? She supposed prostitutes did have sweethearts. Were there people grieving for this girl right now, not knowing what had become of her?

No one had come to the hospital today looking for her. Although maybe that would not be your first thought if someone did not come home one night. Perhaps you might think they had run off somewhere. In any case, the burial would not be delayed. Other than those few shillings in her purse, she was a pauper of no known abode and her body would be disposed of as soon as possible. By this time tomorrow she would be under the ground. If a relative did turn up today, tomorrow or next month, they would be asked to pay the costs and directed to the grave.

Christian raised her shoulders in a sigh of sadness and resignation. There was no point in dwelling on this. She could do nothing more for this girl. She could not even attend her funeral. She might have been able to persuade Betty to come with her – the housekeeper certainly wouldn't let her go wandering through Edinburgh on her own before dawn – if she hadn't other things to do before daybreak tomorrow. She spared a thought for Mr Fox, alone in his chilly cell. Alone and at bay ... and as deadly as a cornered animal. The thought made her shiver.

She had a warm home to go to and a fire she could sit by to lift the chill from her spirits and her bones and she should turn now, leave the operating theatre and go there. She wasn't sure why she had come back up here anyway, except that she had been so upset by Jamie's anger and her own stupidity she hadn't quite known what she was doing.

On Saturday night Jamie had said they mustn't give Robert Catto the slightest piece of information he might piece together with whatever else he knew. *No drawing attention to your skills of draughtsmanship.* So for more than one reason what she was contemplating doing now made absolutely no sense. Yet her hand went to her waist. Pulling a sketch pad and charcoal out of one of the pockets concealed beneath her apron and gown, she began to draw.

24

He had Christian Rankeillor up against the back wall of the anatomical theatre in Surgeons' Hall, and she was begging him for more. 'Harder,' she moaned into his ear. 'H-a-r-d-e-r ...'

'Not yet,' he murmured in return, taking his hand from between her legs. 'You're enjoying this far too much. We can't have that.' Dipping his head, he smothered her protest at the removal of his busy fingers with a long, deep kiss. Then he took her bottom lip between his teeth and bit into it. There should be blood between them. He would let her do the same to him.

He was in his full uniform, still wearing his sword. She was naked. Something about the sheer bloody inequality of that felt so damn good. He was aware of the contrast between the rich red of his uniform and the pale cream of her skin, aware too that the leather of his sword-belt was pressing against the soft roundness of her breasts, squashing them.

The thick edge of the belt caught one nipple and she let out a yelp of pain followed by a moan of pleasure. Pain and pleasure. Funny how the two could be so closely intertwined. Funny how arousing the combination was. He buried one hand deep in the mahogany curls of her hair and drew the other down her body, rubbing his thumb over the wounded nipple, following that deliberately rough caress with a kiss to make it better. Pain and pleasure. Pleasure and pain.

His travelling hand journeyed lower. Tracing the warm curve of her hips, he danced his fingers across her belly and down. Curls here too. His fingers slid through them. She was wet. So very, very wet. He drew the smell of her into his nostrils, lifting his head for a moment to savour that before he went any further. What he saw gave him a jolt. Geordie was walking towards them out of the shadows of the anatomical theatre, emerging like a genie rising through the tiers of wooden seats.

'Bugger off, Geordie,' Catto said roughly. 'This is no place for you.'

The boy's face was white and shocked. 'Ye canna do this, sir. It's no' right.'

'I'll be the judge of that.' Confound it, why did the child have to possess such expressive eyes?

'Don't stop,' she moaned into his ear. 'Keep moving your hand. Harder. Faster.' Catto turned away from Geordie and did as she asked. So very, very wet. Sticky, too. He brought his hand up, placed it between his face and hers. A metallic smell. Why was he smelling something metallic? All the sconces were lit. He could see her and he could see his hand, held stiffly inches from his face. He recoiled at the sight.

'Look at my fingers,' he gasped. 'They're covered in blood!'

'That's what I meant, sir,' cried Geordie. 'Look at her! Look at her properly!'

He did as he was bid. She giggled, and was all at once no longer Christian Rankeillor. 'Well,' she said, 'what d'ye expect, mannie? I am deid, you know. Cut open into the bargain. I'm no' going tae be a very pretty sight, am I now?'

He studied her face. He studied his hand. Blood was dripping down it, staining his white shirt cuff deepest crimson.

'I'm in a much worse state than you,' the trollop said cheerfully. 'Look!'

He lowered his eyes to her stomach. 'Blood and guts spilling out a' ower the floor,' came the cheerful voice again. 'But that'll no bother you, eh? You've seen much worse than this.'

Still smiling at him, she plunged her hands into her open stomach.

'Much worse than this,' she repeated, and brought her full and bloody hands up in front of his face.

Blood and guts. Glistening intestines. The stinking reek of gin and half-digested oysters.

He came awake in the space between one second and the next, pulling himself up to consciousness with every ounce of energy he possessed, snapping up to a sitting position in one rapid movement. For a few moments the only sound in the room was his own rapid breathing. A bad dream. A nightmare. That's all. He kept saying those words inside his head and gradually his heart stopped hammering, his breathing slowed and the nausea wore off. Threading his hands through his hair, he gazed out at the shadows of the room and beyond those to the ill-fitting shutters. They were completely dark. Dawn had not yet broken.

'Captain? Is it no' early yet, sir?'

'Aye,' Catto said into the gloom of the kitchen. 'No need for you to get up yet, Geordie.' Having pulled on the clothes he had discarded last night before he left his bedchamber, he was shrugging his shoulders into his coat. 'I'm going out for a wee while. To … eh … check on something.'

The boy sat up, his slight frame barely distinguishable against the shadowy recess of the box bed. 'Before it's even light, Captain Catto, sir?'

'Aye, lad. I'll be back for breakfast. Expect me within the hour.'

'Captain,' murmured the sleepy sentry as Catto slipped past him. 'You're not requiring an escort, sir?'

Catto shook his head and walked off in the direction of Greyfriars Kirk. It lay no distance from the High Street, although far enough on a morning as cold as this one. He took the full brunt of a vicious shower of hailstones before he reached the tall double gates of the cemetery. Trying an experimental push, he winced as his bare fingers touched frost-coated wrought-iron.

The gate was unlocked. He pushed it open, kicked it shut and walked on up into the graveyard. He already knew his way around this place. Inclement weather or not, early though it was, the town outside the big black-painted gates had been stirring. Once you came in here you left the land of the living behind. The feeling of being in the waiting-room of the next world was strong.

Although, unless he was starting to see – or rather, hear – ghosts, there were other living souls within the still forest of headstones. He could discern the rhythmical sound of a spade slicing through earth. That had to be a hard job on a frosty December morning. He followed his ears and soon saw the flickering light of a lantern in the common ground away in the far corner.

His route led him past some grand memorials engraved with the skull and crossbones, coffins and hourglasses. He remembered those from the kirkyard near his grandfather's house. They were the *memento mori*, the reminders to the living that they too would die some day. One day you'll be nothing but bones, rotting away in your coffin, the sands of time run out. *Your time will come.* Cheerful place, Scotland. Inhabited by people inclined to wild revelry on the one hand and deepest, darkest melancholia on the other. Two sides of the same coin. He was one to talk.

His eyes adjusted now to the gloom, Catto made out two human forms. One was extending a hand to the other, helping him out of the grave. On one side of it stood a mound of earth, on the other the coffin. The lantern flickered on top of the box. As he approached, he saw that it was pretty roughly-hewn. As little money as possible was spent on a pauper's grave.

'Minister not here yet?' he asked in a low voice. There were houses which backed onto the graveyard, the ones which straggled down the brae of Candlemakers' Row. Despite the discreet way in which events like this were conducted, he supposed the people who lived there must often be aware of these pre-dawn burials, had learned how to turn a blind eye. 'Twas a useful skill to have if you lived in a city so overcrowded as Edinburgh.

One of the men spat into the mound of earth at the side of the grave. 'Been and gone, Captain. Said it was too cold to bide. Gabbled a prayer over the coffin, gave us sixpence for something to warm us up once we're finished here and took himself off.'

Catto raised his eyebrows and inclined his head towards the coffin. 'Did he know who she was?' *Or what she was?* He stopped himself from asking the second question. 'Twas no business of the gravediggers what she had been.

'He had no idea it was even a female, Captain,' said the same gravedigger who had spoken before. Gravediggers were like that, he had found. There was always one who was the spokesman and one who kept his own counsel. 'Neither did we. Although we had guessed. Too long a box for a child but no weight in it at all. Why, you could lift her into the grave on your own, sir.'

'I'll leave that to you.' He moved to take up a position at the foot of the grave and stood and watched the coffin being lowered into the earth. The gravediggers knew their business. Each man had the two ends of each rope wrapped around the fingers of each hand and the descent was slow and measured.

'That's her,' said the spokesman and the two of them pulled the ropes up and out. 'Will you do the honours, sir?'

'What?' Staring down into the grave, Catto was lost in thought.

'The earth, sir. Someone maun throw in the first bittie o' earth, sir. Will it be you?'

He raised his head. 'Aye. I'll do it.' Bending forward, he scooped up a handful from the mound at the side of the grave.

'Will you say a puckle o' words too, sir?'

'Me?' he responded, taken aback. He shook his head. 'I'm not qualified to do that.'

Lit from beneath by the lantern which now stood at the head of the grave, the man kept looking at him. 'It's no' right that ony Christian soul should be planted in the earth without someone saying a few words ower them.'

'I thought the minister said a prayer.'

'Aye. And then buggered off.' The gravedigger spat again before lifting his chin to indicate the occupant of the grave. 'Were ye acquent wi' the leddy in life, sir?'

The lady. Nobody would ever have called her that in life. Not that she'd been much more than a girl anyway. 'Yes,' he heard himself say, 'I knew the lady.'

There was a double meaning in that answer. The gravediggers showed no sign of having caught it. 'A few words, then, sir,' the spokesman said. 'Only a few bitties o' words.'

He was being coaxed into doing it. A gravedigger was coaxing him into doing the right thing. Only a few words. He had witnessed enough burials in the field for some of those words to come back to him. Since he served with an English regiment, he realized the ones he knew must come from the English rite. Was the Scottish one different? He didn't know.

'*Man that is born of woman hath but a short time to live. He cometh up and is cutteth down like a flower.*' He wasn't sure what came after that and settled for: '*Therefore we commit the body of our sister to the ground.*' Our sister! How hideously inappropriate for him to call the girl that.

'The earth, sir?'

He tossed it in, hearing it hit the wooden boards of the coffin lid and scatter over it. Such an awful sound. Such a final sound.

'Earth to earth, ashes to ashes, dust to dust. Amen,' he said perfunctorily. 'Fill it in.'

He waited till the coffin was fully covered, gave the gravediggers a florin each, asked them to keep an eye on the grave for the next week or so and took his leave of them, walking quickly along the cemetery paths to the gates. Once he was on the other side of those, he lifted his chin, stretched his neck and took a long, deep breath. The black sky above his head was streaked with narrow fingers of grey. Dawn wasn't far off.

He would go back to the guard-house, wash, change into his uniform, eat his breakfast and get on with his day and this crucially important week. What he had told Christian Rankeillor yesterday afternoon was nothing but the truth. He had enough to do without investigating the deaths of prostitutes. Especially one who had more than likely died of the cold and who hadn't helped herself to survive by consuming copious amounts of gin beforehand.

Yet when he left the kirkyard gates he found himself heading east instead of north.

25

She had thought the swelling of Mr Fox's ankle bad enough yesterday. Today it had ballooned. He looked up at her from where he sat on the edge of the bunk.

'Not good, lass. Eh?'

'Not good,' she agreed, seeing no point in dissembling. 'Let me reposition these two pillows under your foot.' She glanced at the chamber pot tucked in at the foot of the bed. It was empty. Her eyes travelled from it to him. Seen through the window set high up in the wall the sky was growing lighter. She could see him rather more clearly this morning.

'I did not want to leave it to you, lass.'

'Sir, you must leave it to me. Did you walk to the necessary house?'

'Hobbled would be more apt description.'

'Oh, sir, that must have been prodigious painful!'

'Indeed it was,' he said cheerfully. 'I had to relieve my feelings by muttering curses in a heinous mixture of Gaelic, French and English. Fortunately I found a sweeping brush when I got there which served me as a crutch for the journey back.' He lifted his chin to indicate where he had propped the brush in the corner behind his bed. 'I may start speaking to it soon. For the company. Ach now,' he chided gently. 'That smile's a wee bittie wan. I fear I am causing you sleepless nights, lass.'

'Sir,' she said again, shrugging that comment off, 'you must leave it to me to do this. We have to get the swelling down. If we are to get you out of here as soon as possible you must keep your leg raised and put weight on it only when you absolutely have to. You must also drink the ale and the water I have brought you and use that as frequently as required.' Fighting a blush, she indicated the chamber pot. 'I think the swelling needs some physic too, Mr Fox.' She indicated the medicine bottle she had set on the small table beside the bed. 'Tincture of dandelion, three drops to be taken in water three times a day. It will also encourage you to ...eh ...'

He held up a hand. 'I understand, lass, and I shall follow my very kind doctoress's orders so I may move easily again and relieve you of this burden I am to all concerned.'

'Sir, I do not mean to be inhospitable-'

'But you are worried,' he said softly, 'as well you might be.'

She sat down on the narrow wooden bench fixed along one side of the cell, too scared to be able to pretend otherwise. 'I fear they may search the hospital.'

'And if they find me you fear the repercussions for those you hold dear.'

'Aye,' she said, looking at him. 'Exactly that. Although for other reasons too. There are people you must speak to in the north, are there not, someone in Edinburgh too before you leave us?'

He nodded. 'A gentleman of great wealth and influence. A member of your local gentry. You are quite right, lass. All of this must be sooner rather than later. How are we to help me on my way? I must confess I find myself vastly interested in the subject.' He pulled a comical face, drawing a wry laugh from Christian.

'Indeed sir, I wonder that you did not ask me yesterday.'

'Preoccupied with other things. Although my departure from here is now at the forefront of my mind. You know what the plan is?'

'Parts of it are by way of being my plan. Unfortunately I think those parts resemble a colander.'

'Full of holes? Then let us talk it over and see how we might stop those up.'

Do what you have been asked to do, Kirsty. No more! Yet she had to discuss this with Mr Fox. She was the go-between. Jamie could not run the risk of coming here till it was time to move their guest. Maybe not even then. Mr Fox listened attentively as she spoke, without naming Anna, of how a pass might be obtained, and of how they might take advantage of the confusion of Daft Friday.

'So the main problem is me not being able to pass as a woman and not being able to walk easily by Friday. Which is not looking terribly likely at the moment. Nor am I in any fit state to scale a wall, or lower myself out of a high window. I'm probably also a good twenty years too old for such capers.' He laughed. 'I've seen the day but now it's night. So we have to get me through the gate and to the gate. A sedan chair?'

'In the hospital's sedan chair,' she confirmed, 'which we use to move patients going for treatments from one floor of the hospital to another.' That had been Jamie's suggestion. Hiring a chair would alert the town's caddies to a journey being made from the hospital to one of the city's gates. When she had asked who would carry their chair he had told her she could leave that to him.

'We cannot avail ourselves of the chair until the early evening. It is not supposed to leave the hospital and it would only be later in the day that its absence would go unremarked.'

Mr Fox tapped one long finger against his lips. 'The town gates close when?'

'Ten of the clock.'

'So somehow we must also fit in time for me to speak to this gentleman of Edinburgh and also work out where he and I shall have our conversation.'

'It cannot be here. We believe the hospital is still being watched. There is yet another problem. A man or woman on foot can merge into the crowd. People tend to notice sedan chairs.'

'Even on Daft Friday?'

'Especially on Daft Friday. We have this ball in aid of the Infirmary,' she explained. 'People are always keen to see those going to it and admire their finery.'

'I can understand that,' Mr Fox said. 'Especially when the finery is worn by a young lady as attractive as yourself.' He made her a gallant little bow, adding wistfully, 'I've been known to wear finery myself. Is it a masked ball?'

Christian nodded. 'Yes. We take our masks off at nine, before we go in to supper. Although I often think it is evening wigs and powdered hair that renders gentlemen not so recognizable even to their closest friends.'

'It all sounds very elegant.' He glanced down at his plain dark breeches and grubby shirt. 'Far removed from the poor showing I'm making of it at the moment, without even a change of linen to smarten myself up.' He glanced at his portmanteau.

'You have spare linen in there?'

'Yes, but in need of a laundress.'

'I could take some of it home with me,' she began doubtfully. 'Or bring you one of my father's shirts and other necessaries.'

'Too risky. How would you explain either away if your basket were searched? Tell me more about this problem with chairs on Daft Friday.'

'People don't only look into chairs on Daft Friday. They tend to peer into them.'

'That being the one night of the year when we can guarantee that everyone goes a bit, well, daft?'

'Some folk are daft every night of the year.'

'That's very true.'

He gave her the laugh she had earned and once again she was aware of the charm. Charming but ready to shoot a man dead if he had to.

'What if it were given out that I was suffering from some terrible ailment? Smallpox, perhaps. Going home to die. Surely people would be happy to see me leave the city, not come near me for fear of infection.'

'We considered that too, sir. Were we living two hundred years' since, you might have disguised yourselves by means of a plague mask, but the only way we can think of how you might keep people at bay is to have a medical escort who would keep warning them of your supposed condition. Here we hit another problem.' She and Jamie had discussed all of this, tossing ideas backwards and forwards. 'That escort could only be one man.'

'Our young medical friend?'

'Indeed, and he is expected at the Daft Friday ball. He has to be there, especially in the absence of my—' Once again she caught herself on. 'He has to be there, must see and be seen by many people. Especially when we unmask and sit down to supper at nine o'clock.'

'Not only for the sake of the hospital but for the sake of acting normally?'

'Yes, and this leads to a further problem.'

'We seem to be encountering a lot of those.'

'Indeed. The most logical gate by which you should leave the city, the nearest to the hospital and the bagnio, is either the Netherbow or the Cowgate Port. The former would be best for you to head down to Leith, where you might be concealed until you could be got aboard the ship before she sails on Monday morning. The ball is held at the Assembly Rooms, up near the castle. For your escort to leave there for long enough to collect you from the hospital, fighting his way through the crowds as he will have to, would be well-nigh impossible. His prolonged absence from the ball would be noticed too.' She frowned. 'You will have to be someone, Mr Fox. We shall have to give you a name and a place of residence, far enough away not to be able to be easily checked or denied. May I ask you something? Are there people in Edinburgh who would recognize you if they saw you?'

He looked up towards the small high window of the cell in which they sat. 'One in particular.'

'A significant person?'

'So it would seem.'

Would you shoot him dead too?

As the question formed in Christian's head, Mr Fox brought his gaze back to her. 'But perhaps he might not recognize me if I was wearing a suit of fine clothes, an evening wig and an eye mask. Tell me, do all the gentry of Edinburgh attend the ball on Friday?'

Her mouth fell open. 'You are proposing to come as a guest to the Daft Friday ball?'

She had stayed too long with Mr Fox. It was broad daylight now and here she was, hurrying towards the main entrance hall of the hospital from entirely the wrong direction, coming from the inside rather than the outside of the building. With some idea of disguising that, she flipped the hood of her cloak up over her head. Oh, no. Had she done so before the Infirmary's housekeeper had stepped into the doorway of her room off the entrance hall?

At the south-west corner of the building. A rowan tree and half-a-dozen whin bushes. Where Catto stood had to be where the girl had breathed her last. What he hoped to achieve by visiting the spot he did not know. Although something had occurred to him on the way here. She didn't appear to have used his money to buy those copious amounts of gin, nor that of any of the other men who'd rented her body on the last night of her life. He had seen her purse, its contents emptied onto a table in the operating theatre. His florin and four shilling pieces. There had been no small change. So someone else must have paid for the gin.

Why did a man ply a woman with alcohol? The obvious reason didn't make sense here. The girl had been a whore. All she asked in return for sex was money. If a man had bought her the gin, 'twas not that he did not have money or wanted to take his pleasure without paying for it. He had wanted her not in command of her wits. In order to kill her with as little resistance as possible, smother her with no defensive wounds, disguising murder as death from the cold?

The day was hovering on the cusp between darkness and light and Catto had endured another hailstorm on his way here, forcing him to lower his head against the onslaught. It had stopped now, thank God, although his hands were raw and stiff from the bombardment. He held them up in front of his face. There still wasn't enough light to see them properly but he knew they would be red. His hands would be red-raw. Or as red as blood.

He gave himself a shake. Why was he mooning about here? He didn't have time to investigate the girl's death. No one was asking him to, anyway. Except Christian Rankeillor. Except maybe his own conscience. Visiting the site where the girl's body had been found when there wasn't enough light to see properly was however serving no useful purpose. He was lowering his hands and turning to go when something caught his eye.

It was lying at the foot of the rowan tree, a blur of white or maybe blue. 'Twas hard to tell in this light. He was walking forward to take a closer look when instinct kicked in, a split second too late. Spinning round, one arm raised in instinctive defence, the sole of one buckled shoe lost purchase on the slippery pile of dead leaves under the tree, making his turn awkward and slow. Too late to see his attacker, he took the blow to his left temple.

Another shower of hailstones restored him to the world, aware in a quite detached way that he was lying on his back on cold hard ground and that there was something amiss with his head. 'Twas not sore exactly … but there was definitely something wrong. When he raised a hand to it his fingers came away covered in blood.

'Not sore yet, then,' he muttered, knowing from past experience it wouldn't be too long until it was, as soon as the initial shock wore off. His hair was already plastered to his scalp by the hailstones when Mother Nature gathered up her skirts and redoubled the ferocity of her attack.

Scrambling to his feet to try to escape the deluge, Catto found himself staggering. Lurching towards the slender support afforded by the trunk of the rowan tree, he flung his left arm around it like a shipwrecked mariner clinging onto a spar. He gave himself a moment before raising his free hand once more to the wound. From the feel of it he suspected he might need a stitch or two. Logically, this meant his next step should be to make his way into the Infirmary. He would do that directly. Once he was sure he wasn't going to fall over the moment he relinquished his grip on the rowan tree.

There had been something lying at its foot. It wasn't there now. Leastways, he didn't think so. Adjusting the angle of his head to peer down to look for it brought on a hideous attack of dizziness. He waited for that to pass, took a breath and let go of the tree. Good. He was still standing.

Walking with slow deliberation, he set off towards the corner of the building, rounded it and headed for the front door of the Infirmary. He was sweating by the time he got there, expending vast amounts of energy in keeping the dizziness at bay. He walked under the portico and into the hall. Two women were standing there, talking to each other.

Now he knew for certain the fates had it in for him. One of the women was Christian Rankeillor.

26

She was lowering the hood of a black cloak to reveal a freshly-laundered linen cap identical to the one she'd been wearing yesterday. The woman with whom she was in conversation wore a very plain blue gown, a white linen mutch and a capacious white apron. Both of them turned at his approach.

Under her cloak Catto saw that Christian Rankeillor was similarly attired, although her apron wasn't so large and didn't have a bib. She'd been wearing that dress yesterday too, the one with the quilted flowers and leaves on its hem. With a large wicker basket nestling in the crook of her arm, she looked like a busy young housewife, out running her errands. She must have entered the hospital a mere moment before he had, although he hadn't seen her outside. He was clearly in a worse state even than he feared. She was one person he was sure he would have noticed.

'What are you doing here?' he demanded.

The dark eyebrows rose over eyes which had widened in alarm. He must look a pretty sight. Her voice, however, remained cool. 'I think 'tis I who should be putting that question to you, sir.' She looked him up and down. 'Were it not obvious from your appearance. You have met with an accident?'

'I have met with an assailant. Somebody hit me over the head. Knocked me to the ground.' His voice seemed not to be coming out of his own mouth. 'Twas as though some other man were speaking, one standing a few feet away from him and out of his line of sight. Christ. He was beginning to sway. He sent up a silent plea. *Not in front of her. Please God, not in front of her. Please God, let me not crumple to the floor in a heap at Christian Rankeillor's feet.*

'Mr Catto? Captain?' She came towards him in a blur of blue and white. Scotland's colours, he thought. She's wearing Scotland's colours. There was something else about blue and white, something he couldn't quite remember.

'Can you make it in here, sir?'

'In where?' he managed. Using the small part of his brain still available for logical thought he was aware of some grudging admiration for her continuing calmness. She had neither panicked nor had a fit of the vapours but simply assessed the situation and realized he needed to sit down before he fell down.

'The dispensary.' She issued a swift instruction to the other woman to "*please fetch Mr Buchan immediately.*" ''Tis but a few steps, sir. Pray take my arm.'

'No,' he said, but found she had taken his anyway. One hand was cupping his elbow, the other loosely gripping his arm below the cuff of his coat and under his shirt sleeve, warming his cold wrist. He was aware of her wicker basket, which she had slid round so as to carry it at the front of her body. As she led him into the dispensary he registered walls lined with dark shelving holding a multiplicity of glass phials and pottery jars. 'Twas much like her father's shop.

'Over here, sir.' This was like her father's shop too, only the leather couch to which she was guiding him was green instead of red. 'Let me put my basket on the table here and then we shall get you out of your coat.' Her fingers were already heading for the buttons.

'I'll do it.' His speech was slurred but he succeeded in divesting himself of the leather coat before sinking onto the cool, smooth leather of the couch. She took his coat from him and laid it over the back of an upright chair set in front of the small table on which she had put her basket.

'You should lie back, sir. The couch is sloped here behind your head. Can you manage to swing your legs up or shall I help you to do so?'

Swing his legs up. He had to swing his legs up. He did that, mumbled, 'Don't need any help,' and promptly blacked out.

He was spinning through space, tumbling and falling through azure skies and scudding white clouds. It was happening oh-so-slowly but the motion was making him feel devilishly dizzy all the same. He was glad when it stopped.

He had landed on a surface that was hard and soft at the same time, warm too. Scrambling to his feet, he looked down and saw well-trimmed green grass and, when he raised his head, walls of honey-coloured brick. Joy rose within him like a bubbling fountain. He was in the walled garden, that magical place whose mellow bricks captured sunshine and held it fast. A suntrap. That's what his grandfather called it.

In here he was a child again, taking stiff little steps under the long skirts of babyhood. He was walking with his mother, his small hand in hers, and she was telling him the names of the flowers and plants. She was encouraging him to repeat them after her, telling him what a clever boy he was when he succeeded. She asked him which flowers he liked best.

'The sunflowers,' he said, gazing up at the impossibly tall blooms. 'I like the sunflowers best.'

'Like smiling faces, Bob, are they not?' she asked. 'Happy, smiling faces.'

He looked up into her own smiling face and nodded his small head in agreement. The movement made the rippling chestnut waves of his hair dance and sway. They bounced on his shoulders, caressing his face and neck with silky warmth. He was so happy here. He was adored here. Adored and adoring – but something was happening to his mother. She was fading, beginning to vanish from his sight. He moaned a protest. 'Don't go, Mama. Not yet. Please don't go …'

'Did he just mutter something about his mother? And sunflowers?'

'That's what it sounded like,' Christian said lightly. 'It surprises me somewhat to learn he has the former. I'd assumed he must have ascended fully-formed from the Stygian wastes of hell.'

Jamie's eyes were downcast, his attention and concentration on the wound to which he was attending. 'Want to award a medal to whoever hit him over the head, Kirsty?' He dropped a piece of blood-stained lint into one of the small metal basins on the big round tray she was holding for him before lifting needle and silk thread from another of the little dishes.

'He's currently our patient. Which means we owe him our skill and our care. I'd further suggest the poor fellow is deserving of a modicum of sympathy. Whoever hit him did so with some force. Employing a makeshift weapon too, by the looks of it,' he added, removing a few splinters of wood from the wound.

Stung by the implied criticism, Christian stuttered out a question. 'You d-don't think his assailant m-meant to k-kill him, do you?'

'No. If that's what had been intended, he'd have stayed and finished the job.'

'So why hit him in the first place?'

'I have no idea. Has he been robbed?'

'I don't know.'

'Haven't you checked his pockets?'

'I thought I'd be better occupied in loosening his cravat, Jamie. Then you got here.'

'Where I'd be better occupied in concentrating on what I'm doing rather than indulging in fruitless speculation as to how Captain Catto sustained his injury, Kirsty. We don't know how long he'll remain unconscious. I've enough to do this morning as it is.'

He glanced up, and their eyes met. On the list for today: carry out his multiplicity of medical duties, conceal a fugitive Jacobite and tell the professor of anatomy at Edinburgh University that all dissections now required the written permission of the Captain of the Town Guard.

She was desperate to repeat Mr Fox's plan to Jamie and see what he thought of it. 'Twas a bold one. Daring. Risky. God in heaven, it was hugely risky ... but maybe daring and risky was their only choice. As she watched, Jamie put in the final stitch to close the wound. 'Scissors,' he commanded. 'Are you going to check his pockets?'

'I'll do it once you're finished.'

He fastened off the silk thread and, taking the scissors she was proffering, snipped it neatly. 'I'm finished now.' With a clatter, he deposited needle, thread and scissors back on the wooden tray. 'Someone needs to sit with him. Lest he be sick or dizzy when he awakes. Is there a blanket in here?'

Christian fetched one from the cupboard where a few were kept, waiting while Jamie slipped Robert Catto's buckled black shoes off before unfolding and spreading it over their recumbent patient. 'I'll sit with him.'

Jamie frowned at her. 'No, Kirsty. We both know why that is not a good idea.'

'It's a terrible idea. My heart sinks at the very thought of it. But it's going to have to be me. Everyone else is run off their feet. That's usually the case on a Monday morning, is it not, dealing with the ailments stored up over the Sabbath? Along with making sure all is trig before Professor Monro arrives for his ward round.'

Jamie was still frowning at her. She could see those considerations were passing through his mind too. He would be especially concerned about getting everything ready for the ward round. Professor Monro was a stickler for order and method. Given the news he had to give him about dissections, Jamie could not afford for anything else to be wrong.

The frown had deepened into a fully-fledged glower. That sat so ill on Jamie's boyish good looks. As did the challenging stance he adopted, flinging one arm across his chest to grip the top of the other one. He was in his shirtsleeves as usual, rolled up and secured at the elbows to keep their generous linen folds well out of the way. His hair was tied back but was already beginning to escape from its ribbon, exploding down his back in a riot of shiny brown waves. He wore his usual canvas apron, its fawn strings encircling his slim figure twice and fastened in a bow at the front.

'All right,' he said at last. 'Just don't antagonize him any further. Or put any more cock-eyed ideas to him, like dissecting the body of the girl. I should never have let you persuade me to that.' He lowered his tousled head and transferred the hand gripping his left arm to his nose, pinching it between his thumb and his forefinger.

'Do you have a headache?'

'Yes.'

'Can I get you something for it?'

'No. I have to go back to the wards now. I was in the middle of attending to another patient when you sent for me.'

'I didn't send for you. I asked if you could come.'

'You're my master's daughter. You sent for me.'

That again. She had never been able to convince him of the level of esteem in which she held him. She had never been able to convince him that in no way did she regard him as her inferior. He was sensitive about his social status, she knew. His pedigree might be impeccable but his family's devotion to the Stuart Cause had cost them dear. Yet his own loyalty had never wavered.

'I can cope here,' she assured him, wanting nothing more than to share the burden with him. 'I'll clerk him in. Prepare some physic. He's going to have a headache too when he comes round. Would it be an infusion of willow bark you would advise, Jamie?'

'Aye.' He was still pinching his nose. 'But you of all people have no need to ask me that, Kirsty. You ken as well as I do what to give him.'

'I'll not say anything I shouldn't to him. I promise.'

He dropped his hand and raised his head. 'Send for me again as soon as he regains consciousness. The moment he regains consciousness.'

She stood at the door of the dispensary looking after him as he walked across the lobby, watching as he mounted the grand staircase. He stood back against the banister to allow the hospital's sedan chair to pass him. If only she had been able to put Mr Fox's plan to him now. Turning, she looked across at Robert Catto. Even in this unconscious state, his physical presence was powerful. Men were so … big.

She walked reluctantly towards the couch, lifting his riding coat from the chair at the foot of it. She did not relish the idea of checking his pockets. The task seemed altogether too intimate. Settling for patting the smooth leather, she encountered the hardness of what had to be a coin purse. Extracting it with some delicacy, she laid it on the table next to her basket before taking the coat over to the hooks on the other side of the open door. She hung it up, fetched his shoes and placed them beneath it before walking back to the couch.

As she had surmised on Saturday night, he did have an abundance of hair, quite gloriously wavy hair. He was handsome too. That she could not deny. The very northern European cast of his countenance put her in mind of the coloured plate of an angel in one of the religious books Betty had read to her when she'd been a little girl. Either that, or he looked like one of the Norse gods. Battle-scarred and bruised. The wound on his left temple was discolouring before her eyes.

He lay with his head towards the wall, the gleaming chestnut waves spilling over his shoulder. They were half in and half out of the black ribbon which had slid down towards the ends of his hair. It must have come dislodged when he had been hit or perhaps when he had fallen. The strip of satin was badly creased, narrowed to half its width.

On Saturday night he had worn a sharply-pressed bagwig. Yesterday too she had noticed that his hair ribbon was crisp and neat. From such details and his clothes in general, both in uniform and out of it, she had concluded that when it came to his personal appearance he was a fastidious man.

Yet she could not help but notice that the linen cravat she had loosened and which hung now on either side of the open neck of his shirt was also crumpled, and a little grubby. So too was the shirt itself. The chest rising out of the grey blanket Jamie had spread over it was clad in a plain brown waistcoat, the same one he'd been wearing yesterday. Nor had he shaved this morning. His jaw was lined with stubble.

There was another conclusion to be drawn here. He had risen from his bed this morning and pulled on the clothes he had cast aside the night before, crumpled hair ribbon, grubby linen and all. He had risen early and gone out early, presumably intending to return to wherever it was he lodged, shave and make his toilette, change into fresh linen and put on his uniform. So he had planned to be out only for a short while. In the dark of the morning. Before dawn had broken.

His hands were lying loosely across his middle, where Jamie had placed them, one on top of the other. Like the rest of him, they were big too, but finely shaped, long and slim. You might expect a surgeon to have hands like that. Or a musician. The fingers of the topmost hand twitched. He was beginning to stir.

His shoulders shifted. He turned his head and she saw a quick frown furrow the pale and high forehead. Reaction to pain, she presumed, and thus an indication that he was returning to consciousness. Any minute now he would open his eyes.

The prospect was a daunting one. Christian straightened her shoulders and drew in a breath. She couldn't allow herself to be daunted. She must appear cool and calm, not at all like a woman helping conceal a known rebel under the same roof as Captain Robert Catto. No more than a few minutes' walk away.

She laid a calming hand on her stomach and reminded herself to act naturally. She'd be sympathetic. He was a fellow human being who'd suffered a nasty injury and whatever she thought of him, he hadn't deserved that.

His eyelids were fluttering. *How are we feeling, Mr Catto?* No. *How are we feeling, Captain Catto?* One designation acknowledged that he was a gentleman. She supposed. The other recognized his authority as Captain of the Town Guard. So she would address him as such. His eyes opened, found her face and focussed on it. Words floated out of Christian's mouth. They weren't the ones she'd been rehearsing. 'You went to that girl's funeral this morning, didn't you?'

'I wouldn't dignify the event by calling it that,' he murmured. 'How long have I been insensible?'

'About fifteen minutes.' Ready to pounce on that incautious response, she remembered what Jamie had said. *The two of you clearly strike sparks off each other. Don't antagonize him further.* 'How are we feeling, Mr … eh … Captain Catto?'

He shot her a withering look. 'How do you think I'm feeling?'

'You remember what happened to you?'

'Of course I remember what happened to me.' The leather beneath him creaked as he shifted position. 'Someone hit me over the head.'

'Aiblins you would like to tell me about it, sir. We should see if you can remember what you were doing before you were set upon.'

'What I was doing before I was struck is none of your business, Miss Rankeillor,' he retorted, the deep voice growing stronger with every word. The moment of weakness which had given her the answer to her question hadn't lasted long. He looked past her, towards the two long windows at the other end of the room through which the winter sun was now pouring. 'What time is it?'

'It must now be approaching half past nine. What happened to you is my business. When patients have been knocked out by a fall or a blow it helps us assess the level of injury if they can tell us what they remember.'

'Helps *us*? I didn't know there were any physicans who wore petticoats.'

'Are you always so ill-mannered?' The question was out before she could stop herself. So much for not antagonizing him. Although, given the tenor of their relationship thus far, she was acting naturally. They both were. 'I wouldn't want to be a physician anyway.'

'What?'

'Never mind. I am trying to help you, sir.'

'I don't need your help. I need to get out of here.' He sat up, and froze into position. 'God Almighty,' he breathed, the words expelled on a ragged gasp of pain. 'My head really does hurt.'

'Well, of course it does, Captain Catto. What do you think you're doing?'

For he was moving again, swivelling round to swing his legs over the side of the green leather couch. 'Getting out of here. That's what I know I'm doing.' Finding himself tangling with the blanket as it puddled up into his lap, he muttered something. A curse, no doubt. Probably only in one language. Or maybe not, considering he must have racketed about rather a lot of Europe.

'You'll leave the hospital when Mr Buchan of Balnamoon says you can.'

He had managed to push the blanket out of the way. Now he was bracing himself, both of those long-fingered hands curled around the edge of the couch as he readied himself to stand up. 'I'm leaving now, madam. This very minute.'

She eyed him up. His whole posture, every inch of him stiff and tense, was eloquent of the pain he must be experiencing. Beads of sweat stood out on his forehead, a response to the effort of shifting his position even as little as he had. He was probably still in shock. She took in the look of grim determination on his face and knew none of that was going to stop him.

He was a strong man and this weakness was only temporary. He might make it. On the other hand, he might stumble, fall and sustain another injury, which would serve him damn well right. Except that he was indeed currently her patient. For his own good, she would have to stop him.

The couch was a high one. As his stocking-soled feet made contact with the floor he lowered his head – very slowly – to look at them. 'Where are my shoes?'

'On the other side of the door. On the floor below where I have hung up your coat.'

He raised his head with the same caution with which he had lowered it. 'Bring me my shoes. And my coat.'

'No. You are not yet recovered enough to leave the hospital. If you will lie back and rest I shall go and find Mr Buchan and ask him to come and take a look at you.'

'I don't need Mr Buchan to come and take a look at me.' He took a firmer grip of the edge of the couch. 'Are you going to bring me my shoes and my coat or do I have to fetch them myself?'

She had half a mind to let the stubborn oaf do exactly that and see where it got him, two steps from the couch before he dropped like a stone to the floor, probably. Would she have to attempt to physically restrain him? 'Twas not a prospect to be relished.

'This really is not advisable, sir.' Perhaps an appeal to reason might persuade him to bide where he was. 'You have taken a severe blow to the head, you know. You've got stitches.'

'Both of which eventualities I've experienced before, madam, and more than likely shall again.' How could a man manage to sound so condescendingly dismissive when he was in sufficient pain to be making him slur his words?

'Besides,' he said, with a passable attempt at an unconcerned drawl, 'it doesn't feel as though I've got that many stitches.'

Her eyes fixed on his face, Christian noticed the exploratory hand rising only as it reached the wound. 'Don't do that!' she yelled. 'Och, you stupid, stubborn man, dinna do that!'

27

'Oh, God,' he groaned, 'oh, sod it …'

Eyes the colour of a summer meadow … her face swimming in and out of view … she looks so solicitous … as though she really does care about me …

As though she really cared about him? Why the Devil should she? Had he given the bloody woman any reason to care about him? He was damn sure he hadn't.

'Mr Catto? Captain? Can you hear me, sir?'

'Of course I can bloody well hear you. You're screeching right in my damn ear.' Oh, and his head was hurting like buggery … and yet he was still aware of her hand … that neat but surprisingly strong and capable hand she'd laid on his chest, her fingertips resting on the exposed skin of his chest. Had it been her who had loosened his cravat?

She had untied his cravat, now her cool fingertips were on his warm skin and even with his head hurting like buggery he was feeling the stirrings in his breeches. He was a hopeless case. *Think about something else, Catto. For God's sake, man, think about something else!* He would touch the wound again. That should do the trick.

It did. Quite royally. Pain ricocheted round his head and zigzagged down through his neck and chest for good measure. His eyes watered with the intensity of it. Waves and waves of pain. 'Bloody hell,' he breathed. '*B-l-o-o-d-y* hell …'

'Please stop touching the site of your injury, sir.' She sounded exasperated with him. Small wonder. If he was her he'd be exasperated with him too. If he was a gentleman he supposed he'd be offering up an apology for swearing in front of her. If he had any kindness left in him, he supposed he'd be apologizing for how harshly he'd spoken to her yesterday, and for that foul name he'd called her the day before. He looked at her, wondering if she expected him to do any of that. There appeared to be two of her but both seemed only a little startled, nothing more.

'You have tears in your eyes.'

'It hurts.'

'So I gather. Let me help you.' She slid one arm under his in what felt like a practised gesture. 'Gently does it. Once you're lying down again you'll feel an awful lot better.'

'Don't *soothe* me,' he muttered. She didn't like him, did she? Hated his guts, in fact. Loathed, despised and looked down on him. So he could do without her damn womanly sympathy.

After a moment he opened the eyes he had closed. The room had stopped spinning and there was only one Christian Rankeillor. One was more than enough. She was frowning at him, although it wasn't addressed to his face. 'The blanket's all bumfled up around your middle.'

'*Bumfled?*' He took a chance and cocked one derisive eyebrow. Good. The reckless gesture hadn't given rise to a fresh bout of vertigo. 'Is that a term you female physicians use?'

'Haven't I told you I'd never want to be a physician? A surgeon or an apothecary, yes. Far superior beings.' Those neat and capable hands were heading towards the blanket's crumpled folds. Catto's brain shrieked a protest. *No, no, a thousand times no!*

'Let me do it!'

'And how do you propose to achieve such a feat when you're lying down?' she demanded. 'Dinna be daft.' It took only the brush of her fingers on his thigh for the damage to be done.

He wanted to die. Failing that, maybe some passing magician could leap into the room and, with a swirl of his sun, moon and stars cloak, conjure up a puff of smoke into which he could disappear. Or perhaps there might be an earthquake, and he could fall through a hole in the floor and emerge somewhere an awful long way from here.

Don't notice. Please don't notice. He darted a glance at her and couldn't decide whether she had or not. Her colour was certainly high. In her modest blue dress and white linen cap she looked like a rosy-faced nun.

No, she didn't. She looked nothing like a nun. Well, maybe she looked like the nun in the series of coloured prints he'd discovered in a locked cupboard in one of the booksellers' shops in Marlin's Wynd while he'd been looking for other things. That nun's habit had been rather less than modest, arranged, or disarranged, to permit her to attend to a priest's rather less than spiritual needs. And thinking about those illustrations, crude in one way and meticulously fine in another, was doing nothing whatsoever to improve the situation.

'I shall fetch you some water.' She spoke like a woman making an important announcement. 'I shall also inform Mr Buchan that you have regained consciousness. Can I trust you to lie there whilst I do so?'

'I don't know,' Catto said, doing his damnedest to brazen it out. 'Can you?'

'It's for your own good.'

He waved a hand in dismissal. 'Go. I shall endeavour to contain my impatience until you return.'

She muttered something he couldn't make out and left the room. As soon as she'd disappeared through the open doorway he adjusted the blanket over himself as best he could and released a heartfelt groan. To have reacted to her touch like that was humiliating in the extreme. It was bad enough to have been lying here out of his wits with her watching over him. Under a sodding blanket like a babe having a nap, for God's sake.

Letting out another groan, he willed his traitorous flesh to shrink. He baulked at the idea of touching the wound again. He'd have to try thinking horrible thoughts. An ample supply of those were waiting in the wings of that private playhouse in his brain.

The sun coming in through the tall windows stopped shining, shut off as swiftly as though someone had snuffed out a candle. The weather had clouded over again. *Our sister?* Would his hypocrisy in referring to the girl as such stick forever in his craw? He hadn't used the lass as any man would want his sister used.

His sister. Those two words set him off down another road. He pulled himself back, not prepared to embark on that mental journey. He would concentrate on the girl instead, face up to that image of her lying on the table under Balnamoon's knife. Used and sullied. Naked and bruised.

The somewhat unforgiving combination of a hard stone wall and a forceful partner.

Guilt flooded through him. She'd been such a little thing too, a mere slip of a girl. Taking one last look at her before he had left the operating theatre, she had put him in mind of a doll, a broken one, abandoned by those who had previously played with it. Wasn't that exactly what she had been, a plaything to be tossed aside without a second thought once the spoiled children who owned it had no further use for it?

He tried telling himself he couldn't have been the only man to have pressed her up against a hard stone wall. Her life must have been full of squalid couplings in the street with rough and careless strangers, men who didn't even know her name and were not interested enough to ask. Men like him.

He tried telling himself she'd been willing, she had approached him, that he had vastly overpaid her. Much good the money was going to be to her now. It was all so sad. So unbearably sad. Someone coughed.

Christian Rankeillor was standing at the foot of the couch with a tray in her hands. An earthenware jug and beaker stood on it. 'Is aught amiss, sir?'

For a few reckless seconds he was tempted to confide in her, to share at least the tale of the girl's burial and how he had felt as he had seen that pitifully small coffin lowered into the ground. Only for a moment. It was easier to once again raise the derisive eyebrow, more comfortable to keep his thoughts to himself. 'Apart from having been cracked over the head, you mean? What happened to the money in the girl's purse?'

'We put it into the box in which we collect donations. The Infirmary is always short of money and we shall have to pay for her burial. Were you thinking about her just now?'

He could hardly deny it. 'Yes.' Moving cautiously, he raised his shoulders up off the couch.

'I'm not sure you should be doing that. Not yet, anyway.'

'I'm fine,' he said, relieved to find he had brought himself to a sitting position without experiencing any further dizziness. Drawing his legs up, he rested his wrists on his bent knees. Christian Rankeillor hadn't moved. She stood there with the tray in her hands and looked at him. He saw her swallow, knew she was getting her courage up to ask him something, knew also what the question was going to be.

'Did you know that girl?'

His head ached. His heart ached. He had to tell someone. 'Yes,' he said. 'I knew her. Although only on the one occasion.'

Outside the dispensary, the hailstones started up again.

28

Christian Rankeillor's face flooded with colour, leaving Catto in no doubt she had caught the nuance of meaning the gravedigger hadn't. For a moment she said nothing. She might have been choosing not to compete with the racket of the hailstones clattering against the windows. Somehow he didn't think so. It wasn't the noise which was stopping her from speaking. She didn't know what to say. His answer to her question had embarrassed her, quite hideously embarrassed her. No longer feeling in the least aroused, he raised his own voice against the onslaught of hailstones. 'The water?'

'Of course.' She set the tray down, poured the water out and brought the beaker to him. He was careful to take it from her without touching her fingers. 'Mr Buchan will be along directly.'

He watched her walk across the room and reach up for a large ledger from one of the shelves. Bringing it over to the table and opening it, she picked up a quill from the small inkstand at the back of the table. 'I have to clerk you in.' She dipped the quill in the inkwell. 'Robert Catto.' Competing with the hailstones, she too was forced to raise her voice. 'Is that your full name?'

'Yes,' he lied, watching her as she wrote his name in the book.

'It's an unusual name.'

'Not to me.'

A little sigh before the next question. 'May I know your age?'

'Twenty-four. Very nearly twenty-five.'

'How nearly is very nearly?' She asked the question without looking up.

'My birthday is on Old Year's Night.'

'Old Style or New Style?'

'The former. So I do not share a birthday with your hero.'

The quill paused. 'What makes you think he's that?'

'Isn't he?'

'Maybe it's a lot more complicated than that. A lot more complex.'

'Is it?'

'Do you really think I'm going to discuss this with you? May I know your place of residence in Edinburgh?'

'Any message or communication sent to the Town Guard-House will find me.'

'You live at the guard-house?' That had raised her head.

'It's comfortable enough,' he said, and heard how defensive he sounded. Reminding him of a small dog he had once known emerging from a lochan after a swim, she gave herself a little shake and reapplied herself to the ledger.

'Next of kin?'

'I have none.' That was another lie, though he seldom now thought of it as such. 'Twas so long since he had offered up any other answer to that question.

'You have no living relatives?'

'No.' Third lie. 'Do you?'

'A few. Although not all of them talk to us.'

'Why's that?'

'Because my mother eloped with my father. Her family thought he wasn't good enough for her. He was only a surgeon's apprentice back then. Now he's successful and one of the managers of Edinburgh Royal Infirmary some of them have changed their tune, of course.' She raised her head again and gave him a very level look. 'But I expect you know all this already. Given that you do seem to know rather a lot about the Rankeillor family.'

Catto had indeed known the story. The Lord President had told it to him. He gestured towards the ledger. 'Have you finished clerking me in?'

'Not quite. I have to record the cause of your injury. You were set upon by an assailant, you said. At the back of the Infirmary?'

'Yes.'

'This assailant struck you with a weapon?'

'A piece of wood, I think. Maybe a fallen tree branch.'

'You say that because it felt rough?'

'Also because I noticed there were several of those lying on the ground. Sheared off in the last storm, I presume.'

She wrote a few more lines in the ledger, blotted them, laid down the quill and pushed the book to one side. She rose again and began to move about the room, collecting a series of objects: a pestle and mortar, three small glass phials, one larger one and a blue and white pottery jar. Bringing them to the table, she sat down and slid her basket out of the way.

Extracting what looked like a small fragment of wood from the pottery jar, she dropped it into the mortar before adding a few drops of liquid from the larger phial. After she had replaced its stopper, she lifted the pestle and began grinding the two ingredients together. Catto watched her for a moment, aware that his scrutiny was making her uncomfortable. He was feeling pretty uncomfortable himself. They both started speaking at once.

'Are you—'

'I am mixing—'

'You are mixing up some physic?' he supplied. 'Is that what you were about to say?'

She nodded without raising her eyes. 'Yes. It's for you.'

'I don't much care for taking potions.'

'You are not alone in that. But if you will consent to take this one I can guarantee 'twill ease the pain in your head. Your head is painful, I take it?'

'You might say that. I, on the other hand, might say a lot worse. Although I'll restrain myself.'

The hailstorm ceased as abruptly as it had started, making his voice suddenly too loud, and if he'd been hoping to raise a smile with that last comment, his strategy hadn't worked. 'What's in that potion you're mixing up for me?'

'Willow bark. A substance which is most effective in the relief of pain.'

'Ah, yes. I have known army surgeons who swear by it.'

'I shall give you some now and some to take home with you. To be used as required.'

'Thank you,' he said gravely. Those words earned him a sharp glance. Because they were perhaps the first civil comment he had made to her over the course of their short but spiky acquaintanceship? 'You know a lot about physic and remedies?'

She shrugged. 'I have always helped my father in his work.'

'Always?' Catto queried, finding himself seized with the determination to make her look at him again. 'Even when you were a babe?'

'Almost. He let me help him from an early age. From the time when I was more of a hindrance than a help.'

He'd succeeded in his aim, although he didn't fool himself he had anything to do with the smile now curving her mouth. That had to be coming from fond memories of her father. He flicked the fingers of the hand which wasn't holding the beaker of water towards the table. 'Is that what's in your basket? The wherewithal for lotions and potions?'

'We prefer to call it physic. But yes, that's why I'm at the Infirmary this morning. It is our turn for the next fortnight.'

'Your turn?'

'There is a rota. A group of apothecaries who take it in turns to supply the physic the Infirmary requires for its patients.' She lifted her left hand off the mortar and tapped the edge of the wicker basket.

'Not a whole fortnight's worth of physic, I take it.'

'No. There is physic which keeps well and physic which must be prepared and used within days, or even hours. I shall be in and out of the Infirmary every day over the next two weeks.'

'Even although Daft Friday and Yule are almost upon us?'

'People do not stop falling ill because it is Yule.'

'I suppose not.' That was interesting. She had now told him twice that she had a legitimate reason for coming backwards and forwards to the hospital over the next two weeks. Yet Catto found it hard to believe Rankeillor would involve his adored daughter in something so dangerous as giving help and succour to one of the King's enemies. It wouldn't hurt to slip her a question or two as the conversation went on, though, see how she reacted. It might also help him claw back some authority.

'You seem very much at home here.' He flicked his fingers again, indicating the ledger before lifting the beaker once more to his lips. 'Clerking me in as well as preparing my physic.'

This time she looked him straight in the eye. 'Well, Captain Catto, even a privileged and protected young lady such as myself cannot sit around drinking tea all day. One would be swimming in the stuff. And like most of her tribe, my cat sleeps more than she is awake. There are days when I fear she must have passed away during the night, she is so still. There isn't much fun to be had in inviting a cat who has apparently consumed a sleeping draught to chase a length of string.'

He couldn't stop the laugh. It made the water under his mouth bubble. When he looked at her over the top of it, he found himself laughing again. She was trying to look cool and disdainful but she couldn't hide the gleam of triumph in her eyes. Getting her own back on him. 'Touché, Miss Rankeillor,' he said softly, and raised the earthenware cup in salute.

She dropped her eyes, unstopped the larger phial and poured some colourless liquid from it into the mortar. Had he embarrassed her all over again simply by making that little toast to her? Curious. Maybe she was more of an innocent that he thought.

'What's your cat called?'

'Lucy.'

'Lucy Locket?' he hazarded.

'Lucy short for Lucrezia.'

'As in Borgia?' Then, when she nodded: 'Let me guess. She's a ruthless murderer, came to you as a grown cat and not a kitten and presented you with one of her victims as an enticement to be taken in?'

'Correct. No rat or mouse is safe when she's around.'

'As long as she hasn't consumed her sleeping draught? What's that you've added to the willow bark?'

'Distilled water. Nothing more.' Pulling another beaker towards her, she tipped the contents of the mortar into it, stood up and walked over to stand by the couch.

He looked up at her. 'I can trust you not to poison me?'

'I don't know. Can you?' She had given him back his own words, the ones he had addressed to her before she had left the room, along with: *Go. I shall endeavour to contain my impatience until you return.* Out of nowhere, it came to him what she had said to him in reply. *Thank you, oh great one.*

He was seized by an insane desire to grin at her. He didn't act on it. Holding out the cup to him, she looked decidedly fierce. Which was perhaps not to be wondered at when he considered what she now knew about him. Why in God's name had he blurted out that confession, and to her, of all people? Why, after that confession, were the two of them holding this calm, if somewhat odd, conversation?

'Give me the beaker. I'd suggest you down this in one.'

'Without even a wee piece of tablet afterwards to take the taste away?' he asked as they exchanged cup and beaker. This time their fingers did touch. Hers felt cool. Cool and competent. He was in safe hands, which was an absurd thought, unsettling and comforting at the same time.

'Is that what your mother used to do? Give you a wee piece of tablet to take the taste away?'

'My mother?' Gazing quizzically up at Christian Rankeillor, he found himself smiling after all as the memory of childhood illnesses came back to him. He'd always rather enjoyed being ill, the convalescing afterwards, at any rate. Sitting up in bed playing with his toy soldiers. Being read to. Having little tantalizing tidbits of food brought to him on a tray. Having his mother's undivided attention. 'She did, as a matter of fact.'

'Mrs Catto is no longer with us?'

'Why do you assume that, Miss Rankeillor?'

'Because you just told me you have no living relatives.'

'So I did,' he replied, and put an end to any further discussion by putting the cup to his lips and swallowing her potion. 'Yeuch,' he muttered, employing one of young Geordie's favourite exclamations of disgust. 'And twice yeuch.'

Her lips twitched. Or maybe his wits were still wandering off with the fairies and the elves and he was imagining his reaction to her potion had amused her. 'You're not finished yet.' She returned to the table, brought back the jug of water, poured some of it into the beaker and swilled it around. 'Drink all this down too. So none of the physic goes to waste.'

'Why do I get the distinct impression you're enjoying this Miss Rankeillor? Having me at your mercy?'

'Do I have you at my mercy?'

'Ask what you want to ask, madam.' He was pretty sure he knew what that was going to be.

'Drink this first. Then I shall pour you some fresh water. Not as good as tablet at taking the taste away but 'twill help a little.'

He took his time. The chance to reverse his threat to police all dissections would be more than welcome. In reality he didn't have the time or the manpower to do it in any effective way. He had probably missed one dissection last night, that of the cadaver they'd carried away from the Royal Infirmary. He wasn't going to let her know any of that, as he wasn't going to give in too easily. She'd have to work for it, convince him of the justice of her cause. When the question came, however, it wasn't the one he'd been expecting.

She took a run at it, rattling the words out as though she feared her courage might fail her if she didn't. 'Sir, since you must know that girl's name, could you not make it your business to find her family and let them know of her sorry fate?'

'I don't know her name,' he said, startled into giving her an honest answer.

'You don't know her name?' She was staring at him in incomprehension, as though he were speaking a foreign language of which she understood not one single word. Oh, bloody hell. He was going to have to explain this to her.

'The … eh … exchange of names is not necessarily a feature of such … eh … transactions … as that girl and I had.' His voice was very dry. So was his throat. He took another sip of water. Christian Rankeillor was blushing again. He wondered if her face could go any rosier.

'Would the people at the house not know her name?'

'The house?' he inquired, aware of a creeping warmth in his own cheeks. He hadn't known he was still capable of such a reaction.

'Sir,' she squeaked, 'you know what I'm talking about!' Lowering her voice, she hissed the words at him. 'The-house-of-pleasure!'

'Ah,' he said. 'I'm … eh … afraid such transactions also do not necessarily take place inside houses. Or indeed inside anywhere.'

Her face could go rosier. Thinking of the picture he had undoubtedly now planted in her mind, he discovered his could too. Balnamoon's words were ringing around his aching head. *The somewhat unforgiving combination of a stone wall and a forceful partner.* He could almost see them dangling between him and Christian Rankeillor, written in large black letters on a huge sheet of paper. No, make that red letters. Blazing, shameful, giant red letters. When she went very still, he realized what else she might be seeing. 'Ask your next question, Miss Rankeillor,' he said drily.

'How do you know there is one?'

'Because,' he said, continuing to look her in the eye, 'I can see you're wondering if any harm might have befallen her at my hands.'

'You were … with … her on Saturday night? After you left our house?'

Damn. Damn. Damn. He'd thought he was taking control of this conversation. Was this girl regarding him so earnestly some sort of a witch that she had made him blurt out this second confession? 'Aye,' he said, and rushed on before she could draw any conclusions from that. 'And she was fit and well when I left her.'

Fit and well. Not perhaps the best phrase to have used. From the look on her face, Christian Rankeillor also had a private playhouse in her brain and he kept giving her pictures with which to fill the stage of it. At least this anguished interrogation had to stop now. There was nowhere she could go from here. Unless it was to pick up the jug of water, throw what was left in it over him before telling him to sod off and never darken the doors of her precious Royal Infirmary of Edinburgh ever again.

He had underestimated her. Despite the excruciating embarrassment by which she so obviously was gripped, there was somewhere she could go from here. 'Captain Catto. Do you think the assault on you has any connection with the death of the girl?'

'I think a lot of things, Miss Rankeillor.' None of which he was going to share with her. He might have been thumped on the head because he'd been getting too close to a hiding place. 'Twould be a clumsy way of going about things, serving only to alert him further. If the Jacobite plotter was in the hospital and his friends so desperate to protect him, why not simply finish off the man they feared was getting too close?

His attacker could easily have wielded a knife instead of a tree branch. Because they didn't yet have the stomach for cold-blooded murder?

He was also trying to drag out of his memory what it was he had seen lying at the foot of the rowan tree seconds before he'd been struck from behind. It had been white and crumpled, like a sheet of discarded paper, but that was as far as he could go. There was something at the back of his mind, something to do with Christian Rankeillor lowering the hood of her cloak.

'But that is what you were doing this morning, isn't it? Examining the locus of this unexplained death?'

'I don't think it is unexplained. It does seems more likely 'twas misfortune that killed her. Being in the wrong place at the wrong time.' He gazed once more at the tall windows. Bright sunshine again. 'Out there on such a cold night. Alone in the darkness.' He was silent for a moment, thinking about that.

'Mr Catto? Captain?'

'What?' He transferred his gaze from the windows to her. 'What?' he asked again.

'No matter. If she had not been rendered incapable of leaving, do you not find it odd that she should have chosen to stay outside in the cold and the darkness when she had money in her purse?'

'From what Mr Buchan has discovered, she had consumed a lot of gin. She may have become befuddled, too confused to find her way home or to a lodging house.'

'I suppose so. By the way, you too have money in your purse.' She pointed to it, lying on the table beside her. 'Did you also have a pocket-book with you?'

'I did not bring it out with me.'

'So whoever attacked you did not do so in order to rob you.'

'They might well have attacked me for other reasons.'

'Such as?'

'They might hate the Town Guard. They might dislike me personally.'

The dark eyebrows drew together in a frown. 'You are being flippant?'

'Not at all. Both prejudices are to be found in Edinburgh, I believe. The place is full of Jacobites and people disaffected to the government, you know. Some of those people also find me rude and overbearing. Completely lacking in manners. Hard to believe, eh? Have you got him hidden in the hospital?'

'Who?'

'The man your father met at Surgeons' Hall on Saturday night.'

'What man?'

He gave her a sardonic smile. 'You're learning.'

'Always. Although I have no idea what you're talking about. Would you like to check the contents of your purse?'

'No. I can see it is as full as it was when I left the guard-house.' He corrected himself. 'Or when I left the graveyard.'

'You gave the gravediggers some drink money?'

'Aye, and as payment for them to guard the grave for the next week or two.'

She shifted from one foot to the other, setting her blue skirts swaying. 'I would hope no one would disturb that girl's rest now.'

'Why would they not, Miss Rankeillor? A fresh body is a fresh body. Despite Mr Buchan's work, there would still be parts left to be dissected, am I not right?'

She made an exclamation of disgust.

'Come, come, Miss Rankeillor. Did you not tell me that grave-robbing is a necessary evil? Is that not what you believe?'

'Yes,' she said. 'That is what I believe. Especially when it is so difficult to find subjects for dissection. Especially when there are so many restrictions placed upon the procedure.' She leaned forward, the eager supplicant. 'Captain Catto, will you please change your mind about imposing yet more restrictions?'

'Yes.' So much for making her work for it. His swift surrender had surprised her. When he heard her next question he realized it had emboldened her too.

'Will you please also make some enquiries about the girl? Even if 'tis only to discover her name and who her family might be?'

'You can surely do that yourself, Miss Rankeillor. Mr Buchan said he recalled treating her. Would she too not have been clerked in?'

'Yes, but there are so many names in the ledgers of the Salivating Rooms. I would have to ask Jamie to look through all of them and see if he could put a name to her face.' She murmured her next words but this time Catto heard them clearly. 'And I've already had my head bitten off this morning.'

A shadow fell across the room. Someone was standing in the open doorway of the dispensary. 'I'm glad to see you restored to consciousness, Captain Catto,' Jamie Buchan said as he walked into the room. 'Not only restored to consciousness but conversing with some animation with Miss Rankeillor. I hope she has not been plaguing you with questions. Annoying you when you ought to be resting.'

It was said with a little laugh but Catto didn't miss the admonishing glance being directed at Christian Rankeillor. Nor her eagerness to please young Mr Buchan of Balnamoon. He wondered if the two of them were lovers. Whatever the nature of their relationship it was clearly a close one. So she was bound to tell Balnamoon about his encounter with the dead girl. Oh, God. What sort of a dolt was he?

'Captain Catto has agreed to reverse his decision on dissections, Jamie. Is that not wonderful news?'

He could have struck a bargain with her over that, her silence about what he had told her about himself and the prostitute in exchange for it. Why the Devil had he not thought to do so?

'It is indeed,' Balnamoon said gravely. 'I thank you, Captain. I thank you most sincerely. How are we feeling?'

'I have absolutely no idea how you're feeling,' Catto retorted. 'As for myself, I'm perfectly well.'

'Not exactly perfectly,' Jamie Buchan demurred, approaching him with a pleasant smile on his face. 'Let's have a look at you.'

Balnamoon proceeded to carry out what seemed to Catto a largely unnecessary series of tests. A visual inspection of his head wound and the man's own stitching was fair enough. Why he then had to sound his chest front and back, look down his throat and peer into his eyes was beyond comprehension.

Submitting to the whole rigmarole with barely-concealed impatience, his responses to the questions being put to him were growing increasingly testy. 'You are now holding up three fingers,' he snapped. 'I can see each one quite clearly whether they're directly in front of me, off to the right or off to the left. Can I go now?'

Hell's teeth, why was he asking if he could go? Medical men. Acted as if they were God Almighty Himself and expected to be treated with the same reverence.

'I'd prefer you to stay here for a while. In the afternoon we'll take another look at you and see if you're fit to be discharged.'

'In the afternoon? It's out of the question for me to stay here that long. There are urgent matters which require my attention now.'

Balnamoon moved his unruly head from side to side, obviously weighing up the chances of persuading his rebellious patient to do as he'd advised. 'A compromise, then. If you will agree to rest here for the next couple of hours, we shall send a message to the guard-house to let them know what has happened and to ask them to send an escort to accompany you back thither.'

Catto opened his mouth to say no. There was no way on earth he was going to show such weakness in front of the men. On the other hand, reaching the guard-house and falling down in a dead faint as soon as he got there wouldn't look too impressive either. A flash of inspiration struck him. It was nice to know the blow to his head hadn't irretrievably addled his wits. 'One hour.'

The balancing gesture again. 'I'd prefer two.'

'One hour,' Catto repeated. He knew very well he ought to rest for longer but he wasn't going to do it here. He would do his recovering on his own and in private, as he had always preferred. 'I'd be obliged if the messenger could ask for Master George Maxwell who should meet me here at the Infirmary at half past ten.'

'Make it half past eleven,' Balnamoon said. 'It wants but a quarter to ten now.'

'Eleven o'clock. Not a moment later. If I might be left in peace I shall use each one of those intervening moments to their best effect.'

'I shall go and see about sending the message to the guard-house.'

'Do so with all dispatch, Kirsty. I suspect we're not going to be able to rest until we know we're going to be able to make good our escape from us as soon as humanly possible. Am I right, Captain?'

Catto fixed Jamie Buchan and his convoluted syntax with a baleful look. Then he pointedly closed his eyes.

29

She was in the hospital's library and teaching room, diagonally opposite the dispensary. With the door open, she could keep an eye on that, make sure Robert Catto wasn't disturbed. If only he had returned the favour. Standing in front of the tall bookshelves which lined the wall of this room, Christian tilted her head back against them.

She could barely believe he had asked her outright if they were hiding someone in the Infirmary. Nor could she believe how she had so calmly pretended ignorance. Or that he had let her do so. Could Jamie possibly be right, that he was on their side? He might equally have been trying to entrap her.

Yet there had been nothing calculated about his telling her about himself and the prostitute. He had told her because he had no one else to tell. He had looked like an overgrown schoolboy sitting up on the couch in the dispensary, wounded, sad and very alone. Dear God, she could not possibly be feeling sorry for Robert Catto. As for his body responding to her touch …

Hot with embarrassment, Christian blew out a breath, stopped staring at the ceiling and walked forward to restore the handful of books lying on the study tables to their rightful places on the shelves. Professor Monro never used the teaching room on a Monday but that was no reason why it should not be tidy. The task did not take her long, leaving her cooling her heels until half past eleven. She might go and make herself useful elsewhere in the hospital but she'd probably only be in the way. Tempers tended to fray when Professor Monro was expected.

So she could do nothing but wait. She didn't have the patience to read, not when thoughts were whirling around her head, not when her frustration was mounting at not having been able to talk to Jamie about Mr Fox's plan. He had asked her to see their unexpected patient off the premises at half past eleven and dashed off. He had no choice but to leave it to her now. Professor Monro's ward round would be in full swing by half past eleven.

Her eyes went to the cabinet where anatomical drawings were stored. Last night she had secreted her sketch of the dead girl in there. She walked across the room, extracted the drawing, laid it on top of the wooden cabinet and stood looking down at it.

Somewhere not too faraway a clock struck the quarter hour. Moving with slow and careful deliberation, Catto got up from the couch and walked across the dispensary to where his shoes and coat were. It took him more time to reach them than it ought to have, as it did to slide his feet into the former and shrug his shoulders into the latter. Christ. He was as weak as a newborn kitten. As least he had managed to get himself into his coat without Christian Rankeillor doing up his buttons.

Seated once more on the edge of the green leather couch, he retied his cravat and gathered his hair back, loosely enough to allow a thick strand to fall forward over his brow. As he finished doing that the door of the dispensary was nudged open and her neatly-capped head appeared round the edge of it. She opened it fully when she saw he was up and awake.

'I had thought to give you a bandage, sir.'

'No bandage. I shall endeavour to keep the wound clean without one.' Acutely aware of her, he was doing his damnedest not to look directly at her. Why was the bloody woman still here at the hospital?

Didn't she have any household chores to attend to? Why in the name of God and all His angels he had chosen to unburden himself about his encounter with the prostitute to Christian bloody Rankeillor he did not know. The only excuse he could make for himself was that he must have been rendered temporarily insane by the blow to his head.

'Very well,' she said doubtfully. 'But we must make an appointment for you to return to the Infirmary in due course to have the stitches removed.'

'I'll do that myself,' Catto said as he rose from the couch, managing to do so without falling over. 'I've done it plenty of times before.'

She was frowning at him. 'I really think you should come back to the Infirmary to have your stitches taken out, Captain.'

'I don't. Please do not let me detain you further, Miss Rankeillor. Thank you for your care of me. Please convey my thanks to Mr Buchan of Balnamoon also.'

He'd meant that little speech, even the delivering of such a few words taking it out of him, to be a valediction, but as he walked into the lobby and made his way out of the hospital she stayed with him. As they stepped out into the quadrangle, he stopped and turned to her. 'As I said, I think I need detain you no longer, madam.'

'You have been in our care,' she said gravely. 'It is my duty to see you safely on your way. Although I wish you would have stayed with us a wee while longer.'

'I'm fine,' he said tersely. 'Fighting fit.' *And lying through your teeth, Catto.* Her potion had taken the edge off the pain in his head but the injury was still throbbing. The wound in his thigh was also making its presence felt. He must have jarred it falling to the ground after he had been struck. All he wanted to do now was crawl into some warm, dark place where he could shut the world out until he was ready to face it again.

'Good-day, Miss Rankeillor.'

'Before we part, there are some things I must give you.' Holding out her cloak, she slid her hand into a deep inside pocket and brought out a small roll of some quilted stuff. 'Three doses of the same physic you have already ingested. To be taken as required.'

'I won't need 'em.'

'Please take them all the same. In case you do. Mayhap at midnight tonight when your head is really sore. I do not like to think of anyone being in pain when they might have the means to alleviate it.'

Taking the small parcel from her, he slid it into his pocket. It was still warm from hers. He wished she would stop being kind to him. He wasn't sure how much longer he could take it. As he wasn't sure how much longer he could stand here and stay upright or how many more times he was going to have to say, as he did now, 'Good-day, Miss Rankeillor,' before she would let him go.

'I have something else for you.' Head bowed, she was extracting two small pieces of heavy card. 'I have put it between these to stop it from becoming creased or crumpled. I have made it small so you might keep it in your pocketbook and thus also keep it in good condition.' She handed it to him. 'It is a drawing of the girl's face. There are two copies, one below the other.'

'So I see,' Catto said, separating the two pieces of card.

'Is it a good likeness, do you think? I ask because I saw her only in death.'

He had seen the girl only by moonlight but he knew this was one face that was going to stay him forever. 'It is an excellent likeness.' He looked up from his scrutiny of it. 'You did this?'

'I have some small talent for drawing.'

'You have some very large talent for drawing, I should say.'

She shrugged. 'I hope you will find it useful. If you should lose or pass on either of these to someone else, I have the original drawing and would be happy to supply you with more copies.'

He tapped the edge of the drawing with his fingertips. 'You drew her last night?' Then, when she nodded: 'Why do you care so much about a girl you never knew, Miss Rankeillor?'

'A guilty conscience, perhaps. When her body was discovered yesterday morning my first thought was not for her. 'Twas how I might use her death as a means to achieve my own goals. Persuading you to change your mind about dissections,' she added hastily. 'At the moment I am finding it quite hard to forgive myself for that.'

I used her a lot worse than you did. You need have nothing on your conscience in comparison to me.

'Captain! Are you all right, sir?' Hurrying up to them, concern was writ large on Geordie's face as he peered up at Catto's brow. 'Yeuch! That looks gey nasty.'

'I'm fine, Geordie,' Catto assured him, already heartily sick of those words. 'Apart from someone bashing me over the head.'

'Someone bashed you over the head?' The boy looked outraged. 'Did you apprehend the evildoer, sir?'

'I'm afraid not. The … eh … evildoer knocked me unconscious.'

'So that's why ye didna come home for breakfast. I was starting to get real worried about you, sir. I was that relieved when I got the message. I've bespoke a chair to take ye back to the High Street. So ye willna have tae walk when you're feeling a wee touch weakened, like.'

'You've done what?'

His face falling, the boy stuttered a repetition, indicating the chair and the two caddies waiting by the Infirmary's gates. Catto's mouth set in a grim line. 'I am perfectly well and perfectly strong and I am not going back to the guard-house in a damn chair, Geordie. You had no business ordering one.'

'Och, but Captain Catto, it's an excellent idea. The young man has done well to think of it.' She flashed a dazzling smile at the boy and received an equally dazzling one in return. 'You have taken a nasty blow to your head—'

The skirts of his leather coat spun out as he rounded on her. 'I am not an invalid. I do not require to be carried through the streets of Edinburgh. Chairs are for gouty old gentleman. Or,' he added in scathing tones, 'young ladies of fashion whose ridiculous clothes prevent them from walking where they want to like normal people.'

He heard the little gasp, saw her stiffen. Good. That would disabuse her of any notion that a truce existed between them or that she in any way now had the upper hand. She could tell the whole of Edinburgh he had fucked a girl in the street for all he cared.

Sucking on clay pipes which must once have been white but were now stained to a sludgy brown, the two caddies leaned against the chair, their expressions a mixture of boredom and shrewdness. They'd get their hire fee anyway, no matter the outcome of this argument. The longer the debate went on, the more money they could legitimately demand.

'But Captain,' Geordie protested, 'ye shouldna tire yersel' when ye've been hurt. I can see that was a right nasty blow just by looking at it.'

'Will you stop arguing with me, boy?' He pointed an accusing finger at the lad. 'You had no business ordering a chair. I am not going back to the guard-house in a damn chair.'

'Mr Catto?' came a low voice at his elbow. ''Tis not that the cost of the chair is a problem? I could easily put it to the charge of the hospital—'

'I thought the hospital was always short of cash.'

'We have a fund for eventualities such as this.'

'Save it for someone who needs it.' He dug out his purse, extracted a silver coin and tossed it to one of the chairmen. 'Enough?'

The man looked at the half-crown, bit it and grinned. 'For this we'll carry you to Leith, young gentleman. Halfway back too, if that's your pleasure.'

'You can carry fresh air to wherever you damn well please. As far as I'm concerned, you're dismissed.' Turning to Christian, he made her a jerky little bow. 'Madam. I thank you and Mr Buchan of Balnamoon once again for your care of me. Neither of you need feel any further responsibility for my health.'

'But you have reversed your decision on dissections?'

'For God's sake, have I not already said so? Yes, I have reversed my decision on dissections.'

'And the other matter?'

'Is something I am prepared to discuss with you no further, Miss Rankeillor.' God Almighty, but she was like a dog with a bone. He snapped his fingers at the waiting boy. 'Geordie. Now.'

30

'Captain? Are you all right, sir?'

Catto raised his head towards the sound of the boy's voice and immediately regretted the gesture. The kitchen of the guard-house and its entire contents were swirling around him like a maniacal whirlpool: furniture, pots and pans, the plates on the dresser. Instinct had him stretching his hands out, seeking safe anchorage. His fingers closed around a piece of wood. The edge of the table. He was grounded again.

'I'm thinking it would be better if ye would sit doon, Captain. I've put the chair right behind ye.'

'I'm all right. Leastways, I soon will be. Any second now. As soon as the room stops spinning.'

'Sit doon, Captain. I'll guide ye into the chair.'

'That's better,' Catto said a moment later, opening his eyes and giving the hovering Geordie a reassuring smile. He was remembering his walk back from the Infirmary, plunging down the hill into the Cowgate and climbing back up into the High Street, determined to reach the guard-house by sheer will alone if he had to. Despite the punishing pace he had set, the boy had been with him every step of the way.

'Ye had me gey worried for a moment there, Captain.'

'I had myself gey worried, Geordie. Maybe I should go through to my bedchamber and lie down for a wee while.'

'But you'll bide at the table for a minutie, eh? Then ye'll mebbe no' be so dizzy when ye stand up again.'

'That's a good idea, Geordie,' Catto said, humbled by the boy's concern for him. 'Your idea about hiring a chair wasn't a bad one either. Except that I didn't want to look like a gouty old gentleman or some sort of an invalid. It wouldn't be good for the men to see me like that.'

Geordie had moved away from the table, was at the door hanging up Catto's coat. As when he had returned from the dissection yesterday, he had no recollection of having taken it off. Completing the task, the lad turned and looked at his master. 'Ye didna want yon Miss Rankeillor to see you like that either?'

'What did you say?'

Geordie moved to stand on the other side of the table. 'I said I thought ye were concerned as to what Miss Rankeillor thought o' ye, Captain.'

'I have absolutely no interest in Miss Christian Rankeillor's opinion of me!'

'Aye, sir. Of course, sir. She's real bonnie, though, eh?'

'Is she? I hadn't noticed.'

'No, sir, of course you hadn't. She's a kind lady too, I'm thinking. Will ye tak something to eat afore ye go through to lie down?'

'I don't want anything.' He was once more seeing the hellish procedure he'd witnessed yesterday afternoon. Not only seeing it. Smelling it too. Listening to Balnamoon enumerating the contents of the girl's stomach. Watching the man stirring those cold, dead innards around with that wooden pointer—

Hot, swift and unstoppable, the meagre contents of Catto's own stomach rose in his throat. He leaned forward, retching over the table. That hurt almost as much as his head did. Having barely eaten anything over the past twenty-four hours, he had very little to be sick with.

'Here ye go, Captain.' A basin was slid under Catto's mouth, a small cool hand laid on his forehead.

'Nothing more to come, I don't think,' he said a moment or two later. The boy cleared up what mess there was, took it and the basin away and came back with a tankard of water and a wet cloth. 'Thanks, Geordie,' he said, taking the latter and wiping his face. He gulped down a swig of the water. 'You're getting to be my right hand man, eh?'

The boy flushed with pleasure. 'It's no bother, sir. None o' it's any bother. I'll see ye through to your bedchamber now.'

'No need for that, lad. I'll manage fine by myself.'

'I'm doing it anyway, Captain. There's no point in arguing wi' me. My mind's made up.'

Able as he always was to recognize when the battle was lost, Catto made no further protest. In truth he was glad of the lad at his back, absurdly reassured and comforted by the skinny arm stretched out ready to grab him should he stumble.

'Shall I tell onybody wha asks that you're busy working on your papers today and canna be disturbed?'

'Excellent idea, Geordie. I'll maybe show my face around the gates this evening in case there's been any gossip about what happened. The way rumours fly about this town I might well be dead by this afternoon.'

'I'm no' sure if you should go out tonight, sir. Besides, everybody'll see you at the Daft Friday ball at the Assembly Rooms and ye're bound to hae recovered by then.' The intelligent little face brightened as the boy pulled back the quilt on the box bed. 'Ye've that to look forward to, sir.'

Catto bit back the sour comment which sprang to his lips. This bright and inexplicably devoted boy deserved more than to always be on the receiving end of his sarcasm and ill humour. Perching on the edge of the bed, he allowed Geordie to ease his shoes off. 'I'll need to be out and about well before Friday, Geordie. Is my suit for the ball back from the tailor's yet?'

That was something Duncan Forbes had insisted upon. In the face of Catto's protests, he'd also paid for the new clothes. '*Want you to make a good showing, laddie. Once they start noticing you, we want them to really notice you! Show the buggers the Town Guard's coming up in the world and a force to be reckoned with!'*

'It's promised the morn. Will I help you off wi' your waistcoat, sir?'

Catto unbuttoned it, tugged off his cravat and handed both over. That was two people who had helped him undress today. As he lifted his legs up onto the bed the boy was there again, pulling the quilt up over him. 'Can I fetch you anything, Captain?'

'Maybe more water,' Catto mumbled, exhaustion, shock and reaction beginning to claim him. 'Bring that tankard through, will you?'

'Right away, sir.' Fitting Catto's brown waistcoat over the back of the chair in front of the desk, he came back to stand by the bed.

'Something on your mind, Geordie?'

'No, sir. Water, ye said?'

'Captain,' Geordie began when he returned to the bedchamber a moment or two later, 'there is something I need tae talk tae ye—' The words died on his lips when he saw that his master was dead to the world.

He went back through to the kitchen and out into the internal courtyard, standing for a moment listening at the door to the rest of the guard-house. Stepping over to the holly bush and the ruined stairs, he issued a soft instruction. 'Come into the warm, now. I've some soup for ye.'

'All right, lass?'

'Fine,' Christian said as she walked into the kitchen. 'Something smells good.'

Little Tibby blushed. 'I've made cock-a-leekie soup for our dinner, Miss Kirsty. First time I've done it all on my own.'

'I've baked some gingerbread to have after the soup,' Mary said proudly. 'First time I've done that all on my own.'

'You've been keeping them busy, Betty.'

'Weel, ye ken whit they say. The Devil makes work for idle hands.'

'Anything left for me to do?'

'Nothing but sit doon at the table and eat your dinner. Am I to serve the soup or you?'

'Why don't we let Tibby do it? Is your gingerbread cool enough now to slice into nice, neat squares, Mary?'

Tongue poking out of the side of her mouth in concentration, Mary set about slicing the gingerbread. Tibby solemnly ladled the broth into the big blue and white tureen before putting its lid on and carefully carrying the soup to the table. Betty and Christian exchanged smiles. Somewhat shaky ones.

Unless they were entertaining visitors, the Rankeillor household customarily all ate together in the kitchen, Patrick at the top of the long table which stood in the middle of it, Christian and Betty to his right and left, with Mary and Tibby beside them and opposite each other. Today Betty gestured towards the top of the table. Christian shook her head but, with a significant glance towards the two young maids, Betty silently insisted.

'Can a place be set for a hungry man?' called a familiar voice. 'Temporarily head of the household, Kirsty?' Jamie asked as he came into the kitchen.

'Looks like it,' she agreed. 'How did the ward round go?'

'Very well. Thanks, Mary,' he said as the girl set an extra place and Betty fussed around him, ushering him into the chair which was normally Christian's. 'Professor Monro didn't shout at anybody. Which is always a bonus and has put me in such a good mood I thought I'd come and help you open the shop this afternoon.'

'Are you not having a bit of a busy day as it is, Jamie?'

'Think you're having the same, Kirsty. I can spare an hour.'

'He asked you that?' Jamie gave a long, low whistle. 'How did you answer him?'

Christian repeated the little interchange. She had just served the first customer of the afternoon, who'd been waiting at the shop door when Jamie had unlocked it. The woman had bought some tincture of rhubarb and hurried off.

'He did not press the point?'

'No. You think that's significant?'

'Could be. If he were on our side …'

'It would make all the difference in the world,' she supplied. 'But how can we know he's not trying to trick us?'

'He stood down the guard on the hospital.'

'And is probably still watching it and us. You said that yourself, Jamie.'

'If I were him I'd be watching us too. Doesn't necessarily indicate which way he might jump if push comes to shove.'

'I'm not so sure there's any doubt about that,' she said, frowning at him. 'But there is something else I must tell you. Our visitor has come up with an idea. I had to speak to him about it, Jamie. He needs to know what is to happen and you cannot go and discuss it with him.'

'I know. Have I been like a bear with a sore head, Kirsty? I'm sorry.'

'Och, but Jamie, I understand why! You've so much to contend with.'

He smiled at her from under his untidy hair. 'Speak. Quickly, before the next customer comes in.'

'The Daft Friday ball,' she began. His eyebrows rose as she spoke but he allowed her to continue uninterrupted as she told him Mr Fox's idea. That, dressed in her father's evening clothes, he should be carried up to the Assembly Rooms in the hospital's sedan chair, a gentleman suffering from the gout but still wanting to see the merriment. With luck, he would arrive unnoticed among all the other guests and Christian would discreetly help him into one of the smaller reception rooms where he might speak with the gentleman he needed to see before he left Edinburgh. 'You'll know who that this, Jamie? He'll definitely be at the ball?'

'Never misses it. Although he likes to arrive late at such events. Make an entrance.'

'So it might look suspicious if he got there unusually early?'

'Not necessarily. He might have decided on a whim to arrive earlier. It's the sort of thing he does. A greater difficulty might be in separating him from his entourage.' Jamie said the word with some disdain. 'He always goes about with a tail of followers. Like a Highland chief. Although I can enlist the help of one of those followers.'

'You're sure you can trust him?'

'He's one of us, Kirsty.'

'A member of this Association?'

Jamie nodded. 'We would have to secure one of the smaller reception rooms and get the key to it.'

'I could do that this week. Say we want to privately greet our most generous donors to the hospital.'

'That could work. As long as we don't actually do that.'

'How long will this interview take?'

'I think we dare not allow more than twenty minutes. Too long an absence would be noticed. After they've spoken we will arrange for Mr Fox to be carried down to the Netherbow, get him out of Edinburgh well before the gates shut for the night. He'll be fit to ride once he gets through the gate?'

'Aye, although 'twill not help the swelling of his ankle.'

'Better a swollen ankle than a stretched neck.'

She gave him a speaking look. 'Our visitor said something very similar. He'll need help to mount the horse.'

'He'll have it. That part of his journey is already arranged.'

'What about getting him through the gate?'

'A pass signed by the provost would certainly help. Mr Coutts is due to attend the ball?'

'I believe he and his wife return to Edinburgh on Friday for that express purpose.'

'Then ask Anna to call on them in the early afternoon and request a pass from Mr Coutts for a Mr Duff of Banff who has been in town for the treatment of his gout. Let him be one of her numerous relatives, not fit to visit the provost himself and a nervous traveller, hence his desire for a pass. Our visitor would change into your father's evening clothes and wig at the bagnio?'

Christian nodded. 'I would take them over there when I take my own, hidden between the folds of my gown. If we can get him there sometime towards the latter part of the afternoon, he could change and wait in the gentlemen's bathroom while Anna, Meg and I bathe and change. If I ask Meg to come to the bagnio at two o'clock there would be no danger of her running into him. It's already arranged that we three are going up to the ball in hired chairs at four. I would make sure Meg is in the first, Anna next and me in the last one, with our visitor following on in the hospital's chair, which we could put round the corner out of sight of the real caddies. Which leaves the problem of how Mr Fox and the hospital's chair are to pass from the Infirmary to the bagnio unnoticed.'

'I'll take care of that.'

'Jamie, how can you? We cannot know you will not be seen. Four o'clock is also too early to arrange some kind of a distraction.'

'It'll be getting dark by four o'clock. That will help. Robert Catto turning a blind eye would help even more.'

'We cannot know that he will, Jamie!' Christian burst out, beside herself with anxiety.

'Then we have to find out.'

She swallowed hard. 'So we're going to do this?'

'I think we have to do this. I think it's our only option. Dinna look so worried, Kirsty.'

'It's hard not to be worried.' She pulled a rueful face. 'Worried being vastly too mild a word.'

'I know.' One hand fluttered onto her shoulder in a gesture of reassurance. 'Concentrate on the details. That'll help. How we're going to do this. Did Robert Catto tell you anything about himself, Kirsty? Where he comes from, even?'

'Only that he has no living relatives.'

'Is that what he said? Lonely position to be in. Can't be easy being the Captain of the Town Guard either. Not an office which inspires much affection.'

Christian grimaced. 'As Captain Porteous found out.'

'Exactly. Nobody's going to invite his successor to supper or exchange Yuletide gifts with him, are they? The office Mr Catto occupies makes him *persona non grata* at both humble and exalted tables. Not unless they want something from him, of course. Shall I put this away for you?' he asked, reaching for the blue and white porcelain jar which held the tincture of rhubarb. 'Bit far for you to stretch.'

'We want something from him.'

'You think we should try to make friends with him?'

'I wouldn't go that far. Jamie, I asked him if he could find out the dead girl's name and if she had any family. I think he was upset by her death. Moved by the death of someone so young, I mean,' she added hastily.

Jamie turned from replacing the tincture of rhubarb on the highest of the shelves behind the counter and looked at her.

'I'd like to be able to give her a name, Jamie. That's all.'

'Nobody's going to raise a stone over her, Kirsty. She's buried in common ground.'

'A pauper's grave,' she agreed, and for a moment could say nothing else.

'Och, Kirsty Rankeillor,' he said gently. 'You've such a soft heart.'

She took her hand from her mouth. 'So have you.'

'Maybe once upon a time. Not any more.' He lifted his chin in the direction of the hospital. 'Working over there I've had to harden my heart. Not become too involved. Not care too much. When you see how illness attacks those who don't deserve it …'

'Does anyone deserve it?'

'No. Although sometimes it seems to be those with the blackest of hearts who survive.'

'Life's not fair, Jamie.'

'That's a certainty.'

'But don't try telling me that you don't care. Every time I see you with a patient it's obvious how much you do. Are you angry with me for asking Robert Catto about the girl?'

'No.' Jamie's face took on a thoughtful look. 'In fact, we might be able to use that to our advantage. If he comes back to you with a name he might also come back to you with a message, make it clear where his sympathies lie. Upset about the girl, was he?'

'I think so,' Christian said, wondering how she could explain that Robert Catto was very unlikely to come back to her after how they had parted in front of the Infirmary. He'd probably tossed her drawings on the fire by now.

'We certainly need to find the chink in his armour. Troubled he may be but he's also very controlled, don't you think?'

Now. She would tell him now about Robert Catto and the prostitute. Why was she even hesitating? The bell on the shop door jangled. Another customer.

31

Catto woke to find his bedchamber flooded with light. Confused, he shifted his head on his pillows, tracking the source of it. 'Ow,' he muttered. '*Ow, ow, ow, ow, ow.*' The pain catapulted him into a rushing remembrance of the events of the day – hadn't this happened yesterday, too? – and why he was lying in his bed long before it was over. Broken up by its vertical black bars, sunshine was spilling through the unshuttered window. As day gave way to the long winter's night, the sun was making one last, glorious stand before it set.

He tried moving his head again, winced, and drew his breath in on a hiss. It still hurt like buggery. Perhaps he might succumb to one of the witches' potions … given to him by the wee witch herself. Oh, God. He didn't want to think about her. Mostly he didn't want to think about what he had told her. Why the Devil had he done that? 'Twas not a story he would want to reach the ears of the Lord President. Somewhat squalid. Jamie Buchan of Balnamoon had not been wrong.

The door creaked open. 'Geordie?'

'Aye, sir. How are ye, sir?'

'In need of some physic. You'll find it in my leather coat. Can't remember which pocket I put it in.'

'I'll find it, Captain.' The boy was back in no time, his hands full. 'Is the physic in one o' these phials, sir, or in one of the wee packets?'

'What wee packets?' This time he remembered to keep his head still, turning only his eyes towards Geordie to squint at what the boy was holding. 'I'd better sit up.'

'Shall I help ye, sir?' Geordie laid the glass phials and the paper packets down on Catto's night-stand. 'Aiblins if I put my hand under your arm 'twill be easier for ye.'

'Thanks, Geordie,' Catto said, a groan or two of pain and a handful of curses later. 'Don't know what I'd have done without you today.'

'Nae bother, sir. I'm glad tae be o' service tae ye.' Despite his words, the boy sounded oddly subdued.

'You all right, Geordie?'

'I'm fine, Captain. Will ye tak the physic now?'

'Aye,' Catto said, adding a murmured, 'Even without a wee piece of tablet to take the taste away.'

There was clearly nothing wrong with Geordie's hearing. 'We dinna hae ony sweeties, sir, but I could fetch ye a cup o' milk.'

'Water'll do fine.' Catto downed the medicine in one, and handed the phial to the boy. 'Disgusting,' he said. 'Fucking disgusting.'

'As long as it does the trick, sir.'

'Aye, Geordie. As long as it does the trick. Let's have a look at your wee packets now. I know what one of them is. Curious,' he said as he turned the smaller one over between his fingers. 'I think this is made out of a piece of paper I already had in my pocket.' He pressed it gently between his thumb and forefinger. 'There's something inside here.'

'Wee bits o' something,' Geordie agreed. 'Ye didna fold it like this, Captain?'

'No.' Catto opened the packet up and revealed its contents.

'Seeds,' Geordie said. 'Flower seeds. Is that no' whit they are?'

'That's certainly what they look like.' Catto pushed the seeds apart with the tip of his finger, counting them. 'A bakers' dozen of them. Hold out your hand, would you?'

He funnelled the seeds into Geordie's cupped palm and unfolded the paper which had held them. It was the copy he had made of the coded message. 'How very singular.'

One small hand wrapped around the seeds, Geordie leaned over to look. 'What do the marks mean, sir?'

'I haven't had time to work that out yet.'

'It's a code, though? A way o' disguising the real words and letters?'

'You know your alphabet?' Catto asked, surprised by that response.

'I can read and write, sir.'

'You never told me that.'

'You never asked,' Geordie said mildly. 'Why have you circled these symbols, Captain?' He pointed to the ones he meant.

'Because they're the ones which recur most frequently in the message so I thought they might be the letter *e*. That's the one most commonly used in the English language. Assuming the message is in English, of course. What?' he asked, seeing something in Geordie's face. 'Do you think you can decipher it?' He turned the paper so the boy was looking at it the right way up.

'If this symbol is *e*,' Geordie said, 'then we can work back from that to the beginning of the alphabet and maybe see how that works and then work forward to get the other symbols. Aye?'

'Aye. But we have different symbols here, Geordie, not only what looks to be based on a square.'

'So first you use the lines o' a square, then there's squares wi' dots in them, then the circles and then these wee sharp shapes.'

'Triangles,' Catto supplied.

'Triangles,' Geordie repeated. 'They've got dots in them too, so all we have tae dae is work oot the maist number o' dots there are going tae be and the way the symbols are arranged. Whether we run through a' the different varieties o' one shape first or mix them a' up thegither …' He paused and looked at Catto. 'Och, I ken whit I mean, Captain, but I dinna ken the right words tae say it.'

'You're describing it very well, Geordie. But you could say we're looking for the sequence of the shapes and the different permutations of lines and dots of each one.'

The boy gave Catto a quick, shy smile before repeating these new words too.

'What we need to know is whether we work through all the permutations of each symbol in turn, or whether each letter is a different permutation of each different symbol in turn. If that's not as clear as mud.'

'Quill and ink and a fresh sheet of paper, Captain?'

'Exactly. You get those organized and I'll get up.' Sitting forward, Catto swung his legs cautiously over the side of the bed. He accomplished the movement without too much pain in his head or his thigh and with minimal dizziness. He was already on the mend.

'This,' he pronounced as the two of them sat side by side at his desk, 'is really quite humiliating. Why did I not see this as quickly as you did?'

'I'm younger than you.' Geordie offered the words with another shy smile, which grew into a grin when his master pretended to cuff his ear.

'Do the last line, boy,' Catto said with mock severity. 'So far we've got *Ten/Friday/Agreed Place/Bird in the Hand.* What's next?'

A look of concentration had already replaced the grin, Geordie's tongue poking out of the corner of his mouth. Why did people do that when they were exercising their brains?

'L-o-s-e,' the boy dictated. 'N-o.'

'Lose no,' Catto repeated, writing the words down.

'O-p-p-o,' Geordie began.

Catto's head snapped up. Shite. He'd have to stop doing that. Geordie was two letters on by the time his vision and thought processes had cleared.

'r,' Geordie said. 't.'

'u-n-i-t-y?' Catto asked, rattling out the letters.

'u-n-i-t-y,' the boy confirmed a moment later. 'You were ahead of me there, Captain.'

'Only because someone said these exact words to me yesterday. Several times over, in fact. *Lose no opportunity.*' In his mind's eye, Cosmo Liddell's face hove into view.

He thought back, trying to remember exactly what the man had said to him. *Lose no opportunity. A good maxim for life, I've always thought. Are you a broad-minded man, Captain Catto?* His affirmative answer had raised the curtain on a series of dirty jokes, all a lot filthier than they were funny.

'Do you think there's a connection, sir?'

'There already is.' Catto tapped the coded message with the tip of his index finger. 'This was sent to the man who told me to lose no opportunity. The man who sent it to him repeated the phrase.'

'What d'ye think it all means, Captain? The seeds must mean something too. They must signify something.'

'Aye,' Catto agreed, once more appreciating the boy's quick wits. He indicated the seeds, lying now on the table in front of them. 'If I don't miss my guess, these are sunflower seeds.'

'Do sunflower seeds signify something in particular, Captain?'

'They're a symbol, Geordie. A symbol being another kind of a code,' he added in response to a look of enquiry. 'Do you know who the Old and the Young Pretender are?'

'The King Over The Water and his son Prince Charlie.'

The promptness of that response was followed by a little pause, and when Catto did speak, it was in a deceptively mild murmur. 'Who is it you know that calls them by those names?'

'I maybe shouldna tell ye, sir. I'm no' wanting tae get anyone into trouble.'

Catto met Geordie's clear blue gaze and felt a very unwelcome thought slide into his head. Who would have noticed a young boy hurrying through a darkened Edinburgh to deliver that warning to

Surgeon's Hall on Saturday night? He spoke his next unwelcome thought aloud. 'I'm beginning to wonder if I should be discussing all this with you, Geordie.'

'You can trust me, sir.'

'Can I?'

'You've been good to me, Captain, and I'm right grateful for it. I would never betray you, sir, nor repeat anything ye've tellt me that I ken needs tae stay a secret. Never,' he repeated.

Catto waited, sensing something else was coming.

'I'm thinking you'll be good at keeping secrets, Captain.'

'I've had lots of practice at it,' he agreed. 'Is there something you want to tell me, Geordie? I'll not be angry with you, whatever it is. Well,' he said, trying to put the boy at his ease, 'I'll maybe shout at you when I first hear it but I'll calm down soon enough.'

The boy opened his mouth and closed it again. Catto studied the pale little face and wondered why the answer to his next question should matter so much to him. 'Can I trust you, Geordie?'

'Aye, sir. On my honour.' He lifted one hand to his chest. 'Cross my heart, Captain.'

Catto looked at the boy and went with his gut instinct. 'I'm glad to know there's at least one person in this benighted town I can rely on.'

Geordie blinked at him and posed another question. 'Do you think it was the gentleman who told you to lose no opportunity who put the sunflower seeds there, Captain?'

'It could have been. I played skittles with him and his friends and my coat was lying folded over a chair. One of them could easily have put them into the letter and slipped that back into my pocket whilst my attention was on the game.' He clicked his tongue against the roof of his mouth. 'My coat was also hanging up out of my sight at the Infirmary this morning.'

'You think it could have been Miss Rankeillor, sir?'

'Or the surgeon who stitched up my head.'

'Some sort o' a message tae ye?'

More than a message. A question. As one of the most well-recognized symbols of the Stuart kings in exile, the sunflower seeds had to be asking him where his loyalties really lay. His pulse quickened. What he had to do now was deliver his answer to that question to whoever had put the seeds into his pocket.

Christian Rankeillor acting on Balnamoon's instructions? She'd had more opportunity, although they would have been taking a hell of a risk in doing something so easily traced back to its source. Cosmo Liddell then, thinking himself powerful enough to take the risk and bored enough with his pampered existence to be willing to play at plotting?

Liddell's letter to Arthur Menzies of Edmonstone was clearly about a meeting, one which probably had taken place last Friday, the night before the one Catto had interrupted at Surgeons' Hall. Might there have been a similar rendezvous on Friday involving Cosmo Liddell, bird in the hand referring to the Jacobite messenger? Yet why run the extra risk by holding two meetings rather than one? Nor, in this connection, did the maxim to lose no opportunity seem relevant, unless it meant lose no opportunity to take action, show your support for the Stuart Cause. That didn't quite seem to fit.

Acting so quickly to put the seeds in his pocket might imply the Associators already knew who he was, which would be bloody quick work. Or maybe they thought they had no time to waste if they were planning on smuggling a Jacobite messenger out of Edinburgh on Daft Friday and hoping he might allow or even help that to happen.

'What's in the other packet, Captain?'

'A drawing, Geordie. Here, take a look. Recognize her?'

The boy shook his head. 'Canna say I do, Captain. Who is she?'

'Was, Geordie. The body found at the hospital yesterday.'

'You're good at the drawing, sir.'

'Not me, Geordie. Miss Rankeillor—'

'Captain?'

'The map,' he said. 'She drew the bloody map. But that's between you and me and the gatepost, Geordie. If you're asked, you know nothing about any map. All right?'

The boy nodded. 'Secrets are important, sir, eh?

'I'd say so, Geordie.'

'Ye canna trust everyone tae keep them, though.'

'Some people are constitutionally unable to keep them. If you want the whole world to know something without it appearing to be you who told them, swear those people to secrecy and they'll do their dirty work for you. This,' he said, 'I have learned from my years in the army.'

'Are ye hungry, sir?'

'Ravenous.' Scooping the seeds up in the paper, Catto laid them to one side and threw the boy one of his own expressions. 'Hungry enough that I could eat a scabby dug. What time is it?'

'Four o' the clock, Captain.' Geordie rose from the table. 'I've plenty ragoût left over from dinner time. I only had Lieutenant Liddell and Private Stewart in today.'

Liddell. That name again.

Catto breathed in a mouthwatering mixture of beef, carrots, herbs and doughballs. 'How is it that you're such a good cook?'

'We're all good at something, sir. Wi' me it's cooking.'

'Aye, but who taught you, your mother?

'I dinna remember my mother. Is the physic working, Captain?'

A past master at turning aside enquiries about his own family and background, Catto recognized the skilful use of diversionary tactics. Geordie had used the technique on him several times. 'Twas intriguing that a humble cook-boy was so adept at blocking any attempts at finding out more about him.

Even before he had flinched away on Saturday night, there had been hints Geordie had suffered cruelty in the past: a wariness in his eyes, a shrinking back when there were raised voices in the guard-house, a flash of fear in his eyes when something startled him. Maybe the secret he wanted to share had to do with that rather than anything he had overheard at the guard-house.

Catto liked the boy. The feeling seemed to be reciprocated. God alone knew why. 'What,' he asked, on a sudden rush of good feeling, 'would you say to you and me keeping Christmas, lad?' For even if he struck lucky this Friday, he didn't think he'd be leaving Edinburgh until some time in the new year.

Geordie's freckled nose wrinkled in perplexity. 'Keep Christmas, sir? How would we do that?'

'Have all manner of good things to eat and only do the work necessary to cook them and put them on the table. I'll help if you like. Don't look so doubtful. I can cook. Not as well as you, maybe, but if you're a soldier you have to know how to feed yourself. If you keep your nose clean between now and Yule Day I might even teach you how to play chess.' He caught himself on. 'Assuming you don't know already.'

It didn't do to make assumptions about people, as he had so recently been reminded. It also tended to blind you to possibilities. Christian Rankeillor had drawn the map. That would be why she had been so jumpy when she had spotted the document cylinder.

'I don't know how to play chess, sir,' the boy said solemnly, 'and I'd like that fine.'

'So we'll keep Christmas?'

'Aye, sir, if that's what you want.'

'Don't bowl me over with your enthusiasm, Geordie.' What was wrong with the child? So lively when he had been helping decode the letter, now it was as though a light had gone out.

'I'm sorry, Captain. I dinna mean tae be ungrateful. It's only that the minister was preaching awful hard against celebrating Christmas last Sunday, sir. Said it was superstitious and heathen.'

Sod the minister. Killjoy Presbyterians. Catto stifled the words unsaid. He had learned over the past month that Geordie set great store by his Sunday mornings at the kirk. 'What if I could present you with some arguments to convince you there's absolutely nothing wrong with the keeping of Yule Day? Would you trust me to do that?'

'I'd trust you to do anything, sir.' Once again the boy blinked solemnly at him, like a fair-haired, freckled owl.

'Geordie,' Catto said gently, 'if there's something bothering you, you know you can tell me, don't you?'

'Aye, sir, I ken that. About those seeds. Would yon Miss Rankeillor no' ken for certain whit they are? If she's tae dae wi' the Infirmary, she mebbe kens something aboot physic and suchlike.'

'She kens a lot about physic and suchlike, Geordie. Her father's a surgeon and an apothecary. I think she's by way of being an apothecary herself.'

'So ye could ask her, and maybe get a wee idea if it was her wha put the seeds in your pocket. Frae the expression on her face, like.'

'Good thinking, Geordie.' It would also be a excellent way of giving his response to the question being asked by the sunflower seeds. Subtle. Christian Rankeillor, lady apothecary, would be intelligent enough to get the message. If she deigned to speak to him. *Lose no opportunity.* He'd lost one this morning when he'd allowed his feelings to run away with him. First he'd told her too much, then he had lambasted her. Not clever, especially as he had no choice but to approach her again. Speaking to Balnamoon himself was too direct. An idea slid into his head. If he managed to find out the name of the prostitute, went to the apothecary's shop, gave her that information, pulled the sunflower seeds out of his pocket, didn't threaten her … aye, that could work.

That wasn't the only reason why he was going to make some discreet enquiries about the girl. Doubts were creeping in as to whether she had died of the cold. Even Godlike medical men could make mistakes. Someone had been following him this morning, that much was clear. The attack on him smacked of panic. If it had been provoked by fear that he was too close to a hiding place then it was pretty bloody clumsy, serving only to alert him further to the possibility that someone was indeed hiding in the hospital. So had there been another reason to knock him out?

It came to him what he had seen at the foot of the rowan tree. A crumpled piece of paper with some blue writing on it. It could have been a name. He had a hazy image of capital letters. Could the girl have been murdered and dumped at the hospital, her killer losing a letter out of a pocket and only realizing when he saw what Catto was looking at?

That would mean it was the girl's murderer who had been following him. Or someone who was in on the plot. Had they been waiting at Greyfriars to see if Catto put in an appearance at her burial? But why? To see if he cared enough to go, because they knew he'd had her on Saturday night?

That didn't seem to make sense. Nor could he see how it would help their Cause. He might not want the story of his encounter with the lass to reach the ears of the Lord President but 'twould hardly shock that gentleman into sending Catto back to Europe like a schoolboy guilty of some misdemeanour. 'Twas not enough for them to be able to blackmail him into helping them.

What if they had pushed the girl into his path? Once again that faltered on the value of what she had done. He'd hardly been going to confide in her, tell her his secrets—

God Almighty. It had been the other way round. She had threatened to tell him their secrets. She had seen something on Saturday night – and that had to have been the Jacobite agent being hurried into the Royal Infirmary. What else could she have known that was so important they had to silence her?

The hairs were standing up on the back of his neck. His quarry was still in Edinburgh and Daft Friday was their only opportunity to try to get him out. So he would delay his answer to the question posed by the sunflower seeds until Wednesday or even Thursday. Keep them dangling for as long as possible and they would be desperate for his help.

33

It was late, but Christian was no closer to falling asleep than she had been an hour earlier. Admitting defeat, she sat up, provoking a growl from Lucrezia Borgia. 'Sorry, baudrons,' she murmured, 'I canna seem to get to sleep. Not a problem you ever have, eh?' Swinging her legs over the side of the bed, she felt on her nightstand for tinder box and candlestick.

'I look a bit startled,' she told her reflection in the cheval glass. 'And hideously wide awake.' Thinking. That was the problem. That had always been her problem. Not to mention imagining. All manner of thoughts and pictures were running through her head. 'Twas like the most crowded of thoroughfares in there, the High Street in the busiest part of the morning, or how it would be on Daft Friday. Daft Friday when they were going to try to smuggle a man with a price on his head out of Edinburgh.

Panic flooded through her as the enormity of it struck her afresh. She wondered how much Robert Catto knew, wondered if he was playing with them as Lucy might play with a mouse. Let the poor creature think it had escaped, only to pounce and snuff out life and hope. She was also wondering why she had not told Jamie about Robert Catto and the dead girl.

'Twas not embarrassment that had stopped her. Used as they were to meeting over the naked cadavers of both men and women, there was not much of that between Jamie and her. What had stayed her words had been the sacred duty of confidentiality. Anything a patient told you was not yours to repeat. People could confide their deepest secrets when they were in pain or distress. Except that Robert Catto was the enemy and all was fair in love and war.

Nor did he deserve her discretion. Marching about this house last Saturday night as though he owned the place. So arrogant. So contemptuous of her. Looking her up and down at Surgeons' Hall on Sunday afternoon and clearly finding her wanting. Telling her she was a privileged and protected young lady.

Striding off across the High School Yards this morning with the tails of his big horseman's coat flying out behind him and the boy struggling to keep up with him. Making that caustic remark about chairs being for gouty old gentlemen and young ladies of fashion who wore stupid clothes. His sheer dismissal of her.

He had come swooping into her world like a gale-force wind, scooping up all sorts of terrifying things in that long grey cloak of his and depositing them in her lap. Yet he had brought clarity with him too, sharp as glass. It had cut through the sense of foreboding which had been besetting Christian for weeks. Better to be scared out of your wits than live with nameless unease.

The events of today had given her some very different pictures of Robert Catto. Sitting up on the couch in the dispensary with his wrists resting on his drawn-up knees looking like that overgrown schoolboy. Sitting up on the couch in the dispensary looking so sad and alone.

'You cannot let yourself do that.' Christian shook her head and reproved her mirrored self. 'You cannot let yourself feel sorry for him.'

She knew that she did. There was something about him, some air of mystery and melancholia. She knew too why he had reacted so badly to the boy bringing the sedan chair to meet him. Right at that moment, Captain Robert Catto had been at the end of his tether, mentally as well as physically. She had been brought up helping minister to the sick and ill, and she seldom had any difficulty in reading the signs, even when folk were doing their damnedest to hide them. Especially then.

He'd been so pale, so stiff and tense, the effort of simply staying upright manifest in every line of his tall frame. There had been a rigorous self-control at work there, not to mention an iron will. Men so hated to admit to any weakness. She had wanted to tell him to get off his high horse, come back into the hospital and lie down for another hour or so, not be so daft. She had done none of those things, recognizing that he particularly hadn't wanted to demonstrate any weakness in front of her.

Could Jamie possibly be right, that he was subject to divided loyalties, stretched to his limits by the impossible task of trying to serve two masters? Today he had suggested she might be the recipient of a message as to where Robert Catto's loyalties really lay. Yesterday he had angrily observed that the two of them seemed to strike sparks off each other. They did. Yet this morning they had conversed at some length even after that astonishing confession, not to mention the unfortunate incident of the smoothing-out of the blanket.

'Too hot,' she muttered, 'I'm too hot.' Pulling off her nightcap, she tossed it down the bed, provoking another growl of feline displeasure. Leaning to one side, her legs lifting, she plucked the cap off the cat and dropped it onto the quilt before straightening up again. Nightgown ruched up around her knees, legs dangling over the side of the high bed, she continued her conversation with her reflection.

His reaction to the touch of her fingers had been instinctive, quite indiscriminate. If the lady governess or any of the nurses had readjusted the blanket his body would have reacted in exactly the same way. Men were like that. Her father had explained this to her a long time ago.

On the day after her eleventh birthday he had sat down with her, she on one side of the library fireplace, he on the other, and told her what she needed to know. One day soon, although it might not be for a year or two, she would find herself bleeding from her vulva. He had always used the proper anatomical terms with her and had already explained how babies grew in the womb and how they came into the world. He had shown her some coloured plates of exquisitely detailed draughtsmanship showing how a child grew and developed within its mother's womb. She always attributed her love of drawing to her study of those beautiful illustrations.

This bleeding she was going to experience was because women were the bearers of children. As she grew older, her womb would prepare itself every month to receive the embryo which would grow into a baby. The blood was that embryo's nourishment. When it wasn't required, the body would very cleverly expel it and this would happen once a month. It was a perfectly natural process which happened to all girls and women until they were no longer young enough to bear children. Christian should welcome these monthly bleeds as a sign that she was making the transition from being a girl to becoming a woman.

'As such,' Patrick Rankeillor continued, a little embarrassed but determined on imparting the information, 'it is important you should know about certain other things, my dear. 'Tis not good for girls or boys to know Latin and arithmetic and philosophy yet remain ignorant o' their own bodies.' He explained to her how men and women joined together in sexual congress and how this could result in the getting of a child.

'And for the man to be able to enter the woman's body, he must be in a state of readiness?' eleven-year-old Christian asked gravely, for she knew how much her father appreciated what he called her enquiring mind. 'This readiness being the result of excitement?'

'Indeed,' Patrick ran a finger around the inside of his shirt collar. 'This is where you must be careful, lass. When a young man is in this state of excitement and readiness he will promise the young woman who has aroused it many things. The earth, if necessary,' he muttered. 'I'm afraid he willna always be speaking the truth. There is an old saying—But we'll leave that tae one side. D'you understand what I'm saying tae ye, Christian?'

'I think so, Father.' She wasn't entirely sure but she knew it must be something serious if he was addressing her by her full given name. 'I am not always to believe what boys say?'

'You should certainly be very dubious of anything said … in the heat of the moment.'

She nodded. 'Very well, Father. I shall bear that in mind. Thank you for explaining it all to me. What shall I do when I start to bleed?'

'Do?'

'For the mess, I mean.'

'I think the best thing will be for you to go to Betty. She will advise you.'

'Very well, Father. When the time comes, I shall go to Betty.'

'Good,' he said. 'That's settled, then. No other questions?' He stirred the air with his finger. 'About any aspect o' this?'

'No, Father.'

'If you think of any you must come to me wi' them.'

'Yes, Father.'

She never had. She had thought of various questions over the years but they weren't the sort you could take to your father. What if someone slides his hand down your bodice and squeezes your breast and you don't like it? What if someone slides his hand down your bodice and squeezes your breast and you do like it?

And she was still hideously wide awake and sitting on the edge of her bed studying her own reflection and thinking about Robert Catto. He had been in this room. He had seen Lucy. Yesterday he'd been interested enough to ask what her name was, which meant that he liked cats. If he liked cats, and Lucy had been where she spent twenty hours out of twenty-four, he had probably knelt on this bed and stroked her, rubbed his knuckles down her bony little head and made her purr. Christian glanced down at the cat. 'Traitor,' she muttered.

Outside the window, an owl hooted. 'Twas an eerie sound. It put you in mind of ruined castles and moonlit beaches and graveyards. Along at Greyfriars, that girl was lying in the cold earth. What a life she must have led. Not even plying her trade in a house of pleasure. Not even, at the very least, safe and warm. Not even comfortable. *The somewhat unforgiving combination of a hard stone wall and a forceful partner.*

Christian tried to imagine what that might feel like. It sounded very different from what she had read of in books like Mrs Haywood's, which spoke of amorous conversations, rapture and the ruinous ecstasy to be found in a man's arms. She couldn't imagine what that felt like either, had never really wanted to know. The risks always outweighed the promised pleasures. She'd seen the consequences of succumbing to that rapture. Ruinous was the right word.

She had been touched and she had been kissed, but it had been furtive and swift and she had always been too scared to go any further. She had never wanted to go any further.

'Until now.'

She had spoken those words out loud. She clapped her hands over her mouth as though to deny them. 'Oh, no,' she murmured to her reflection. 'Oh, no.'

34

'Aye Captain, I would certainly say 'tis a good likeness of the poor lass. Ye're skilled at the drawing, sir.'

'Not me, Sergeant. So all you can tell me is that whenever you saw her it was in the Grassmarket?'

'Aye. That's where she had her pitch.'

As street girls the world over did. Having a couple of shadowy corners nearby where they knew they could take the man and remain undisturbed. Although, if Livingstone was right, the girl had been out of her territory when she had approached Catto.

'No name for her?'

'I cannot think I ever heard one, sir,' Livingstone answered in his Highland lilt. 'Nor have I any idea where she might have bade. Likely in the Grassmarket but that does not help us much. Floor upon floor and stair upon stair in that den of thieves.'

'Is there anything you can remember about her, Livingstone? The smallest detail might help.'

'I used only to exchange the time o' day with the lassie. She was a bright wee thing. Cheery. Forbye I once had to break up a fight atween her and another girl.'

'Quarrelling over who had to the right to work the pitch?'

'Indeed, sir. I had to give both o' them a good talking-to. Turned out the dead lassie had got there first, so I told the other one she'd have to move on.' He and his Captain looked at each other.

'You'd recognize this second girl again, Sergeant?'

'I'm not going to hurt you. I want to talk to you, that's all.' He had the girl Livingstone had pointed out to him five minutes ago backed into the corner of a stone courtyard and her eyes were wary and full of suspicion.

'Whit could I have tae say that would interest a gentleman like yourself?'

He held his hands up, palms outwards to show his non-aggressive intent. 'You might be surprised, lass. I want you to look at something. Let me just get it out.'

Her eyebrows lifted and her features relaxed. Realizing later than he should have the obvious *double entendre*, Catto tried his best disarming smile. 'A picture. I want you to take a keek at a picture.'

She started when he showed it to her but tried to dissemble. 'Never saw her afore.'

'Now, then. That's not true, and we both know it. The two of you fought over your pitch. My Sergeant saw you. Tell me what you know about this other lass.'

'Nothing.'

'Och, I think you do. Give me her name, now.'

The girl looked up at him. He looked down at her.

'Jeannie,' she said. 'Jeannie Carmichael.'

'Where did she live?'

'Here. In the lodging hoose on the tap flair.'

'No family?'

'Only one she ran away frae. It was her mother and father that first sold her.'

'Know where that was?'

The girl shrugged. 'By her way o' speaking, she came frae Fife.'

'Did she have a lover?'

He was on the receiving end of a very cynical look. 'One that didna pay for it, ye mean?'

'Aye. That's what I mean.'

'She thought she did. Hauf a year ago. She was going tae gie up the streets. Sullied though she was, he was going tae be gracious enough tae mak an honest woman o' her. Stupid wee bitch believed him.'

'He left her?'

'Aye. Taking all the money she'd earned, forbye. Then she came doon wi' the pox.' More relaxed now, his informant folded her arms. 'Although she went tae the Infirmary and got herself cured o' that.'

'When was that?'

'Couple o' months ago.'

Thank God for small mercies. With a bit of luck, Jeannie Carmichael had still been clean when he had met her.

'Did she leave any possessions behind?'

'Nothing much. A spare skirt and bodice. A change o' linen. A few ribbons. The other lassies and me have already divided those up atween us.'

'No letters or papers? No books?'

She gave him a disbelieving look. 'No.'

'Anything else you can tell me about her?' Catto let the resulting silence grow and got his reward. The desire to pass on a juicy nugget of information could be a powerful impulse.

'There was one thing. She'd been gey cheerful for the past week or 'twa. Was boasting last week that she'd soon be getting oot o' here.'

'Another man?'

'No' one that I ever saw. Moving on, that's what she said she would be doing. Moving up. Daft wee bitch,' the girl said again. 'None o' us gets oot o' here.'

Catto dug into his pocket, pushed open the strings of his purse and felt round for a shilling. His fingers found a florin first. 'Here,' he said, handing the two coins to the girl. 'Take this in exchange for the information.'

Three shillings. It was what he had paid Jeannie Carmichael.

'Captain.' Clearly nervous, Liddell stepped into the guard-house kitchen. Seated at the big table, Catto did not invite him to join him.

'An explanation, Liddell,' he said crisply. 'What I require from you is an explanation.'

'I have none, Captain. I made a mistake and I'm very sorry for it.'

'Why did you join the Town Guard, Liddell?'

'Because I wanted to help, sir.'

'You wanted to help?'

'Help keep the peace, sir. Help apprehend wrongdoers.'

'Because you thought that would be exciting, Liddell?' Catto asked, puzzled.

'Because I thought it was a worthwhile thing to do. I still do.'

Idealism. He hadn't expected that.

'Captain, may I make one request?' The words were rattled out. 'If I am to be put on the horse, please make it soon, sir, so I can get it over with!'

The man was pale to the lips. Catto gazed up at him and sighed. 'I'm not going to put you on the horse, Liddell. Sit down, if you please. Opposite me.' He indicated where he meant. Liddell stayed where he was.

'N-not going to p-put me on the h-horse, Captain?'

'Bad for morale. Bad for the standing of the Town Guard in the eyes of Edinburgh's citizens. Besides which, you're an officer. Sit down, Liddell. Geordie will warm you some ale.' He looked up at the boy. 'And then make himself scarce.'

Geordie nodded.

Archie Liddell was idealistic when it came to politics too. Naïve, but idealistic. He was a proud Scotsman, regretted the loss of nationhood but whole-heartedly supported the Protestant succession. His religion and his liberties were important to him. The naïveté showed when he expanded on that. 'Kirsty, Miss Rankeillor I mean, is always trying to persuade me those would be safeguarded—'

As he ground to a red-faced, horrified halt, Catto gave him a cool smile. 'Your religion and liberties would be safeguarded if the Stuarts were restored to power. Is that what Miss Rankeillor always says, Liddell?'

'C-Captain,' Liddell stuttered. 'I sh-should not have said that!'

'Indeed you should not. Tell me something. Do you continue to disagree with Miss Rankeillor and, I presume, Mr Buchan of Balnamoon, on this subject?'

'Aye, sir. I do. But Kirsty and Jamie are rare talkers.'

'Meaning?'

'I do not think they would ever actually do anything. They are both too sensible.'

'We have to hope everyone will be sensible, Liddell. Including your cousin Cosmo.'

'Cosmo will always do what's best for the family, sir. You can depend on that.'

'And in your considered opinion, what's best for the family would be a continuation of the present settlement?'

'I don't think any sensible person could doubt that.'

'Don't you?'

Liddell looked puzzled. 'Captain?'

Catto let the silence hang for a few seconds.

'You're a student at the university, Liddell?'

'Aye, Captain.'

'But you do not study medicine, I think.'

'No. Law.' Liddell was looking puzzled again.

'Although as a scholar you naturally feel a loyalty to the whole College.'

'Of course.' Realization dawned. 'Och, but Captain, if you're thinking I might have warned the Professor we were coming, that I did not!'

'Somebody did.'

'Not me, sir.' Liddell shook his head. 'I wasn't happy when I found out where we were headed but duty is duty, sir. You have to believe me!'

'I believe you, Liddell. Although sometimes duty can be a harsh mistress.' Once again he allowed a little pause to fall. 'Sometimes we can find ourselves facing dilemmas. Duty versus conscience. Duty versus conviction. Duty,' he added, 'versus friendship and family loyalty.'

'Duty is duty, Captain,' Liddell said stubbornly.

'I'm very glad to hear you say that. Finished your ale?'

The younger man took that for the dismissal it was, and stood up. 'Captain, what I said about Miss Rankeillor and Mr Buchan ...'

'You didn't tell me anything I didn't already know, Liddell. Good afternoon to you.'

35

'You paint a very vivid picture, Captain Catto.'

Surrounded by a group of mainly young men, all of whom seemed to be hanging on his every word, Catto adopted a suitably modest expression. His talk on Dettingen had been received with rapturous applause and declared a triumph. Considering he'd had no time to prepare and had delivered it completely off the cuff, he was feeling rather pleased with himself. He had concentrated on the battle rather than the politics and pulled no punches in describing the grim realities of modern warfare. Let them get a glimpse of what it's really like. Might make some of them think twice.

He was realizing now that his blood, guts and gore descriptions had exercised that impact on some of his listeners and the opposite on others. The Honourable Cosmo Liddell and his friends seemed still determined to see battles as romantic and heroic. Obviously he hadn't painted that picture vividly enough.

It was all too vivid inside his own head: the deafening noise of conflict as swords clashed against swords, the whistle of musket balls and bullets, the thud of cannon fire, the smell of gunpowder, the stench of death, the whinnying of wounded horses. Oh God, the horses … Sometimes he lay awake at night thinking about them. What misbegotten bastards men were to bring such wonderful creatures to the places of carnage where so many of them fell along with their riders.

'Captain?'

Plastering a look of interest on his face, Catto allowed himself to be introduced to yet more of Edinburgh's *prominenti*. Half-an-hour later, he was in possession of three more invitations. One was to deliver the same talk to a group of gentlemen in South Queensferry, whenever was convenient to him. He would stay the night, of course. They could guarantee him a good supper and it would be their pleasure and privilege to ensure he was as comfortable in the accommodations they would provide as they could possibly make them.

He was also bid to sup one evening at his very earliest convenience at the house of Professor MacLaurin, who wanted to discuss with him the terrible state of the city walls. The good professor seemed very concerned about them. It was nice to know someone was.

The third invitation was the most intriguing. He was asked to the private dinner of a club which met in a tavern in the Parliament Square. The busy little man who issued the invitation was infuriatingly coy, not even naming the club or saying very much about it.

He was skirting and dancing around the subject to such an extent Catto was currently fighting the impulse to grab him by the throat and demand that he speak plainly. Look! Just tell me! I have an appointment with the buxom and very obliging Lizzie Gibson within the hour and I don't want to miss a single second of her delightful company!

Cosmo Liddell sidled up, clapped him on the shoulder and laughed both at the busy little man and the ill-concealed impatience on Catto's face. 'I know, I know, Catto. We are being very mysterious.' He tapped the side of his nose. 'Have to keep this out of female sight, that's the thing. Not for the eyes or ears of the petticoats.' He stepped closer and lowered his voice. 'The Beggar's Benison. That's the name of the club. Keep it to yourself. If you're a broad-minded man with an eye for the ladies, as I think you are, you won't want to miss it. Will you come? Tomorrow night? Hideously short notice, I know, but we don't meet that often and we're very keen to have you as a member.'

Well. His social stock was certainly rising. Whether this particular invitation meant anything more significant was yet to be discovered.

Lizzie Gibson lifted her head off Catto's shoulder. Raising herself up, she placed one hand flat on the bed on either side of him. 'How did ye enjoy that, Captain?'

He smiled up at her. 'As if you didn't know, Miss Gibson.' Reaching up, he twirled a strand of her hair around his index finger. Her shining locks were not unlike his own, both in length and in terms of the deep waves which tumbled over her luscious breasts. Her hair was fair, although he suspected some artifice had been employed there. The evidence was to be seen elsewhere on her glorious body. 'Did you enjoy it?'

'Very much, Captain. You're a grand lover.'

Catto's smile didn't falter. 'I'd wager you say the same to all your gentlemen friends.'

The dimple in Lizzie's right cheek put in an appearance. 'Aye. But sometimes I mean it. Will ye get up now and slip on a robe and I'll ring for our supper?'

He administered a playful slap to her well-rounded rear. 'If you'll get off me.' As she eased herself off him, he put his hands behind his head, staying on his back while she untied the thin pink satin ribbon from the membrane covering his shrinking cock. He suppressed a grimace of distaste as Lizzie peeled it and its now unwanted cargo off and whisked it all away in the direction of the two small basins on the other side of the bed.

'Thank you for agreeing to wear this, Captain.'

He waved a hand in acknowledgement and dismissal of her thanks, something she had expressed on each of his visits to her. He'd found her via a very helpful little book entitled *A Guide to the Ladies of Pleasure of Edinburgh*. That bookseller in Marlin's Wynd had pressed it into his hands as a gift, babbling with gratitude when Catto told him it wasn't exactly within his remit to be bothered about the questionable literature the man had in his backshop. He'd had some idea of working his way through the ladies listed, as it were, finding it useful to know in advance which of them had good teeth and a pleasant disposition, but on his first foray he had found Lizzie and liked her.

On his previous visit she'd asked him to stay on to supper tonight, which had at the time filled him with unholy glee. They'd both been stark naked, Lizzie bent over his cock, full breasts dangling. Yet she'd issued the invitation with such gentility, as though she'd been asking him to come and take tea with her in a parlour full of chaperones.

The debris Lizzie was disposing of now would have shocked the chaperones. He didn't like wearing armour, no man did, but it protected them both. Not that it was always foolproof. 'How's your boy, Lizzie?'

'He's well and happy, sir, thank you for asking. Soon be out of his petticoats.' She smiled. 'I'm going down to Leith over Yule to spend a few days with him and my mother.'

'Does he think she's his mother too?'

'It has to be that way, Captain,' Lizzie said, slipping into her own robe and dropping another on the bed for Catto. 'Folk are that quick to judge, ye ken?'

'Aye,' he said, sitting up and pulling on the robe while she walked over to the bell-pull. 'Let he who is without sin cast the first stone. That was quick,' he said a moment later in response to a sharp rat-a-tat-tat. Launching himself off the edge of the bed, he crossed the small room and swung open the door.

It was the madam herself who was bringing their supper. His stock must be rising here too. That might be because he was turning into a regular customer. Or because they'd also heard the story of last Saturday's sortie and were thinking an influential Captain of the Town Guard might be of use to them. As they might be to him.

'Can you wait a moment?' he asked as the madam deposited the tray on the small table in front of the window. 'There's something I want to ask you. Both of you,' he said, including Lizzie in the request. His coat was hanging on the back of a chair. Bringing out one of the drawings Christian Rankeillor had made, he showed it to them. 'Do either of you recognize this girl?'

'Who wants to know?' Lizzie asked, adding an apologetic, 'I'm no' wanting to get anyone into trouble, Captain.'

'She can't get into any more trouble, Lizzie,' Catto said drily. 'She's dead.'

'Was she one of us?'

'A street girl. I was hoping you might know her all the same. Her name was Jeannie Carmichael and she lived in the Grassmarket.'

'Don't think I know her,' Lizzie said, studying the drawing. 'Knew her, I mean.' She looked up. 'Was she done away with?'

'That's what I'm trying to find out.' Catto turned to the madam. 'How about you?'

'Don't think I know her either but if you leave this with us I'll ask my other young ladies to take a look, Captain. I'll let you know on your next visit if any of them recognized her.' She looked at Lizzie and back at him again. 'Or am I assuming too much in thinking you'll be visiting us again?'

He grinned at her. 'Oh, there'll be another visit. Quite a few, I hope.'

Catto watched Lizzie putting out their supper, lazily enjoying the view of bouncing hair and bouncing breasts, peeping out from the middle of the unfastened robe. 'Thanks,' he said as she handed him a plate. 'Now get your own and come and sit on my lap to eat it.'

'Ooh,' she said, obeying that instruction, 'ready for more, are ye?'

'Always.' Bending his head, he raked each of her nipples with his teeth before lifting a slice of toasted bread and cheese and taking a healthy bite out of it.

'Dinna do that the other way round, Captain.'

'Wouldn't dream of it,' he mumbled through toast and cheese.

'Have you,' he asked once he had chewed, savoured and swallowed it, 'ever heard of a gentleman's club called the Beggar's Benison?'

'Dinna tell me they've asked you to become one o' their knights?'

'One of their knights?'

'Ye dinna ken onything aboot them?' She laughed. 'Och, Captain, you are in for a treat!'

As he walked back to the guard-house through the chill of the night, he wondered if Archie Liddell were sharp enough to have got the subtle messages he'd sent across the table to him earlier in the day. Failing that, he'd have to hope the man would repeat their conversation to Balnamoon or Cosmo Liddell or that those two would make it their business to get it out of him. They were bound to be watching the guard-house, would know Archie Liddell had spent some time there today.

He needed the message to get through. To be sure that it did, he would have to call on Christian Rankeillor. A series of images of her began to glide through his head. Miss Hoity-toity Rankeillor in her daft hooped skirts, looking down her nose at him. The earnest girl trying to convince him of the benefits of dissection. The neat young apothecary's daughter, lowering the hood of her cloak. The distressed girl with her back turned to him, that one mahogany curl so dark against her creamy skin as they stood together in the darkening quadrangle of the hospital. The kind girl who had given him something to lessen the pain in his head.

And how had he responded to her kindness? By snarling at her. Which was as nothing compared to what he might be going to do to her now. If things went to plan on Friday night she stood to lose all that she held dear. If the Jacobite agent was still in Edinburgh, Catto would have to arrest not only him but Balnamoon, Patrick Rankeillor too when he returned from Glasgow. He'd have to put her under house arrest and armed guard to prevent her from trying to get a warning to her father.

What would happen to Balnamoon and Rankeillor after they were arrested was not Catto's decision to make. Rankeillor had influential friends. That might help. Or it might not. At the very least both men would be imprisoned. So she would lose her father, Balnamoon, her home and her status. Would Edinburgh Royal Infirmary still see her as a member of their family after that?

He was about to ruin her life.

If he didn't, she might go on to suffer unspeakable horror.

Do you know what can happen to girls and women in time of war, sir?

Before he could stop it, he was seeing what had happened at the farmhouse in Saxony happening to her. Shaken, he struggled to banish the obscene images, using all his willpower to summon her up as he had seen her today and this week. He had to focus on those pictures, not some hideous future he was imagining for her. He had to focus on how she was now.

The skilled healer, preparing him physic. The kind girl, giving him that physic to lessen the pain in his head. The neat young apothecary's daughter, lowering the hood of her cloak-

Lowering the hood of her cloak but coming from the inside of the hospital. He hadn't seen her outside the building because she hadn't been there. She'd been inside and had flipped the hood of her cloak over her head to disguise that fact. She was taking food and drink to the fugitive. It had to be her. Balnamoon would be too much noticed. So she was giving aid and comfort to one of the King's enemies. A hanging offence.

They hanged women for a lot less.

Lizzie Gibson looked up as her door was pushed open. 'Och,' she said, 'no one else tonight. We agreed—' Her voice changed. 'Oh. How did you get in here?'

The man closed the door behind him and walked forward to where she sat in front of the fire. 'It's a bawdy house, Lizzie. I paid to get in here.'

'I'm not lying with you!'

His eyes slid up and down her generous curves. 'You're not to my taste, Lizzie.'

'I was good enough for your friends,' she said bitterly.

'They paid you well.'

'Not well enough for what they did to me.'

He shrugged. 'You're a whore, Lizzie. Your body's for hire. What did he want?'

'Who?'

'Don't be stupid, Lizzie. Your last customer.'

'What do you think he wanted? As ye said yersel, this is a bawdy-house. We didna sing the psalms thegither.'

'Watch your mouth. Did he want anything else?'

'I don't talk about my gentlemen!' She realized too late that the drawing Robert Catto had left was still lying on the table in front of the window, saw her visitor's eyes go to it. Lizzie sprang to her feet but he got there first.

'He asked you about her, did he?'

'That's nane o' your business!'

'Och, but it is.' He looked at the drawing for a moment before striding over to the fire and throwing it onto the glowing coals.

'I'll tell him you did that!'

'No, you won't. How do you think I recognized her?'

Lizzie's eyes widened in horror. 'You did away wi' the lassie?'

She got no answer to that, only a question in return. It was the same one Robert Catto had put to her, only delivered with chilly menace. 'How's your boy, Lizzie?'

36

A hanged man was a vile sight. A hanged woman was immeasurably worse. Obscene. Disgusting. Unnatural. He could see her, twisting in the wind, her neck broken by the fall and the cruel jerk of the rope, her head at a hellish angle, her dark hair spilling out of a white linen cap. He'd been seeing that unholy vision of her all night, tossing and turning as sleep eluded him.

He tried telling himself she was a lady and that they didn't hang ladies. Not any more. He tried telling himself that both she and her father had influential friends, not least the Lord President. Then he remembered what Duncan Forbes had said, his voice shaking with emotion, about how the might of England would react to any rebellion in Scotland. The velvet glove would give way to the mailed fist, the response brutal and vicious.

The people the Lord President called those buggers in London were smug about Scotland now. Their troublesome northern neighbour had been broken, tamed and brought to heel. Rebellion would prove them wrong. Rebellion would scare them witless. Rebellion would be crushed without pity. There would be trials and hangings, confiscation of houses and estates. Even the seeds of a rebellion would be crushed without pity. Catto's eyes went to his desk and the neat little packet lying there.

'Captain Catto.' Her voice was as cool as that drink of water she'd given him on Monday.

'I'm afraid so.' He closed the shop door and, as its bell continued to jump and jangle, nodded a greeting to her customer. 'Pray continue with what you are doing, Miss Rankeillor. I can wait.'

'Oh, thank you. That's most gracious of you.'

Ouch. And twice ouch. He was grateful for the distraction when the bell rang with renewed vigour. The first person to enter was a young black boy, richly dressed in wine-coloured velvet, curled white wig, swirling black cloak and tricorne hat. Removing that with as extravagant a flourish as Catto had ever seen, he held the door wide, bowing his mistress into the shop. The entrance of the Queen of Sheba. Otherwise known as Charlotte Liddell. Sister of the Honourable Cosmo and foremost of Edinburgh's Jacobite misses. Catto recognized her immediately.

'Kirsty,' she said, sweeping over to the counter in a rustle of flowered silk. 'My dear! How are you? I hear you had a most unpleasant experience last Saturday night! A quite dreadful ordeal! You must tell me all about it! Unburden yourself!' She continued without drawing breath. 'I have brought the ticket money from myself and my friends for the Daft Friday ball. Is that not good of me?' She beckoned the boy forward. 'Joshua has it.'

'Good morning, Charlotte. I shall take the money from Joshua in a moment. As soon as Mr Murray and I complete our transaction.'

That response hadn't gone down too well. Not that Charlotte Liddell's smile had faltered. If anything, it had grown wider. Pity it hadn't reached her eyes. When she spoke again her voice was steely. 'I should like to give you the money now, Kirsty. I would have thought you might be grateful to me for collecting it. The patronage of myself and my friends is important for the Infirmary, is it not?'

'Indeed it is, Charlotte. We at the Infirmary are very grateful for all the support the hospital receives. However, I am in the middle of serving Mr Murray. His wife is sick and he is understandably anxious to get back to her.'

'I c-can w-wait if you like, Miss K-Kirsty,' the man stuttered.

'Someone who knows his place,' Charlotte Liddell said. 'How refreshing. Increasingly I find that people don't.' Now she was giving Christian Rankeillor the top-to-toe treatment.

Any minute now. Catto wasn't disappointed. The haughty chin went up.

'I know my place very well, Charlotte. Right at this moment it's behind the counter serving Mr Murray.'

Oh, it was tempting. He could stand back and watch them fight it out. Or he could behave like a gentleman for a change and defuse the tension. One small thing he could do for her. He coughed, and brought Charlotte Liddell spinning round. He wasn't unfamiliar with women looking at him and liking what they saw. He saw it now as she took in the elegance of his uniform and the stiff black bow of his bagwig, the switch from bitch to coquette. Not a pretty sight. 'Sir?' She didn't have nearly so pleasant a voice as Christian Rankeillor.

'Madam,' he responded, making her a little bow.

She put out the tip of her tongue and licked the underside of her top lip. Too obvious. Much too obvious.

'I did not see you there, sir. Must I wait my turn behind you too?' The smile had become charmingly quizzical. Wondering how she would react if he came out with, 'Aye, you must, you spoiled wee brat,' he saw her toss an instruction over her shoulder. 'Pray serve Mr Murray, Kirsty, but kindly introduce me to this gentleman first.'

'Twas a pity she couldn't see the expression on Kirsty Rankeillor's face. Or maybe that was just as well. Catto suspected she really couldn't afford to antagonize this unpleasant young woman. So he would ride to her rescue, turn on the charm. He must be able to remember how to do that. 'If I may make so bold, madam,' he drawled to Charlotte Liddell, 'perhaps I may introduce myself.'

Her eyes grew very wide when he did.

Catto closed the door behind Charlotte Liddell and her young footman. Christian Rankeillor had her back to him, replacing jars and bottles on the apple-green shelves behind the counter with rather more force than was necessary.

'I thought Charlotte Liddell was a particular friend of yours.'

'Did you? Fancy that.'

'You share each other's politics, do you not?'

'I believe I have already told you I am not prepared to discuss such matters with you.' One more blue-and-white apothecary's jar was banged down on the shelves. 'You do not share her politics yet you seemed to be getting on famously with her.'

'You may have noticed that I did not satisfy her curiosity about what happened at your house on Saturday night. One should not always believe what one sees, Miss Rankeillor.'

'Regarding politics?'

'Regarding liking and disliking. I cannot abide young ladies like Charlotte Liddell.'

'What sort of young ladies are those?'

'Spoilt and unpleasant ones. With not an ounce of kindness in them. Please turn around. You've put all the lotions and potions away now.' She did as he'd asked, although she was bestowing one of her best glowers on him. Unlike Charlotte Liddell, she had absolutely no inclination to flirt with him, that much was obvious. Given that he'd invaded her home, told her he'd coupled in the street with a prostitute and been breathtakingly rude to her each time they'd met, he supposed that was hardly surprising.

That was only the start of what he was going to do to her. He would hang no one but in his actions here this morning and over these next few days he would fashion the noose. He could do nothing else. Liddell had said it. Duty was duty. His task now was to inveigle her into trusting him. Lay the trap and watch her step into it.

'Would an apology get me anywhere?'

The dark eyebrows shot up. 'I shouldn't have thought you the type of man who goes in for apologies. Nor should I have thought you one who sets much store by kindness.'

'Then you are wrong. I consider kindness to be a much under-rated virtue.' *Although what I'm doing here is the opposite of kindness. You should not trust me, Kirsty Rankeillor.*

'Really? My acquaintance with you thus far would not have inclined me to think that of you.'

'Perhaps you should not judge a book by its cover.'

'I tend to judge people by their actions.'

He laid a hand on his chest, acknowledging the hit, hating himself for the gallantry. She would know him soon enough for what he really was. Her sworn enemy. 'As for apologies, I've been known to offer them now and again.' His thoughts flashed to Geordie. 'When I really owe one to someone.'

She folded her arms. She wore a dress the colour of buttermilk today, its bodice decorated with a row of rich brown velvet bows, her hair covered by her usual neat white linen cap. She looked fresh and pretty and innocent. Still fierce, though.

That fighting spirit wasn't going to help her at all. She'd be defiant, speak out, say exactly what she thought, talk back to arresting officers, gaolers, lawyers and judges. Influential friends might plead for her, he might say she'd been acting under the command of her father. Hell would freeze over before she would agree to that: and she'd get herself hanged for it.

'Aiblins you offer an apology when you want something from someone.'

'Don't we all change our tune when we want something from somebody else?'

'I helped you on Monday. I didn't get much thanks for it.'

'I apologize for behaving like an ungrateful oaf on Monday.'

'Only on Monday?'

Ouch again. On Monday the after effects of the blow to his head had made him see two of her. Today he felt as though there were two of him. His thoughts were running on one track, dark and dangerous and to be concealed at all costs from her. The words coming so fluently out of his mouth were his method of concealment. Lies. Half-truths. Betrayals.

'I apologize if I have made the situation more awkward for you by being here when Charlotte Liddell called.'

'I cannot say I am looking forward to the Daft Friday ball as I normally do.'

'Because you will be the subject of gossip?' he asked, pretty sure she had a lot more to worry about on Friday night than wagging tongues. She was dissembling too.

'That seems inevitable.' She gave herself the little shake he was beginning to recognize as one of her mannerisms. She did it when she shifted from one subject to another. 'But why should that concern you? Is that not the result you wanted, to purposefully make the situation awkward for me and mine? You were not very kind on Saturday evening.'

'I was doing my duty on Saturday evening.'

'You appeared to me to be taking considerable pleasure in it.'

'Appearances can be deceptive.' *Oh, and they can also be exactly what they seem.*

'Can they? How is your head, Captain Catto? Do you require more physic?'

'My head does very well. Thank you,' he added.

'Then why are you here?' She glanced over her shoulder through the window between the shop and the house. 'If you tarry much longer, I fear Betty may feel the need to come in here to safeguard my honour.'

'Heaven forfend,' he murmured, and felt his heart turn over when the comment drew forth a tiny smile. If she only knew what he was really doing here. 'There is something I wish to ask you. I also have some information for you. I have found out the name of the girl. She was Jean Carmichael. Jeannie.'

Christian Rankeillor sank back against the high stool set behind the counter. 'Jeannie,' she repeated. 'Jeannie Carmichael.' She looked up at him. 'You found her family?'

Catto shook his head. 'Another girl who stayed in the same lodging house in the Grassmarket. 'Twould appear Jeannie Carmichael had no family worthy of the name.'

'They were cruel to her?'

'They introduced her to the life she led. She ran away from them – she was from Fife – and came to Edinburgh.'

'Where she followed the same kind of life?' She'd pulled a handkerchief out of her pocket.

'I think she probably had no other choice.'

'She was not very old, was she?'

'No. She was not very old.'

Christian Rankeillor put her handkerchief to her nose. 'Thank you,' she said after a moment, returning the scrap of cloth to her pocket. 'For finding out her name. And for coming here to tell me what it was.' She rose to her feet. 'You mentioned something you wanted to ask me about?'

Bringing the seeds out of his pocket in the fresh packet to which he had transferred them, Catto emptied them onto the counter. 'You know a considerable amount about plants and remedies, I believe. Can you identify these for me?'

She reached out with thumb and index finger, picked one of the seeds out of his palm and held it up to the window. 'These are sunflower seeds.'

'I thought they were.'

'How did you come by them?'

'Someone put them into the pocket of my coat either on Sunday or Monday.'

She turned from the window and looked at him. 'That big leather riding coat?'

'Yes. I thought you might have put them there. Or Mr Buchan of Balnamoon.'

She waited a second too long before answering him. 'Why would either of us have done that?'

'You tell me. Or perhaps you might ask him.' Their eyes met across the counter. 'You drew the map, didn't you? And don't say *what map*? You know more than I thought you did.'

'I cannot possibly know what you thought, sir. Have our overlords in London now decreed it is against the law for a Scotswoman to draw a map of Scotland?'

'It may arouse suspicion if that map comes with a list of military garrisons and their strengths. Ah,' he said, watching her reaction, 'I didn't think you had added those. They are done by a different hand. Although it worried you when you saw me holding the map. Why was that, I wonder?'

She didn't answer him. No matter. He had worked this out since he had realized she was the cartographer. It was giving him a tiny spark of hope for her. She had not knowingly drawn a map intended to be used by the officers of a rebel army. If she could be persuaded to say as little as possible after she was arrested, not speak out, that ignorance of the purpose of the map might work in her favour. He would attest to that himself, put it in writing. Hellfire, he'd find some way to stay on in this bloody place so he might give such evidence at her trial.

'You're a woman of many talents,' he said lightly. 'Although some of those might get you into trouble. Like drawing naked bodies. Of men as well as women.'

'Only among the narrow-minded.'

'Pity they are often also people of power and influence.'

'Are we striking a bargain here, sir?'

'We could be. Perhaps we can help each other. Believe me, Miss

Rankeillor, nothing would please me more than to find myself in a position where I might be able to help you.' He saw the confusion in her eyes, did not know why he said what he did next. 'In the meantime you might tell me, if you please, what purpose sunflowers serve. In terms of physic, I mean.' Using his palm as a funnel, he poured the seeds back into their packet and returned that to the pocket of his uniform coat.

'Many and various. One may employ the seeds directly or the flowers themselves. A very efficacious oil may be extracted which can be used both internally and externally. An infusion of the leaves can be very effective in treating the whooping cough. Sunflower ointment is very soothing if one is footsore— Oh.'

'Oh?' he queried.

'It's nothing.'

'You have piqued my curiosity. 'Twould be cruel not to satisfy it.'

She spoke with obvious reluctance. 'While you were insensible you murmured something about sunflowers. Something about your mother and sunflowers.'

He remembered now. Funny how a dream evaporated so quickly when you awoke, yet could be recalled hours or even days later.

'Sunflowers were a feature of your mother's garden?'

'My grandfather's.' For once he didn't turn the personal question aside. He wasn't thinking straight. ''Twas a walled garden. I loved it, the sunflowers especially. They were so much taller than I was. Yet I always thought they were such friendly flowers.'

'Because they seem to have smiling faces.'

'Aye,' he agreed. 'Because they seem to have smiling faces.' He registered that she had moved nearer to her side of the counter, the two of them close enough for him to be able to see her beautiful eyelashes, thick, dark and lustrous. God, but she had a lovely mouth too, one made for kissing … and he had no business to be thinking of her in this way. Especially not when that vile picture of her dangling from a gibbet had slid once again into his head.

'Mr Catto? Captain?'

He raised his eyes. 'Were you not running quite a risk by obliging Charlotte Liddell to wait until you had served the customer who was here when she arrived?'

'Och, yes! But there are times when I cannot thole having to defer to her and people like her. The Infirmary is so dependent on donations. We get many small ones from folk who cannot afford to give us much but desperately want to contribute to the work of the hospital.'

'The widow's mite?'

'Aye. To be fair, there are wealthy people too who give out of the goodness of their hearts and brush aside any thanks offered to them.'

'But Charlotte Liddell and her kind aren't numbered among the latter?'

'No. They expect something for their largesse. To be bowed and scraped to. Fawned over. Told their terrible poetry and their awful drawings and paintings are wonderful. Och,' she said, 'how I loathe people like that! How I loathe it when they are so haughty and condescending to good, honest, folk. I despise people who look down their noses at other people. Have I said something amusing, sir?'

He folded his arms across his dark red chest. 'If you don't know I'm not going to tell you.' Nor could he fathom how he could be finding anything funny, although he was thanking God that the image of her looking down her nose at him on Saturday night had replaced the other picture. 'The physic you gave me helped the pain in my head. I should pay you for it.'

'No one who is treated at the Infirmary is required to pay for their treatment or for their physic.'

'Your father does not supply the latter gratis, surely?'

'Of course he does. It is for the Infirmary.'

She said that as though it were an article of faith, a central tenet of her creed, as he supposed it was. Unfolding his arms, he dug into his pocket for his purse. 'You will permit me to make a donation to the hospital in lieu of payment?'

'Donations to the hospital are always welcome.'

'As long as I do not expect you to defer to me in return?'

'For preference.' Lifting the circle of keys at her waist, she went to a cupboard, unlocked it and brought out a money box with a slit in its lid. Returning with it, she laid it on the counter in front of him and he dropped a few coins into it. They did not have far to fall, and made the unmistakeable sound of landing on other coins.

'Pretty full.'

'Our customers are generous.'

'Grateful too, I imagine. You were very kind to that man who was in here just now.'

'His wife is dying of the canker. He is in sore need of kindness.' Another tenet of her creed. 'Was there anything else, sir?'

'Yes. What am I to do with these seeds?'

'You could always try planting them. That is generally considered quite a sensible thing to do with seeds.'

'Really? I should never have guessed. I shall do so as soon as I return to the guard-house.'

'No, you won't.' She spoke in tones of amused scorn. 'That would be daft. Wait until next spring. Put them in little pots on a sunny windowsill until the weather's warm enough for them to be planted outside.'

Next spring. When he would be long gone, back in Europe. When Christian Rankeillor might no longer exist, all her fiery life and spirit quenched, scattered to the four winds.

'The guard-house doesn't have much by way of a garden.'

'Sunflowers don't need much of a garden. They flourish on the stoniest soil.'

He had to force himself. 'Then you will be hoping they take root. Sunflowers also have a symbolic meaning, do they not?'

'Unswerving loyalty.'

'To a political cause, for example?'

'For example.'

'Do sunflowers as a symbol of unswerving loyalty have a particular significance for any particular political cause?'

'I think you know the answer to that, sir.'

'As do you, Miss Rankeillor. I underestimated you, didn't I?'

'I'm used to that.'

'So am I. Miss Rankeillor, let me say something to you.' He spoke urgently, lowered his voice. 'Do you really want to see Scotland plunged into bloodshed for nothing more than a change of kings? Do you really want to risk everyone and everything you hold dear?'

'A change of kings,' she repeated. 'You think that's all this is about?'

'What else?' he demanded.

'Reclaiming ourselves. Our name and our pride, our ability to care for our people, to devote ourselves to the common weal, to move forward, to progress.' The proud chin went up. 'You are a Scotsman too, I think. You're happy for your country to be ruled by others?'

'I take no interest in politics.'

Her eyes flashed. 'Then you take no interest in life!'

Suddenly he was angry with her. She spoke so passionately of life yet was prepared to throw away her own on the bloody Stuart Cause. Had that accursed family not ruined enough lives? He wanted to take her by the shoulders and shake some sense into her. He wanted to yell at her, demand to know why she had no fucking sense of her own safety and self-preservation. He wanted to warn her, tell her disaster was heading straight for her if she didn't step out of the way. He wanted to tell her to leave Edinburgh and stay away until it had all blown over. So he could not trust himself to say anything at all.

She had gone very stiff. 'You are a busy man, sir, with places to go and people to see. So I shall bid you good day.'

'Jamie, I did not know what to say!'

'You did very well by the sound of it, Kirsty. Said neither yea nor nay to him. Leave this to me now. I'll take it from here.'

'You will approach him more directly?'

'The sunflower seeds were an approach. Which he seems to have come to the shop today to answer.'

'Seems to have? We cannot rely on how things seem, Jamie!'

'We may have to. He is the Captain of the Town Guard and a serving army officer. He cannot afford to overtly state his position. He must needs hint and allude. As he did to you this morning.'

She shook her head, not convinced. 'It was you who put the sunflower seeds into his pocket?'

'No, but I know who did. If 'twill reassure you, I can tell you that person also plans to approach him more directly tonight and will be more confident in doing so after I have told him what you have just told me.'

'That person must remain on his guard. As you must too, Jamie. Robert Catto confused me with what he said.' She frowned. 'Confused me greatly.'

Jamie lifted her hand to his mouth and kissed it. 'Leave this to me,' he said again. 'I am not relying only on Robert Catto. Got some other tricks up my sleeve. What you must do now is confirm the details of the plan to Mr Fox. Only two more days to go, Kirsty. Two more days and we may breathe freely again.'

37

He'd been in some tight corners, strange places and downright odd situations in his time. He had never experienced anything quite so bizarre as this. He was in the upstairs room of a tavern in the Parliament Close, sitting at the head of a long table set for an elaborate supper. As yet, neither he nor his twelve fellow diners had embarked upon that.

It was the centre-piece of the table which was drawing Catto's gaze. Displayed on a wooden model of a human head, he was staring at an old-fashioned full-bottomed wig. The head was set on a stand a foot tall. Despite that, the wig's cascading curls brushed the table. He had registered it and its somewhat piebald appearance as he sat down, ushered into the place of honour by his host, whom Cosmo Liddell introduced as the sovereign of the club. That gentleman explained to Catto why the wig was composed of hair of different hues.

'The pubic hair of Charles II's mistresses?' He roused himself to comment. They would expect that of him. 'Well, we all know the merry monarch had an eye for the ladies but even for him it must have taken some time to gather together enough hair to make this. I wonder if Mistress Gwyn and Milady Castlemaine flinched when they saw the king approaching them yet again with a pair of scissors in his hand. Delicately wrought of the finest silver though those undoubtedly were.'

Looking up in response to the laughter his musings provoked, he found the other men sitting around the table smiling broadly at him. Apart from Cosmo Liddell, Hector Grant and Arthur Menzies, they were all quite a bit older than him. They might have been kindly uncles giving a favourite nephew a treat.

The evening's entertainment had begun with the ushering into the room, from a closet in the corner of it, of two naked girls. With the stern admonition that there was to be absolutely no touching, Catto had joined the members of the club in filing past the young ladies as they struck various illuminating poses. He had looked his fill, striving to fill his head with warm, living female flesh, not those foul visions which continued to beset him. As he was doing his utmost to concentrate on the here and now.

The stories Lizzie Gibson had told him about the proceedings of the Beggar's Benison had been hair-raising. Although apparently it was not one's hair one might be called upon to raise. It was not that he doubted his ability to do so. 'Twas only that he preferred to keep such matters between himself and the girl he might be with at the time. Or his own good right hand.

The sovereign was pushing his chair back, lifting some objects from the table as he stood up. Catto watched warily as the older man approached him. Lizzie had said something about measurements being taken, and mentioned a platter in which one's … production … was gathered and compared with that of the other members of the club. Catto was hoping to hell she'd been having some fun at his expense. Stopping at his chair, the sovereign bent forward in a bow.

'Sir. We are honoured that you have agreed to be invested as a knight of the Ancient & Most Puissant Order of the Beggar's Benison. To this end, we beg you to accept these tokens of membership.' A strip of silk was placed around his neck, something halfway between a collar and a cravat. Better than having it put around another part of his anatomy. 'We beg you to accept these medals.'

Catto took the first and examined it. On one side were two naked figures who must represent Adam and Eve. He drew that inference from the engraved banner around the edges of the medal, *Be Fruitful & Multiply.* Turning it over, he found another male and female figure. The woman sat with her legs splayed, holding a purse in her right hand and using her left to point at the man's genitals. The words in the banner above their heads read *May Prick & Purse Never Fail You.*

'Thank you,' Catto said gravely. Judging by the expectant looks, more was required of him. 'A most … eh … appropriate motto for any man.'

The man sitting to his left clapped him on the shoulder. 'Although I canna think a handsome young chiel like yourself ever has to worry about the former!'

Catto managed a laugh in return. Oh God. He could come up with some bawdy stories if he had to. He didn't want to have to come up with anything else. The sovereign took the medal from him and fastened it to the silk collar. He was handed two more, both showing Adam and Eve on one side but with different designs on the reverse. The first showed an anchor with an erect phallus laid across it, a bulging purse hanging suggestively from its tip.

The second depicted Venus asleep, Cupid at her side and Adonis the hunter stealing up behind her. The banner above his head read *Lose No Opportunity.* Catto repeated the words and looked up. Cosmo Liddell smiled at him. 'Another most appropriate motto for any man.'

Low already, his spirits plummeted further still. Was that all the coded message had been about, the arrangements for a meeting like this one? Was he sitting through this bloody flummery only to learn nothing?

'Finally, sir,' the sovereign said, 'we ask you to accept our official diploma.'

Catto took the black leather document roll and once again noted the air of expectation.

'Open it, sir,' urged one of his fellow knights. One of his fellow knights? He was as crazy as they were. He wondered if they celebrated sex in this way because they weren't actually getting very much. Or any. Liddell, Grant and Menzies excepted, probably.

'Read it out to us,' drawled Liddell. 'This is all part of the initiation ceremony.'

'He must toast the wig first,' someone said.

All eyes swivelled back to that remarkable object. A glass brimming with claret was put into his hand. It was shaped like a penis. Down to the last detail. Or details. 'Twas not easy to decide where to hold it. He raised it. 'The wig.'

'The wig,' came the various responses. With mock solemnity, Cosmo Liddell stood up, bowed to the wig and placed it carefully on Catto's head. It was big enough to fit easily over his own hair. 'You must see yourself in it. Fetch the looking-glass, somebody.'

'You look not unlike the merry monarch yourself, sir,' one of the kindly uncles said, obeying that casually autocratic order.

Even in the wig, he looked nothing like Charles II, although he supposed the comment had been meant as a compliment. What brought him up short was how like the portrait of his great-great-grandsire he looked. He hadn't thought about that portrait in years, or the castle whose walls it adorned, that rugged fortress in the north-east.

Best not to think about that. 'Twas always best not to think about that. Fortunately the wig was providing him with an excellent distraction. Here he was, about to read out loud an undoubtedly obscene document whilst wearing a wig made out of the pubic hair of Charles II's mistresses. 'Twas almost like tipping the velvet to those legendary courtezans.

Unrolling the document, he began to read out loud that he had been created, admitted and received as a *Knight Companion of the Most Ancient & Most Puissant Order of the Beggar's Benison and Merryland* which, apparently, entitled him '*...to enjoy the celebrated territory of Merryland with privileges of ingress, egress and regress from and to all* *of the harbours, creeks, havens and commodious inlets of the extensive territory at his pleasure...'*

These excrutiating puns were almost as bad as that terrible Jacobite poetry he'd had to read.

'Not that I imagine you've ever needed a diploma to enjoy the delights of Merryland, eh, Catto?' Cosmo Liddell murmured the words in his ear as they clattered down the narrow wooden staircase from the supper room. 'Sorry if you found that a bit tame but I thought it might amuse you. We have something rather more exciting planned for Friday night. Not with that lot up there, of course. Like to come along?'

'It's Daft Friday. Aren't you going to the ball at the Assembly Rooms?'

'While you're keeping the peace? You'll be able to do that and join us. Arthur, Hector and myself prefer the dead of night for our occasional little adventures.'

'Those adventures comprising what, exactly?'

'Something more suited to a man of action such as yourself,' Liddell said silkily. 'Where we require the trollops to do more for their five shillings than simply stand there. Get the little bitches hot and sweaty and working for their money. If you catch my drift, sir. Fancy going on somewhere for a drink or two before we say goodnight?'

Catto did catch his drift. He didn't much like it, as the last thing he wanted to do now was go carousing with Liddell and his acolytes. Liddell laid a hand on his shoulder.

'Come on, Catto. Lose no opportunity, eh?'

He looked into the man's eyes and could not tell whether he was seeing hidden depths or hidden shallows. So he could not risk calling it a night just yet. There might be more to be found out here. Duty was duty.

'I'm drunk as a lord,' he announced to the assembled company.

'Fou',' someone said.

He nodded. 'Fou'. Full of claret and full of brandy. If we were in Prussia or Saxony I'd be betrunken. Or besoffen. Those are both good words, don't you think? Befuddled. That's a good word too, ain't it?'

'Drunk as a puggy,' offered the man sitting beside him.

'Whassa puggy?' Catto demanded.

'A unicorn,' came the reply. 'Like the one on top of the mercat cross.'

'Whyzit called a puggy?'

'No idea. Think I need a wee sleep now, sir.' The man closed his eyes and promptly nodded off.

'Not very friendly,' Catto complained, pushing his now silent companion's head off his shoulder towards the wood panelling on the other side of it. It landed with a crack which failed to disturb its owner. 'Eshpeshially when I wash having an intelligent convershation with him.'

'No,' agreed the voice to his left. He peered at the face. It was very gloomy in this tavern. No unnecessary money wasted on candles in here. 'Although perhaps you could be doing with a wee sleep yourself, sir. Shall I walk you back down to the guard-house?'

'Uncommonly shivil of you,' Catto said as he rose unsteadily to his feet. 'Uncommonly shivil. Tell me something. What happened to Captain Porteoush?'

'The mob hanged him.'

'Really?' He swung wildly round to the first person who'd given him a straight answer to that question. 'Why'd they do that?'

'He crossed them,' his informant said. 'A man in his position can't be too careful, sir. Your position too, eh? The door's over here.'

'I knew that,' Catto said, gasping as the freezing night air hit him. 'Shometimes,' he confided, listening to the sound of two pairs of footsteps on the cobblestones, 'it's very hard to know who's who and what's what.'

'It's wise to be cautious.'

'Absholutely.'

'And a man has to look to his own future, wouldn't you agree, sir? Know which side his bread's buttered. Know when to turn a blind eye.'

'Absholutely,' Catto said again. 'When should I turn a blind eye?'

'Friday night would be good. At the Netherbow Port. Gentleman going home early from the Daft Friday ball. Needs to be on his way to Leith. And a word to the wise, sir. Don't waste your time investigating the death of a whore. Nobody cares. Here we are at the guard-house. We can only hope you're going to remember this conversation come the morning. You don't know who I am, do you? But you'll remember about turning that blind eye? You might get your reward sooner rather than later. We won't forget our friends.'

Catto peered into the gloom. Once he was sure he was alone he stepped back into the shadows around the guard-house door and straightened up. He'd had a few but he was neither fou', betrunken, besoffen or befuddled. The floor of the tavern in which they'd spent the last couple of hours had been filthy. It had been easy enough to drizzle half his drink onto the dirty straw which covered it.

He wasn't the only one who'd been acting a part. So had Arthur Menzies of Edmonstone. Smart enough to affect the manners of a fop and slide them off when not required, but an inexperienced plotter nevertheless. Asking Catto to turn a blind eye when he believed he might be too drunk to remember their conversation the following morning, betraying secrets too.

Friday night would be good. At the Netherbow Port. Gentleman going home early from the ball. It made sense. One man in a mask and evening wig might easily blend in with other men similarly attired. The ball would also offer excellent cover for a final meeting with Edinburgh's Disaffected, especially those unwilling to risk being compromised by meeting other than in such a public place.

So now he knew for certain that the Jacobite spy was still in

Edinburgh. As he knew for certain that Jeannie Carmichael had been murdered.

He came to with a start on Thursday morning, knowing he had slept late and instantly aware of his injured head. He'd drunk enough last night to take the edge off the pain but the alcohol had worn off now. He'd almost forgotten what it was like not to have a sore head. Maybe he'd been born with one.

He'd been dreaming again, of himself going down on Nell Gwyn. Catching the dream before it tore itself into fragments and floated off into the clouds, he knew he and Nell had not been alone. Christian Rankeillor and Geordie had been there too, standing at the top of the stairs in the tavern where the Beggar's Benison had held their meeting and pelting him and Nell, enjoying *soixante-neuf* at the foot of the stairs, with oranges. The brain did funny things with the information you took in during the day.

At least it had spared him gibbets and nooses. Or murdered prostitutes. Did Arthur Menzies of Edmonstone have the balls to have done the deed? Seemed more likely he'd hired some lowlife to get the girl drunk and then smother her. Balnamoon had covered it up, knowing what he was going to see outside the Dispensary window. Easy then for him to suggest that death was due to natural causes.

Consumed by sadness over Jeannie Carmichael's fate, Catto lay for a moment listening to the sounds drifting in through the ill-fitting shutters from the street. He heard the call of a coal-seller, then a woman's voice, politely asking if she might see Captain Robert Catto. His eyes snapped open. Bloody hell. *Bloody hell!*

He jumped out of bed. No time to get dressed. Only enough to shrug his shoulders into his dressing gown. As he swept out into the kitchen Geordie's head snapped up. As did that of the girl sitting at the kitchen table.

38

Christian knew what fear looked like. She had seen it many times, in the startled reactions of children when a disturbance erupted in the street, on the faces of the relatives of a patient lying in the Infirmary in the grip of merciless illness, in the tight-lipped pleas of callers to the shop like Mr Murray yesterday that surely there must be some other kind of physic to try. Never before had she seen quite such a look of terror as there was on the face of the golden-haired young woman who sat at the table in the kitchen of the guard-house. She had to be related to the cook-boy. The resemblance was unmistakeable.

'Geordie,' boomed Robert Catto, 'what is going on here? You will tell me and you will tell me *now*.'

The girl moved only to shrink deeper into the folds of the grey blanket she was clutching around her skinny shoulders, her eyes as wary as those of a woodland animal. Yet when Robert Catto strode towards the table, the bright silk of his dressing-gown sweeping out behind him, she sprang to her feet and put herself between him and the boy.

'Dinna touch Geordie. This is no' his fault!'

Walking forward from where she stood with the Sergeant who had ushered her into the kitchen, the white-haired and bearded one who looked as you imagined God might, Christian walked round the other side of the table and took hold of the sleeve of Robert Catto's dressing-gown. 'You're frightening her,' she murmured, pulling it and him towards the door out into the enclosed courtyard. 'Can you not see that?'

'Aye,' Geordie said, casting a grateful glance at Christian. 'Stay where you are now please, Captain. Although ye've no need to be scared o' him, Alice. Have I no' tellt ye he's no' like yon other gentlemen?'

Robert Catto, Christian and the Sergeant exchanged a look. Realizing her hand was still on the smooth sleeve of that surprisingly sumptuous dressing-gown, she removed it before she spoke again, keeping her voice as low and neutral as possible. 'Perhaps we three should retreat to the other side of the door for a moment. Geordie?'

When the boy nodded his agreement, she led the way out into the courtyard. As the heavy wooden door swung shut behind them, Robert Catto propped himself against the windowsill to the right of it. 'Make yourself at home, Miss Rankeillor. Don't mind me.' His eyes flickered to his Sergeant. 'We'll have to discuss how Geordie managed to smuggle a young girl into the guard-house, Livingstone, but not now. Not a word to anyone about this. All right?'

'Sir,' the man said, and withdrew.

'Are you quite well, Captain Catto? You look a trifle pale.'

'My head hurts,' he said tersely.

Her eyes went to the fading bruise. 'From your injury? Or because you imbibed a drop too much claret or brandy last night?'

He shot her a dirty look, glad she still had the power to annoy him. 'Why do you leap to that conclusion?'

'Because I often see gentlemen suffering from that ailment. They call at the shop first thing in the morning looking for something to take the pain away. Generally also looking more than a little sheepish. Always galling when you've done the damage yourself.'

'On this occasion you're wrong.'

'Then I beg your pardon and wish I had brought you some more physic. Yon other gentlemen?'

'Aye,' Catto said grimly. 'Have you leapt to the same conclusion as I have, Miss Rankeillor?'

She met the sombre grey eyes. 'Putting them together with how frightened she looked when she saw you?'

'Aye.' He gathered the bright folds of the dressing-gown around his body and wrapped his arms about himself to secure it.

'You are feeling the cold, sir. Should I perhaps step back into the kitchen and see what stage the negotiations are at?'

'No. Geordie will come for us as soon as he can. Anyway, I'm not cold.' He glanced down at himself. 'Not in this.'

'It is indeed a splendid garment. A pattern of dragons,' she said, studying it more closely. 'How wonderful. I could wish you would not lean against a stone wall whilst you are wearing it. The fabric will rub.'

He shrugged. 'Hardly a major disaster if it does. Not compared to what seems to have befallen that girl in there.'

I'm only making small talk. Trying to carve out a brief respite from finding out exactly what has befallen that girl in there.

'Whilst we are waiting for Geordie perhaps you might tell me what it is that has brought you to the guard-house this morning, Miss Rankeillor.'

''Tis of no moment,' she said hastily. 'Not now.'

He tilted his head, the better to survey her. The gesture made his unbound hair dip to one side like a gleaming coppery curtain. 'I should like to know what your purpose was, all the same.'

Don't ask me what my purpose was. I don't know! I'm obeying an impulse, born of fear and panic. Albeit an impulse that required a certain amount of preparation and some sneaking around so Betty wouldn't guess what I was up to. If she ever finds out I called at the guard-house to see you, unchaperoned and alone, I'll be in real trouble. Although not as much trouble as you might be going to land us all in.

'I came to bring you a wee Yuletide gift. A bit early I know, but there you are.' *But there you are?* What did that mean? She was rambling, made uncomfortable by the way he was looking at her. More than uncomfortable. Uneasy. 'One for you and one for young Geordie.' She scooped them up out of her basket, two flat boxes fashioned from card, each tied up with narrow ribbons, one red and one green. 'Tablet,' she said, and held both boxes out to him.

Coming to the guard-house this morning, she'd thought of the tablet as a talisman, an offering to the gods. *Please be on our side.* Or maybe she'd been going to ask him outright whose side he was on.

As he took the boxes from her and bent his head to study them, the fronts of his dressing-gown fell open again. She saw his nightshirt and the exposed skin at the neck of it. 'Twas darker than her own, a smooth, pale brown with a feathering of tiny coppery hairs. She had a sudden vision of him lying in his bed, his nightshirt gaping open and that gleaming curtain of hair spilling over the pillow. She blinked to banish it.

He looked up. 'You made me tablet,' he said, those grey eyes fixed on her face. Bracing herself for the sarcastic comment and the disdainful look, she rolled her bottom lip under her top.

'Don't do that.'

'Don't do what?'

'Bite your lip. You've left a mark.' The boxes of sweets secure in one hand, he reached out the other and put his thumb to her bottom lip. His touch was as light as thistledown. His touch was as strong as steel.

39

For a moment neither of them moved. Grey eyes met green. Green eyes met grey. When the kitchen door swung open, they jumped apart like guilty lovers.

'Miss Rankeillor? Captain? Alice is more composed now.' Geordie ushered them in, somewhat, Catto thought, in the manner of a diplomat brokering peace talks after a decisive battle. 'If you will sit next to me, sir, and Miss Rankeillor next to Alice?'

'Alice,' Catto said as he sat down, consciously trying to keep his voice gentle and his person not too intimidating. He saw the girl spare one hand to reach along the table to Geordie. The boy put his over hers, although when Catto looked from one young worried young face to the other he thought it was a matter for debate as to who was clinging onto whom. The girl was older than her brother, perhaps fifteen or sixteen. 'Would we be right in thinking it's Alice Maxwell?'

'It's no' that simple, Captain.'

'It never is.' Catto sighed. 'Start at the beginning, Geordie.'

'Alice is my sister, Captain. But our name is Smart.'

'All right,' Catto said, rolling the two words around his mouth. 'So who's looking for Geordie Smart?'

'I'll have tae tell him, Alice,' the boy said. 'The Captain's been real good tae me and he deserves the truth.' A flicker of the eyelids from the girl. Permission granted. 'I didna want to lie to you, sir. I really didna want to do that. You've been right good to me and I appreciate it. Mair than ye'll ever ken. But I was feart, Captain. Feart o' them coming after me. I'm bought and paid for, ye see.'

'Bought and paid for?' Catto stared at him, not understanding. 'Nobody can own another person, Geordie. Not unless one of those persons is unfortunate enough to have been born a black slave.' He thought of Charlotte Liddell's young footman Joshua, wondered what his story was.

'I know what he means. Geordie, where are you and Alice from?'

'Prestonpans, miss.'

'You were born into a mining family?' When the boy nodded, she gave him a smile of encouragement. 'Explain it to your Captain, Geordie. Tell him how it works.'

He nodded his bright head again before addressing himself to Catto. 'You see, sir, when I was born my father was given money for me. In the kirk when I was baptized,' he explained further, clearly not seeing any understanding of what he was telling him dawning on Catto's face. 'In return for the money he had to promise I would become a collier like him. Like his father afore him and his father afore that. Way back to the olden days. Only our father wanted something better for me.' He squeezed his sister's hand. 'For us.'

'Your sister had to work down the pit too?'

'Oh, aye, sir. It's the women and girls wha carry the coals up to the surface. My father could read and write and he taught the both o' us. Used to say that if you were able to read, the world would open up tae ye.'

'Your father was right, Geordie. He must have been a very wise man. Smart by name and smart by nature. Like his son.'

The boy slanted him a smile. 'He was a good talker too, our father. Persuaded the big hoose to take Alice on as a scullery maid and kept me oot o' the pit as long as he could. Said he needed me to keep house for him and our uncle. He lived wi' us too,' the boy explained. 'Our mother's brother. That's how I learned to cook, sir. Looking after the both o' them after Alice went tae the big hoose.'

'Your mother's dead?' Christian Rankeillor asked gently.

'When I was born, miss. I never knew her. Alice did, although no' for very long. When our uncle died the colliery manager said I had to go doon the pit in his place. It wasna good doon there,' he said quietly. 'I didna like it. I wasna always working alongside my father and some o' the other men were gey rough. Then my father died and I was going to have to go and bide wi' another family. But I didna want to do that and I didna want to stay down the pit. So I ran away. Alice hid me and fed me for a week near the big hoose. She could have lost her position for doing that, sir, so we decided I should come to Edinburgh.'

'How did you end up at the guard-house?'

'I was going round everywhere looking for work and they needed a cook-boy here. Talked my way into it, ye might say. I think maybe I take after my father in that respect.'

'I'd say so, Geordie.' Catto lifted one of the boxes of tablet. 'All right if we open this now, Miss Rankeillor?'

'Please,' she said, shaking her head as he offered the sweets first to her. 'Go ahead.'

'I'm real sorry I didn't tell you straightaway about Alice, Captain, but she was so scared. Feart on my account, too. If they find out where I am, they'll take me back.' A shudder ran through the small frame. 'Send me back doon the pit. Gie me a flogging afore they dae it.'

'They will do either of those things only over my dead body, Geordie. Here, have a sweetie. Miss Rankeillor's brought them for both of us. All three of us now, I suppose,' he added with a wry laugh.

'Ye dinna understand, sir. They still own me. I'm their property.'

'Unless he can stay away for a year and a day. That's the law.'

'Is it?' Christian Rankeillor turned to the girl. 'How long till that year and a day is up?'

'Nigh on four months, miss. He left the big hoose on the morning o' April Fool's Day past.' Alice Smart laughed, although the sound was devoid of mirth. 'Although it's me wha's been the fool. I didna live up tae oor name.'

Christian Rankeillor and Robert Catto exchanged another look. 'But,' she said, pushing the box of tablet towards the girl, 'how would his master find him? Unless anybody sees you together, why would they connect what happened to you with Geordie?'

'Because of who did this to her, miss.'

'Who was that?' Catto asked. Geordie's answer sent both him and Christian Rankeillor rocking back in their chairs.

'Cosmo Liddell?' Catto said. He and Christian Rankeillor had retreated once again to the courtyard. 'The Honourable Cosmo Liddell?'

'It's awful,' she agreed, 'although I cannot say I am surprised.'

'There have been stories about him before?'

'No. I've always had this feeling about him, though. That something very dark lurks beneath the surface charm. You would discount such feelings and instincts?'

'Not in the slightest. Acting on instinct has saved my skin on more than one occasion.'

'When you become aware a sharpshooter has you in his sights?'

'You describe one such incident exactly. In addition to which, I have some instincts of my own about Cosmo Liddell.'

He was thinking back to that comment Liddell had made. *Get the little bitches hot and sweaty and working for their money.* He had found the words and the attitude behind them as distasteful as the filthy jokes Liddell and his acolytes had recounted. Now he was finding them chilling. 'I think he is the kind of man who does not really like women.'

'I've always thought the opposite. That he likes women rather too much.'

'In one sense, yes, but I do not think he really likes them in the sense of enjoying their company.'

'As you do?'

'As I do,' Catto said absently. 'I have just realized I have in my possession something which might be evidence of this assault on Geordie's sister. A coded letter which refers to a rendezvous last Friday night. She did not say when the assault took place, did she?'

'She did not say very much at all.'

'Except that she had been a fool.'

'Implying that he charmed her, enticed her to go away with him somewhere?'

'That could be.' Propped once more against the windowsill, his legs draped in the vivid splash of colour of his dressing-gown, he tapped one long finger against his lips. 'I've thought of something else. Although I find myself hesitating to share it with you, Miss Rankeillor. ''Tis of a somewhat less than delicate nature.'

'I am broad-minded, sir. I am a surgeon-apothecary's daughter. I am not quite so naïve as you seem to believe.'

'Very well,' he said, making up his mind to tell her. 'This coded letter—'

'Which you intercepted and decoded?'

'I did the first part, 'twas largely Geordie who accomplished the second. He has a good brain. Do you wish me to continue with this explanation?'

'Please do.'

'The letter gave a time, mentioned an "agreed place" and included some words, innocuous in themselves, but which I now believe indicate the rendezvous had to do with matters of a sexual nature.'

'What were the seemingly innocuous words?'

'Do you have to know?' He answered himself. 'Stupid question. Of course you do. That's what you're like.'

'Is that a compliment?'

'Interpret it any way you like, Miss Rankeillor. The final line of the message read *Lose No Opportunity.* 'Tis one of the mottoes of a gentleman's club known as the Beggar's Benison.'

'You have attended a meeting of this club?'

He gathered the red and turquoise dragons more closely about himself. 'I did not say that.'

'No. You did not say that. You seem somewhat discomfited, sir. Forgive me, but our acquaintance thus far would not have led me to believe you to be so proper about such matters.'

'The activities of the Beggar's Benison sit at the opposite end of the spectrum from proper, Miss Rankeillor. The word *frankness* does not adequately cover their proceedings. Or alleged proceedings,' he added, seeing the light of curiosity dawn in her eyes.

'Could you give me some idea what we are talking about, Captain Catto? I ask not out of salacious interest. I ask because I would like to help that girl in there. I think I could do that better if I knew something of what she had been through.'

'Very well. I am going to speak very plainly.'

'You have my permission, sir.'

'Among their activities, the Beggar's Benison number the examination of young women and girls.'

'Some raillery and banter, Mr Catto? That does not sound so awful.'

'I mean a physical examination, Miss Rankeillor. The young women present themselves naked for the delectation of the gentlemen of the club.'

Her face went as red as an autumn sunset. He could only admire the way she kept her composure. 'Present themselves? That sounds as though a voluntary principle is involved.'

'Money changes hands, I believe. Money can buy anything. Even willingness.'

'You think that might be what Alice meant when she said she had been a fool? That she agreed to one thing and found herself subjected to another?'

'It's a possibility. I wonder if she has told her brother what happened.'

'I think she might have felt too ashamed to tell even him more than the bare facts. It happened to one of our maidservants. Well, she didn't work for us when it happened. We took her in afterwards, when her family wouldn't – and we were criticized for it. As though,' she said bitterly, 'it were Tibby who ought to bear the shame and not the young man who had forced himself upon her.'

'I don't think that's right either. I've never thought that way.'

'Nor has my father.' Her voice dipped. 'Tibby tried to take her own life afterwards. She failed, thank God, but ended up in the Infirmary. That is how we found her. We knew who her assailant was, one of the sons of the house where she was working at the time. My father wanted him arrested and tried.'

'It would never have come to court,' Catto said with a grim laugh. 'A poor girl accusing a young gentleman of mistreating her would find no helpers. Look what happened to Lucky Kennedy. One law for the rich and one law for the poor. The law should be one law for all.'

She threw him a curious look. 'That's what my father said. He took some persuading to drop such a foolish notion that a poor girl might seek justice and redress. Everyone was called in to convince him to let it go. Mr Drummond, Professor Monro and the other managers of the Infirmary. Everyone.'

'We return to the distributors of largesse who must be deferred to?'

'Aye, although 'twas also the case that Tibby begged my father not to proceed. She could not bear the thought she might have to repeat to a lawyer or worse still, in open court, the dreadful things that had been done to her.'

Catto raised a hand and jabbed his thumb in the direction of the kitchen. 'I suppose that girl in there might feel the same.'

'With the added complication that her brother is a runaway and from the family of her attacker. In the eyes of the law, he does belong to the Liddells.'

Catto snorted in disgust. ''Tis a barbarous arrangement.'

'But it is the law as far as the miners are concerned. Their legal status is that of serfs. You are the Captain of the Guard and an officer of the law. You could not be seen to be conniving at the breaking of it.'

'Let me worry about that.'

Perhaps we can put on something rather more exciting for you next time. Myself, Arthur and Hector like to have the occasional little adventure together. More suited to a man of action such as yourself. Where we require the trollops to do more for their five shillings than simply stand there. Get the little bitches hot and sweaty and working for their money. If you catch my drift, sir.

Did Liddell and his two friends have another bout of forced and brutal sex planned for tomorrow night, one in which they believed Catto would be willing to participate?

'I think you are using me as a thinking post, Captain Catto.'

'I beg your pardon, Miss Rankeillor. 'Tis a bad habit of mine. What did you say to me that I did not hear?'

'I said I believe you have an immediate problem you need to address. I do not think you can keep a young girl in the guard-house.'

He blew out a breath and ran a hand through his hair. 'No, I cannot. But I am loath to take her to the poorhouse. I wouldn't take a dog I liked to that place. If they find out that she has been ruined, as they inevitably will, her life in there would be made even more of a misery.'

'I could offer you an alternative to the poorhouse.'

'You surely do not mean that you would take her in?'

'I mean exactly that.'

'Why would you want to help me, Miss Rankeillor?' He adjusted his position, replanting his feet on the beaten earth of the courtyard and leaning forward. 'Ah, I see. It's the girl you want to help.'

'Aiblins I want to help both of you.'

'In the hope that I might be grateful?' He saw it in her eyes. That wasn't why she had offered to take Geordie's sister in but the thought had occurred to her now. 'Are we,' he asked softly, 'striking another bargain here, Miss Rankeillor?'

'Maybe we're striking the same one.' The words came out in a rush, as though she'd had to take her courage in both hands and run with them. She paused and composed herself. 'Are you willing to strike that bargain, sir?'

'Yes,' he said, and hated himself.

'Are we both talking about the same thing here? Not only about Alice Smart?'

'Yes,' he said again, and hated himself even more. 'You do realize the girl could be with child? Or–'

'Poxed?' She did not blush. She had more important things to worry about now. 'Both those thoughts have occurred to me. In either case, Alice would be well-placed to find help to deal with either of those eventualities if she was under our roof.'

'What about the wagging tongues?'

Her chin went up. 'Let them wag. This girl needs help. I am in a position to offer it.'

'Your Christian duty?'

'If you like. Mayhap also my duty as a daughter of Eve. Should we now put our proposal to Alice and Geordie?'

Catto rose to his feet. 'I do not think Geordie will take much persuading. Nor his sister either.' He glanced round the courtyard, indicating the old stone steps. 'He must have been hiding her out here.'

Christian shivered. 'Where she must have been very cold and scared and lonely.'

'Aye,' Catto said. 'Please step back into the kitchen, Miss Rankeillor. Once we have explained our plan I shall ask Sergeant Livingstone to hire chairs to take you and Alice back to the High School Yards. Best be discreet. Especially as the lass seems to be barely clad.'

'One chair will look more discreet than two. I can walk beside it, as though I am accompanying a patient who is too unwell to walk. Besides which,' she added, 'I am not wearing my ridiculous clothes today. I can get where I want to go like a normal person.'

Aye, she still had the power to annoy him. He did not rise to the sally, only looked at her as she looked at him. He knew what she was doing, distancing them both from that touch. Neither of them could afford that complication. He waited, made her ask the next question.

'We have a bargain, then?'

'It would seem so, madam. I expect Geordie will want to follow his sister to your house.'

'By all means,' she said.

'Is that you back, Geordie?'

'Aye, sir,' came the unusually subdued response. 'Shall I come through?'

'No. I'll come to you.' Dressed as far as his shirt, breeches and waistcoat, Catto slipped his arms back into his dressing-gown.

'Shall I get you some porridge, sir?'

'I've already had some. Has your sister settled in at Miss Rankeillor's?'

Geordie's face brightened a little. 'Aye, sir. It's all women in that house right now. Miss Rankeillor made a point of explaining that to Alice. She's real kind, Miss Rankeillor, sir.' A single tear ran down one smooth young cheek. Catto had been about to start the interrogation. Not any more.

'Come and sit by the fire, Geordie. You look cold. Have you had any porridge this morning?'

The boy shook his golden head. 'What will happen to Alice now, sir?'

'I don't know,' Catto said, picking up a bowl and ladling a dollop of porridge into it from the big black pot still simmering on the range. It was thick enough now to pave the causeway outside but the lad needed something inside him. 'Perhaps Miss Rankeillor can find her a position, maybe even in her own house.'

Geordie brightened again. 'That would be grand, sir.'

Except that Miss Rankeillor might soon not have a house. Geordie didn't need to worry about that yet. His sister would be safe there for a while, especially once Catto put a guard on the place. Its mistress would not throw the girl out onto the street from spite towards him. She wasn't made that way.

What Geordie would think of him was another question. Splashing in some milk and sprinkling a generous pinch of salt over the porridge, he handed over the bowl and a horn spoon. 'Why did you not tell me what had happened and that your sister was here?'

'At first because Alice begged me not to, sir.' Geordie's face crumpled. 'I keep wishing I hadna come to Edinburgh and left her alone, sir. Maybe this wouldna have happened if I'd bade where I was.'

Pulling another stool out from beside the fire, Catto sat down next to the boy. 'Geordie, what's happened has happened and none of it is your fault. You are not to blame in any way. Do you hear me, Geordie?'

'I hear you, sir.' A second tear ran down the boy's downy cheek.

'Eat your porridge.'

'Aye, sir,' he said, although he took only one spoonful and then sat motionless, staring into the fire.

'Another spoonful,' Catto coaxed. 'And another one after that.'

Again the boy obeyed him, only to drop the spoon into the bowl and turn from his study of the crackling flames to look at Catto. 'I did try to tell you a few times, Captain, but somehow I never managed it. I was feart you'd be angry, sir. If you're going to put me on the horse, can you please do it now and get it over with?'

Aghast, Catto stared at the boy. 'Put you on the horse? What sort of a brute do you take me for?'

'I'm sorry, sir. The Captain in charge before you came put me on the horse.'

'*He put you on the horse?* What had you done?'

Geordie's apparent calmness dissolved, his eyes brimming with tears. 'He said I was cheating him on the food money, sir. Making a skin. But I wasna, I really wasna. It was his reckoning that was at fault.

When I told him so he got real angry wi' me. But I wasna cheating. I really wasna. Ye have tae believe me, Captain. Ye have tae!'

'Geordie,' Catto said. 'You're babbling. Stop it. I know you weren't cheating him. You don't have that in you. I'm not going to put you or anyone else on the horse. Although don't tell the men that.' His robust tones had stopped the tears. Geordie gave him a shaky smile and drew the back of one small hand across his eyes. 'Finish your porridge. And stand up to do it. You should always stand up when you eat your porridge.'

'Why, sir?'

The power of curiosity and the chance to learn something new to distract and soothe an inquiring mind. He had observed the phenomenon before. 'Did you,' he asked, 'ever hear tell of the Border reivers?'

40

Attractive and animated, her gleaming brown curls a striking contrast to the azure blue of her skirts, Anna Gordon's eyes were fiery with indignation. 'Kirsty, what in the name of Hades is going on? Meg and I have been subjected to what can only be called an interrogation at the West Port. And,' she demanded, 'what's this we've heard about a Town Guard raid on your house? Your father said nothing about that when we met him in Glasgow.'

Meg Wood tapped her arm and shushed her. 'I'm guessing the Professor did not want to alarm us, Anna. Give Kirsty a minute. She'll tell us everything in her own good time.'

'I do have rather a lot to tell you,' Christian said wryly. 'It has been a somewhat eventful week. Come upstairs and we'll have some tea.'

Crouched in front of the fireplace in her bedroom a few moments later, she used the hooked cleek to draw back the hinged iron plate on which her little brass kettle was coming to the boil. Laying the cleek along the hearth, she lifted a folded cloth to protect her hand before moving the kettle onto its stand on top of the blue and white Dutch tiles. 'Say something, ladies.' For she had started her story with what had happened to Alice Smart and the other two girls had fallen silent, their faces sombre.

'It's bloody awful,' Anna said in her rich Buchan accent, 'the poor quine. Where is she now?'

'Tucked up in bed with a warm stone piggie at her feet and Tibby sitting beside her. The two of them have an unfortunate bond.'

Meg Wood nodded. Both she and Anna knew Tibby's story. 'Are you wanting this teapot now, Kirsty? She has no chance of any redress, I suppose.'

'Could some money be got out of Cosmo Liddell?' Anna asked. She shuddered. 'We've never liked him, have we?'

'It wasn't only him.'

'There was more than one of them?' Meg asked, her face white and shocked.

'Two more,' Christian said, pouring boiling water onto tea leaves. 'Three, including Cosmo Liddell.'

'Oh, that's awful!' Meg shivered. 'Horrible!'

'Do you know who they were?' asked Anna.

'No. Alice has not yet felt able to tell us the whole story.'

'One can hardly blame her. Although we all know who his closest friends are.'

'We must not accuse them without evidence, Anna!' Meg exclaimed.

'Mustn't we? You do not think there would be any point in laying a complaint against Cosmo Liddell, go to the Town Guard about it?'

'There's a bit of a complication there.'

'Ah,' Anna said. 'Because the raid on this house and Surgeons' Hall was led by the Town Guard?'

Christian nodded. 'In the person of Captain Robert Catto. Senior officer of the aforementioned Town Guard.' She was struggling not to show her reaction to speaking that name. *Not in front of my friends, please God. I'm not ready to tell them how I feel about Robert Catto. Not when I don't know myself. Not when I keep remembering how it felt when he touched my mouth, how it sent a tingle running through my entire body ...*

'Betty said he wasn't much of a gentleman.'

'She's right. Och, and she's not right! On the one hand, Captain

Robert Catto is a harassing, hectoring bully, sharp-tongued, inhuman, condescending in the extreme and a pig-headed Whig to boot.' Christian threw Meg Wood an apologetic glance. 'Sorry, Meg.'

'Pour the tea and I'll aiblins forgive you,' Meg said drily. 'I think we could all be doing with a cup.'

'And on the other hand?' Anna queried as Christian poured the tea into dainty china cups.

'He's been a gentleman about this,' she said, unable to deny him that. Damn him. 'The other complication is that Alice was hiding at the guard-house. That's where I found her.'

'Hang on a wee minute,' Meg said, 'why were you at the guard-house?'

'I was enquiring after Robert Catto's health.' *And his intentions. Don't know I'm yet convinced as to where his true loyalties lie. Not sure about that at all. Not sure where my response to him is leading me either, except that it's to a dangerous place. He's dangerous.*

'This is getting confusing, Kirsty.' Anna frowned in perplexity. 'Why were you enquiring after his health?'

'Because he'd been a patient at the Infirmary. After someone hit him over the head when he was looking at where the dead girl was found.'

'What dead girl?' asked Anna and Meg simultaneously.

'Sure there's nothing I can do, Kirsty?'

'Only keep this quiet, Meg, at least for the moment. I haven't even told Jamie about Alice yet.'

'Of course.' Above the colourful red-and-black checked riding habit in which she had travelled through from Glasgow, Meg looked pale and drawn. They all did.

'I had thought of asking him to examine her, to see if she is … damaged … in any way but I think now she would be terrified of any man. Especially given the necessary intimacy of such an examination.'

'Poor lass,' Meg said. 'Perhaps she will let you look at her, Kirsty.'

'Perhaps. I thought too she might bathe in the bagnio tomorrow.' Christian raised her shoulders in a gesture of uncertainty. 'In the perhaps vain hope of washing away some of the horror of the experience as well as allowing her a physical cleansing of her body. She and Tibby will go across in the late forenoon and have their baths.'

'Let us hope that may help. What time should I come to the bagnio on Friday?'

'Let us make it two of the clock. The second cistern of water will be fine and hot by then.'

Meg looked troubled. 'Going to the ball seems somewhat frivolous now.'

'We have to go,' Christian said quickly. 'For the sake of the hospital.' *For Mr Fox's sake too. It's a matter of life and death for him that we go to the ball!*

'There is another reason why we must go.' Anna leaned forward as she emphasized her point. 'When terrible things happen we have to keep going, continue to do the normal things. It helps balance it all out somehow. So that the darkness does not win.'

Meg considered that, nodded her agreement. 'Cosmo Liddell will be at the ball.'

'None of us shall dance with him.' Anna raised a hand. 'I know, Meg. That is not much in return for this vile thing he and his friends have done.'

'Nor will it stop them from doing it to some other girl. Can we not at least let him know we know about this vile thing, make sure no one dances with him or any of his friends, shame them?' Meg spoke passionately, until her face fell. 'Oh,' she said, 'you will not want any trouble at the ball. The Infirmary cannot afford to cross the Liddells.'

'How I wish that were not true, Meg!' Christian spoke with equal passion. 'But we must keep this quiet, not only for Alice's sake but for her brother's too. The Liddells could take him back, flog him, force him back down the mine. They would have the law on their side, forbye.'

Once again Meg pondered what had been said and sadly nodded her agreement. 'You're right, Kirsty, of course you are. Och, but these have been difficult days for you!' She gave Christian a swift hug. 'Stay here by the fire, you two. If I know Betty Gilchrist, she'll be standing by to see me out.'

Christian stood up. 'I'll see you to the bedroom door at least, Meg.'

'We leave the bagnio for the ball at four?'

'Aye. Where we shall put a brave face on it.'

'Indeed. Continue to do the normal things. In which endeavour I shall depart now to pay my duty calls, leaving you two to talk treason as usual.' She kissed both girls before stepping over to the bed and tickling Lucy the cat behind the ears. 'Fare thee well, baudrons,' she said, pulled on her gloves and was gone. Christian and Anna gazed at each other in silence until they heard her taking her farewell of Betty and the sound of the front door closing behind her.

'Did we know we were both such good actresses? *Leaving us to talk treason as usual*?'

'Always a jest between the three of us,' Christian agreed. 'Until now.' She closed her bedchamber door and walked back to where Anna sat by the fire. 'You know, then?'

'I know. Before you ask me what I know I shall tell you. There is to be an attempt in the spring, maybe earlier. There is a man in Edinburgh who has to be helped on his way north if support is to be won in the Highlands for that attempt. I also know I may be involved in helping him get there. As I surmise you already are, Kirsty.'

'Och, Anna,' she breathed, 'it is such a relief to be able to talk to you about it!' Then, as Anna sprang to her feet and threw her arms about her: 'Anna, I am so scared!'

'So am I, Kirsty.'

'But you're always so brave.'

'You can't be brave without being scared. The two go hand-in-hand.'

'I hadn't thought of it that way.'

'Does it help?'

'A little.'

'Tell me what I must do, Kirsty.'

'Let's sit down again, then. There's a lot to this.'

'So,' Anna said once Christian had finished speaking. 'I shall obtain a safe conduct for a Mr Duff from Provost Coutts, which paper I shall give to him or Jamie before we leave the bagnio.'

'To Jamie. To minimize your involvement.'

Anna gave Christian the words she had given her father. 'I would play my part, Kirsty.'

'You have the heart of Bruce, Anna. We all know that. But 'tis safer for you to not meet Mr Fox, I mean Duff.'

'We'll see. Sometimes things dinna work out as planned. When we get to the Assembly Rooms, I shall distract Meg while you escort Mr Fox now Duff to one of the reception rooms.'

'I have been calling him Mr Fox all week. I shall have to drum his new name into my head. What if Meg wonders where I am off to with a man she does not know?'

'The gentleman is one of you and your father's patients and you are helping him see the merriment, as you said. As Mr Duff, he is one of my numerous relatives, too distant for me to know well. Meg need not know anything about me securing a pass for him.'

'She must not. For the same reason as before. What if she mentions him to someone else or asks why he does not appear in the ballroom? Or asks why I do not?'

'Dinna worry about Meg. She is observant, as we know, but there is much else to catch her eye at the ball. With everyone in masks or with their hair powdered, 'twill not be so easy for her to distinguish him among all the other gentlemen. Or distinguish that he is absent from the ballroom.'

'Even though she will see no one with a badly swollen ankle?'

'As I understand it, the plan is that she will not see him as we leave the bagnio. She will barely notice him or his swollen ankle when we arrive at the Assembly Rooms, especially if I distract her as we get out of the chairs. Take the two of us very quickly up the stairs into the ballroom, where she will soon be too busy dancing to notice anyone who is not doing the same. Ye ken how she loves to dance. Jamie wants you to stay with Mr Duff for how long?'

'Until this gentleman with whom he must speak arrives. Then I am to leave them alone to their discussions.'

'You do not know when this other gentleman will arrive?'

'No. Apparently he is one of those who consider it fashionable to arrive late, although Jamie has asked him to come a little earlier than usual, although not so early as to arouse suspicion.'

'So that Mr Duff may be got out of Edinburgh early in the evening,' Anna said, repeating what Christian had told her. 'Via the Netherbow Port?'

'It is the easiest of access from the Assembly Rooms.'

Anna nodded. 'Straight down the High Street. There will be crowds there but there will be crowds on the approaches to all the gates. You are worried by the choice?'

'A little. 'Tis the largest gate and will be well-guarded.' Christian raised her shoulders. 'Although they all will be that. Robert Catto will make sure of it.'

'A pass signed by Provost Coutts will get Mr Duff through and since the pass must also request safe conduct for him to Inverness from Leith, 'twould be odd if he did not leave by the Netherbow. In any case, I thought your Captain Catto had agreed to look the other way.' Christian looked at her. Anna blew out a long breath. 'You fear you cannot trust him?'

'That's exactly what I fear.'

'But Jamie is convinced?'

'Or chooses to be. Och, I have to move, I'm too restless to sit still!' She stood up and laid one hand on the mantelpiece. 'Anna, something has changed in Jamie since this all started.'

Anna looked up at her. 'That's understandable, surely. Are we not all as much excited as we are scared?'

Christian shifted the two pewter candlesticks which stood at opposite ends of her mantelpiece, then moved them back to their original position. 'It's more than excitement. It's a recklessness. He seems willing to take risks, which is not like him. Jamie has always been so very careful.'

'Jamie has always had to be careful. His position has not been easy. You don't need me to tell you that, Kirsty.'

'I have always tried my best to give him his place.'

'Indeed you have. You have always acknowledged that he is Mr Buchan of Balnamoon. Even though Balnamoon is now no more than a pile of stones in a field.'

'He is sensitive about that.'

'I know someone else like that.'

'Och, Anna,' Christian said with quick sympathy, turning from the mantelpiece and sinking down onto the footstool next to the armchair. 'You've loved Alick Forbes all of your life. Since you were wee bairns playing together. Falling in the burn and tearing your clothes as you chased each other through the whin.'

Anna nodded and swallowed hard. 'Those were happy days!' She coughed and spoke more clearly. 'Since we left childhood behind it has become increasingly hard to convince the stubborn fool that I do love him.'

'He knows your family do not see him as a suitable suitor. But if the restoration happens not only the King will come into his own again. A suitor unacceptable to your family may become acceptable.'

'Or give his life for the Cause.'

'As Jamie may too. And Meg's brother Andrew.' For Andrew Wood, Glasgow shoemaker, did not share his sister's pragmatic politics. He was a passionate Jacobite. 'My father is probably negotiating the purchase of shoes with Andrew as we speak.'

'And Andrew will be agreeing to supply them, whatever the risk to himself.'

Christian spoke in an anguished whisper. 'We might lose them all. There's your father and mine too. Och, Anna, how could we bear it?'

They reached for each other's hands. Anna recovered first, lifting those joined hands and giving them a shake. 'We will not think that way, Kirsty. We cannot allow ourselves to think that way.'

'Can't we?'

'Only in private. Only when none of the men are about. Now and again we shall permit ourselves a fit of the vapours. Tell me about your Captain Catto. He can't be all bad, with a name like that. Must come from my part of the world. There's a clutch of Cattos around Methlick. What age is he?'

'Twenty-four. Twenty-five on Old Year's Night. Old Style.'

Anna raised her eyebrows at her. 'He specified? For the avoidance of doubt with whom he might share a birthday?'

'Exactly that. We had a rather strange conversation. He and I have had one or two of those.'

'Tell me more.'

'I think I've told you too much already. Do you think you might know him?'

'No, and if he's that age and a Buchan loon I would do. Although there's something about his name – Catto, I mean – some story.'

'What sort of a story?'

'I'm associating it with a scandal. Years ago now. Before our time. Might have nothing to do with your Captain Catto.'

'Stop calling him that. He's not *my* Captain Catto.'

'Although you find yourself attracted to him, Kirsty, do you not?'

'How did you know that?' demanded Christian, jerking upright and pulling her hands away.

'Because I'm a witch. Do you think he returns your feelings?'

'Anna …' Christian stood up again, threw herself into the other armchair.

'Would it help to talk about it? I'll not tell a soul. Not even Meg if you don't want me to.'

'If you've noticed, she probably has too. Anna, I don't understand myself, or my reaction to him. I find myself very attracted to him …' She blushed. '… in a very physical way.'

Anna laughed softly. 'There's nothing wrong with physical attraction, Kirsty.'

'Anna, have you and Alick ever … you know …' Her hands flew up to her mouth. 'I'm sorry! I should not have asked you that!'

A gleam of mischief shone in Anna's eyes. 'We've taken a few steps along the road. But never travelled right to the end of it.' Her voice softened. 'Does it scare you, Kirsty? Because of what happened to your mother?'

Christian nodded. 'That. And in a different and yet more awful way after what happened to Tibby and has now happened to Alice.'

'That had nothing to do with love. Or love-making. 'Tis different when you both want it.'

'I'm not in love with Robert Catto.'

'It's purely physical?'

'I dinna think there's anything pure about it.' She frowned. 'Yet there's more to it than that. There's something about him that tugs at my heartstrings.'

Anna tilted her head to one side, the better to survey her. 'But you're not in love with him.'

'Dinna be daft, Anna!' Christian blew out an exasperated breath. 'I've known the bloody man for less than a week. And dinna look at me like that, or say anything about love at first sight, either. That is a totally irrational belief.'

'Maybe not, if we've all been here before.' Anna raised a hand. 'I ken fine you think that's a totally irrational belief too. And I didn't say a word. I think you're saying them all.'

'There could be nothing between him and me, Anna. What would my father say?'

'The Professor might find him an acceptable suitor. Depending on what happens tonight. On how Captain Catto acts tonight.'

'Robert Catto would never be an acceptable suitor to me!'

Anna said nothing, only gave her the most mischievous of smiles. 'Show me the gown you're wearing to the ball.'

'Is Meg not right, Anna? Should we be caring about such frivolities?'

'I think we have to keep living, Kirsty. As normally as possible for as long as possible.'

'Keeping the darkness at bay?'

'Aye,' Anna agreed. 'Keeping the darkness at bay.'

He had wanted to kiss her. As they had stood together in the courtyard of the guard-house he had wanted to replace his thumb with his mouth, gently explore her lips, slide his arms about her waist, feel the softness of her breasts against his chest. He thought she had wanted to kiss him too. Maybe he was fooling himself.

There could be nothing between him and Christian Rankeillor. Wrong time, wrong place. Wrong man, wrong woman. Wrong situation. That was a masterpiece of understatement.

The stage was set and there wanted only a few short hours before the last act in this drama would play out. By this time tomorrow it would all be over. He saw no reason why he should not bring matters to a successful conclusion. They thought they had him in their pocket. As he had allowed them to think, using her to get the message across.

So tonight he would arrest the Jacobite messenger, Balnamoon and Arthur Menzies of Edmonstone and confine them to the Tolbooth. He had already alerted the gaoler, told him to expect at least three prisoners late in the evening. If he caught any of Edinburgh's Disaffected red-handed, in conversation with the Jacobite messenger, he would arrest them too. As he would arrest Christian Rankeillor, have her escorted home under armed guard. With a bit of luck that might allow him to stop her from damning herself out of her own mouth.

She would give him no help there. He knew she would refuse to plead that her father had coerced her into helping. Her father, on the other hand, would plead anything that might save his beloved daughter from prison or the gallows. Even if they had to physically gag her to stop her from contradicting him. Catto's eyes narrowed. Or he could find a way of convincing her she would help her father and Balnamoon most if she kept her mouth shut.

He had no idea how he was going to do that. By this time tomorrow she would hate him as much as she had done last Saturday night, would not be prepared to listen to anything he said. He could not and would not jeopardize tonight's mission by giving her any sort of a warning. That was unthinkable. Yet he had been perilously close to doing exactly that in the apothecary's shop yesterday, when he had allowed his emotions to get the better of him. He would not do that tonight. So she would walk into the trap he had set for her. She had to.

He was not in love with her. How could he be? They had known each other for less than a week. She touched something deep within him, that was all, reminded him of how life could be. *That was all*? Dear God in Heaven, what had his life become?

He sank down onto the edge of his bed and bent his head to stare at the floor. She reminded him of what it was like to have a home and a family, to live among people who cared about you and about whom you cared in return. It had been a long time since he had known that.

He could not afford to think like this. It weakened him. So he had to remind himself of all the reasons why she infuriated him, what a bloody fool she was, one of those idiots determined to hurl themselves to hell in a handcart. He straightened up and squared his shoulders. 'Twas neither his fault nor his responsibility that fate had brought the two of them together in this time and this place. He had not sought this mission. Every bone in his body and every drop of his blood had protested against it.

His blood. The words brought another consideration, another he had to push away. No emotion, then. Duty only – but he would see her one last time before she looked at him for ever afterwards with hate in her heart. He would see her one last time before he betrayed her.

41

'But Miss Christian is still in her dishabilly!' The little maid was flustered, clasping and unclasping her hands in front of her apron.

'At ten o'clock in the morning?' Catto queried, choosing to forget that he had been in his *déshabille* at half past ten the previous one. 'I still require to see her. Fetch her now.'

'But, sir …'

'Fetch her now,' Catto repeated. He hadn't raised his voice. He had merely looked her in the eye. It had the desired effect. She lifted her skirts and clattered up the stairs. Oh God. He had just realized she might be the girl Christian Rankeillor had spoken of yesterday, the one who had been raped and who, like Geordie's sister, was now scared of all men. He didn't suppose having a house full of them last Saturday night had done her much good.

Perhaps it would help if he adopted a less threatening pose. He propped himself against one of the broad windowsills which flanked the front door. The one he chose already had an occupant. 'Lucrezia Borgia,' he murmured, pronouncing the name in the Italian way as he tickled the little cat behind one ear. 'How are you this fine morning?'

His fingers stilled on the cat's head. This might be the last fine morning its mistress would ever know, and coming here had been a mistake. He knew that. All the way from the guard-house he had kept telling himself not to be so bloody stupid, to turn around and go back.

His feet had continued to lead him to her house. He could hardly leave it now. The little cat seemed to agree. Deigning to fancy some human company, she put out an exploratory paw and followed it with the rest of her sinuous body.

'You've found a somewhat precarious perch, puss. My legs are at too much of a slope for that to possibly be comfortable. Come up here.' Lifting his head as a movement caught his eye, he saw Christian Rankeillor's housekeeper descending the stairs. He was surprised she hadn't flown down on her broomstick.

'Miss Christian is still in her dishabilly,' she announced, her eyes rising from the cat to his face.

'I am already apprised of that fact,' he said crisply. 'I still need to see her.' He had an excuse ready, that he wanted to enquire after Alice Smart's welfare without worrying Geordie.

The housekeeper glowered at him. 'Come back this afternoon, then.'

'I don't have time to come back this afternoon. Kindly summon your mistress forthwith.'

The hands were on the non-existent hips now. 'Summon her? Summon Miss Kirsty? Ye dinna ken her very well, dae ye? What dae ye want to speak to her aboot?'

Catto rolled his eyes, wondering for the umpteenth time why servants in Edinburgh had to be so damned unservantlike. 'My business with Miss Rankeillor is none of your business, goodwife.' He threw her a cynical look. 'Although you probably know all about it anyway.'

'I ken everything that goes on in this hoose. Which is quite a lot at this moment.'

'Good for you. This morning, however, I am going to speak to Miss Rankeillor alone and I'm going to do so now. As soon as humanly possible. Kindly tell her I am waiting for her.' He glanced across the gleaming floorboards of the lobby to the stairs he had walked up last Saturday. It felt like a lifetime ago. 'Otherwise I'll go up there and tell her myself.'

'You will not!'

'I will if you don't go and fetch her right now. I do know the way to her bedchamber.'

More muttering, although his threat to mount the stairs himself had worked. The little woman headed back up and reappeared on the landing a moment later, exercising what power she could by making him wait till she was at the bottom again before she spoke. 'She says she will be down directly. She says I am to offer you some refreshment. Though why I dinna ken.'

'I can do without refreshment.' His arms being occupied in providing a level shelf for Lucy the cat, he flicked his fingers at her. 'You're dismissed.'

'Dismissed? It's no' your place to dismiss me, young man!'

'Oh, go away!' he said, exasperated. This was descending into farce. He hadn't come here to argue the toss with a housekeeper.

'Betty? Have you offered the Captain some refreshment?'

'He says he doesna want any.'

Catto turned towards the stairs. She was coming down them. In her dishabilly. Which was not as exciting as it sounded. Her high-necked cream-coloured dressing gown was so adorned with frills and ruffles it was hard to make out any shape in the body beneath it. She wore a nightcap too, larger and vastly more fussy than her neat daytime caps. So he was not going to see her hair loose and tumbling about her face. Above the dressing gown she wore a bluey-green tartan plaid fastened with a silver pin at her bosom. He knew she had a bosom, he had seen it last Saturday night. He had seen a lot more of it when she'd been wearing an evening gown than he was seeing now.

'Mr Catto,' she said, gliding across the floorboards towards him. 'Captain.' She extended her hand. Should he kiss it? He settled for gripping her fingers for a few seconds and bending over them in a perfunctory bow. More perfunctory than it might have been for fear of squashing the cat.

'Kindly dismiss your housekeeper. I've tried to, but she won't go.'

'You could always have threatened her with your sword.'

Their eyes met. 'Miss Rankeillor. I wish only to have ten minutes conversation with you.'

'Betty, 'twill be all right. Do you go back up to Alice. Captain Catto and I shall be in the library. I need to speak to him too.'

'Very well,' the older woman said. 'But I shall fetch Mary to sit here in the lobby. You'll leave the library doors open, Miss Kirsty. You'll stand in the doorway, forbye.'

'For God's sake,' Catto howled. 'It's ten o'clock in the morning. Broad daylight. Must we be so nice about the proprieties?'

'I'm afraid we must,' Christian Rankeillor murmured. Her back to the housekeeper, her words were intended only for his ears. She watched until the older woman went through to the kitchens. 'Please sit down, sir.'

'I cannot sit while you are standing.' Passing her in the open doorway, he saw her raise her eyebrows.

'Really? I don't recall you having such scruples on your previous visit to this house.'

'That was different,' he said, turning to face her. 'Please come into the room and sit down, Miss Rankeillor.'

'I can't. Betty would have apoplexy.' She threw a glance over her shoulder. 'Here comes Mary to stand guard.'

'Very well, then,' he said tersely, propping himself against the edge of her father's untidy desk.

'You don't have to keep carrying Lucy.'

'What? Oh. Yes.' Bending forward, he lowered the little cat onto the rug. When he straightened up he found Kirsty Rankeillor watching him with an odd look on her face. 'Something the matter?'

Her expression altered. 'You mean apart from the obvious?'

'She has spoken to you of what happened?'

'Yes. That is why I am still in a state of undress at ten o'clock in the morning.'

Catto tucked his hands under his arms. They were cold now they were no longer holding a warm furry body. Christian Rankeillor took one step into the room, put her hands behind her back and leaned against the open door. 'Alice woke the whole household at four of the clock this morning.'

'She was in the grip of a nightmare?'

'Aye.' Her eyes fluttered closed. By the time she opened them again he had launched himself off the desk and was standing in front of her. 'You are very pale, Miss Rankeillor. Will you not sit down?'

She shook her head. Through the thin material of her nightcap, he could see her abundance of dark curls.

'I'm all right.'

'I think you are not all right. Come into the room and sit down. Let us trade places. I shall stand in the doorway and you shall sit in one of the chairs by the fire. Come,' he said again, coaxing her to move. When she did, he took up the position she'd been in and looked at her over the monumentally untidy desk. 'Thus are the proprieties observed.'

'We are so nice about them, are we not? Yet for some women and girls there is no propriety whatsoever.'

'Go on,' he said grimly.

'She calls them gentlemen.' Her voice shook on the word. 'Though their behaviour makes them savages.'

'Cosmo Liddell and how many others?'

'Two. Three, including him.'

'Did she know the other two?' Catto asked, watching her face. She was carefully not looking at him, and she was still too pale.

'They called each other by name as they urged ever greater outrages on her. The names they used were Arthur and Hector.'

'Arthur Menzies and Hector Grant?'

'They are his most intimate friends. You know them?'

'Aye. I will not say I have the honour of their acquaintance. All three of these so-called gentlemen … participated?'

Christian Rankeillor sucked in a breath. 'Yes. All three of them subjected her to a horrifying, bestial assault. They violated her in every possible way. One after the other. Taking turns to restrain her. Then at the end when she was exhausted and had no resistance left in her, all of them at once …' She stopped, bent her head and put her hand over her mouth. The cat leapt onto her lap, curled up and began to purr.

Rage surged up inside Catto. Rage that Geordie's sister had suffered such a brutal violation. What they had done to her body was horrific but over the next days and weeks it would surely heal. Would her broken spirit ever do the same? That was without even taking into account that she might be poxed or with child.

He stared at Kirsty Rankeillor's bowed head. Distress was evident in every line of her. He wanted to cross the room, pull her up out of the chair and wrap his arms around her. Sod the proprieties. Sod this whole bloody situation. Sod everything. That was exactly what he was going to do.

Her head snapped up before he was halfway there. One slim white hand followed. 'No,' she said. 'Please don't come any further. Betty really would be shocked and she doesn't need to be any more shocked than she already is.' A wan smile. 'As we all are.'

Catto stopped, caught between the plea in her eyes and the overwhelming need to offer her what comfort he could. 'May I not at least call for the maid to bring you a glass of something? Or if you will tell me what to fetch I shall go through to the shop and procure some sort of a restorative.'

The wan little smile danced along her lips. 'I do not think there is any restorative for what ails me at the moment. But I'm all right. I only listened to what happened. Alice endured it.'

'Where did it take place?'

'At a deserted cottage on the coast somewhere. She is not sure exactly where. She was blindfolded when she was taken there.'

'Although she went voluntarily?'

'In a manner of speaking. It was as you thought, Captain Catto. She had agreed to pose nude. In return for five shillings.' She sent him one of her fierce looks. 'I do not think she should be judged for that.'

'No more do I,' he said gently. 'Five shillings would be a princely sum to a girl like Alice. Enough to enable her to come to Edinburgh and find her brother.'

'That was her plan. Although she had a tussle with her conscience about the method of earning the money. Cosmo Liddell persuaded her there was nothing wrong in simply removing her clothes. Pointed out to her some of the paintings of nudes in his house, told her they were beautiful and she was beautiful too. What was wrong with showing that beauty to two or three gentlemen who would admire it, not touch her, and give her five shillings into the bargain?'

'Only what happened to her after she took her clothes off was anything but beautiful.'

'The ugliest thing imaginable.' She shivered and drew the bluey-green plaid more tightly about herself.

'How did she get to Edinburgh?'

'After it was over, she was once more blindfolded, bound and thrown into a covered cart. She was taken to a house from which she subsequently escaped.'

'How did she manage that?'

'There was a woman there who was quite drunk. After she fell asleep, Alice took the key from her belt and slipped out in the small hours of the morning.'

'Can she pinpoint the house?'

'Only that it was within the sound of church bells.'

'Everywhere in Edinburgh is within the sound of church bells. How does she know the house where the attack took place was near the sea? If it was from hearing seagulls she might as easily have been a mile or two inland.'

'No, it wasn't that. She could smell salt in the air and also hear the waves as they broke against the shore and went out again over shingle.'

'So it was probably somewhere on his estate. Near Prestonpans.'

'Probably,' she responded, her voice dull.

He could see her thoughts were in the same place as his. With a terrified young girl in a hut or hovel near the beach being raped over and over again by men much bigger and stronger than her. Being violated, as Kirsty Rankeillor had put it, in every possible way. *The ugliest thing imaginable.* Had listening to the waves allowed Geordie's sister to escape for even one second from the dreadful reality she had been experiencing? He could only hope so.

'The house in Edinburgh was a house of pleasure?'

'Aye. The woman told her she would now live there and work for her. That 'twas surely a better life than carrying creels of coal up out of a pit or working like a wee slavey at the big house.' She laughed a bitter little laugh. 'Alice keeps saying how dirty she was when she worked down the mine but not nearly as dirty as she feels now. She says she will never be clean again.'

The grandfather clock ticked. The cat continued to purr. Catto kept wanting to enfold Christian Rankeillor in his arms. Especially when she looked up again with a brave little smile on her face. 'She is going across to the bagnio this afternoon. We are all hoping that may make her feel a little better.'

'You use the bagnio?'

'Now and again. I have two friends coming early this afternoon to do so. Before we all go to the ball. The one I no longer feel like going to.'

The ball you have to go to. Balnamoon can't do this without you. It's at the bagnio, then? That's where you're making the transfer, probably giving him your father's evening clothes and wig to change into. You'll all be going up to the Assembly Rooms in chairs. Probably the man too. More discreet. So I'll ask William Angus Stewart to make sure he's one of the caddies carrying those chairs.

There was anguish in her eyes. He put a gentle question to her. 'How are you, Miss Rankeillor?'

'Sad for her. Angry at them that they think they can do this to a young girl and get away with it. Because they are rich and she is poor they consider themselves above the law. Angry that they have done this to other girls. Or plan to do so.' She raised her hand in a jerky movement, indicating the outside world. 'Girls who are happily living their lives out there all unknowing what hideous fate may be lying in wait for them if they have the misfortune to do nothing more than be in the wrong place at the wrong time. Or in need of five shillings. That's all it takes to fall foul of savages like Cosmo Liddell and his friends.'

'They're not going to get away with it.'

She stared at him. 'But what can you do? The Liddells are too powerful.'

'I'll think of something.' He already had.

'He has influential relatives.'

'Don't you all?'

'He is pretty influential himself.'

'So he will have all the further to fall when I make sure as many people as possible know what he and his friends did to Alice Smart.'

'He will hate you for it.'

'Undoubtedly.'

'He may try to revenge himself on you.'

'He may.'

She gave herself the little shake. 'When do you plan to do this, Captain? You will be on duty tonight outside the Assembly Rooms?'

'You may see me there, yes, but I shall do nothing to disrupt the ball. Neither of us would want that, I think. I shall not act tonight, Miss Rankeillor.' He saw from her face that she had taken the meaning he wanted her to take from that.

He did not know if he was lying to her about not disrupting the ball, did not know if there was any hope of carrying out tonight's arrests discreetly. All he knew was that this was the last occasion on which

Christian Rankeillor would be willing to speak to him with cordiality, the last occasion on which she would look at him without hatred in her eyes. And suddenly he knew he could stay here no longer.

'I must take my leave of you, madam. You had best not show me out. I should not like to be responsible for your housekeeper having apoplexy over you seeing me to the door in your dishabilly.'

'Then we shall say goodbye here, Captain. Where I shall offer you my thanks for what you plan in respect of Cosmo Liddell and his friends. And for what you plan not to do tonight.'

Oh, you should not be thanking me for that. All I can offer you is this balancing of the scales of justice. If it damns me and my military career, so be it. Maybe one day, and oh God, how I hope you will live for that day to be years from now, you may find it your heart to realize I had no choice but to do my duty.

'It's only *auf Wiedersehen*,' he managed.

'Is that German?'

The power of curiosity and the chance to learn something new to distract and soothe an inquiring mind. He had observed the phenomenon before. 'Yes. It means until we see each other again.'

'Say it once more so I may hear how it is pronounced.' When he did so, she repeated the German farewell. '*Auf Wiedersehen*, Captain Catto. Until tonight.'

He walked away from her house knowing he had to put her out of his mind. He would spend the rest of the day finalizing his plans for tonight, making sure everyone was where he needed them to be. He would spend the rest of the day ensuring the success of his mission, holding his nerve, and locking his heart up forever.

42

'Will ye bide still, young Captain Catto? We'll hae powder a' ower the place, else!'

Catto took the protective mask from his face and snapped back. 'Surely you've finished by now. I've been biding still for hours!'

'Dinna exaggerate, laddie. I've been here nae mair than twenty meenits.' The wig maker was dancing round him, making tiny adjustments to his own handiwork which all seemed to Catto to be cancelling one another out. As his impatient customer shifted from one foot to the other, the man tutted in exasperation. 'Noo see whit ye've done! The powder's spilled onto your brow.'

'I'll do,' he said shortly.

'Indeed you will not. Hold still! There's nae point in daein' ony o' this unless it's done properly. We hae tae hide this bruise on your temple, forbye. Ye got that prowling around poking your nose into other folks' business, I'll be bound. It'll only take a wee minutie mair. A wee dab o' potamum's what we need.'

Catto sighed, replaced the protective mask and resigned himself to the procedure. He had to look the part tonight. 'Twas crucial as a way of keeping them in the dark for as long as possible as to his true intentions. He would resume his role as Captain of the Town Guard only at the last possible moment. His eyes slid sideways to his sword, lying with its white leather belt on top of his desk. He would have to take it off before he went into the Assembly Rooms but instead of depositing it in the cloakroom he would hand it over at the door to Sergeant Livingstone. The Sergeant would remain there, well within hailing distance, until he was called for.

Neither Livingstone nor the platoon he would have with him should excite any special interest. There was nothing unusual about them being there, ready for any trouble which might bubble up among the crowd gathered to catch a glimpse of the ballgoers. More guards were already stationed at the small post situated conveniently close to the Assembly Rooms. He'd put Rintoul in charge of the detail at the Netherbow Port, had all the town's gates as tight as a drum and was confident they would stay that way. The outcome of his visit to Provost Coutts' house this afternoon had been an unexpected stroke of luck. He'd impressed upon all the men that unless they received specific orders from him they were to remain at their respective stations no matter what.

The wig maker whisked away the cloth tucked in around Catto's neck to protect his evening clothes. 'That's you. Tak a look at yersel.'

Legs dangling, Geordie was sitting on the edge of Catto's bed, watching him being transformed for the ball. 'Ye look grand, Captain. Really grand!' Having made his pronouncement, he sank his teeth into the apple he held.

Catto was glad the weight of the world seemed to have lifted, if only for a while, from Geordie's small shoulders. He begged to differ from that *ye look grand, Captain.* He was used to check his appearance in the cheval glass every morning but only in a purely functional way. He liked to wear clean linen and a fresh shirt, cravat and hair-ribbon each day. He liked his breeches, waistcoats and coats, uniform and otherwise, to be smart, well-brushed and uncreased. He never looked in the mirror for the sake of vanity. 'Just as well,' he muttered.

'Eh?' queried the wig maker.

'Nothing. How much do I owe you?'

Waiting until the man had left, hurrying on to his next client, Catto laid his purse down and turned again to his own reflection, aghast at the sight of his hair powdered white and curled at the side of his head. 'I look like a complete fop. 'Tis worse even than that. I look like a molly.'

'You look like a young gentleman of fashion, sir,' Geordie pronounced between munches of apple. 'There's a difference.'

'There is?' Catto asked, still surveying himself with a look of horror on his face. He was wearing the dark green and silver brocade frock coat the Lord President's tailor had made for him. Below that, the colours reversed in their swirling pattern, was a satin waistcoat. A pleated white linen stock and dark green satin breeches completed the ensemble. Apart from the embroidered ruffles at the cuffs of his shirt. Those foamed out like snowflakes over the backs of his hands.

'I look like a molly,' he said again. There were decorative knots of smooth green satin ribbon on his shoulders, for God's sake, at the top of his arms. They served no practical function. Because women wore stupid clothes, did that mean men had to?

'No lady would ever mistake you for a molly, Captain.'

Catto looked at him in the mirror. 'It's not the ladies mistaking me for a molly that I'm worried about, Geordie.'

The boy grinned at him. 'Well, sir, it's only Miss Rankeillor you really hae tae worry aboot and I dinna believe she'd ever think that. I can tell by the way she looks at ye.'

'Geordie,' Catto said, 'sometimes you leave me speechless.' He picked up the green satin and velvet mask the tailor had also supplied and tied it on. If only it were that simple. If only he were going to this ball tonight with his only worry that Kirsty Rankeillor might consent to dance with him, allow him to escort her home afterwards.

If all went to plan, he would be escorting her home: only he would have her under armed guard.

Lizzie Gibson was sitting with her feet on the small stone hearth of her fire but she still didn't feel warm. She hadn't been able to get warm since Tuesday night. That threat to her son had chilled her to the bone.

Her boy meant everything to her. When he came running towards her out of the low door of her mother's cottage down by the shore, Lizzie's heart leapt. He could never know that she was his mother – how could she tell him she did not know who had fathered him? - but he loved her all the same. She thanked God every day for that, and for him. He was a bright child, clever and kind, and she was determined he would have the choices in life poverty had denied her. Although she might have to admit that allowing herself to be seduced by a winning smile, empty promises and her own youthful stupidity hadn't helped.

She earned well, though, enough to allow her son to be educated. Combine his intelligence with learning and he would be able to steer a steady course through life. Who knew how far he might go? Education, a respectable living, health and happiness, that was what she wanted for her boy.

Now all she wanted for him was his life and his safety.

'Ready? You know what you have to do when you get to the Assembly Rooms?'

Christian nodded, more nervous than she had ever been in her life and doing her utmost not to show it. Meg and Anna had left a moment before, leaving one sedan chair waiting outside the doors of the bagnio and the hospital's chair just round the corner, out of sight. They were going to have to hope nobody would notice it or its caddies in the crush of arriving ballgoers up at the Assembly Rooms.

Christian stood now inside the bagnio with Mr Fox and Jamie, both almost unrecognizable in their evening finery. Mr Fox wore Patrick Rankeillor's white evening wig and leant on an elegant black cane Jamie had produced from somewhere. He had also found the time to have his hair powdered and his dark blue evening clothes looked fine.

They were not in the height of fashion but they were not shabby. He did not wear them often enough for that.

Mr Fox smiled at Christian under the flickering light of the lantern burning in the lobby of the bagnio. 'Almost over, lass.' He spoke softly. 'You will be glad when life becomes a wee bit less exciting. I would thank you now. In case I do not have the chance to do so later.' He reached for her hand and lifted it to his lips. 'I shall never forget my kind and brave doctoress.'

There was a lump in her throat. 'I wish you a safe onward journey, sir.'

'Aye, and a successful one too,' Jamie said. 'Off you go, Kirsty. I'll see you into your chair.'

'Jamie,' she murmured as they walked out into the darkening afternoon, 'what shall we do about not having the pass from the provost?'

For Anna had arrived at the bagnio with the devastating news that Mr Coutts and his wife had not yet returned to Edinburgh. Their housekeeper had heard there had been heavy snowfalls in East Lothian and suspected they were either snowed-in or had decided not to risk the journey. The woman had also heard that snow was expected to fall on Edinburgh overnight.

'I have an alternative plan.' Jamie handed her into the chair.

Christian looked up at him. Under the light of the lantern above the bagnio door he seemed calm, a man who knew what he had to do and was resolved to do it. 'One of those tricks you have up your sleeve?'

'Aye. Maybe more than one. On you go, Kirsty. I'll not be far behind you.'

The threat to her boy made her blood run cold but Lizzie Gibson's conscience would not let her be. Robert Catto was in danger and she had the power to warn him. She had grown fond of the Town Guard Captain over the past month. Inside the man there was something of the lost boy. Men lowered their defences when they were in bed naked with a woman who posed no threat and whose job it was to pleasure them.

Lizzie walked over to the window of her room. It was getting busy out in the High Street. She watched as several sedan chairs were carried past, caught glimpses of their occupants. A ring sparkled on a woman's white hand. A man's silken sleeve and lace cuff rested on the window of another chair. He pulled back the curtain, exchanged some banter with a group of Lizzie's friends, gathered at the close mouth beneath her window to watch the guests going up to the Daft Friday ball. She knew Robert Catto was going there too. He had told her, making a joke about having to get himself dressed up in fancy clothes.

She took a step back from the casement when she saw the other man, the one who had threatened her boy. He might be in silk, powdered hair and a mask but she'd have recognized him anywhere. She stood watching him, thinking about how he had handed her over to his friends. They too had worn silk. Fine feathers did not make fine birds. Her heart and her body burnt at the memory of how cruelly they had used her.

The man who had threatened her boy must have known how they were going to treat her but he had wanted something from them and had traded her in return. Her pain and humiliation had been of no concern to him. He hadn't cared.

Robert Catto would never treat a woman like that. Robert Catto cared. Oh, he was a tough soldier, but his instincts were to protect those who needed protection. That was the sort of man she wanted her son to grow up to be.

She kept back, expecting at any moment that the man in the street below would look up at her window, reinforce the threat he had made. He didn't, just kept walking on up the High Street. So he thought he had dealt with her. Pure, hot and cleansing, anger surged up inside her.

She waited until he had gone out of sight, snatched in a hurried breath, ran to her door and clattered down the stairs. She got out to the street just in time.

'My, do you no' look braw! I'd fair like a Daft Friday kiss from you, sir.'

'Is that right, sweetheart?' Catto turned and stepped towards Lizzie Gibson. 'Surprised you recognized me in this get-up,' he murmured as he drew closer to where she stood in the lee of the close leading to the bawdy house.

Lizzie was also keeping her voice low. 'Ye're a lang lad. A heid taller than a lot of folk. Something I need tae tell ye. Pretend tae kiss me and I'll whisper it in your lug.' She gave him a name and a warning. 'I think he did away wi' yon lassie ye were asking aboot. Dinna turn your back on him.'

Their journey up the High Street was not too difficult, the crowds growing but not yet raucous or causing much obstruction. Christian lifted the blind covering the chair window and gazed out at Edinburgh, hoping Mr Fox was resisting the temptation to do the same. A tall man in dark green evening clothes, embroidered white cuff ruffles and powdered hair was embracing a woman, his hand resting casually on her behind, bunching up her skirts in what looked like a familiar grip. She dropped the blind.

When they reached the Assembly Rooms, she was relieved to see no sign of Anna and Meg in the entrance lobby. With a word to one of the attendants, she helped Mr Fox upstairs and into one of the reception rooms off to the left of the ballroom and round another corner, locking the door from the inside as Jamie had instructed. She wasn't to unlock it unless and until she heard three quick knocks followed after a little pause by two.

They came what seemed like ages later but might only have been half an hour. Mr Fox seemed uncharacteristically disinclined to conversation. Jamie stood there beside a tall man, though not the one she had seen in the High Street. This man was dressed equally elegantly but was not unrecognizable. Cosmo Liddell.

43

Catto stood in the Assembly Rooms, every sense alert. He had positioned himself in the open double doorway of the first floor ballroom from where he had line of sight along the landing to the kitchens and supper room on one side, the three reception rooms on the other and down the central stairs to the lobby. That was where the caddies set their chairs down, allowing passengers to disembark out of the chill of a December afternoon fast turning into a dark, although not too cold, evening. It did feel as though the predicted snow was on its way.

Sergeant Livingstone was in the downstairs lobby, holding Catto's sword and ready for anything. His platoon stood feet away, outside the doors into the street. A moment ago and with no sign of recognition, Cosmo Liddell and Arthur Menzies of Edmonstone had mounted the stairs and walked past Catto along the corridor to the reception rooms. If you already knew someone, and were watching for them, 'twas not so difficult to discern who was behind the masks and under the powdered wigs and hair. How people walked was also a giveaway. Liddell affected his usual relaxed saunter. Edmonstone was more tense tonight.

Catto followed them with his eyes until they turned the corner and went out of sight. He had the bastards. *He had them!* He had allowed the four chairs from the bagnio to arrive before he got here but he knew who was waiting for them in that room along the corridor. On a nod from William Angus Stewart, Livingstone had watched Christian Rankeillor help a man with a gammy foot or leg up the stairs and then turn left.

Whoever the man was, he wouldn't be running away. He would have to come limping back along this corridor. They would have thought that room around the corner more discreet but did not seem to have considered that there was no other egress from it. Catto had checked. He'd put three men below its window, just in case.

He glanced around the ballroom, brilliantly lit from the numerous sconces reflected in the mirrors around the walls. The great and the good of Edinburgh at play, all unaware of the drama being played out under their noses. Sleepwalkers. It came to Catto that their safety was in his hands tonight, as was Edinburgh. God help them all.

Archie Liddell wore rubbed purple silk and a mask of black satin. 'Twas the nervous demeanour as much as his worn evening clothes that gave him away. Catto was about to make him more nervous still. He lifted his chin, indicating that Liddell should come to him.

'Captain?' he murmured.

'Don't call me that. Going to need you very soon. Stay close.'

Christian gazed in horror from Cosmo Liddell to Jamie. 'This is the man Mr Fox must meet? Do you know what kind of a man he is, Jamie? Do you know what he did last Friday night, him and his friends Arthur Menzies and Hector Grant? They raped a young girl, Jamie. Used her hard and sore.'

Cosmo Liddell looked down his nose at her. 'What is this deranged chit talking about, Balnamoon?'

'Dinna try to deny it!' Christian said hotly. 'I have the story from the girl herself!'

'Kirsty,' Jamie said. 'Come with me. Now.' He turned to Mr Fox and Cosmo Liddell. 'We'll leave you gentlemen to talk.' As he hustled her out of the room, she heard Cosmo Liddell speak to Mr Fox, a smile in his voice.

'Girl's got hold of the wrong end of the stick. You know what they say, sir. When a woman says no, she means yes.'

Catto turned from his apparently casual glance around the ballroom. He had no trouble recognizing the girl who had this minute arrived at its door. He'd know that determined chin anywhere, not to mention the lovely mouth above it. She glided past him in her hooped petticoat, reminding him of the automata you saw in toymakers' windows in Italy and Switzerland, dancing ladies who twirled tirelessly on the tops of music boxes.

She hadn't noticed him, too intent on reaching two other girls in the opposite corner of the ballroom. They made space for her, standing as close to one another as their skirts would allow. Those were less wide than the yellow silk she'd been wearing when he had first met her. Dame Fashion deigned to rein herself in to allow for dancing.

The vivid colours of her and her friends' gowns spilled out in reflection onto the highly-polished wooden floor like blossoming trees reflected in a burn. She wore a rich and vibrant pink. Catching the light of the sconces, the material shifted and shimmered, as alive as a garden full of rosebuds. The metaphor had occurred to someone else.

'Three bonnie blooms in a garden of bonnie blooms,' said a man standing somewhere behind him. On the other side of the room, the three bonnie blooms were fluttering their fans. All three pairs of masked eyes lingered on him. All three pairs of masked eyes passed on. Christian Rankeillor's gaze returned to his face and he saw the start of recognition. Grimly amused, he placed one hand on his overdressed chest and made her a little bow. She hadn't expected to see him here tonight.

'Something amusing you … Captain Catto?'

'Mr Buchan of Balnamoon. You seem surprised to see me here.'

'Relieved would be a better word. Good evening, sir.'

'Good evening. As to what is amusing me, I am merely enjoying the view.'

Balnamoon laughed, and clapped a hand on Catto's shoulder. The bonhomie was a little forced. 'You're human, then. That's a relief.' He took a step closer. 'We can rely on your discretion this evening, sir? Perhaps rather more than that?'

'I hope I am always reliable,' Catto said, meeting the other young man's gaze through their respective masks. 'What happens now?'

'We wait. While we do so, shall I take you over and introduce you to Kirsty's friends?'

'Does that not rather defeat the object of a masked ball? Introduce me, if you please, as Mr rather than Captain Catto. I do not wish to excite too much interest on my own account this evening. I trust I may rely on you there, Mr Buchan.'

'You'll be lucky. A tall and handsome stranger in our midst? I expect the mamas and duennas are already sizing you up as a prospect for their daughters. Even before you remove your mask. A man might make a good marriage in Edinburgh, sir. If he knows the right people.'

Was Balnamoon offering him an entrée into Edinburgh society as an additional inducement to help them tonight? Ye gods. He'd have to be bloody desperate: even leaving aside the fact that the only families with whom Balnamoon would have any social *cachet* would be of the impoverished Jacobite variety. As Catto followed the man across the floor he was hoping to God this wasn't a feint, distracting his attention and moving him away from the doors. He was also hoping to God he was right to put his faith in Archie Liddell. He remained uneasily aware that he had yet to discover who had sent the warning to Surgeons' Hall last Saturday. If one of the links in his chain failed he could be in trouble tonight.

He reminded himself that Balnamoon needed him to get the Jacobite messenger out of Edinburgh, especially when that man couldn't walk very well. He certainly wouldn't be lowering himself down the walls on a rope. He'd have to go with his gut on Archie Liddell.

Emulating Balnamoon, Catto saluted all three girls with a kiss on the back of the hand and was seized by a vision of them in the bagnio a couple of hours earlier, naked and splashing about in hot water and soap bubbles. Christ, he really was a hopeless case.

'Catto,' one of them mused. 'You must surely hail from my part of the world, sir. 'Tis a name particularly found around Methlick in the shire of Aberdeen. Perhaps I may know your family. Where do they reside?' She looked at him with the air of expectant relish all Scots did when they posed that question, settling in for an interminable discussion about family connections. Only there was more to it than that. From her accent she must be Anna Gordon, daughter of the banker with suspected Jacobite sympathies and links. She had a purpose in trying to find out more about him.

'I regret to disappoint you, madam,' he said smoothly. 'I believe my forebears did originate from Buchan but the connection is now purely historical.'

'Young gentleman!' came a shout from the podium at the opposite end of the ballroom. 'Tall young gentleman in the green and silver. I dinna think I ken you.'

Bloody hell. This was the tamest masked ball he'd ever attended. In London and Paris it amused some men to secure tickets to the same entertainment both for their wives and their favourite doxies. The danger that they might meet was part of the fun. Sad, he'd always thought, how cruel some men could be to the women they married.

Sitting on the podium to one side of the musicians, the rather formidable lady directress of tonight's revels called out again. 'Who are your people, sir?'

That bloody question again. His mission here tonight could founder on it. He was racking his brains for how to answer when Christian Rankeillor spoke.

'I know him, Miss Nicky. I'll vouch for him. Here is the music starting up,' she said brightly. 'We promised each other a dance, did we not, Mr Catto? Let us take this one.' She whisked them both away from her friends and Balnamoon to join a set of couples already forming on the dance floor.

'We didn't promise each other a dance.' His heart was pounding. That had been a close shave. 'You didn't expect me to be here.'

'I know. But I'm not quite sure what I'm doing this evening.'

'Thank you. That's most flattering.'

She could still glower, even with a mask on. 'Miss Nicky might have tried to throw you out.'

'Because the Captain of the Town Guard cannot possibly be of a high enough social status to attend your ball, Miss Rankeillor?'

'I did not say that is how I think. Maybe I was also rescuing you from those troublesome personal questions you so much dislike. You are quite the debonair gentleman this evening, sir.'

'I look like a molly, you mean.'

'I would have to disagree. There is nothing which so brings out the manliness of a man as ruffles at the wrists. Dresden work, I think, and very fine. I hope your lady friend appreciates the effect.'

'My lady friend?'

'The lady I saw you embracing with some fervour, not to mention familiarity, in the High Street when I passed in my chair. Tell me, sir, are you acquainted with all the ladies of pleasure of Edinburgh?'

'Not all of them. The dance is starting. Not sure I know how to do this one.'

She gave him a little shove. 'Step back and bow to me.' She sank down in a deep curtsey to him. His own personal rosebud. The thought of how different things might have been was a dagger to his heart. She came back up and extended her right arm to him. 'Now we turn each other, and then again, only with the left hand. We do not grip each other's fingers quite so firmly as that, Mr Catto.'

'I beg your pardon.' She wasn't the only one who was tense. 'Tell me what to do now. In the dance, I mean.'

'You and I walk up to the top of the set.' They separated and took their places at the head of the line of couples, too far apart now for conversation. The dance continued until each couple had taken their turn to head the set. It seemed interminable to Catto. When it at last ended and bows and curtseys had once more been exchanged, he returned her to Balnamoon, who was standing on his own next to the doors out into the corridor. He had an odd little smile on his face. 'Time for commitment, Catto. Don't you agree?'

'It would seem so.'

'Then come with me. Both of you.' He led them out into the corridor, along and around the corner. He knocked on the last door, three short raps followed after a pause by two more.

Arthur Menzies of Edmonstone opened the door. Behind him, Cosmo Liddell turned to look as Balnamoon ushered him and Christian Rankeillor into the room. Pushing himself up on his black cane, Mr Fox rose to his feet. Robert Catto's eyes found his unmasked face and stayed there.

Father and son looked at each other.

44

Robert Catto tore off his velvet and satin eye mask and threw it onto a side table. Like Mr Fox, Cosmo Liddell and Arthur Menzies had also removed their masks. As Jamie followed suit, Christian untied her own and slid it into the concealed pocket at the waist of her gown.

'John Roy Stuart,' Robert Catto said, his eyes still fixed on Mr Fox's face. 'That's his real name. Expect you know him by one of his many aliases, Miss Rankeillor. He's had several of those. They're a necessity in his line of work. But that stops here.'

She had never seen such a sad smile. 'You're not here to help me, Bob?' asked Mr Fox.

'I'm here to arrest you. And don't call me that.'

'I aye used to call you that. When you were but a wee laddie.'

'You were never there.'

'You choose to forget those times we shared?'

'I choose to forget all of it. I choose to forget you. Do not pretend to have a claim on me.'

'You cannot deny the claims of blood, my son.'

Robert Catto was very pale. 'I deny any such claim. I am not your son. You are not my father. I never had one worthy of the name. John Roy Stuart, I hereby arrest you on suspicion of plotting armed rebellion against King George. You will come with me.'

Christian looked from Robert Catto to Mr Fox and back again. She should have realized before. Unlike Geordie and Alice Smart, this resemblance was not unmistakeable. There were little clues, though. One man with red hair, the other chestnut. The height. The strong mouth and chin. The way they held themselves, a proud stance which could become an arrogant one.

Jamie stepped forward. 'You will not betray your own father, man!'

'Watch me. Watch me arrest all of you. As I'm now about to do.'

'Och, I don't think so.' Jamie spoke in a voice that chilled Christian's blood. 'We're four to one, Catto. The odds are against you.' As he raised his arm from his side she saw that he was holding a pistol. It was one of Mr Fox's. She recognized the hearts engraved on its barrel. He lifted his left arm, bent his elbow, braced the gun on his forearm, pulled the cock back and aimed at Robert Catto. He threw Jamie a look of contempt.

'You're really not very experienced at this sort of thing, are you? The instant you fire that the noise of the report will sound the alert.'

'Not if I wait till the music is too loud for anyone to hear the shot. And I've still got a pistol aimed at your heart, you bastard.'

'Do you think I came in here unprepared? I have people waiting outside the door. You have to go out through it. There's no other exit from this room.'

Arthur Menzies stepped over to the window, pulled back the curtains, looked down into the street and stepped quickly back. Cosmo Liddell had neither moved nor spoken. He did not look scared. Arrogance, Christian thought. Whatever might be going to happen now, he expected his wealth and status to protect him from any harm.

'Aye,' Robert Catto said. 'I have men there too. So, I repeat. I'm arresting you all.'

'Your own father?' Jamie said again, the pistol still raised. 'They'll hang him, you know.'

'They'll hang you too, Balnamoon. Actions have consequences.' The mouth she knew could broaden into a grin or open into a laugh was tight set.

Mr Fox – John Roy Stewart – looked at his son. 'That's a rigorous philosophy, Bob. Unforgiving.'

Robert Catto's eyes flickered to him. 'I believe I have told you not to call me that.'

'Don't like being reminded of the duty you owe to your family?'

'You're one to talk. Enough. You will all come with me. Miss Rankeillor, you will remain here. I'm arresting you too. I shall lock you in and come back for you later.'

'There are more ways to dispatch a man than by shooting him.'

One hand on the back of his chair for support, John Roy Stuart turned, winced, but got the words out. 'You'll not run my son through!'

Jamie lowered the pistol and shrugged. 'I would if I had to, but we have no swords. We'll have to overpower him.'

'Then you must do something to render him insensible. He's my own flesh and blood, lad!'

'He's ready to see you hang, sir. The Cause comes before everything, Mr Stuart. As I know I need not remind you.'

'Oh no,' Robert Catto said. 'He's never needed reminding of that.'

Jamie swung round to the window and lifted a cushion from its seat. Christian stared at him, not understanding what he was doing.

'He's strong. It'll take the three of us.' As he glanced towards Cosmo Liddell and Arthur Menzies, he sounded perfectly calm. 'Pity I did not think to bring some laudanum with me.'

'Or that you don't have time to get me drunk. That is how you murdered Jeannie Carmichael, isn't it, Balnamoon? Got her drunk before you smothered her?'

Christian felt the blood drain from her face. 'Tell me he's lying, Jamie. *Tell me he's lying!*'

Jamie took a firmer grip on the cushion. 'I had to, Kirsty. She threatened to tell him where Mr Stuart was. She'd seen us bundling him into the Infirmary.'

'You took a life, Jamie? No. That cannot be true. Not you, Jamie!'

'There was no choice. As there is none now.'

'There's always a choice! You could have offered her money to keep quiet!'

'Apart from the fact that I have none.'

'You could have come to me for that.'

'Cap in hand?' he asked bitterly. His voice hardened. 'I had to be sure of her silence. What sort of a life was she going to have anyway? She'd have been dead of the pox before she was thirty.'

'Not your decision when her life should end. Not your decision, Jamie!'

'I'm making the same decision now.'

'Jamie, no! There must be another way!' With no clear idea of what she intended to do, Christian stepped back towards the door.

'There is no other way, Kirsty. Do not meddle with this. 'Tis men's business. Gentlemen?'

Arthur Menzies looked half-horrified, half-excited. The gleam in Cosmo Liddell's eyes was chilling. 'Well,' he drawled, ''twill be a new experience, to be sure. We've never gone quite this far, Arthur, have we?'

'But you won't get out! He has men posted who will intercept you! You cannot smother all of them!' Her fingers were gripping the key in the door. She could turn it now, call for help. If she did that she would damn Jamie and Mr Fox. If she didn't she would stand here and see bloody murder done.

She looked at John Roy Stuart. He nodded. She unlocked the door and pulled it open.

Archie Liddell burst into the room.

45

'Livingstone,' Catto said, as the Sergeant followed Archie Liddell into the room. 'Take charge of these men, those two first.' He lifted his chin to indicate who he meant. 'The one with the cushion in his hands and the one standing to his left. I am taking them to the Tolbooth. You have rope to bind their wrists?'

'Aye, Captain.'

'That one will need to go in a chair.' He jabbed a finger in the direction of John Roy Stuart. His hand and arm were rock steady. 'He cannot walk very well.'

'There are several downstairs, Captain. We can easily commandeer one.'

'We'll need two. Liddell, pick up that pistol and the portmanteau lying next to it. Put them over on that table behind me. Once you've done that, search Mr Buchan's pockets.'

'You're still outnumbered, Catto.' Balnamoon looked at Archie Liddell. He too had discarded his eye mask. He looked back at Jamie Buchan, then turned to face his cousin. Cosmo Liddell wore a supercilious smile.

'Thought you'd see sense, Archie.'

Archie looked at Catto, who met his gaze but for once could not read it. If he had misjudged the Lieutenant, this was all over.

Pale but resolute, Archie spoke. 'I'm sorry, Cosmo. That goes for you too, Jamie.'

'You cannot mean what I think you do, Archie.'

'I have to do my duty, Cosmo.'

'Your duty lies to your family, Archie!' Ready to bully and hector, Cosmo Liddell's expression changed as he studied his cousin. 'I'm sure we can come to some arrangement to persuade you to see that. Some financial arrangement.'

Archie shook his head. 'I don't think we can, Cosmo. There are some things money can't buy.'

'Every man has his price. I'm sure Captain Catto does too.' He did not include Livingstone in the offer. The Sergeant was beneath his notice.

'You have nothing I would want, Liddell.'

'I could ruin your military career. We all could. Especially now we know who your father is. That's going to call your loyalty into question forever more.'

'Not if I hand him over to justice. Livingstone, secure these two men now. Liddell, go as discreetly as you can and bring up two men from the Sergeant's platoon. They will guard this other pair. Who are also under arrest.'

'You can't arrest us, Catto. Are you mad?'

He ignored Cosmo Liddell's protest. 'Miss Rankeillor, you will come with me. I would not leave you alone with these two.'

Her chin went up. 'Are my hands to be bound too?'

'Not if you give me your word of honour to walk quietly down the stairs with me.'

'Honour? Is that a word you understand, Captain Catto?'

He did not flinch. Not outwardly. Balnamoon gave her a look as hard as a blow. 'Do you understand what you've done, Kirsty?'

'Jamie, I'm sorry! I could not stand by and watch you commit murder!'

'Enough,' Catto said. 'Livingstone, these two.' He pointed at Cosmo

Liddell and Edmondstone. 'They are the men who raped that young girl we know.' He saw Livingstone look at them with disgust and contempt in his eyes. 'We can throw them in the Tolbooth tonight but their friends will probably get them released tomorrow. They'll likely go unpunished. Do you think that's fair, Livingstone?'

'I could suggest a punishment, young Captain Catto.'

'Thought you might be able to.'

'I have your permission, sir?'

'I'm ordering you to do it, Livingstone.'

'No orders required, Captain.' Livingstone sketched him a salute, walked over to Cosmo Liddell and kicked him hard between the legs. As he crumpled to the floor, the Sergeant doled out the same punishment to Arthur Menzies.

'I'm thinking that's not really enough, Captain,' Livingstone said as he looked down at where they writhed in pain. He wasn't even out of breath.

'I'm thinking you're right, Sergeant. Give 'em a few more. They deserve a good kicking.'

Two young women stood, unmasked, on the landing of the Assembly Rooms. One was Charlotte Liddell, her face alive with malicious interest. Anna Gordon started forward. 'Kirsty?' When she spotted Jamie with his wrists bound her anxious frown deepened.

'Anna,' Christian Rankeillor said urgently. 'Say nothing!'

'Good advice,' Catto said. 'I'd take it if I were you, Miss Gordon.'

'Where are you taking them?' Anna demanded.

'You need not concern yourself with that. Your friend will come to no harm.'

She was facing up to him. Birds of a feather flocked together, it seemed. 'Can you guarantee that, sir?'

'I guarantee it, Miss Gordon.' He looked at Charlotte Liddell. 'Whereas I am afraid harm has already befallen your brother and his friend, madam. My Sergeant is currently kicking them in the balls. You might tell Mr Grant of Soutra he's at risk of the same treatment. Don't think any of them will be feeling like forcing themselves on any defenceless girls for quite some time.'

'Lieutenant,' he said, turning to Archie Liddell. 'I'm leaving you in overall command here.' He reached out a hand, squeezed the young man's shoulder and murmured a word or two of thanks and encouragement. Archie looked at him and nodded in acknowledgement.

She was in one chair, John Roy Stuart in another. Robert Catto walked beside hers and she could just see Jamie, wrists bound, walking in front of him. The whole caravan was surrounded by men of the Town Guard. Oh God, what had she done?

'Our betters been up tae nae good?' called a rough voice. 'Let's hae a wee look, then!'

'Keep walking,' growled Robert Catto.

That was easier said than done. The crowd covered every inch of the High Street and many were emboldened by drink. 'Och, let's see wha's in the chairs, sir,' called another man. 'It's Daft Friday. Gie us our fun.'

'Keep back or I'll give you a taste of my sword, you bugger.' Carrying that, he extended the naked blade in further threat. She saw the menace in his face and was not surprised when the group of revellers pulled back – or tried to. There was nowhere for them to go. He muttered something under his breath before barking out an order. 'To the guard-house. That's as far as we're going to get.'

They had to squeeze through the crowd to get to the guard-house door. Robert Catto hustled them all into the guard-room, where the portly Sergeant he had told to gag Betty stood with nine or ten other guards. They held their Lochaber axes to their chests, expressions of grim determination on their faces.

'Captain,' the Sergeant said, whirling round and saluting his

Captain. 'We were just aboot tae tak those buggers on. Afore this turns ony uglier.'

Pale and anxious, Geordie sat on one of the smoke-blackened settles which lined the walls. Clearly confused, it was Christian to whom he spoke. 'It's awful noisy oot there.'

The words were barely out of his mouth before a small stone shattered the glass of the window and came flying through the guard-room to hit her on the temple. She cried out and stumbled sideways. Robert Catto threw Mr Fox's portmanteau onto a table and pushed her down onto the settle next to Geordie, untied and tugged off his pristine white stock. 'Hold this to your head. It's bleeding.'

'I'm not bleeding into fine linen!'

'You already are. Crichton, secure the shutters. God damn it, why were they not already closed?'

'We didna want that lot tae think we were feart o' them, Captain.'

Angry shouts were floating through the broken window, the noise of the crowd outside building into a menacing growl. Some voices rose above the others.

'High time we burnt this bloody place doon.'

'Long past time. Hell and damnation to the Town Guard!'

'Aye! Let's dae it! Let's dae it noo! Show them we've had enough o' the Town Rats!'

'Fucking hell,' Catto muttered. 'You two,' he said to Jamie and Mr Fox. 'Sit down. Crichton, check their wrists are still securely bound and then follow me and the men out. Load my rifle for me and bring it with you. Geordie, help Miss Rankeillor.'

The crowd fell silent when he walked out of the guard-house. Hearing that from the other side of the wall, Christian could visualize him ducking his head as he went through the low door, drawing himself up to his full height before he spoke, making them wait. His voice was loud and resonant. 'I order you to disperse. Get about your lawful business.'

For a moment, as the crowd stayed silent, Christian thought that was going to be enough, his confidence and physical presence sufficient to cow the troublemakers. Until a voice rang out. 'Who the fuck are you to order us about? You're nothing but a big nancy in satin and lace. A lang streak o' pish and wind, that's all you are.'

Laughter ran round the crowd. Christian had recognized the voice. She looked across the guard-room at Jamie. He gave her a tight little nod back. 'Twas one of his friends, one of the two who had acted as caddies tonight.

'Untie us, Kirsty,' he mouthed. 'Now.'

Catto's eyes ranged over the crowd. He made sure to look directly at as many people as possible. Holding his nerve. Showing them he wasn't feart of them. Asserting his authority. He lifted his sword, drew it round in an arc. That sent some people stepping back as far as they were able, onto the toes of those behind them.

'I am the Captain of the Town Guard of Edinburgh and I'm ordering you to disperse and be about your lawful business. If that's getting rat-arsed and too stupid to know what's good for you, go and do it somewhere else. Away from the guard-house.'

That earned him some laughter but the same voice spoke again, educated but trying to sound rougher than it was. 'Who have you got in there?'

'That's my business, not yours.' He took the rifle Crichton was handing him, swapping his sword for it. 'If you don't disperse I'm going to shoulder this rifle. Which one of you would you like me to shoot first?'

'He thinks he's Captain Bloody Porteous!'

'Aye, and we all ken whit happened tae him!'

Those were different voices. Others joined in. Jeers. Insults. Threats.

'You've only got one shot in that gun. We willna gie ye time tae reload!'

'Ever been on the wrong end of one of those?' Catto glanced at the guards and their Lochaber axes. 'It's not pretty.'

Inside the guard-house Geordie had laid the linen stock to one side and was holding a folded square of damp cloth to Christian's brow. With a speed that allowed no escape, Jamie brought his bound arms over Geordie's head, forcing the boy to his knees.

'Now, Kirsty,' Jamie said. 'Untie us now. Unless you want to see us hang.'

'This bugger means it. I'm off!'

'One sensible man,' Catto said coolly, his rifle still raised. 'If you all want to live to see another day you'd do well to follow his example. Men,' he added in softer tones, 'fan out. Push them up the High Street and back into the closes, down into the Cowgate and the Grassmarket. Crack a few heads if you have to. Scare them shitless. Chase them to their own front doors. Prop my sword against the guard-house door before you go, Crichton.'

He watched as the men moved forward, their weapons at the ready. By the light of flambeaux being carried by some in the crowd and the lanterns burning above tavern doors, they looked as they had looked last Saturday at Surgeons' Hall. Ferocious. Already the crowd was beginning to thin, many deciding for themselves to slip down the closes off the High Street to escape the attention of the Town Guard.

Catto lowered his rifle, lifted his sword and walked back into the guard-house. Jamie Buchan of Balnamoon was waiting for him. Stepping out from behind the door, he brought the pistol butt down hard on Catto's right hand.

46

'You do realize you won't get through the Netherbow, Balnamoon?'

'That's why I'm taking some insurance.' Jamie had the pistol pointed at Geordie now. In his other hand he held Robert Catto's sword. 'First you'll bind your Captain's hands and feet, boy.'

His chin trembling, Geordie looked in mute appeal at Robert Catto.

'Do as he says, Geordie. But know this, Balnamoon. If any harm comes to this boy I shall come after you and hunt you down. Even if I have to travel to the ends of the earth to do it.'

John Roy Stuart laid a hand on his shoulder. His son's shoulder. Christian saw how that son stiffened at the contact.

'I'll see that no harm comes to the boy.'

'Really?' Robert Catto shrugged him off, held out his hands for Geordie to tie together, drawing his breath in on a hiss as the rope went over the bruise on the back of his hand. 'And how will you do that, pray? Mr Buchan of Balnamoon seems to have taken leave of his senses.'

'Bob,' John Roy Stuart said, 'believe me. I'm sorry it's come to this.'

'Get the hell away from me. It's all right, Geordie,' he said to the boy, now kneeling at his feet, shakily wrapping rope around his ankles. 'Do it. Do everything you're told to do.'

'Mr Stuart,' Jamie said. 'Go out to the sedan chair. My friends will be waiting for you there.'

'Jamie, lad, you won't …'

'No, sir. I won't. Please go out now. We have no time to lose. Kirsty,' Jamie said as John Roy Stuart limped out, 'you're coming with us.' His eyes ranged over her. 'Pity you're not more practically dressed.'

'Jamie, I can't come with you. How could I leave Betty and the girls?'

'Then I'd better give you this.' He handed her the pistol. 'It's cocked. All you have to do is squeeze the trigger. Aim at his head or his heart, a little below either. The gun will go up as you fire it. Be ready for that. Hold it down with your other hand.'

Geordie whimpered. Christian raised horrified eyes to Jamie's face. 'I can't, Jamie. I can't!'

'Then you'll see your father hang. If he doesn't baulk at seeing his own father swing, do you think he'll have any scruples about the Professor? You have no choice.' He gave her an odd little smile, laid a hand briefly on her shoulder. 'Sometimes we are left with none. Do it, Kirsty. Wait a few moments so that Mr Stuart does not hear the sound of the gun.'

Robert Catto's gunmetal-grey eyes travelled from the pistol up to her face. 'I don't think you've ever fired a pistol, have you? In fact, I don't think you've ever held a gun.'

'Don't move!' she said as he shifted position on the oak settle.

'How can I?' He raised his bound hands and feet. 'Trussed up like an animal going to the slaughterhouse. Not very sporting. Finding that gun heavy?'

'No,' she lied, and raised the pistol by an inch.

'Tell me something, Miss Rankeillor. Are you a student of Machiavelli? Do you believe that whatever evil may be done in the name of your cause is made a moral necessity by the rightness of that cause in the eyes of its adherents? That the end justifies the means?'

'Do you really think this is the time and the place to have a philosophical discussion?'

'What's philosophical about it? It's a matter of life and death for me. Especially with the way that gun's waving about.'

'You were going to hand your own father over to the hangman.'

'I have no father.'

'A convenient fiction.'

'Never was convenient. I never had a father who cared about me as yours does about you.'

'Back at the Assembly Rooms,' she said.

'What about it?'

'I had my fingers on the door key. I didn't know whether to turn it not. Mr Fox – I mean Mr Stuart – nodded to me that I should do it. He cares about you.'

'Oh, that was chivalry towards you. He always had that to spare for others. Never for his wife and children.'

'Children?'

'I had a sister. She's lost to me, too. Sold herself to the highest bidder. Not that I blame her. John Roy Stuart left us with nothing. Dragged my mother through a succession of dingy rooms in dingy streets all over Europe. Shortened her life.'

'Maybe she loved him.'

'She did. That was the trouble.'

'And you've never been able to forgive her for that or him for any of it? Maybe you would be a less troubled man if you did.'

Anger flashed in his eyes. She saw him get it under control. 'I thought we weren't indulging in philosophical discussions. Have you thought about what's going to happen next, Miss Rankeillor? You do realize that Balnamoon's right? You can't leave me alive.'

'Because it's either you or us.'

He raised a quizzical eyebrow. 'Got the stomach for that, have you? Got the stomach to allow John Roy Stuart to foment rebellion, plunge Scotland into bloodshed? Whose side are you on, Miss Rankeillor, the devils or the angels?'

She looked at him and saw only her father, her beloved father away in Glasgow all unaware of what was going on here, her beloved father who could go to the gallows because of what had happened here tonight. She raised the pistol, and fired.

47

The crack of the shot. The flash of gunpowder. A stumble of her foot on the uneven floorboards beneath her as the pistol jerked up in her hand and she stepped back in reaction. When the white smoke cleared Robert Catto was looking at her with his customary cool expression.

'You missed me. Bad luck, madam.'

'I meant to miss you, you bloody fool!'

'Then I should be grateful for your beginners' luck. You might just as easily have killed me. Do tell me, Miss Rankeillor, what is your further strategy as to how this fascinating evening we two are enjoying should progress? If you have some brilliant idea tucked up your silken sleeves I should be prodigious interested to know what it is.'

'Do you always have to be so sarcastic?' She was beginning to tremble. Her fingers opened and the pistol fell onto the floor.

He shrugged. 'It's a character trait. Don't see me sloughing it off now. Why did you shoot to miss me?'

'Did you really think I would happily dispatch you to meet your Maker?'

'There have been times during our short acquaintanceship where I've had that feeling, yes.'

'I don't know why I shot at all. Maybe I thought I could tell Jamie I had tried but failed.'

'We've both failed this evening.'

She sank down onto the settle behind her. 'Forgive me if I do not commiserate with you. I don't know why I'm talking to you like this. Whatever happens, you and I seem to keep talking to each other.'

'And what does that tell you?'

She raised her eyes from the floor to his face. 'Nothing that I want to hear.'

'Me neither. Why has it gone so quiet out there? Untie me, Kirsty.'

'Only if you give me your solemn promise not to go after Jamie and your father.'

'Would you believe me if I did?'

'On the grounds that you have lied to me over and over again?'

'I tried not to do that. You made assumptions based on what I did not say. Or on what you wanted to hear. Did you ever embroider handkerchiefs for Jamie Buchan? With his initials on them?'

'How did you know that? Oh. You found one such by Jeannie Carmichael's body?'

'I spotted one. That'll be why he knocked me over the head. He sent her to waylay me, too.'

'Why would he have done that?'

'To keep me occupied while he ensured the cadaver was stowed away. In case I decided to turn back and look for that or John Roy Stuart. I think she was by way of being Balnamoon's agent. They probably met while he was treating her for the pox. I should arrest you, you know.'

'You already did. Although I think I currently have you at something of a disadvantage, sir.'

'One could see it that way. On the other hand, my men will come back sooner or later. How is this going to look for you then? If you untie me now, there need be no witnesses.'

'What are you going to do about my father?'

'I cannot make any promises. But I shall do what I can. 'Twill help if you will allow yourself to be advised by me on what you should and should not say if you are interrogated by any third party. I also think

Professor Rankeillor would prefer not to find his daughter in the Tolbooth when he comes back from Glasgow.'

She rose to her feet and did as he asked, her fingers fumbling with the knots in the rope. As soon as they began to loosen, he flexed his fingers and freed himself, bent forward to undo the rope around his ankles and stood up. 'Robert,' she began, and slumped against him. 'I have no idea what to do next,' she told him in a whisper, looking up into his face.

'No more do I.' But he slid his arms around her and pulled her into his embrace. He heard her swallow tears, felt her hand on his chest.

'I have no idea why I am talking to you like this and I have no idea why I am allowing you to do this.'

'Because you stand in sore need of comfort and I am the only person currently available to give it to you. Don't worry. I'll not tell anyone if you don't. How is your head?'

'Sore. How is your hand?'

'Sore. My stay in Edinburgh has not been very beneficial to my health.'

He turned at the sound of the guard-house door opening. Geordie stood there, covered in snow.

'Captain! Oh, thank God, Captain, you're safe!'

'Snow's piling up,' Catto said, closing the shutters again. 'Not a living soul moving out there now.'

'You will not pursue them?'

'Not tonight. Maybe not tomorrow either by the looks of that snow. They seem to have got away, Miss Rankeillor.'

'You sound remarkably sanguine about that.'

'A soldier always has to recognize when a battle is lost.' He folded his arms and looked down at her where she sat with Geordie, nestled like a baby bird in the crook of her arm. On her other side, her bright skirts spilled out along the settle. 'A battle only, not the war. You are a somewhat exotic creature to be sitting in my guard-house, Miss Rankeillor.'

She responded to neither of those observations, asking instead: 'Your men will be sheltering somewhere before they attempt to make it back here?'

'They'll have gone home if they've got any sense. Which most of them do.'

'If not the one of whom Geordie has told you?'

For Jamie had not needed Geordie as insurance to get through the Netherbow. Davie Rintoul had let him and John Roy Stuart out, before disappearing with them into the swirling snow. He had muttered a message to Geordie as he had left. 'Tell the Captain I'm sorry!'

'Balnamoon must have had some sort of a hold over him.'

Jamie, oh Jamie, what happened to you? She put a hand up to steady her trembling mouth. She could not think about Jamie now. If she did, she would dissolve. She knew that. But, oh God, the pain this was going to cause her father …

'Men with a cause,' Robert Catto said, watching her. 'They subordinate everything else to that cause. Nothing matters more. Not friend, not lover. Not wife, not children. Not their life, not anyone else's life.' His voice was very gentle. Yet she could tell that fierce emotion lay beneath the calmly-uttered words. Did that come from *his* pain?

'I wonder if those at the Daft Friday ball will be marooned up at the Assembly Rooms.'

'Seems likely. You are concerned about your friends?'

'They will be concerned about me. I hope Betty will think I am with them.'

'You will have a lot to tell her and your friends tomorrow.'

'You think Alice will be all right, Miss Rankeillor?'

'I'm sure she's fine, Geordie. My Mrs Betty and Tibby and Mary will be looking after her. 'Coorie doon,' she suggested. 'Put your head on my lap and close your eyes.'

'I'll no' sleep, Miss. I canna sleep for worrying aboot Alice and thinking aboot everything that's happened tonight.'

'Alice will be fine. You close your eyes and have a wee rest.'

Robert Catto stepped over to the fire. Carefully and quietly, he stirred it with the poker and used the tongs to place a few fresh lumps on the glowing coals. Then he put the pistol he'd previously picked up from the floor into a cupboard, took off his evening coat, laid it on the settle opposite Christian and sat down next to it.

'Is that him away now?'

'Out like a light. He's sound asleep.'

'We shall have to waken him before I escort you back to your house. He will want to come to see his sister. We shall go once the snow allows and as discreetly as possible for the sake of your reputation.' He raised his eyebrows. 'Unlikely guardian of the proprieties though I am.'

'Will you be escorting me back to my house as your prisoner, Captain Catto?'

'You called me Robert a wee while ago, Miss Rankeillor.'

'Heat of the moment. You called me Kirsty.'

'Heat of the moment.'

'Are you going to permit me to receive my friends tomorrow?'

'Probably. Otherwise I have no bloody idea what I'm going to do with you. You did save my life earlier this evening and neglected to kill me a little later. Although I'm still not entirely convinced that wasn't by accident rather than design.'

'But you always do your duty, don't you? Because duty is all you've ever had to hold on to.' Then, as he threw her a speaking look: 'How you hate anyone to know you. How you hate anyone to know anything about you. Or to suspect that part of you is glad your father got away.'

'I think I have already made my feelings clear on that subject.'

'You'd like to think so. But I don't believe you. Why do you hate him so?'

He leant forward, bracing his hands on his satin-clad knees. 'You really want to know?'

'Yes,' she said. 'I really want to know.'

'All right, then. Here's the story. My grandfather never thought he was good enough for her, and he was right. They were too young, for a start, but John Roy Stuart persuaded her to run away with him. He was always good at winning people over. Silver tongue. That's what people say about him. It broke my grandfather's heart when she left.'

'Oh. That's so sad. Did she and her father ever see each other again?'

He nodded. 'There came a time when she couldn't stand it any longer. She left him, brought us back to Scotland, home to my grandfather's house. He took us all in. We could have stayed there. We could easily have stayed there!'

'At your grandfather's house where the sunflowers were.'

'Yes. At my grandfather's house where the sunflowers were and we were all happy.' He threw himself back in the settle, tilted his head against the dark wood and closed his eyes. 'Except that when John Roy Stuart begged her to go back to him she did.'

'She must have really loved him.'

'He didn't love her. Not enough. She was already ill when he got the call to go to Rome. And he went. Nothing,' Robert Catto said bitterly, his eyes still closed, 'could stand against a summons from his Prince.'

Christian's hand flexed on Geordie's shoulder. 'She died while he was away?'

'Aye. With only my sister and me to nurse and comfort her. In a cold, damp room in a noisy, smelly street in Paris and us running out of money to feed her or ourselves.' A tear slid down his cheek. 'She was still trying to comfort us at the end. Right up until she took her last breath. As she kept on hoping till the last moment that he would come.' He opened his eyes and looked wildly at her. 'That's why I hate him so much. He came too late, Kirsty. *He came too late!* His Prince and his bloody cause meant more to him than she did! Or us!'

'Robert,' she breathed, extending her free hand towards him, 'och, Robert …' and in an instant he was kneeling at her feet on the dirty floor, his face against her skirts.

'I do not like you with powdered hair,' she said a few moments later, lifting her hand from where it was resting on that hair.

He lifted his head, rubbed a hand over his face and rose to slide in beside her on the settle, lifting those bright skirts so that they splashed over his legs. 'I hate having my hair powdered.'

'But you had to look unlike yourself tonight.'

'Yes. What am I to do with you?'

'Your duty. So where does that leave us?'

'I have no bloody idea,' he said again. 'I might even be open to suggestions.' His powdered head jerked up. 'What do you mean, where does that leave us? Who are *us*?'

She glanced down at Geordie, snoring gently, his blond waves spilling out over her rose-pink lap. 'I think we're rather bound together now. Don't you?'

'For more reasons than Geordie and his sister?'

'You tell me.'

He raised his hand to her face, dancing his fingertips with infinite tenderness over the bruise at her temple. He slid his fingers into her dark curls, and it was not the pain in the back of his hand that made them tremble.

'It's all right,' she soothed as she gazed at him. 'It's all right, Robert.'

'It's a bloody mess. The whole thing's a bloody mess. You ought to hate me.'

'I know. But I find I can't do that.'

'I shouldn't even be thinking what I'm thinking now. This can go nowhere.'

'I know that too.'

'Even as we sit here, events are being set in motion which will overwhelm and divide us, you on one side and me on the other. You probably know what those events are.'

'Probably I do,' she agreed.

'How are we to find our way through all of this?'

Her voice shook. 'Somehow we'll find a way.'

'My morals are reprehensible.'

'Indeed they are,' she said, regaining some of her crispness. 'We're going to have to do something about those.'

'We?'

'The two of us.'

We. The two of us. The two of whom he now was one – and despite it all, despite this bloody mess, joy was rising within him like a bubbling fountain in a sunny garden, warming his frozen heart. 'You seem to know so much I'm wondering if you know what I'm going to do now.'

'I think I might be able to guess.'

Their heads were drawing ever closer. The delicate embroidery at his wrist brushed her face, and she shivered.

'Don't be afraid, Kirsty.' He glanced down at Geordie and his mouth curved. 'We have our chaperone.'

'I'm not afraid, Robert. I'm not afraid,' she said again, and raised her head for his kiss.

...to be continued.

Author's Note

John Roy Stuart and Duncan Forbes of Culloden were real people. Although I have imagined and assigned to them specific fictional roles in *Gathering Storm*, including giving John Roy Stuart a fictional family, their relative political positions, loyalties and commitment are accurate. Both men played crucial roles in the history of the '45, John Roy passionately in favour of the restoration of the House of Stuart, Duncan Forbes of Culloden passionately opposed. If you would like to read more about the parts they played in those turbulent times, I researched and wrote up their real stories in *Bare-Arsed Banditti: The Men of the '45*.

In the Scottish style, Duncan Forbes of Culloden, Lord President of the Court of Session, was often known by the name of his estate near Inverness, his ancestral acres. This custom continues in farming communities in Scotland to this day. Bonnie Prince Charlie chose to make Culloden House his headquarters when he retreated north in Spring 1746. So it's not entirely an accident of history that the Battle of Culloden was fought where it was. It's certainly an irony of history that the name of the humane Duncan Forbes should be forever associated with this mythic and bloody last battle, the last fought on British soil, and its brutal aftermath.

The Beggar's Benison and the infamous wig Robert Catto encounters in this story were both real. There is a scholarly and highly entertaining account of both in *The Beggar's Benison: Sex Clubs of Enlightenment Scotland and Their Rituals* by David Stevenson. The wig had its own club. For the purposes of this story I have brought the two clubs together. Professor Stevenson notes that the wig was last heard of in the 1930s when it was reported to be in a lawyer's office in Leith. As Geordie Smart might say: yeuch.

Readers not familiar with the Scots tongue might like to know that both *gey* meaning *very* and *gin* meaning *if* are pronounced with a hard *g*. I've allowed myself the pleasure of spelling *courtezans* and *tidbits* in the 18th century way. I've also used *–ize* rather than *–ise* endings, as I was taught at Garscadden Primary School in Glasgow back in the day, because 18th century people favoured those endings – as does the modern Concise Oxford Dictionary – and because I have a penchant for the elegant strokes of the letter *z*.

www.maggiecraig.co.uk

Also by Maggie Craig

Fiction

The River Flows On
When the Lights Come on Again
The Stationmaster's Daughter
The Bird Flies High
A Star to Steer By
The Dancing Days

One Sweet Moment

Non-fiction

Damn' Rebel Bitches: The Women of the '45
Bare-arsed Banditti: The Men of the '45
When the Clyde Ran Red
Footsteps on the Stairs: Tales from Duff House